I0631123

DANGEROUS DEVOTIONS

A D Penhall

First published by Clan Destine Press in 2023

Clan Destine Press
PO Box 121, Bittern
Victoria, 3918 Australia

Copyright © A D Penhall 2023

All rights reserved. No part of this book may be reproduced or transmitted in any form or by any means, including internet search engines and retailers, electronic or mechanical, photocopying (except under the provisions of the Australian Copyright Act 1968), recording or by any information storage and retrieval system, without prior permission in writing from the publisher.

National Library of Australia Cataloguing-In-Publication data:

Penhall, A D

TITLE: Dangerous Devotions

ISBN: 978-1-922904-09-6 (paperback)
ISBN: 978-1-922904-10-2 (eBook)

Cover Design by © Willsin Rowe
Design & Typesetting by Clan Destine Press

Clan Destine
PRESS

www.clandestinepress.net

*In memory of my Uncle Phil who lived with the love of dancing,
music, hard work, and with blindness.*

*And in memory of Cheryl, who never let either living with disability
and subsequent poverty or the stereotyping and moralising of others irritate her too much.*

Thanks to them both for the laughs.

'Tis a common proverb in Italy, that he knows not Venus in her perfect sweetness who has never lain with a lame mistress ... ancient philosophy has itself determined it, which says that the legs and thighs of lame women, not receiving, by reason of their imperfection, their due aliment, it falls out that the genital parts above are fuller and better supplied and much more vigorous ... and come more entire to the sports of Venus.'

—Michel de Montaigne (1553-1592) *Of cripples*

MONDAY

1

An armless Cabbage Patch doll sits on a doorstep. The detached parts are discarded, one leg severed above the knee. Blood – is it real? human? whose? – is splattered across the neck, the chest slashed, stuffing spilling. The doll is propped in a niche, protecting it from the bitter early morning wind that might otherwise topple it.

The house is a refuge for women with disability who are victims of domestic violence. Eight women and eleven children are currently crowded into the mansion that was once home and surgery for a local doctor, later a brothel, more recently a boarding house. A child, hearing daughter of a deaf woman, finds the doll this winter morning, and screams so loudly the nearby windows rattle in their ancient frames. The mother drags her daughter back inside and holds her close. The mother, too, is punched by the horror and emits sounds without words. This is not the first time.

Across the city, it's a cold dawn, a desert wind, a broken-glass brilliance, starved of moisture, a complete absence of playfulness. With strong, well-practised movements, Tom Challinor climbs from the pool and lets the chill splinter against him for a full sixty seconds before wrapping a towel around his large frame and heading for the house. He enjoys the wind, its lack of manners, the way it tears away at the pretence of Sydney as a warm, sea-trimmed beauty. When it comes to tourism, the westerly winds are among Sydney's best kept secrets.

Showered and dressed, Tom switches on the espresso machine. He wants the city and its inhabitants to admit to other secrets, and very soon at that. He calls Warren, who's very good at asking the right questions, or knowing the right people to ask them of.

'Don't you ever sleep?' Warren asks, blurry-voiced.

'Thought I'd get you before your kids were up. I'm hoping you have time for some work over the next few days.'

'Surveillance?'

'Basically.'

'Anything interesting, I'm in. If it's bread and butter, my cholesterol's already over the limit.'

'This one's out of the ordinary. A new escort agency, with an unusual twist.'

'Dunno if that's possible. And last time I followed a pimp I ended up with a closer connection to some asphalt than I generally fancy. Job wasn't for a well-known barrister on the right side of the law like you, Boss; doesn't mean the dangers're any different.'

'No close personal contact involved. There's a van I need you to follow.'

'A van? What kinda escort agency has a van?'

'One that supplies elegant ladies, and the occasional gentleman, who use wheelchairs.' The hiss of the coffee demands attention. 'This agency serves a niche market. Its workers are all people with disability – some have amputations, some spinal injury. There're also people with dwarfism and vision impairment. The clients don't like to see themselves as ordinary punters. They call themselves "devotees".'

'Boss, I know y'might have a personal interest, but brothels aren't illegal anymore. Maybe an escort agency's dodgier. Thing is, people gotta have work. Manufacturing's all gone, you know.'

Tom pours his coffee. Outside, a tree-branch screeches resistance to the wind. 'Agreed. The problem is not with devotees. It's with an organisation whipping up the extremes of fetish and putting workers in dangerous situations. We've been aware of the agency for a few weeks, gleaned what I've told you about the van and the workers and have been putting out feelers for more information. Recently, the ante has been upped. Sit down a minute, I'll give you some detail.'

The story is: late last week, an elderly gent, exercising against arthritis, stumbled across a grotesque scene in Parramatta Park. A young woman was lying, face frozen in fear or death – he couldn't tell which – below the murky surface of a heavily overshadowed, out of the way section of an ornamental lake. A wheelchair was abandoned nearby. The man managed to attract the attention of other joggers. Together they lifted the young woman from the cold water. One applied CPR, another called emergency services. The young woman survived, although it was edgy for a time.

'The police reportedly jumped to the conclusion of suicide. The old gentleman stoically insisted that was impossible – she simply couldn't have pushed herself to the lake. The tree roots were too thick, the ground too broken, debris strewn everywhere. He badgered them at the station. Once they accepted it was not a self-inflicted near-disaster they took more time to get their heads around the fact the young woman – Melanie – wasn't out touring the park with a parasol and hadn't elegantly tripped, rolling involuntarily into the water.

Tom sips his coffee, runs his hand over his short hair.

'They finally noticed it might just be attempted murder. They still appear to be ignoring the information Melanie gave them; that she'd been paid to be in a hotel room with a strange man and with no way of exiting independently. That she'd been taken from the room, involuntarily. They couldn't believe a nice young woman in a wheelchair would engage in anything as sordid or out-there as sex work.'

Tom can almost hear Warren's shrug. 'Boss, they're coppers. They're do-ers, progressive thinking's not their thing.'

'Indeed. However, we're not muscling in on the police investigation, not for the time being. In fact, they have a suspect in custody. Our job is to uncover the mechanisms that allow a middle-aged man to have an assignation with a young woman with paraplegia in a hotel room in the western suburbs in the middle of the day, at an exorbitant fee – with limited, if any, safety support. And, as an imperative, to track down the people who are promoting such threatening situations. They're not simply new pimps on the block, trying out a different sales-pitch: they're very effectively operating off all the usual radars. There's big money involved in this set-up.'

'Well, you got my interest. Isn't this a job for Ivan though? I mean, how they getting the word out? Talking to each other? Bookings must be net-based, hey.'

'Ivan's so far drawn a blank. Net, social media, dark web, all as profligate and dirty as ever – while completely lacking any indication of this particular organisation. His impression is that twentieth century communications are being utilised, keeping everything close and relatively unhackable. Eventually he'll dig something up. In the meantime, there'll be cracks in the agency's armour. After the park incident, the staff will be wary, more likely to talk – if only we can find them to ask. And we've got to get a handle on the agency's customers. Our sources tell us the uptake is extraordinary, frenzied. This agency sells the exotic, the fetishistic, the truly unique. Much more can go seriously wrong. Violence toward people with disability comes cheap. And excites some people.'

'Got the picture. If this agency's spreading its wings or digging in its claws, how come I never heard of it?' Warren sounds seriously aggrieved.

'Your ignorance is a good measure of its discretion.' Tom means this. Warren is a finger-on-the pulse PI.

'Discreet means expensive. I bet they're paying the workers like they're convicts off the First Fleet, though.'

Good, Tom thinks, he'll take the job. Warren cheerfully leaves solving major crimes to the police – when he thinks they can manage the job – but he's always ready to go into bat for the underdog. Tom's father would've liked Warren. Pity Keith Challinor died so young.

'We'd really appreciate it if you could spare a couple of days. They're easily exploited employees,' Tom says with the mild delivery he's carefully cultivated. Few people know what Tom Challinor is really thinking. Except perhaps, on occasion, Warren.

'Yeah. Okay, you've got me. But who's this "we"? You're not in this with your old missus, are you?'

'Clare and I are working on this together, yes.'

'Listen, Boss, you may not've been in the luck lately, but you've never had trouble attracting the chicks. Why don't you leave that one for good and proper?'

'I have left her. And Warren…'

'Okay, okay. None of my business. What're the details I need?'

Tom calls Ivan. Developments are few. Ivan has been posing as a variety of identities, worming his way into various groups, making himself thoroughly disgusted with the world, getting nowhere near an escort agency fitting the description.

'Hard to believe the sexual proclivities of people,' he says, not for the first time. 'Heard about the lot that fancy faeces? Smeared in all the places you can imagine, and more. I stumbled into what looked like a quaint old-fashioned chat room for nice little homos like me. Wrong move. Behind the door, there was shit everywhere. There's a name for it, I checked: coprophilia, also known as scatophilia or scat for short. Man, that's off the planet.'

'You're a champ, Ivan.'

'Guessing that means you want me to keep looking.'

'If you don't mind.'

'You keep paying, I keep looking. It's how the world works.'

'Keep me updated.'

Tom's phone buzzes as the hiss of steam indicates his second attempt at coffee – the first's gone cold – is ready. 'Clare,' he says.

'I've only got a minute. I can't make the Acqui meeting this morning. I've – well, something's come up. I'm really sorry, but are you able to do it?'

Acqui is a group of people with recently acquired disability. Clare had agreed to be a guest speaker at their monthly meeting. Group members are mostly amputees and wheelchair users – the most popular disability "types" in devotism. The new escort agency is likely to have at least one Acqui member working for it.

Clare had been sure they'd gain intel at the meeting; her changing plans this late in the piece surprises him. He wonders briefly if there's a subtext. They'd done everything together, from trekking the Himalayas – not an easy feat for a too-tall blind man and a small, city-bred sighted woman – to voluntarily running investigations into abuses, corruption, malpractice in the disability, aged, women's support and other under-funded sectors. As they were now.

Eventually, like a drug, the marriage had sapped his pride and energy. It wasn't all Clare's fault. She was a giver. She couldn't help it that he didn't want to always be the recipient.

'I can make the meeting, although I'll have to wing it,' he says, business-like.

'I'm sure you'll manage. You're pretty good at keeping control. And this particular investigation is more your scene than mine – all the grimy guts of the underworld on show.' She changes tone. 'I shouldn't've said that, it sounded bitchy and I don't mean to be. Really.'

His coffee's cooling. 'I won't be able to use your PowerPoint? Not set up with sound markers?'

She softens. 'It isn't, and I really am sorry.' Her voice drops. 'You know I don't want to make it hard for you. I'm truly sorry.'

The excess of sympathy irritates him. He is reminded of the sugar he found in his grandmother's pantry one rainy afternoon when he was a kid. The smell, fecund and unfamiliar, pulled his attention from the biscuit tin he intended to raid. The sugar had swelled and spilled in the moist, overheated summer. When his fingers brushed the damp grains, the sensation was repulsive, as he imagined a carcass would feel in decomposition. The acrid smell made him retch. His grandmother had found him, and the mess. There'd been hell to pay.

He murmurs something non-committal.

'I'll talk with Kurt again and see if the police have more detail on that assault,' she responds, 'and follow up with the numbers we've got.'

Kurt? Clare isn't generally so friendly with the police. 'Clare, Kurt's a good contact, but watch your back. Powerful people are involved in this agency. Powerful people have powerful friends, often including police.'

'Kurt's not that high up. And you be careful, too.'

He drinks the cold coffee. It still throws a punch.

2

WARREN MUNCHES HIS BREAKFAST WHILE PONDERING CHALLINOR'S STORY. Do young blokes just wake up one day with a hard-on and a leftover dream about sex with a woman with no legs or a bloke who can't hear them scream? Is that okay? What's it like only being attracted to someone with a very particular disability? Can do if you're a C5 quadriplegic, can't do if you've lost your arm in an industrial accident? Weird. Ponders his breakfast too. Ditto on the weird. Karen's new health kick sure leads to some meal aberrations. In his opinion.

'See ya,' he yells to Karen – who, despite food preferences, is top of the charts in his world. Likes his work, too. Started off as a sports journo, all starry-eyed. Behind the glamour found corruption and drugs, angst and unsavoury sexual exploits. Couldn't spill the beans, no bugger'd listen. Hopped into PI-ing when Karen was pregnant. Pay and conditions suited a young father, so long as he didn't tell his wife the detail of his life out on the streets. Soon he understood there was a thread; he liked trailing those with something to hide, and, when the time and possibilities were right, splattering stories for maximum results. Not always for the worst.

Slips the key into the lock of the old Jag. The Jag's engine purrs. The description's a cliché, ten years of journalism hardly let him forget, but it truly does. Hangs a soft left and takes off down the arterial. A radio shock-jock is banging on about government taxes being a rip off, only there to line the pockets of politicians. 'No taxes, no services, you dickhead,' Warren mutters and shuts the radio down. Bluetooth's a passing phase, not worth installing in the Jag.

Hits a brick – or rather, metal – wall. Stationary cars jammed onto Parramatta Road, a narrow dirt bullock track upgraded to a narrow asphalt one. Challinor's told him to concentrate on the western suburbs, where the standard of hotel's rising quicker than a punter's prick.

Met Challinor in Brisvegas, when he was a journo and Tom the captain of the Australia cricket team. Blind cricket; great game. Worked with him for years now. Man's too curious for his own safety. Nearly got himself beaten to a pulp recently, sticking his cane into a boggy bitta grass that was covering up some seriously deep corruption in aged care suppliers. Metaphorically speaking, o'course. Not the nearly murdered bit – Challinor avoided that only because people think a blind bloke can't fight back, when Challinor sure can – but the boggy grass, that's a metaphor. Warren watches the car in front leap a whole half car-length. Why bother? Hopes the current investigation is less threatening than the aged care gig.

Forty minutes later he's in his unremarkable hatchback, which hides in a hired garage in an area where mortgages threaten to cave in and smother their owners whenever the real estate market has a mild cough. A good place to leave what you don't want looked at. Now he's approving of the slowness of the traffic. Gives him time to check for the van. A mobile brothel, with no internet presence, that does its business during the daytime. No premises, no hanging glamorously off an arm at an event, and no home visits as far as anyone knows.

The boss impressed these facts on him: they define the clientele. Yep, a mobile brothel'd appeal to the most assiduous family man, the politician or priest, the clever bastard who needed to be seen going home to the wife and kiddies at night and/or getting his (her?) mug on the social pages. So long as they have the money and power to take an extra-long lunch, they're home and hosed. As it were.

Warren pulls up (illegal) outside the mega-shopping centre. Sees a couple of interesting girls hanging outside, dressed to the nines, handbags and all. The taller one, a pretty young thing with a serious face, has only one arm. The shorter one – the very short one – has the face and the body of a cherub: a pert, pretty, challenging cherub with gorgeous golden curls. A mini-bus pulls out of a loading zone. Warren whizzes in, illegal still, but safer. Gets out, wanders over, casually checking his phone.

The women are obviously mates. The taller one's called Sonnie: Sonya? Silver cross around her neck. Looks what? Iraqi, Iranian? A few Christian refugees from both countries around, so possible. The other girl's the real talker. Yabberer, more like. Good at it, amused and amusing. Girl who likes life, he figures. Definitely a girl who likes clothes, the subject of their current conversation. Seems Sonnie thinks the shorter girl, whose name is maybe Avril (hard to hear for sure), is wasting her money on so many clothes. The boots she's wearing look pricey, probably specially made. Her legs are too short for off-the-rack boots, and these fit her perfectly.

They complain about their lift being late. The smaller woman steps forward – yep, her name is Avril – as a group of school children explode through the automatic doors, nearly knocking her down. A kid gawks at her, pointing. Warren smiles when she gawks pointedly back. The kids pass, one banging at her with his bag, and Warren's about to step forward, hassle the rude little bugger, when there's another kerfuffle. Some older guy fallen over. 'I can't get up,' he calls, staring straight at the cherub girl. One of his eyes is covered by a patch.

Two women stop. One offers her hand to the fallen geezer. The second grabs her, warning her not to touch a man. The first woman turns, her beautiful eyes under her headscarf seeking help. Avril heads straight for the guy. The kind woman nods her thanks over her shoulder as she and her friend continue into the shopping centre.

The man grabs for Avril, his grasp on her arm tight, demanding. He's middle-aged, very well dressed, even the eye-patch appears designer. Avril's eyes narrow, like she's questioning whether she's seen him before.

'Thank you,' the geezer says, pulling himself up so he towers over her. He doesn't look very hurt.

'No problem.' Avril turns quickly away.

'Could you hold my arm?'

'I'm late to meet m'mates.'

'I need a doctor. I can't see very well, I need help.'

Pigs fly, Warren thinks, but decides Avril is handling the situation.

'Awright, I'll find where there's a doctor.' She turns toward the shopping centre.

'Don't leave me. I might fall again.' The man grabs, pulls her back.

'Piss off,' she says, but he doesn't let go.

The geezer's hand slides down Avril's arm. He slips something small into her hand. She says nothing, turns to grab Sonnie's hand as she moves to intervene.

A short time later, Sonnie and Avril are in a van that matches Challinor's description to a tee. Warren clocks three other occupants already in the back. The driver is a middle-aged Anglo bloke in dark glasses and no facial expression. Warren jumps into his own car. The day's still shaving the end of the morning peak hour and the delivery van is in competition with mums and dads returning from dropping their kids at school and old buggers setting out for a session at the bowls club but he'll stick with it as best he can.

The van nose-dives down a side street, skates down the rear entrance of a large hotel. Warren enters the location intel in his voice recorder – an old-fashioned bit of technology he's absolutely never discarding – and drives past. It's out again in three or four minutes with one less occupant and a new image on its side panel: "Stephano's Fine Foods".

Another three entrances and exits. The signage changes, the number plates too: serious money and planning involved. And a very retro consciousness, someone who's seen a lot of old movies.

Warren's whistling. He records details, never getting too close. One occupant left. Small. The van cruises past several hotels, spins around the roundabout, returns to the swankiest. Parks outside this time. Is the driver aware of the other car Warren is watching – a sleek, low-slung job that could well be tailing the van? The expensive car hesitates, passes on. Wrong angle, too much reflected sunlight to read the number plate. Irritating.

Warren pitches into the hotel driveway. Ignores the offer of valet parking. Watches as Avril climbs out of the van, rearranges her hair and heads inside with a confidence that makes him grin. He waits. The sporty job doesn't reappear. But as he and his car saunter out into the traffic behind the van, he spies the shiny machine entering the conjoined car park of the hotel next door. Interesting.

3

THE SHARP SOUND OF YET ANOTHER CAR HORN HITS TOM'S EARDRUMS. HE replaces the brailled pages in his satchel, pleased he hasn't any major cases on for a short while. After several weeks in court defending a woman accused of murdering her son on the most anorexic of evidence, he needs a few days without a silly wig and bat-cape robe. His client was acquitted and suspicion directed toward a more likely suspect, based on what Tom considers less circumstantial evidence. But cases involving the death of a child are always exhausting.

He tightens the strap on his satchel. The attempted drowning of Melanie, the young escort agency worker, in Parramatta Park means the imagined open space of the week ahead is filling faster than the freeways out of Sydney on a Friday afternoon.

Even before the attempt on Melanie, he – and Clare, who'd first been contacted by a concerned but anonymous escort agency worker – realised they'd have to up the time and effort put into uncovering this new escort service. It's simply too secretive, too able to exploit women and men who survive in a world in which they have little or no power.

In fact, the more he and Clare have gleaned, the more they've understood the potential danger. So, there goes his week in the sun, or of sorting paperwork and having long lunches. Instead, he is back with Warren on a trail.

Tom smiles to himself: chance, unpredictability and left-field possibilities make life fun, and he's always relished the solving of puzzles. He's probably just a frustrated detective.

'Lucky the wind's died,' the cab driver says, pulling up with a flourish, stamping too hard on the brake. Several more horns blast. 'Piss off,' he says to no one in particular. 'You know mate, you don't look blind, 'specially in that coat and with that buzz cut or whatever. You look more like that guy in that old film *The Matrix*, only you're blonde. I hope you don't mind my saying.'

'You're not the first,' Tom agrees.

At 195 centimetres or near enough six foot five in the old money, he has much of his clothing made for him. The expense is worth it for the comfort. He can only hope he looks good – although cab and Uber drivers are always willing to help out with uninvited comment. At least it avoids politics. There are a lot of very conservative drivers these days.

On the footpath he stops, listens. The westerly wind has softened and he is relying on the sun, sound and familiarity for direction. Behind him, the restless sounds of the Quay – with its clutter of buskers, harried commuters, drug peddlers, pickpockets, too-loud backpackers and busloads of tourists – funnel up between the old stone buildings and bounce against the glass facades of the 1980s boom-time business centres and third millennium luxury apartments. The soundscape is messy, but it's still better to be blind in Sydney than London or New York, where the intensity of weather or architecture, or both, would defeat him far too often. Confidently, he turns toward the north-western end of the building.

Inside the conference room, he shrugs himself into advocacy mode. The meeting's running late; a speaker is doing a run-through of paraphilias.

'Acrotomophilia is the term applied by medical and psychological professionals to an intense sexual attraction to persons who have an amputation. Acrotomophilia is a compound from the Greek: *akron*, extremity, plus *tomo*, a cutting, with *philia*, meaning love, or erotic and sexual love of a person, thing, or activity. A person who has acrotomophilia may only be attracted to people with amputations, although some cope by fantasising that their – intact – partner is, in fact, an amputee. In its extreme form acrotomophilia prevents the person becoming aroused or achieving orgasm with any person who does not have an amputation.'

Tom recognises Clifton Johnson, a psychiatrist well-known in the disability field. Middle-aged, old-school in temperament and style,

Johnson worked in the institutions until most of them shut up shop. He potters along in private practice, due to a respectable degree of dedication and the dearth of professionals in the area. As far as Tom can tell, he's a nice enough bloke, although inclined to medicate first and ask questions about efficacy after. Which puts him in step with ninety percent of professionals working with the aged, people with mental illness, any person who doesn't fit in an easily assembled box. Fill them with drugs, keep them quiet, seems to be the philosophy.

'In summary,' Johnson continues, 'paraphilias are as old as sex itself, as far as we know. Paedophilia remains the most readily recognised paraphilia. Remember, paedophilia is the attraction to *pre*pubescent children; it's often confused with hebephilia, or the attraction to teenagers or post-pubescent young people – they are not the same thing.' He quickly lists other high-profile paraphilias – autoerotic asphyxiation is a well-known one – and fetishes such as those around having bugs or spiders crawl over you. Coprophilia is briefly described, as is agalmatophilia, where the erotic interest is in statues or store mannequins, immobile human-like objects.

Tom half-listens, mildly surprised Johnson is speaking at this meeting of self-advocates. The good doctor generally confines himself to more professional engagements. Still, Acqui has some heft – several of its members have high-status positions in the world. These include Caroline Zammitt, Acqui convenor and his fellow law graduate. Caroline likes the world to run according to rules and she likes to be heard. Hence Acqui's monthly meetings – of which this is one – can attract media and government attention. Perhaps Johnson wants to be seen to be doing the right thing. Or perhaps Caroline managed to arrange a suitable recompense for his time.

'There are dozens more, including mechanophilia – a strong sexual attraction to mechanical objects like cars, or parts thereof. Yes, some people really do have sex with their cars,' Johnson finishes up, laughing at his own mild joke.

He sits for the questions he's agreed to take – five minutes only. He turns to Tom while the audience resettles. 'Clif Johnson,' he says. 'Didn't realise you were the next speaker.'

'I recognised your voice. Good to see you again. My partner couldn't make the meeting. Are you staying on?'

'I was planning to dash, but now you're here I might learn something. Yes, I'll stay.'

Quaint, Tom thinks. Who says "dash" these days?

'Great,' he responds politely.

Questions finished, Caroline, chairing the meeting, introduces Tom.

'Taking off from Clif's talk, I'm here to speak about paraphilias that might become exploitation,' Tom says, going on to outline what they know of the new escort agency. 'Our interest is in ensuring safety and decent payment for staff. It's not our brief, or our beef, to make any moral statement.'

'Who on earth are the – is Johns the word? Consumers? Punters? – of this escort service?' Caroline demands, her voice shrill.

Tom smiles. 'This is Sydney. Presumably some consumers are simply sampling the latest – ah – delicacy the city has on offer. Disability is definitely on-trend at the moment. The others are probably a solid base of people with mild forms of paraphilia. Or who maybe just have a thing for diversity. The ones to worry about are the obsessive devotees.'

'What's wrong with devotees?' a woman asks. 'Surely we all have preferences? Blondes, brunettes, muscle guys, cute butts, whatever?'

Tom nods – a gesture he's been expensively trained to use as if it were natural to a blind person. 'True,' he agrees. 'It's the extremes that are the problem, as always. It's definitely dull if I am considered attractive just because I'm blind. I would therefore be interchangeable with any other blind person, or at least any other blind bloke. A relationship on that basis won't go far. Even the sex is likely to be what the partner thinks is how a blind guy should do it.'

'Experience?'

'Maybe.' He smiles (another expensive gesture, at least when it comes to learning good timing). 'Some devotees are low key, fine. Others are fond of stalking – they say it's because their desires are considered strange and they have to be secretive, but it can be very like hunting prey. And I do say that from experience.'

Tom takes the pulse of the room. They're interested enough. 'I'm definitely not here to diagnose or pigeon-hole people attracted to those of us living with disability as deranged or perverted. But being a devotee does not preclude a person from being a predator or obsessive in ways unpleasant for the focus of attention. But before I go on, Clif perhaps you can shed some light on how people become obsessive devotees? Is there any sort of profile, and any set of behaviours to look out for?'

Clif responds grudgingly. 'My work is with people with disabilities themselves. Among my patients, I can't say the question of devotism has arisen and I admit I have only glanced at the literature. However, it strikes me that devotees may well have a misdirected care impulse.'

'Fucking fanatics,' someone calls from the audience.

'Please,' Caroline says, still shrill, 'let Clif finish.'

'I wouldn't describe devotees as fanatics.' Again Clif speaks slowly. 'A traumatic event in childhood, an instance of cruelty directed at them, for example, or the loss of a parent and a desire to atone for his assumed responsibility in not caring enough for his mother or father, may evidence itself later in life as overly solicitous caring for another person.' He coughs. 'The trauma of war perhaps. PTSD could–'

A woman's voice cuts in. 'If you ask me, trauma's wearing thin as the explanation for everything. It's more pervasive than genes-as-destiny by now. And isn't that the problem with devotees – they want to "care for us". They're on a power trip.'

'What about wannabees and pretenders?' a male voice asks, rhetorically as it turns out. 'Some deadbeats convince doctors to amputate a limb or two on account of them being unable to function as an intact body. I heard about a guy who went to Thailand, managed to persuade one of the surgeons who does sex reassignment that he didn't feel right in his body. He needed to have one less leg so he could walk with a stick and sometimes use a chair. That's a wannabee. Pretenders just play dress-ups. Arseholes who get off on being victims.'

'Come on, what's so wrong with being disabled? It's society that makes it hard for us!'

'Oh, please! That's theory. The reality is that with the best ramps and lifts in the world, with all the gadgets and adjustments, I still have more trouble getting around, going on a holiday, not to mention having sex, than abled bods do.'

'Can't we have a coherent position here?'

'Why should we? Every other group is allowed diversity but we're all lumped together. I for one like to wear lacy underwear.'

'We're not interested in your panties,' a woman's gruff voice takes over the room. 'This new agency is about exploitation. These guys, all they want is the disability, the new exotic. They get excited by running their hands over your fanny and thinking you can't feel it because you're a C4 quadriplegic. The fools think all your sensation is gone, and I'm sure they aren't paying enough for the privilege.'

Caroline suddenly intercedes: 'Everyone, we're here to learn. Let's get back to our speaker.'

Why is Caroline so anxious? It's good for people to talk, even to vent. But, realistically, Tom just wants to have some lunch. He returns to script, briefly outlining the abduction and attempted murder in Parramatta Park. He waits for the expressions of shock to subside before asking directly whether any Acqui member has been offered work in the agency.

In fact, he thinks privately, it's possible there's even a recruiter in the room.

A solid wall of denial greets him. He concludes at least one person in the room is hiding something. The questions are what, why and how deep is their involvement.

The other question is how on earth to find the answer to the first three.

4

Ten minutes later Caroline sends everyone out to lunch. She seems eager to get away herself. But then, Tom reflects, she always was conservative, despite rumours of errant sexual proclivities in their student days. He plays with the idea of her being one of the "escorts" – impossible, Caroline is not the underling type – while he waits for the quiet that indicates everyone has left. He begins to make a private call and is mildly irritated by the creak of wheels on the old floor joists.

'Hi, I'm Bec. There's something I didn't mention in the meeting. Do you mind?'

He flicks back through the voices. He can't recall hers. 'Of course not.'

'I've only got a minute. You see, my boyfriend is also a chair user. He's part of a group setting up a house for men with disabilities who're abused. What's interesting is there's been lot of dissension lately. Fights, really.'

He hears movement outside the open door. She stops speaking.

'Someone from the meeting?' Tom asks.

'Yeah, Roger. Maybe he's coming back for something he forgot.'

"Roger" is Roger Macintyre, head of the pressure group AMPS. During the meeting, Roger had declared his interest in being seduced. Very reasonable, but Roger projects a forbidding presence for any seducer. AMPS members are amputees – mostly accident victims and returned vets. Many were angry to begin with – self-selected to join the armed forces, or to ride too fast, too dangerously, good at intimidating. Now they're angrier. Tom should follow up on Roger.

Roger doesn't enter. His uneven tread recedes. Bec returns to her story.

'The arguments are about private funding. One of the group manages homes for the disabled. Through him, they've had an off-the-record offer from a philanthropist willing to buy property *and* provide staff and resources. Hard to believe really. And it's all very cagey, my fella won't even give me a name. You know what it's like though. They're desperate. Some of the guys just want to take the money, pronto, and are really pissed off at those who aren't so trusting.'

'Why do you think this has something to do with devotees? That is what you're thinking, isn't it?'

'I wasn't, until you were talking. It's what you said about the connector – what you might call a pimp. You see, one of the committee's suddenly got a load of new clothes and an adapted car. No new job. He's pushing for a young man's shelter. He doesn't seem to worry about anyone over 25 being out on the streets. It was him who introduced the sponsor guy.'

'New welfare-minded groups are springing up all the time, now the NDIS has brought on privatisation of services in such a rush. Could it be a civic-minded group?'

'Buying property? In Sydney? At best, it's a run-down rental and scrabbling for a computer that's not running on the first ever Windows. And the sponsor guy's making new friends by visiting clients in temporary housing.'

'Private visits?'

'You got it. Look, I've gotta go, otherwise I'll miss my lift and I can't afford cabs right now.'

'Sounds like you're onto something. Is there more you might be able to, um, uncover?'

'Give me a couple of days. I'll follow up as much as I can.'

Tom extricates a contact card from his wallet. 'Can you text your contacts to the number on here? Why didn't you say anything earlier, by the way?'

'In the meeting? You know what it's like, people talk and I didn't want to drop anyone in the shit – especially when I could be wrong.' A sigh; a dry-mouthed swallow. 'What sort of person would be involved in this, this...strange lust?' she asks.

'Who knows where the line is between obsession and ordinariness? In the end, lust comes in many forms. I wouldn't even advocate the escort service must be closed. It's a matter of making sure the controls are good so no one is put in danger. Wait before you feel betrayed.'

'I know, I know. It's silly to think those behind this are monsters with horns and burning eyes or whatever. It's just – oh, who knows what's right in the world anymore?' The old floorboards creak again as she turns her chair toward the door. 'Like I said, gotta go. Sorry about the histrionics; my being in a chair is recent, and it's still messing with my head. Is that a really terrible thing to say?'

'Blindness is not as bad as many think, but it still messes with my head, too, even though that's completely out of fashion to say. Thanks for the information. I've enjoyed meeting you.'

'Likewise. I've texted you my phone contact for work. Maybe it's best if you don't ring my personal number.'

Tom bites back the question, why? Perhaps the friend with the new clothes is her boyfriend?

5

THE CONFERENCE ROOM IS AT THE NORTHERN END OF THE BUILDING, NEAR the café that is the main money-spinner for a museum desperate for income. The cafe's a casual place, with no waiters to show him to a table. Tom folds his cane and listens intently. A table to the left attracts him.

'You startled me,' a woman's voice says as he sits down.

He's surprised by his mistake and amused by her tone. 'I often startle people,' he says dryly.

'I'm large enough, you should have noticed me,' she continues.

He wants to smile, to say something clever. Her voice is resonant, tinged with irony. As he hesitates, a seagull, bored with scavenging the harbour shores, squawks and plummets onto the table. She is eating, he conjectures, waving the bird away. 'I didn't realise the table was taken.' He unfolds his cane.

The intake of breath is contained but definite. She's just noticed the cane.

'Being blind is no excuse for rudeness,' she says evenly. 'You could have asked.'

Whoa: someone brave enough to be neither polite nor solicitous! Very rare. 'Fair comment,' he agrees, the corners of his mouth lifting.

He hears her chair shift back, feels her eyes really look at him for the first time. 'Are you always imperturbable?' she asks.

'I'm working on it. Makes life easier, although some people see it as insensitive.'

'Not as a challenge?'

'Not as a challenge, though that would be preferable,' he affirms. 'Are you always this forthright?'

There's a grin in her voice. Is it a grin a sighted person would call wicked? 'I can't claim to have worked on it,' she says. 'My mother always said I was born rude. I prefer to see myself as determined or frank or some such thing.' Her chair scrapes again. 'I'd better go.' She makes preparations; the sound of keys, a phone collected, knife and fork clattering lightly on a plate.

A shadow crosses and a waitress arrives, radiating annoyance, as if customers should not be allowed. 'Your coffee, madam.'

'Damn,' the woman says, the grin still in her voice. 'Now I'm proven truly rude. Except, I cross my heart, I was about to cancel the coffee. Not because of your arrival – it was taking far too long and I'd already had the most dishonest hamburger I'd ever eaten.'

'A dishonest hamburger?'

'Well, the name was a scam. I wanted minced meat and beetroot, not slivers of wagyu on a bun sprinkled with griddled herbs and seeds and dressed with a salad of greens you've never met before in your life. Fortunately, the gull made off with most of it. They'll eat anything.'

The self-parody in her tone is entertaining. 'Lucky you didn't end up with the vegan option. Do you mind if I order while you're drinking your coffee? I'm starving.'

The chair scrapes again. A bag is replaced on a spare seat. 'Why not? We seem destined.'

Tom holds out his hand, hoping his phone won't ring, the bored waitress will take her time, and the coffee is good after all. Flirting is out of order in this righteousness-driven world but it remains extremely enjoyable. 'My name's Tom, by the way.'

She hesitates, then shakes his hand. 'I'm Julia. And your handshake reminds me I should go to the gym more often.'

Her skin is fine and her grip firm. 'Good. Perhaps we can arrange a time to train together.' He pauses. 'You see, I thought you were annoyed because I might be trying to pick you up.'

'*Are* you trying to pick me up?' she asks, laughter back in her voice.

'I wasn't then. I am now. You've already told me you like old-fashioned ways. Perhaps I could buy you another lunch?'

'Old fashioned? Oh, of course, the hamburger.'

His phone rings. In his life, nostalgia never gets much breathing space. Nodding his apology, he answers.

Warren doesn't bother with preliminaries. 'It's a much better organised operation than the Pentagon, I can tell you. One hand actually seems to know exactly what the other is doing, and nothing leads to a centre.'

'Big money.'

'Mountain ranges of it. Anyhow, seems a cab or two is being used, too. No Uber. Very legit looking. Sub-leased, I'd reckon.'

'Nice touch. Anything I need to know right now?'

'You busy?'

'Yes.'

'Won't ask. Just wanna know which way you want me to go. I can stop and ask a few pertinent questions of a few people, or I keep in the slipstream of the van, see if I can suss out who's handing over dough for services rendered. What'd you reckon?'

Tom wants Warren to get in close, see if he can actually eyeball, even identify a client. But he never overtly directs Warren's investigations. 'Follow your instincts,' he replies. 'You know what you're doing.'

'Got you, Boss. Reckon I might get a bit up close and personal with the buyers. And there's a guy who might be doing a bit of stalking. I'll keep an eye out. I'll email you. Get back to me when you can.'

'Fine. I've got another meeting soon, won't be too long.'

Tom puts the phone down. The warmth of Julia's body disturbs the air around him. 'My phone's off now. Shall we have that lunch?'

'But you have a meeting?'

She is testing him.

'I've arranged to access some documents in the museum. That can wait.' Tom notes the thick scent of a passing group of lunchers in their winter clothing, a gaggle of sounds. He wonders: does she have a husband or partner – of whichever gender? Children perhaps?

'Okay,' she announces. 'I'll pretend to be Alice in another world. For lunch.'

'I think the stairs,' Tom says thirty minutes later as they make their way into the museum proper. 'Lifts make me claustrophobic.'

'Doctor?'

'Oh, you heard. That young receptionist was very formal. Perhaps conveying my cancelling at the last moment was somewhat inconvenient.' He gently kicks the first stair leading to the upper floors, judging the height.

'You were very polite. But Doctor of…? There's about twenty stairs, by the way. Straight up.'

'Thanks. And you?'

'Are you asking about my educational attainments?'

'That sounds terrifyingly formal.'

'I have an idea. Let's not ask any more questions,' Julia suggests. 'I've agreed to another world, for a short time. Let's honour that with an absence of ticking boxes – you live there, I live here, you do this, I do that – or similar fact-finding.'

'We could try it, although I tend to curiosity.'

'This is a grand staircase,' Julia says as they reach the top. 'Someone wanted to make an impression.'

'We could go back down, make a sweeping entry. You'd need a gown. Dior perhaps, not too showy but elegant in the extreme. I could get away with a dinner suit, no need for a tux.'

Julia laughs. 'I agree, a simple, elegant suit would be more "you". But how do you know I wouldn't look like the side of a bus dressed in Dior, or anything else for that matter?'

'I hear buses are very well decorated these days.' His voice drops into seriousness. 'Julia, you respond like a woman who is comfortable in her attractiveness. Would we have chatted so easily if you felt like the side of a bus? And/or – dare I say it – if you'd found me unattractive?'

She considers. 'Sadly, no is the answer. Our response to the physical runs deep, doesn't it? Even if it's a very generic and superficial attractiveness, it has an effect.'

'Indeed. And we'll have to shelve the grand entrance for today. To begin with, the dress would take several fittings. And, after my change in plan, I'm not sure the young woman at reception would appreciate us taking over her access point. She's already annoyed.'

'Jealous, more like. She had to give up the opportunity of taking the arm of a tall, fair, blind and handsome doctor – of something. Could've been very cosy in the lift for her. She'd have insisted on the lift. The proper thing for a disabled person.'

'I can see a little light and shade, enough to make out an outline silhouetted in bright light. Mostly I rely on sound for direction. I hate small, dark spaces that bounce sound around. Don't tell anyone. I usually don't.'

'Why are you telling me? If that's an allowable question.'

'Because you were so rude when we met.'

She laughs. 'That's rather – um – contrary.'

'Let's say because you said – what was it? – tall, fair and blind. Most people pussy-foot around, thinking they shouldn't notice I can't see. It's peculiar really, as if blindness will go away if ignored. Or they think they have to like me because I'm blind. Or despite my being blind. It's often hard to tell which.'

'Stereotyping runs deep in western culture,' she agrees mildly. 'Let's stroll grandly around the displays. I'll do description.'

'You know about blindness, don't you?'

'Questions, questions.' She takes his arm and proceeds into the museum proper. 'I haven't been here for years. We all forget our history.'

The museum is quaintly enjoyable. He wonders who she is and why they have picked each other up in this charming retro fashion. Definitely out of the ordinary. He decides to abandon caution. He is often far too serious. And what could happen in a small museum in the centre of a big city?

She suddenly swings toward him. 'I have to go. This has gone well beyond that hour.'

'Julia, I don't know you well. I do know you're not Cinderella.'

'I really have to go.'

'I won't ask why, it's against the rules. Remember, though, we have a date for the gym.'

A cough echoes from a doorway nearby. They are being told, politely, to be quiet.

She speaks quickly. 'Let's do the same place, same time, next week? I'll be here. I don't break promises.'

6

In the van, they drive down the freeway at exactly the speed limit. Sonya understands the driver is under strict orders never to attract attention, but in Sydney, where it's practically a civic duty to break road rules, it has the opposite effect. Cars slash by on either side, cutting in front of them, blaring horns, flashing lights, or tail-gating them, dangerously close. The mild anarchy shows a lack of fear in the drivers, which cheers Sonya. Eventually they make it to the City-West link and over the Anzac Bridge.

'I don't like it here,' Avril announces as they take the slip road toward Darling Harbour. 'There's only families and foreigners. Are we doing jobs for foreigners?'

Jim the driver doesn't respond.

Avril pulls a mirror from her handbag, inspects her makeup, offers the mirror to Sonya. 'I don't care all that much,' she says. 'The foreigners are better tippers than the Aussies. Only way the Aussies round here can afford their real estate is to be mean every other way. I'm gonna be diff'rent.' She looks hard at the back of Jim's neck as if daring him to comment, before leaning closer to Sonya. 'Got a customer wants some private service,' she whispers. 'Cash in hand, taxi money, and he don't want much, I can tell you. Easy bloody work. Just looks and looks then jerks himself off.'

'Avril, you must not! It is dangerous!'

'I like sunshine,' Avril notes as the sun disappears behind a swiftly moving cloud. 'Don't worry, Sonnie, I said no. But it might be yes next time. We don't know the bosses – why should they make money outta us?'

She returns the mirror to her handbag, placing it neatly beside the flash drive the eye-patch guy pushed into her hand. Is he looking for private work? He's obviously way better off than the other guy. That coat he was wearing – gorgeous, must be worth a mint. And the idea of having control appeals. Yep, with private clients she'll earn more and get away from her parents and the old government housing area they live in much faster. Avril decides to take the flash drive home, to see what it's all about. Later, she'll tell Sonya.

'Cause she and Sonnie share everything, imagine a future together, independence from their families. Avril's parents are born-again Christians; they're convinced her disability is the result of inherited sins. This drives her nuts, particularly as the past sins aren't affecting them – their meanness excepted – and she's the one who can't reach the cupboards or the pedals of a car.

Sonya's family are also Christians. They're refugees from Iraq and civil war, American invasion, religious persecution. Avril can't imagine all that: it's too sad. She and Sonnie are both popular with the clients, and their escape fund is building up. Avril explains the income – some of which she dutifully hands over to her mother – as her working in a factory. Sonya explains hers as payment for a job in a library, sorting books. Sonya's parents are proud she can read English so well. Avril's mother and father just tell her they hope she will stop shift-work soon, it isn't good for her health. A finger up to her health, is what she thinks. She imagines the house she'll buy them one day. That'll show them.

As they squeeze through the clutter of traffic, Avril touches the USB again. Hopes it's a good luck charm.

The van swings into a hotel car park. Avril whistles. 'Swanky.'

Jim jumps out, slides open the door. 'Quick now, we're late. Just Avril.'

'See you s'arvo, Sonnie.' Avril allows Jim to help her out. 'Lie back and think of the dollars,' she adds, grinning.

Five minutes later the van is outside a new apartment building. Dark trim, sleek, views of the city. Yet, for Sonya, the building is forbidding, with its hanging gardens like a long beard trailing over an expressionless face – a living, breathing monster. 'Why are we stopping here?'

'S'where y'going.'

'This is not hotel.'

'Nah. Now Sonnie, don't ask me the ins and outs, if you see what I mean. I'm jus' followin' orders, y'know that.'

'There will be reception, people close?'

Jim shrugs, holds out his hand to help her out of the van.

Sonya hesitates. The work is always meant to be where they can summon help if they need it. They're not working for an ordinary escort agency, they're told over and over. We expect the clients to behave as well as you girls do; any bad business and there's always back-up.

There is no back-up in a private apartment building. Especially not the expensive, thick-walled, sealed-door type she is entering now. Privacy is bought at premium rates in a place like this.

Jim presses the intercom and ushers her toward the lift. 'Tenth floor. Only one flat to a floor, so you'll be right. I'll be downstairs in an hour and a half. Might be a bit extra for you in this one, I hear.' He gently pushes her into the lift.

The lift is low-lit, mirrored. Its size startles her. As does the man who is leaning silently against the far corner. He pushes himself off the wall as she enters, stares. He is in combat fatigues and his body is honed and powerful. Her stomach lurches, but before anything can be said the lift doors open on the tenth. She turns as she exits, looking back to make sure the man is not following her. He is at the lift doors, stationary, a finger on the button that commands the doors to remain open. His gaze meets hers, blank. And then his eyes lift and slip around her, moving to the apartment door. Sonya stays, watchful. When the door opens and a man comes out, the man in the lift gives a slight, sharp nod and lets the doors close.

Sonya fights the desire to run. Is the man in the lift a protector, watching out for her client? He is big enough, he has army hair, he and the client obviously know each other. Still, Sonya does not look behind. Instead she walks, head high, straight to the tall doorway. The man greeting her is finer boned than the lift man, but also well-built. He has a small, neat moustache. Is the moustache a disguise?

'Call me Stephen,' he says, leading her in, offering her a drink. Very politely, as if she is special. Many of them treat her like that, as if she is made out of crystal. It takes them ten minutes or so before they show they want to smash her.

'You will find a dress to wear in there,' Stephen says, becoming business-like when she declines the drink. 'Naturally, I am happy to help you with the clasps. You should call me when you're ready as there are quite a lot of them.' She feels his hand, a sticky moth, as he pushes her toward a half-open door.

She enters a bedroom that doesn't feel lived in. No personal items, no books, no ornaments on the smooth surfaces of the expensive furniture. And no smells. As a child in Iraq she learned the importance of smells. When they were fleeing from one place to another, the safety of a house could be calculated – roughly – by the scent. Children's play smells were reassuring, a woman's perfume signalled a willingness to break with tradition, the odour of closed rooms suggested fear, while the sweat of men had many gradations, from what her father called honest work through to hatred. Sonya breathes in. This room worries her.

On the bed is a dress, one she's only seen before in pictures. A dress made for a queen. For Queen Elizabeth the first, the Virgin Queen. The dress is exquisite, embroidered with jewels, a thick, rich fabric, superbly made. It covers most of the bed. Her breath comes out short and rapid.

Where has Stephen gone? He isn't outside the door, she's fairly sure of that. There could be a spy hole in the room, a hidden camera. Sonya is aware that some clients try to record what goes on. It is one of the reasons the work is in hotels and not in private premises – the agency can keep control, because nothing should be free. Sonya finds the possibility of a recording more disturbing than most aspects of the work.

She struggles to lift the dress. Her own clothes are chosen for ease of removal. Usually, in this one area, her needs and the wishes of the clients meet – they both want clothes that come off with the movement of one hand. This dress makes her dependent. Her shoulders ache with the weight of the heavy fabric. She has to twist and pull and rearrange – the dress seems to have a body and mind of its own – so that she can put it on before the man becomes angry. She is anxious, too, to know what game he is playing.

'I am ready,' she calls, when the bodice is pressed against her breasts and the skirt shivers around her like an animal that might swallow its prey.

Stephen comes in holding a small hook. 'For the clasps, madam,' he says, bowing as if she is truly royalty. She feels the back of the dress being drawn tightly, suffocatingly together. His hands do not touch any part of her naked skin.

'Now, come.' Again he half-bows.

Internally Sonya sighs. Disturbed men talk like this, behave like this. Pretending to be servile, pretending to be someone other than themselves. There is no honesty in this man's speech which, even though her English is not perfect, she can tell is an act. A poor, muddled act – he does not even know who he is making himself out to be. She realises he doesn't even make sense to himself. And she recognises that is dangerous.

He walks behind her, shepherding her into a larger room. It is dark, thick blinds obscuring the daylight, only candles lit. In the middle of the room is a huge chair on a raised platform. A small set of stairs enables her to climb onto the dais and then into the chair, shaped and decorated like a throne. Doing this makes her perspire and the dress cling ever more closely, python-like.

As soon as she is seated Stephen dashes from the shadows and arranges the skirt, lifting and folding and settling, withdrawing if his hands come too near her skin.

'Now, let there be light.' He snaps his fingers and fine beams suddenly illuminate her from head to foot, one bright beam almost blinding her. The dress shines blood red. The stump of her amputated left arm glows too. Sonya is terribly uncomfortable and shifts slightly.

'Stay! You are a queen and a queen knows the power of stillness. A queen can remain without moving for many hours. As you will learn to do.'

An hour and a quarter, or less, she wants to remind him. That's the rest of what you've paid for. Jim will be back then. He'll ring the bell, come up, bang on the door if I am not waiting for him. He is Australian, he will even break the rules if he has to. Or so she hopes.

The man moves backwards and she loses sight of him in the deep web of darkness. His rasping breath remains, causing turmoil in the heavy air. She knows this sound. Soon the pace will increase and the rasping will take on a sharp edge, with cutting, desperate sibilants. A sound without thought, a sound with violence, a sound with no interest in others: he will have that soon, they all do.

'Tell me how you got your injury. '

This is a common demand and she has stories to recite to suit the occasion. They aren't the truth, although the horror and blood and violence she describes are real enough. She begins to speak.

'No. Do not give me facts and figures, who did it. I want to know how the ground felt as you fell upon it, how the stones cut into your flesh, what you thought as you lay beside the putrid meat of corpses, their shit befouling you, how you dragged yourself across fields of spent mortars and cartridges and flesh, knowing that you were bleeding to death, to a place which you thought would offer safety, but where all you could look upon was more defiled bodies, distorted, pierced, broken far worse than your own.'

His breath rate increases as he speaks his strange stilted speech, like he is reading a play. There is another sound, too. Slapping. He is slapping himself. He has fallen into a shaft of light, she can see him now. He is not attacking his private parts. He hits his head and arms. Then he beats deeply into his stomach. Beating and groaning and beating again. Dear Mother of God, she prays.

'Speak, speak,' he screams.

She speaks, trying to make it up, trying to pretend it didn't happen to her. But it did. Just like he said. Her revulsion, her fear, the disgust she feels even now at her own quiet acceptance: it all surfaces and threatens to overwhelm her. She must not move. The slightest twitch of her arm – the stump of her arm that she cannot readily control – is noticed and he screams and beats harder at himself, and she is more and more frightened.

The dress is pushing in on her, forcing her to breathe high and shallow and without hope. She keeps talking, at the same time desperately telling herself to think, to make sense of this man's perversions. A virgin queen, a lighted throne, the talk of blood, the illumination of her injury, the beating. Is she to be a sacrifice? Or, dressed as a queen, is she grand enough to order his punishment? Is this what he wants?

Sonya loses all sense of time. She is a broken woman left on a field whose only chance of survival is to keep awake. The beating doesn't stop, the rasping grows louder and stronger. He asks more and more questions, severing her from the sanity she's maintained so well for so long. Tears are making mud of her makeup and still he persists and persists and persists. 'What was this like, what was that, don't move, remember you are a queen, commander of the sword, remember the blood that was not yours alone.'

The heat of the lights, the weight of the dress, the intensity, the fear:

she is sinking into semi-consciousness. And then, as it had that day when her upper limb was sliced through as if she were nothing more than meat, her anger rises. She is furious that she is treated this way. She swallows the anger, treasures it inside her. It prevents her from falling too deeply into the mire of his perversion.

Suddenly he is in front of her, the effect of the lights severing his head from his body. She recoils. She is amazed, too, that he is still fully clothed.

'Cease,' he says, his voice suddenly, threateningly soft. 'Look.' Swiftly, he undoes his trousers and lets them cascade to his feet. 'Look.'

Sonya looks. She sees scars, healed but hellish. His penis has been cut, and stumped. Scars like her own, a tiny but gaping hole made – by what? a pen knife? – to allow the urine through.

'I was in the peacekeeping force in Bosnia, and then on to the Observation Mission in Iraq. Your people did not like us being there. Your brothers or your relatives or your friends did this to me.'

Her impulse is to cross herself with her remaining right arm. But she senses such a gesture will further disturb him. He clearly assumes she is Muslim. It is dangerous to challenge the assumptions of men naked and vulnerable. And this man has no time for the simple rituals of hope.

'You can go now. Our time is up. Go to the bedroom, I will help you out of the dress.'

When she is in her own clothes again, he shows her to the lift. Quietly.

'You will come again.' It is a statement, not a question.

Sonya leaves, disgusted, saddened, not cowed. Life is, she well knows, a fight to the death.

TUESDAY

7

Avril wakes grudgingly, eyes sore from too much makeup, gut feeling like a fist has been rammed into it. Work was busy yesterday, maybe too busy: a girl can only do so much even for money. And there's the flash drive. She slithers out of bed, tiptoes toward the bathroom. Her mother hears her anyway – like all the other council houses around, theirs has paperbark walls. Genuine paperbark. They stripped large paperbark trees, mashed the bark up and turned it into houses for poor people. The bark attracts the possums that fill the ceiling with shit.

'Avril, what are you doing?' her mother yells.

What the fricking hell does the woman expect at this hour of the morning? 'Having a bloody piss.'

'Don't use that dirty language.'

She'll kill her old lady one day, she really will. As if she and the old man never swear. Despite their God-is-great blather, they're worse than a battalion of troopers boasting about their exploits at a brothel, the pair of them.

She makes it to the bog. Has a gigantic piss. She experiences momentary relief that it doesn't hurt. Reasonably often she ends up with a sore cunt and a urinary tract infection. She's had too many doses of antibiotics to count.

Should she flush the USB down the bog too? Why did she take a video snuck into her hand by some oldie in a suit outside a shopping centre? How fricking dumb is she?

She stays near the toilet. Having a good chunder's an option, inspired by just thinking about the disgusting thing. Completely fricking lucky she'd bought her own laptop a couple of weeks back. Otherwise things might have got really challenging, her old man being obsessed with making sure she never saw the unclothed legs of a footballer, let alone a hundred pics of herself naked as the day. With various pricks and other body parts doing things to her, apparently all in the name of love. Some fool had put the video together with a creepy heart-shaped frame all through it, and with words flashing up – mostly "love" and "my only one" and "my heart's desire" and stuff like that. Of course she wanted love; but no way does this have anything to do with it. This is freako obsession. Without quite intending to, she crosses herself.

The school where she and Sonnie'd met was a Catholic job. Only place that'd have her without shoving her into a "special" class for disabled kiddos. Should she tell Sonnie about the video? The trouble is, Sonnie's protective and a lot more impressed by rules than Avril is; too trusting of authority. It's fricking strange, considering what's happened in Sonnie's life. She'll want to dob to the agency and the police and she'll actually believe they'll do something. That's a joke. You can't arrest a guy for telling you he loves you.

The agency might try to work out who he is, 'cause he's ripping them off, getting images of her for free. Unless he's one of their mates and is paying them for the privilege. Also unless he's used other sources. She certainly suspects not all the pictured women are her. For one, how does she know exactly what her cunt looks like from someone else's point of view? There are no headshots of the females and while all the shots of the being-fucked body – arms, legs, bums and necks – show short stature, some are definitely more classic-shaped than her. She has some syndrome, with a long name she's never bothered to remember – she lives in this body, it isn't some diagnosis as far as she's concerned. Anyhow her body's different from mainstream dwarfism, 'specially her legs and arms. Not to mention her head. Looking closely, there has to be more than one woman of short stature in the video. With or without consent.

That worries her somewhat – being exclusive is important to her maintaining a really good income stream. And that is what she wants to do.

As well as the women, three or four times there's also a clear-enough shot of a man's body. She's definite there's more than one guy. Trouble is any real stuff, like faces or hair or whatever, have been — what's the word? – pixelated out.

Avril's mother calls up to her again. 'I'm getting dressed,' she calls back, rattling her jewellery box to give some authenticity to the claim.

Her mum instructs on her on what to wear. 'It's cold, Avril!' As if she's a fricking kid.

When her mum quietens down, she opens the jewellery box. It holds her music and movie USBs already. Should she add this to the mix?

At the end of the video, a letter had scrolled onto the screen. Creepy stuff about perfect love and destiny and how the world was against them but he would treasure her for ever after. All she had to do was meet him at a hotel she's never heard of near Central Station. The meeting is supposed to be later today and she's supposed to come alone. Making it fricking obvious, somehow — she can't exactly say how — that it's all a kind of threat. She's going to ignore the proposed meeting. This guy's way too weird for her.

Yeah, she'll keep hold of the flash drive. Right now, there's no point in going to the cops. Even if other women and several blokes are involved, the police'll be polite for ten seconds and piss themselves laughing soon as she and Sonnie exit. Exploitation isn't illegal. So right now, it's not worth telling Sonnie either. But who knows what will happen next? The USB might be useful at some time – evidence or something. It truly is a pity the video never shows the faces attached to the pricks.

8

THE WIND IS SETTLING IN LIKE AN AGING RELATIVE DETERMINED ON A LONG visit. The street crowds are thick with extra layers of wool, fake fur, real fur, Gore-Tex and other materials closeted away since last winter. Here and there, the pungent aroma of mothballs is pushed along with the disconcerted crowds. The threat of collision is high, particularly for Tom. He's pleased to arrive in the warmth of his chambers.

Tom closes his door firmly. Janice, the chambers' PA, is – as always – at work sanctimoniously early and he prefers to speak with Warren in private. He also hopes Bec from the Acqui meeting will get back to him with the names of those offering support for the men's group. Could they be real philanthropists? He needs to activate other contacts too.

A call interrupts his musing. Janice puts through Marcia from Women Wear Wheels. Words tumble at him like sharp rocks falling down a steep slope. Hasn't the world heard of text? And that people like to be left alone first thing in the morning?

'Five of them now. This is hell, it's deranged, it's beyond vicious, it's…'

'Marcia, stop. I have no idea what you are talking about.'

Marcia isn't impressed. She's not precisely hysterical but she lets Tom know that she's damn well bloody sure that no-one, not even bloody do-good, smart-arse, Tom bloody Challinor, who clearly can't understand emotion, can do a thing, a single thing, about the stupid, complete arsehole fucker who is leaving these dolls. And something has to be done!

'Dolls, what dolls? I need information, not a diatribe.'

'I can't believe this! All right, all right–'

The story is: five dolls have arrived by various means at the refuge run by Women Wear Wheels. The first, a month ago, was a Raggedy Ann, its arms torn off, the cloth stuffing spilling like stringy grey blood. The second one was a Barbie, ears slashed, crudely drawn hearing aids below the wound.

'To be honest, we didn't take too much notice of the first one – it was pretty horrendous but it's a rag doll and could've been thrown over the fence. Plenty of local kids walk past and some like to hurl abuse at the idiots and cripples, as they see us. The second one was jammed into the letter box. Disgusting, frightening but again we didn't discount local kids–'

'Do the dolls belong to one of the resident children?'

'Come on Tom. They're traumatised kids, don't heap more on them.'

'Could they do it because they're traumatised?'

'Yeah, all right, I agree lots of our kids have some level of behavioural expression. But, mostly it's young kids here now and what kid would come up with this? And it's getting worse. The third doll – another Barbie – arrived five days ago – with an eye missing and head injuries drawn on with felt tip. It came in a package delivered by a courier. Obviously no sender's address. Then yesterday, an old Cabbage Patch doll. On the doorstep again, severed limbs and all. And now, it's vile, there's one of those Hawaiian dolls from the 50s or 60s. Christ, I can't even bring myself to describe it. Hold on a minute.' Marcia's voice retreats, returns. 'That's not the end of it. Actually, I won't read this out; shouldn't give the words airtime. I'll scan it in, you can listen yourself.'

'Marcia, can we back-track here? What are you scanning in?'

Her voice is acidic. 'The doll today was in an Amazon box, addressed to the refuge. One of the kids opened it – all excited it might be a present. It came with a letter, if you can call it that. Before you ask, it's printed on standard paper, in Helvetia.'

'Does the note make actual threats? Any indication of who it is directed to? Can you read it to me after all?'

'Listen, Tom, mostly we manage to keep our address secret, but it doesn't always work and we've had revenge porn dropped in the letter box plenty of times. Sick stuff that describes what the writer will do to the "whore/slut/slag's" genitalia in considerable detail. This is different. All right, all right, listen, I'll read the first paragraph. It's long and seriously perverse. Here goes:'

'You disgust me, your sense of superiority, your self-righteousness. It sickens me that you assume we merely lust for the physical — the glass cunt, the sightless eyes, the silent scream of unbearable ecstasy. How terribly deficient your understanding is. We are not so shallow, so pathetic, so perverse. For as long as there have been humans attracting, procreating or, let us be precise, fucking — behind bushes, in caves, in the shallows of rivers and seas, in beds, flea ridden or luxurious, among the fetid smell of furs upon an ice-cap, in the litter, against the broken wall behind the toilet block — always there have been those in possession of extra perception, of a deeper sense of what it is to be human. We are the gifted ones, we are the anointed. We supplicate, we care, we sacrifice. We slave for you, we work day in, day out to eliminate your suffering. We lead the blind, the lame, we intervene and communicate for the deaf and mute. We find beauty in the abnormal, the infirm, the misshapen. We are prepared to carry a broken body on our shoulders, to lower that body gently down, to place it on pelts and entering it, to bring it to pleasure. We are prepared to give you everything and to give up everything for you. What more could you want! Why are you hidden behind those walls, cowering in self-pity? Where is your gratitude? Why have you no devotion when I have so much?'

Tom runs his hand over his head while listening. The note certainly takes an Oscar for unusual. 'An articulate, educated, entitled, very serious devotee.' The psychiatrist Clif Johnson's words slip into his mind. Devotism as over-zealous caring. Slated to childhood trauma of some kind. Maybe Clif wasn't so far off the mark after all.

'You might say devotee. Other descriptions spring to my mind. Impotent wanker arsehole prick is the kindest among them.'

'Indeed. Have you any idea who it is directed to?'

'Good question. Fuck knows the answer. Could be any one of the women here. Might be the refuge itself. Look at the reference to self-righteousness. We get that all the time — partners who hate us for providing a safe space for the women they've dragged through life by the hair. Every so often they try to whip up hysteria in the media. Lesbians, feminist cows, men haters denying them their rights to their kids; it's a winning line these days.'

'So there's protection in place for the staff as well as residents?'

'Of course. But Tom, what is it about these devotees? This prick seems to think he's a priest of some totally fucked mix of religion and evolutionary biology. It's like the fucking pro-paedophile lobby.'

'The self-justification? You're not wrong. So, some of the dolls were on your doorstep?' Tom asks. The refuge fence is astronomically high, the gates perpetually locked. The women who live there are often very afraid, specifically of the partners who have inflicted violence on them, and generally of a world that is unsympathetic to women with visible difference. Even the children are hyper-vigilant about security.

'Yep, the dolls appear as if by magic – evil magic. Must be in the dead of night. The gates are untampered with, the lights don't go on as they would if someone were inside the fence. Conclusion – a man with a magnificent aim throws them in. We've gone over the security footage. We think there could be a figure. It's too dark for any detail.'

'The delivery company? Did they have a name?'

'Privacy, privacy. I tried.'

'They probably don't even have the information. You'd have to think catching him throwing one in would be the best bet.'

'We've put extra staff on overnight.'

'Good. Now, setting aside your magic theory, the most plausible explanation is a furious ex-partner. Have you spoken with all the residents?'

Marcia's voice grates. 'Of course, and we can't harass them any further, they've been through enough!'

'I understand – as much as I can. However, as you know, having a disability or being the victim of violence doesn't automatically make you a nice person, considerate of the needs of others. People who are victims are still people with personalities and their own behavioural tics, some of which are exaggerated by being victims. If there is a resident who knows the origin of the dolls, they should speak up, for the benefit of all.'

'Tom, you're a wealthy bloke. Life's different here. The women are scrabbling for safety, for a place to live. They don't have the energy to think about others. Still, I get your point. We'll try again – carefully. We've got to stop this.'

'I'll see if I can help out with surveillance. Do you remember Warren? He has other commitments tonight, but he'll have an associate who can help out, and we could cover the rest of the week.'

'Thanks, but we won't have a man in here, much as I like Warren. What if I ask the elderly couple next door if he can camp there? Their place has good sight lines and I don't mind explaining the problem to them.'

'Warren's got an appropriate car, with equipment. Use of their facilities is good, but not essential.'

In the background, a woman asks Marcia something. Unhappy tone, demanding. A child crying. Tom would hate to do her job.

'Police?' he asks when she can talk again.

'Come on, Tom, by this stage of their lives, most of the women who live with us'd swim the Amazon – the real, predator-filled river – before dialling triple O. And, believe me, we can't get the cops to respond when violence is actually happening in front of us. I've tried for this. They shrugged and said it was a practical joke, LOL, ha ha ha. They didn't lift a finger. Complete dickheads.'

'From what you say, what's happening is forming a pattern, heading to a crescendo. That's more worrying, and evidentiary, than a single incident. Police aren't all bad. They will respond if you push them into it. Which you can do.'

'You saying I'm pushy?'

'That's one of the reasons we get on.' Tom hears Marcia laugh. 'On a related issue, I spoke to you about a new – what you might call radical – escort agency?'

'Related, you're implying? The agency's set the cat among the pigeons? Because a few women want to earn a living, some dead-beat decides all women living with disability are betrayers of innocence and should be punished? It wouldn't be the first time.'

'Maybe, although correlation doesn't mean causation. The fact that the escort agency and your dolls follow each other doesn't necessarily mean one set off the other. The vindictiveness you're experiencing is specific, I think. I spoke at the Acqui monthly meeting yesterday. Afterwards a relatively new member brought some concerns to me. Including the possibility of the agency recruiting workers through refuges.'

'Presuming you're intimating our residents could have been approached? Makes sense. Poverty and fear make people vulnerable to any good offer. Against it, I'd say the current residents are fairly long stayers. Most of them hardly go out. We generally get new phone numbers for them when they come in here. Safer.'

'Fair enough. But–'

'I agree, it's still possible. Perhaps probable. Thing is, the dolls and letters are predatory behaviour, Tom. They're not sexual, they're all about power. At the same time that leads me to think your escort agency – yeah, it's not yours as such – might actually have kick-started something. Any fella who thinks his partner is even imagining having sex with someone other than him is an angry man. A man who often sees himself as diddled by the whole, wicked female sex. Imagine how angry a fella might be if he imagines, or knows, his partner is making money out of sex. All his devotion gone to waste. Makes me want to puke.' Her voice is like steel wool scraping a dirty saucepan. 'Right now, I gotta go. I'm fucking exhausted, Tom. This is such madness. I'll talk to the neighbours and follow up with all the other shit.'

'The shit includes calling the cops?'

'All right, all right, jesus, with a small j, between you and the residents I'm the meat in the sandwich. I'll get the police back. We've got Gertrude coming in for night duty tonight; we'll seat her literally by the front door. Now you tell me who's the best person in the force to get onto the job.'

Ah, she wants to use his contacts. That, and Warren's services, are at least partly why she's called him. Good one, Marcia.

9

Tom opens the ABC listen app. The familiar news theme flows effortlessly through his excellent speakers, yet he misses analogue radio. The older form held a certain magic. People speaking into a small device in a small studio, sending that voice into homes, cars, the corridors of power, the confined cells of a correctional centre, all day, every day, fascinates him. Speaking for public consumption is intensely intimate. Analogue sound, less pristine and controlled than digital, conveyed that intimacy more intensely.

This morning the newsreader is a young woman, her voice languid with vowels that travel from Byron Bay to Birdsville in the length of a word. So much for the old BBC voice Australian newsreaders were forced to adopt. If only the robotic voices that read out emails and internet pages to him were like this woman's – individual in timbre and tone, layered with place and culture.

The final item in the brief bulletin is the announcement of the release of the Royal Commission report into sexual abuse in institutional care. He needs to read the report. Soon, soon, when he has time.

A half-cup of coffee later, Tom calls Warren. He hears mildly fractious children in the background. Tom's met Warren's kids, but Warren as a father remains an incongruous concept. He's all overcoats and dark alleys in Tom's imagination. 'You're back at home?'

'Yeah, been out, come back to be with the kids till Karen's sister can take them. Karen had to get off to work and it's school hols.'

'Can you talk? Good.' Tom runs over the issue at the refuge.

'Wow, is that what the pollies mean by a sense of entitlement? Some bozo who thinks they own someone else's body?'

Warren agrees to Thursday overnight at the refuge, suggesting his mate Al can probably do Wednesday, Friday as well, if necessary, he'll suss it out.

'How was yesterday evening, this morning?'

'I've been across the bridge and back near half a dozen times – those nice family types on the North Shore are eager little buggers – and to the eastern suburbs more often than a Pommy backpacker. I reckon you're not far off the mark about a hornet's nest. Only it might be wasps of the killer variety. Way it goes is, the workers head in, disappear to a room, sometimes with the assistance of the driver. I've picked my teeth in a couple of lobbies. Seen bugger all in the way of punters. Guessing they're already in the room or lurking in a corridor upstairs. Bookings're paid for in cash. I haven't seen every time, possible there's other payment means. And there's always a room vacant, often wheelchair accessible, too. How come they hit bingo every time?'

'Possible they book online. When you say North Shore, where do you mean?'

'Cammeray mostly, Willoughby too.'

'So, well-heeled but low-key areas. Eastern Suburbs?'

'Coogee, Bondi.'

'Never the CBD? North Sydney? The Cross?'

'No. I wonder why? Ah, got it. They aren't going near the usual red-light districts or the places serviced by your run-of-the-mill high-class escort agencies. Low profile, keeping clear of the competition. Makes sense.' Warren considers. 'Be interesting if the hotels have overlaps in ownership or management. We should dig a little.'

'And they stopped work around six?'

'Yep. I followed the van from Parramatta. Gets parked in an underground carpark attached to one of the mainstream hotels – sort you pay for a space by the month. It moved out again early this morning, started collecting girls from as far out as Penrith. Brought them back to another carpark attached to another hotel. They all sat and gabbed in the back for a bit. A taxi came in, picked up a couple. The rest were distributed around soon after.'

'Does the same driver pick them up again?'

'Good question. He can't, not every time, 'cause he's doing more drop-offs. Like I said, there's at least two vans, some taxi transport. Hey, did'ya get those names I emailed you, from the side of the vans?'

'Thanks, yes. As you'd expect, they're all false or untraceable. Still, such well-prepared signage tells us they're highly organised crooks. I'm going to speak with a friend of mine who might help with the hotel ownership, and a solicitor who specialises in shelf companies. He'll take some persuading to give over info. I'll give you more details when it's less murky.'

'Gotya. Soon as I off-load these little blighters, I'm off out to the wild west again. Hoping persistence will help. Got a meeting with Lexi this arvo. Anything else you reckon I should do, immediate-like?'

Tom considers the attack on Melanie, the almost frenzied use of the agency, the mutilated dolls – even if they are not all connected, violence around people with disability is escalating and could soon be out of control. As yet, though, no clear direction presents itself.

'What you're doing is probably the best bet for now. How do you think Lexi might help?'

'Could be long odds, but she's out in the field, keeping an eye on the workers. She musta heard some goss.'

Tom nods to himself. The world needs more women like Lexi. She's done her time in the industry and now protects the street-workers as fiercely as she guards her own daughter.

Janice, the chambers' PA, comes in, noisily dropping a pile of papers on his desk. While the Braille machine in her office is highly efficient, she likes him to remember that learning to use it wasn't in her job description. This isn't undiluted discrimination against a blind man – she also reminds anyone who needs it that her job description doesn't include replacing the photocopier toner, emailing messages to them (she only agreed to a paper system) and a dozen other seemingly reasonable tasks. Janice, more than any lawyer in the building, is a letter-of-the-law addict.

'Could you ask Lexi to, ah, utilise her connections to find a couple of workers willing to have a chat with Clare or myself? I realise it'll be delicate,' Tom asks when Janice leaves.

'Call me Roger Moore.'

'Wasn't Bond always blowing up boats or cars?'

'Bond was just cheap trickery. Roger Moore was also *The Saint* and that's me, here with the wee children. It might take longer than a builder's smoko – and cost around the same – but I'll get you there.'

'Thanks, I don't know what I'd do without you. I'm seeing Clare soon. If anything urgent comes up, call.'

'Gotya. Talk to y'soon.'

Tom turns his chair to face the window, letting his retinas detect the little light they can. He dwells briefly on the memory of lunch with the attractive and amusing Julia. A seductive voice, a quick wit, he'd like to know more of her. As it is, without her last name he can't even Google her. Her suggested meeting – same place, same time, next week – is already in his diary. Should he go? Her reticence about giving over personal detail makes him uneasy. Is he simply too old or too jaded? Or is there something more to it?

10

At lunchtime, Tom leaves his chambers, scarf wrapped securely around his neck, head dug into the wind. Snow is reported in the mountains, although it isn't sticking to the harsh rocks and scrubby bush.

His knock on Clare's door is hard, to be heard above the bluster.

'You haven't been here for a while.' She speaks flatly enough to make several interpretations possible.

'How're the renovations?' he asks, walking down the hallway.

'Good. The new bathroom's going in next week.'

Her evident agitation makes him want to ask what's wrong, can I help? It is a trap he sets for himself, tumbling through the soft leaves of her unspoken needs, back into the pit of the relationship. He'll avoid it this time.

In the living room, Tom reaches for the couch, but its position has changed. 'Where do I sit?'

'To your right. A metre.'

He describes Warren's observations, the steps he is taking. 'Clif Johnson was at the Acqui meeting, speaking about paraphilias,' he also notes.

The cane of the wicker chair Clare prefers creaks. 'Caroline didn't mention he was speaking. Do you think that's odd?' she asks.

'Odd that Acqui is suddenly interested in devotism? Or odd that Clif was their chosen speaker?'

'Both. Although Clif is more appropriate than most shrinks, I suppose.'

'Agreed. He made a couple of interesting points. And was defensive about devotees, explaining their attraction as possibly linked to childhood trauma.'

'How on earth?'

'His main example was the loss of a parent resulting in an exaggerated impulse to protect. Neatly situating people with disability as dependent, needing care.'

'Could he have been excusing himself? Is that what's behind Clif's dedication to people with disability?'

'Possible. I'll get Warren to do some background – when he's got the time.'

'Good.'

Tom wishes she'd offered him a coffee. The associated activity might reduce the tension. 'Are you able to ask around about Caroline? I don't want to overload Warren and you know more of her current colleagues than I do.'

'When there's a moment. She doesn't strike me as a priority.'

'Word is – or was – that Caroline's prim exterior comes with a darker inner person. Fond of bondage, which is up to her of course, but with a tendency to apply – ah – undue pressure on others to participate.'

'I'd never have guessed,' Clare responds, her voice flat. Was she indicating irony or surprise?

'Roger McIntyre also struck me as a possibility – as a worker or a recruiter.'

'Roger's way too self-centred to recruit – he'd have to think someone other than himself was sexy.'

'Point taken. Like most of us, though, he likes money and power. He could convince friends and colleagues that agency work might be worth their while. Ivan's looking into his online presence.'

'Noted. From my end, Kurt says the guy from the park's going to plead guilty to a lesser charge,' Clare moves the conversation on. 'He claims he was taking her to the station when she fell out of her chair and rolled into the pool. The station isn't even in that direction across the park. His story is that he tried to rescue her but when someone spotted him, he ran. He couldn't bear what he'd done.'

The cane chair protests as Clare's distaste expresses itself in uncomfortable movement. 'What he couldn't bear was that he'd had sex with Melanie. He seems to find sex with a woman with paraplegia more shameful than murder.'

'He's going to plead under mental health then?'

'You got it. He has a paraphilia, can't stop himself, has to have women who can't move their lower halves. Has to have a frozen pussy, is what Kurt reports.'

'I wonder who'll conduct that defence. Do you have any more details of how the meeting was arranged?'

'No. Melanie's clammed up. All we've got is that she was taken in through an underground car park and up in the service lift. Hotel unnamed. The perp says he was dropped off by a friend who gave him a room key. He didn't note the name of the hotel either.'

'Christ, how ridiculous. I suppose he says the friend arranged it all and now this convenient friend's left the country.'

'He has a lot of friends, our perp. In high places, naturally. Kurt's getting everything word of mouth and we're lucky to have any of it. The cops've put a gag on it.'

From the house next door comes the sudden blast of a TV advertisement, the volume too high. The home Tom had shared with Clare is an end terrace of mid-Victorian vintage. Not too many gargoyles, a small balcony, and a courtyard with space enough to grow herbs and house an exercise bike. Tom had enjoyed its orderliness and predictability. The lack of imagination and the noise of the neighbours, a gay couple with a part-time child and a fondness for retro commercial television, were the down sides. Out of habit, he waits for the television to be adjusted – there's been a problem with their remote for years.

'We need to know why the gag. Is Kurt able to find out who the friends in high places are?'

'I was only using a turn of phrase. Come to think of it, if some sort of rule-bending is protecting the alleged perp, you could be right. I'll talk to Kurt. In the meantime, he's warned us to be careful who we speak to. In short, he thinks we're likely to have connections with the brains behind the agency, even if we don't know it. His theory is that people in the disability field are behind the start-up. It could be someone in the not-for-profit or volunteer sectors, but Kurt's favouring the public sector.'

Tom considers. 'Could be,' he shrugs. 'Paraphilias are hardly confined to any one group, class or profession. Nor is rampant money-making. Is Kurt suggesting–?'

Clare's phone interrupts. She apologises, responds, sounds annoyed, hangs up. 'Sorry, where were we?'

'Clare, what's going on?' All his experience tells him she is holding herself in – or together.

'Oh, Tom, leave it. I'm sorry, I appreciate you asking and I understand I'm being difficult. Don't worry, I'll be professional and get on with all of this. This agency didn't seem so bad to begin with. Now it is disturbed, maniacal. It can't go on, more people will get hurt. I don't know how we can let the world do this to people!'

Her distress is genuine and stinging. He remembers that he'd loved her sincerity, the strength of her emotions, her willingness to take on a cause with a fervour and dedication he is sure he can never match. An impulse to hold her crosses his mind. Old habits, old loves. Nostalgia doesn't satisfy the appetite, he reminds himself. Didn't he say something like that to Julia?

'I hate to say it, but there's more.' Tom details Marcia's call, the dolls with their intimate defilement, the contrast with the almost literary warp of the accompanying note. Clare is horrified. 'By now it's peculiar enough to snag police attention. Marcia's onto that and I've got Warren involved. You know he's the proverbial terrier. He won't let go until he's really made his mark.'

'Are you spending another inordinate amount of your own money on this?'

'It's very reasonable that I do. I earn an outrageous amount for something I thoroughly enjoy doing. And, as you know, I am the son of raging old Marxists. I believe in the redistribution of income.'

The sigh of the wicker chair again. 'I thought it was me who really pushed this kind of advocacy. Now you're…. you're more dedicated than I am.'

Tom is irritated with all the serious, swirling emotion. Their break-up was relatively amicable, for heaven's sake. The memory of Julia reaches out to him again: her voice filled with laughter.

'We can keep each other up to date,' he says, standing to go. 'Take care,' he adds, trying to convey something – sympathy, empathy? Nothing more, no regret. 'I know I – we all – can trust you.'

She leaves him to walk to the door alone.

11

THE SUN SLIDES FROM THE SKY AS WARREN MEANDERS ALONG DARLINGHURST Road, behaving like any interstate tourist checking out which strip club to visit after dark. (The newer drinking spots don't have good old-fashioned strip clubs, he reminds himself, with mild satisfaction).

Odd story, this one about devotees. Maybe Lexi can throw some light on the situation. She's turned up excellent intel for Tom before. Lex hasn't been on the game for years. She sells connections and information and provides care for the women around her. Warren suspects she's taken a shine to the boss. A left-field thought – is a bit of matchmaking in order?

At this time of day, plenty of sex-workers are shopping for ingredients they'll cook for dinner in neat little kitchens before starting work, while school kids make their desultory adolescent way home to the more salubrious parts of Potts Point or Elizabeth Bay. Warren recognises a couple of likely lads he's seen peddling poor quality marijuana outside a local school. Eyes them for a few seconds and they melt in among the other young men who gather in groups, dressed super-cool, faces rigid. Warren smiles; if you grow up in certain 'burbs, the Cross is still where you show you can make it. Only then can you call yourself a man. Trouble is, what used to be an economic exchange – buying your first or least emotionally demanding sexual experience – has become a rite of passage through alcohol and violence.

Tourists are more pleasant. Even with the up-market bars moving out, even with brothels now lining the arterial roads all the way to the edges of Sydney, even with girls as eager to have a go as the blokes, not to mention the phone, net, social media, porn and online dating agencies, the good old Cross is still the place for the outta towners to come. Kinda nice.

Warren gradually makes his way to the El Alamein fountain. Lexi lives nearby but it's worth his PI licence to be seen knocking at her door. The signal is for him to ring a number, not wait for an answer, to walk nervously round the fountain and then back again, acting like he's a bloke trying to decide whether or not to have a quickie without his wife's permission. It's corny, appeals to him.

Lexi appears, kneecaps frizzled with cold, top-half encased in a short, acrylic leopard-look coat. Waltzes past him, chewing gum, sits, flinging one leg over the other, on the edge of the fountain. She chews gum, looks him up and down and grins.

'Wanna walk?' she asks. 'I'll shout you a coffee.'

They take the main drag. Lexi walks slightly ahead, appearing to lead her client, until they reach a café on the other side of Darlinghurst Road.

'So, how's things, Lex?' Warren asks as they sit down.

'Real good. Tina's doing great at school. She loves the crappy uniform and made me buy her those leather shoes we used to hate so much. Bata Ponytails, they were in my day, and still are. Don't know what the boys' version was.'

'Me neither; didn't come from that sorta family. My kids like school, too, though I reckon Louis'll get himself into trouble later on. Motor mouth, that kid.'

The coffee shop is buzzing. Warren and Lexi both lift eyebrows in greeting here and there. 'Only place in town I don't have to get a double-double-shot,' Warren says, referring to the coffee, which comes out with a thick, luscious crema.

'World's changed, Waz. There's a zillion coffee shops and some have real coffee, even in less dramatic parts of town.'

'Thought you never left the Cross.'

'What a boy doesn't know. What've you got for me today?'

'I'm looking into a new service in town. Mobile. Not run locally, s'far as I can work out. Figured you'd be the person to know someone who knows someone. The workers all have – um – unusual credentials. Amputees, chair users, blind or deaf people. The clients call themselves devotees.'

'You doing this for the sexiest man alive, by any chance?'

Warren grins. 'Myself, you mean. Nah, you're on the money.'

'Guarantee me a drink with him and I'll do it.'

'You got more in mind?'

'Nah, don't bother. He spends too much time working for my taste. I like a man who has a bit of fun. Tom could have it with the right girl but that's not me. He'd find talking about Descartes relaxing. His girl'll have to have real class and real brains.'

'You've got class, Lex. And brains.' Warren isn't trying to be sleazy; he admires Lexi no end.

'Yeah, pigs take showers, and Australia is a classless society. It's no problem. I don't want his life any more'n he'd want mine. Gees I need a ciggie. There's laws against everything these days. Everyone says all this shit about flexibility and individuality but you can't breathe without a friggin' law telling you how to.'

Warren peers over the head of the junkie at the next table, fallen asleep bolt upright, to the street. Tables are shaking in the wind, chairs sparkle with spots of rain. Hopefully Lexi can last without a fag for a few minutes longer.

'Boss's looking for someone he can talk to. A worker. Can you put one of your elegant little tentacles out?'

'Sure, anything to be described as elegant. It'll take time.'

'Fair enough. You got any goss on this agency?'

'A rumour here and there. It's not centred round here, I know that. What've you got on it?'

'Main business is out of vans, and yeah, regional.' He lists off areas, hotels, MO. 'Still can't find how they're getting staff and customers. Even Ivan – you know Ivan? – can't find a cyber route.'

Lexi surveys the people around her. 'There's a shop, got plenty of specialist stock – callipers, crutches, false arm things like out of Captain Hook, all glittery, spangly,' she says. 'It's way more under the counter than most – double plastic bags, and both of them black. The word is you need a secret password for the good stuff.' She pats the pockets in her jacket. 'Hey, let's go out and have a ciggie.'

'It'd freeze the balls of a brass monkey out there.'

'Your wife'll thank me for a quiet night.'

The smattering of rain stings his face but it isn't all that long since he joined the ranks of the reformed, so Warren can't complain.

'Do you know who runs the place?'

'Might be able to find out. It's never bothered me before.'

'What about the clientele?'

'I'd say not many pimple-faces, more on the crinkled side. I've seen a couple of chicken-up-the-arse blokes going in. Expensive suits, bum cheeks squeezed. It's funny really, these days they can get anything they want through the net, but some of them only seem to get excited when they think they're slumming it.'

'Are they doing massage, escorting as well?'

Lexi shrugs. 'A few girls and a few of the guys have always dressed up, sat in a wheelchair, acted blind, that kinda thing. I dunno if they're getting work through the shop. Hang on, give me a mo. I know someone who knows things.'

Lexi sends a text, follows up with a call, murmurs assent, hangs up, turns back to Warren. 'My mate's got a mate who's aware of transactions going on through the shop. I should've known that.'

'Says heaps that you didn't – whoever's selling is well outside the ordinary loops. Might go pay a visit. Lex, don't forget what the boss's ordered, someone he can talk to.'

Lexi stubs out her cigarette, pouts her lips. 'Wouldn't want to let the boss down,' she says, then laughs and straightens up. 'Gotta go. Clarrie's cooking tonight, 'fore she goes out. I've gotta get back for Tina. When I can get my nose out of the homework I'll see what else I can turn up. Hey, how come parents have to do so effing much these days? My old lady never did this kinda thing.'

'Maybe you're just a better ma than your old lady was.'

Lexi gives Warren a thumbs-up. 'The thing I like about you, Wazza, is you know what really matters to a girl. Be seeing you.'

12

COOKING AND KIDS' HOMEWORK ARE CALLING HIM TOO. WARREN HEADS home, whistling, wondering if any super-tough, domestically alienated PIs are left. They sure make good movie characters. They never need to eat, shit, or earn money, and only have sex with crims, pros or women who are gonna get them into trouble. His mates in the trade are much like him – boring, average, fond of a comfy bed with a good old lover beside them.

After tea, reading to the kids, watching telly with Karen for a bit, he returns to the red-light district, dressed in a cheap leather bomber jacket scored in an op-shop. Style wise, it's sad, but near enough to what he'd have worn if his life had taken a few different turns.

Sex shops are losing custom to online stores; still they're hardly shy in this part of town. Warren walks by a few (all looking murkier, more desperate than they did in the day). He leers lightly, doesn't get in too close.

The shop – Lexi's lead – fronts a side lane. It sports an air of decrepitude, the sort of place he remembers from his teenage years.

He saunters in. Quiet, no music either blaring or sickeningly intimate, guy behind the counter on a stool. Without doubt the place trades on nostalgia that appeals both to old geezers and to young ones who want to feel they're in a B-grade movie. Sure looks like a film set. Or a hipster paradise.

Warren grazes through the ordinary and extraordinary: dildos, vibrators, whips, cuffs, lacy bras with nipple holes, nurses' costumes, corsets that'd mould the body so tight they'd surely kill. Additionally, bondage equipment specially designed for wheelchairs, jewelled clasps for leg stumps and skin-tight sheaths that hold an arm doubled back, giving the elbow the appearance of a badly healed amputation. Specialist clothing too, including sequined pussy suits for people with dwarfism. Expensive.

Only a couple of other customers, ordinary enough guys. That's the thing with perverts, the leery looking ones aren't half as much trouble as those who look all neat, tidy and repressed. He notes faces, clothing, the state of the hands, rings. Notes who's inspecting items like one-legged fanny-less tights, lacy bras guaranteed to enhance the talents of those with the most severe scoliosis. Another thing about perverts, Warren thinks more cheerfully, is that you always catch them in the end because they can't resist temptation.

One of the blokes slimes up to the counter, grasping a pair of tights and asks something Warren can't hear. The guy behind the counter says a few words back. Some sort of spy movie code. The customer hands over cash and is handed a package wrapped in black plastic. More nostalgia thrown in for free.

When the customer leaves Warren heads to the counter. Leans, chews. 'Hear you might have stuff I need,' he mutters, keeping his head down so his cap shades his face. Standard, of course. But CCTV can't see through hats.

'What might that be?' the counter guy asks.

'Suited to my interests. DVD.' Warren suggests. Reckons that's what was in the plastic.

Counter guy eyes the shop, sniffs. 'Plenty of stuff out there for you, mate.'

The grain of the voice tells Warren this is the end of the conversation. He nods, like he just thought it worth a try. Stays nearish the counter long enough to look relaxed, then slips down the aisle, avoiding a bloke who's letting the cold air through the door like he owns the place. Nice coat, shiny shoes, neat tan leather briefcase. Heading straight to the counter. Nothing is said. Cash changes hands. The bright green of hundred dollar notes. A number of them. The man is handed a card, not a plastic bag.

Warren swallows; he wants badly to cough but doing so'll attract attention he can live better without. A card? A name, an address? A receipt for money paid for services not available on the premises? Very smart, he thinks. Make sure all transactions are cash and fragmented so that the chances of tracing clients are very, very low. Ivan's onto something, saying it's all twentieth-century tech. How are the preferred customers recognised? He figures Challinor'll manage to put all the bits together. With a bitta help from Lexi, who could make the asphalt spill its secrets.

Reckons he's worn out his welcome. Warren exits quietly. At least his information gathering is bearing fruit. Just has to hope he hasn't attracted too much attention.

13

TOM MAKES HIS WAY BETWEEN THE ROWS OF AEROBIC MACHINES TO THE free-weights area. This gym has learned to accommodate his blindness, with raised tape to define walkways and rules about weights that benefit everyone. He always keeps to script – walking straight through the gym to meet his martial arts instructor or working out with a friend. Safer for all concerned.

'Hey, Tom, over here.'

'Serge.'

'Where've you been?'

'Sorry I'm late. Work, and that project with Clare I told you about. You remember – the investigation into the new escort agency. Ready to start?'

Serge hands Tom a pair of weights. 'Twenty reps, a set a piece.'

They work hard for fifty minutes, occasionally muttering about work, Serge's kids, a new music venue tucked away in industrial Marrickville.

'Time,' Tom says. 'I need food and drink.'

'Fine by me.'

Tom wipes his towel across his head and shoulders. What is Serge doing now? How is he standing? Arms folded, feet planted apart? Or hands on hips? Whichever way, Tom can feel a distinctly questioning glance.

'Something's on your mind, Challinor. And it's not the project. Or Clare.' Serge pauses. 'It's a woman, isn't it? I've got it, haven't I? It's all over your face. You know, I don't believe Clare made you look like that. Not for a long bloody time, at least.'

'Ever?'

'Wow, there's a question. The great retrospective; was I really in love? Then? With her? Was it all an illusion? For chrissakes, who in their right mind would try to answer that one?'

Tom laughs. 'Fair enough. Besides, I haven't come to talk about my love life. I need a favour in relation to this investigation. Do you have time for a beer?'

'Just this once.'

The pub is full of young things out to have a dazzling time, as Serge puts it. And so they should, while they can, he adds, himself having two noisy kids at home. Serge maintains he's had it with sobriety and the New Man.

Tom laughs. 'You and Imogen are like Romeo and Juliet without the tragedy.'

'You should have kids, Tom. Bloody hassle they are, but you'd love them.'

'A male immaculate conception, now that'd be a miracle of modern medical science.'

'Smart-arse. What're you drinking?'

'Whisky, malt, neat.'

'Can't argue with that. What's all this about?'

'I've been speaking with a young woman. Her story gave me a thought about real estate.'

'This the young woman who's distracting you from upping your bench press weight?'

'This is a pleasant, serious young woman with a boyfriend and concerns about what he's getting himself involved in.'

'If not love then, you're considering property speculation? Guess all lawyers do it some time.'

'As do mum and dad investors, superannuation funds, mechanics, bakers van drivers, aspirational immigrants, everyone. Real estate is Australia's, and particularly Sydney's, favourite get rich quick scheme. That makes it also our best money laundering scheme. Which brings us back to the young woman. She suggests an unexpected new kid on the block is hankering to play on the disability support field. No known credentials but they're offering to fund refuges for men with disability who are the victims of serious bullying or violence.'

'You don't want this? Aren't you pleased the public is getting behind people who could do with greater recognition and resources? I thought altruism was the new black.'

'Indeed. And, showing it, approximately ten new charities are registered every single day across the country. If you don't have your cause, your *passion* – well, you might as well take yourself off all social media and take up wearing ironed shorts and knee socks. However, despite all the need for self-definition through helping the less fortunate, the woman in question thinks this situation stinks like your uncle's unwashed fishing clothes. She brought it to my attention yesterday, then rang today, saying she couldn't drill down anymore. The men's group who'd been offered the refuges clammed up, told her – with some force – to keep her nose out, et cetera.'

'All right, I'm following you, but it's not much to go on.'

'I agree. But she did get that this new philanthropist insists on having a hand in running the refuges. They also want no media announcements, no public acknowledgement. Why – in the world of shouting your passion – the secrecy? You have to agree it suggests ulterior motives – like money laundering. Which they could do while also cleverly establishing a close connection to potential workers with disabilities, particularly ones who are pretty much guaranteed to be both distant from their usual connections – they've had to fetch up in a refuge after all – and in need of money.'

'That's got some logic to it, I admit. So, how do I, an architect employed at the public's expense, help you be super-sleuth?'

'Before the shutters came down, my contact saw three development applications for refuges had already been submitted to councils you're associated with. Refuges are marginal investments; three is more than you'd expect. Are you able to sight these DAs? If we find companies, consortia, the people behind them, we'll have a starting point.'

'I'll think on it."

Tom drains his whisky. 'I'm not trying to nab some small guy with a backyard operation. We're looking for people or groups with money and organisational strength. Someone or someones who know your part of town.'

'You're suggesting a common denominator. A person behind it who knows the Inner West better than any other part of Sydney.'

'Crims, like the rest of us, tend to shit in their own patch. They are likely to live or work there.'

'Reasonable. Anything else?'

'I'll buy you another drink.'

'I take that as a yes.'

'Yes. One more thing – Warren's got a list of hotels. We're looking for links in the ownerships. In your ambit?'

'More or less. Can get it seen to anyway. That it?'

'I'm forever in your debt.'

'You always were too fucking polite.' Serge drains his drink. 'Now, enough of the serious stuff – tell me about this new woman.'

The waiter interrupts with their tapas, the food sending out seductive aromas. He assiduously arranges the plates out of Tom's easy reach. 'Don't want you to get your fingers burnt,' the waiter explains.

Serge puts a hand to Tom's shoulder. 'He'll learn. Eventually,' he cautions. 'So?'

'So, very clever, and correct, as far as it goes. I have indeed met an intriguing woman. Amusing, smart, attractive, and not ridiculously young.'

'Mate, two new women – some people have all the luck. We'd better order another drink. Don't forget you're paying. When're you seeing her again?'

'Soon. My guess is that she's married.'

'You haven't asked? You haven't found that out for a fact? What is going on? What're you going to do about it?'

'Hope, I suppose.'

'Now I've heard every damn thing. How did you meet her?'

Tom smoothes his hand over his head. 'She just materialised. You know that I don't usually have trouble working out where people are. I sat down at a table – the café outside the Sydney Museum, you know it? – and there she was. She was – I don't know – sharp, yet not serious. I've had it with being serious all the time. I was thrown by not noticing her.'

'Maybe she jumped into the seat, to have a go at chatting you up.'

Tom puts his glass down. 'That's what worries me. What if she did sit down for that reason?'

'You've lost me. No, you haven't. You're getting obsessed with this devotee stuff. Come on, Tom, I bet this woman – what's her name, by the way? – I bet she didn't even notice you can't see. And even if she did, so what?'

'Julia. She said blindness was no excuse for rudeness. In the most beautiful voice.'

'You'd've loved that.'

'I did.' He thinks for a moment about how Serge's voice also has a complex timbre. Unfortunately, not the sort of thing you mention to a male friend. 'It's likely nothing will come of it.'

'I expect a report back this time next week. Now, shall we have one for the road?'

'You're on. Mind you, I hope it's not you I'm drinking with next time I go out.'

'Whatever happened to male bonding?'

'We're doing it now. I can't do it every night. The drinks are too expensive.'

WEDNESDAY

14

THE PERPETRATOR'S LATEST DELIVERY GOES UNNOTICED FOR AN HOUR OR more. Maryam, one of the residents, sets out for an early trip to the supermarket. She closes the refuge gate behind her and nearly rolls her chair over a bucket as she moves forward. In it, arms, legs, severed nipples, feet and hands, of a life-size baby doll. The head is absent. Maryam doesn't bother with histrionics. She mouths her disgust in language not nearly as foul as what she is staring at.

The temptation is to scoop up the mess, bin it: the women she lives with don't need this. Instead, she reminds herself the evidence is important. She steels herself and takes several shots of the jumble of plastic body parts with her phone.

She scours the area for any clue to who deposited them. In her estimation, they could still be watching. It's the sort of thing her ex would take great pleasure in. Does that mean she could be rushed as she turns and punches in the gate's code? She stays still for several seconds. Then decides to call the staff, have one of them come out before she tries to re-enter the premises. There are two women rostered on at the moment. One supposedly keeping a look out for this very event.

The workers take their time coming. Maryam begins to wonder about the staff.

A few kilometres away, a man calling himself Robin takes the stairs to his office, admiring the way the balustrade reflects the early morning sun. He is a medium sized man, fit enough, good looking enough, still young enough to cut a fine figure, while not standing out from the crowd unnecessarily. He considers this an advantage.

In the office, he hangs his coat – Italian-made, Australian merino wool – and passes a hand over the fine fabric of his shirt. Robin has achieved what every entrepreneur dreams of – he has found a market hitherto untapped, unturned, left fallow – and has had the acumen to develop it. *Helpmates* is his very own creation, and he is proud of it. This despite having been forced to find first one and then another partner – the first having turned out to be stubbornly interested only in his own proclivities. Or perhaps "obsessed with" was a more appropriate description than "interested". Partners mean the increased risk of exposure, he is well aware. But a financial backer is essential to support the responsive and immediate procurement of staff, equipment and support services for the astonishingly rapid expansion in business.

The number of bookings attest to *Helpmates* being a service that caters to a market thrilled to be noticed, after years, lifetimes, of socially and often practically enforced denial of its deepest desires. *Helpmates* supports, too, a workforce previously neglected: men and women enthusiastic to be recognised and well-paid. Robin is doing good, bringing together devotees and workers with disability. Hence the acquired name – Robin – and his more recent partner's adopted appellation – John. Robin Hood and Little John, taking (gently) from the rich to give to the poor. He likes that. But he does feel some trepidation about John.

Robin nudges the desktop mouse. The official screen offers itself. His legitimate business is at the forefront; all else is in apparently unrelated files or on his personal computer. Entry to that computer is well-protected and the machine itself locked away in its specially designed and secreted compartment. Robin specialises in the use of old-style codes, which he considers much more sensible than cloud storage, despite encryption. He alone has the keys to these codes. Robin concentrates on his work.

At first he does not notice John's arrival. The man's wheelchair is new and fabulously streamlined. He wheels silently into Robin's office. John has a strange wasting of the legs. No diagnosis, cause or prognosis has been alluded to. The symptoms came on suddenly, also seeming to affect John's personality. Does this indicate a neurological disorder? John's fortune has been made in "complimentary medicine"

– specifically the manufacture and distribution of herbal and other alternative drugs – and he does not like to be seen consulting traditional medical practitioners. But there must be some significant reason for the adoption of the chair.

Robin eases the collar of his shirt. For as John's mobility has become impaired, so it seems has his mental acumen. John has transformed from a man any aspiring businessman would want as a mentor to a man who is unreadable, unpredictable and arrogant. First Gus – his original partner – and now John. Still, Robin thinks, it may be a temporary result of treatments unnamed. He smiles and removes the chair opposite his desk. John moves in as close as possible.

'There are problems.' John's until recently urbane delivery is decidedly taut. The police, he tells Robin gravely, now realise the girl found in Parramatta Park is a working girl and are convinced she isn't working alone or for a back-street pimp. They've got wind of an organisation.

Robin smiles again, comfortable that, in this, his chess pieces are almost in mate. The girl, Melanie, is smart, educated, and he has arranged for a very suitable amount to be deposited into her bank account as a thank you for fielding enquiries in an appropriate manner. Although it is true she let a few details slip before the message and promise reached her, with luck – no, with his excellent organisation – none of it will go beyond the police station. However, there is the question of how John was informed.

'The young woman is well taken care of. Nothing damaging will come out,' Robin says calmly.

John, perfectly kitted out for luncheon at the yacht club, raises a manicured eyebrow. Not so long ago, Robin imagined himself in similar attire, with a similar sized boat and similarly well-heeled friends. Now, he recalls his school principal – a petty tyrant if there ever was one – having the same lift of the brow when he was trying to diminish an errant student who was, in reality, beyond his control. This makes him smile internally: he begins to relax just as the bite comes.

'There is, unfortunately, my friend, no concrete proof that is the case,' John declares. 'It has been a shock of some magnitude that you could allow such an event to occur.'

Robin recoils. At this juncture, with their massive expansion over the Harbour Bridge into the comfortable northern suburbs, John's continued financial banking is paramount. John must have faith in Robin. But the man, it seems, is scenting blood and cannot resist coming in for the kill.

'The chap in custody is not the culprit in the attempted drowning,' John continues. 'Robin, there is a potential killer on the loose. Our staff are at risk. As are we.' Then John's eyes swerve away from Robin's.

He has, Robin thinks, said more than he intended. The man is losing control. At the same time, the information is devastating. Robin swallows. Has John arranged a fall guy? Gone behind his back, found someone to be framed and destroyed, or a man handsomely paid to be arrested but whom the evidence will not convict? A decoy, in short. A cover. That implies there is someone to cover for. That someone must be close enough to John for him to bother with. He is not an emotionally generous man. Perspiration collects under Robin's superbly crafted shirt collar.

'As I was saying,' John changes tack, 'the police are under pressure – we don't know from where – to investigate the claims the young woman made before we convinced her otherwise. Even if we are able to stop an investigation – and let us hope we can – we must conclude that someone, somewhere, knows more than we want them to.'

'Where on earth have you heard all this? How can you be sure it's the truth?' Robin asks, immediately regretting the innocence of the questions. His role is to be all-knowing, or near enough.

'I protect my sources. They are, I assure you, absolutely to be trusted. They are also, of course, sworn to secrecy.'

Sworn to secrecy? What has happened to their agreements, their careful planning? Does this new version of John imagine he is part of a special society with funny handshakes and charming rituals? Perhaps he does. Perhaps he has sent the decoy in to deflect attention from one of his friends. Unlike his previous, ultimately unreliable partner, John has shown no interest in using *Helpmates* services. This has been very reassuring. However, it has become apparent that John's friends are a different kettle of well-dressed fish.

Questioned on this – discreetly of course – John was defensive. In fact, he explained the voracious use of *Helpmates* – by *all* the hundreds of committed customers – as evidence that there were many, many men who dreamt of engagements that soar far above the average; who desired interactions that fulfilled needs greater than the mere sexual. Engagements that approached the sublime in their sympathy and willingness to treat the impaired, the infirm, the unseeing, as angels, was how John put it.

John had also forcefully requested details of precisely which friends of his are *Helpmates* clients.

Robin had politely resisted divulging names. This was his side of the business: the development and protection of the business model, its operations, and its data, including protecting the privacy of the customers. Heaven knows they have enough customers without John's fancy friends, but Robin has stored their names for future reference, perhaps evidence, which may come in useful one day. In Robin's estimation, they are in no way chasing spiritual satisfaction; they are simply bored, above all with themselves. They simply find it mildly exciting to have a secret life that is singularly exotic. They would go elsewhere if a more nearly unique alternative presented itself. There is not an iota of nobility in any of it. No doubt, though, they could be convincing themselves that they are special, almost anointed. And, Robin suspects, this could ruin everything.

'John, listen to me. We have spent considerable energy, in every possible monetary and personal way, ensuring maximum discretion. This has meant, to date, that you and I have been open with each other. You do understand the absolute importance of continuing that openness? We're like a dual-hulled Titanic: if one of us sinks, there are too few lifeboats.'

John raises that eyebrow again. He's enjoying making Robin beg for information, that much is obvious. Equally obvious: he has something to hide.

Robin thrusts his hands in his pockets; a gesture he would normally eschew. It ruins the line of his suit, but right now the desire to shake, even strangle the man opposite him is threatening to take over from his common sense and decency. Robin likes to be decent. He searches his brain for a way to ensure John does not continue operating behind his back, keeping information within his secret society friends.

'We will, of course, immediately increase security for all our suppliers and customers. Given you have more information than I do, perhaps you have some suggestions of the best ways of going about this?'

This hits a mark. John reddens. 'I wasn't suggesting I *know* there'll be more attacks.'

Robin doesn't remind him that it is precisely what he did say. 'It seems most appropriate to build in an awareness of, and prevention strategies for, the possibility,' he says instead. 'Unless you have some guarantee that this was a one-off incident.'

'Of course not! Be careful what you insinuate, Robin. My concerns lie more in the possibility of data breaches.'

Cheap deflection, Robin thinks. 'I can assure you, the minimal electronic data we hold is disguised. The most innovative or experienced data analysts or hackers would pass by it without a second glance. However, there remain real people going about their business in the real world. They are both more vulnerable and more likely to expose us. These real people include you and me and your colleagues and friends. No matter what, we must increase our security, and particularly our means of ensuring privacy and personal protection. We can readily absorb the expense. Leave it with me.' Robin hopes he projects confidence. He is walking on a narrow bridge over a deep ravine, after all, with piranhas in the river below. 'However, to get us properly started, you need to tell me what you know.'

15

Julia Prettie takes the ferry to work. She has a parking space under her building – a status symbol if ever there were one – but this morning she hankers for the beauty of the harbour, the sigh of the water as the ferry slices through it, the moment of being shocked, almost anew, by the immense simplicity of the bridge as the ferry turns toward it. She wishes, too, for the anonymity of the early morning commuters, all wearing earbuds, staring across the water after a too-short sleep, checking their social media before work.

She finds a narrow space on an outside bench. Cold, windy, pleasant. She draws her coat around her. Will the short trip ease the confusion that has fluttered around, pecking like a pack of persistent pigeons ever since Monday? Meeting Tom Challinor like that, interacting as they had; it was all far more than she could have expected. He was too attractive for safety.

Soon the ferry, wind-buffeted, thumps against the dock. Soon the brisk walk to the less salubrious edge of the CBD is over.

'Hi,' she says to Vanessa, her executive assistant. Vanessa looks up, faint lines of disapproval around her mouth. Surely she is allowed to be the tiniest bit late now and then. 'Something's up?'

'A man, a Peter Thompson. Who insists. Your diary is full. Completely.'

'Pete! He's back. I have five minutes for Pete.'

'He said that, and he barged in.'

'Ah, sorry, remnant from my less formal past. He'll be fine, Vanessa, don't concern yourself.'

A faint aroma of male sweat makes her office seem unfamiliar but not unpleasant. She grins at Pete's broad-shouldered back as he sits in the visitor chair. 'What are you doing, panicking Vanessa like that? She's a wonderful woman.'

Pete jumps up, gives her a hug, and holds her at arms' length. 'Well, you are looking – ah – fabulous.'

'If a public servant, in the pay and sway of the government of the day, *can* look fabulous, I presume is your implication. And if you can be totally un-PC.'

'No, yes, both. Either way, it's grand to see you.'

'You too. Pete, I really do only have a few minutes. Vanessa's not the only one who'll blow a valve.'

'Quaint. Valves, that is. Very pre-millennial.' Pete hands her a black coffee. 'Hope you still drink it straight.'

'More than fabulous, you are. How was the trip?'

Pete begins talking. She's half-listening, thoughts on the meeting ahead and the outcomes of the meeting behind. Maybe she's avoiding listening too closely because his life is much more exciting than hers these days. Is it also more – ah – rewarding? The tinge of envy she feels surely indicates it is.

Pete is her old world, her pre-department world, the days when she was too young to be CEO of a medium-sized aid organisation, but was anyway. Before the organisation was gobbled up by a bigger organisation, religious in orientation and bureaucratic in practice: so much money wasted. It was probably no excuse for going into the government sector, but it seemed reasonable at the time. You have to be in the system to really effect change; that sort of argument.

Pete had jumped ship too, taken a job with a secular charity that quickly showed itself corrupt if you peeked millimetres below the surface. Now he's back with their old aid organisation, arguing they've got their act together, smoothed out the wrinkles and gone all ecumenical, supporting diversity, actually getting things done. When she has the time, which is rare, she is mildly envious of his ability to keep going in the Not For Profit sector, with its infighting as extreme as the public or corporate sectors, its monetary rewards much less and its needs so much greater. At least sometimes, though, with so-called outcomes that are almost decent.

Right now, Pete's back from a fact-find up in the Northern Territory. Despite their avowedly international focus, the organisation – he's telling her – has an increasing emphasis on the needs of Indigenous Australians. Water supplies in the NT are as bad as in the Sahara. More infrastructure is desperately required.

'So, you're a walking web of information then?' she asks.

'Too right, and cheaper than those experts you government lot employ. A million times more effective. Bet you're green.'

'Haven't time for envy. Besides, you know I hate sand. How's Matt the cat, did he survive your absence?'

'Just, just. Wasting away. My poor mother, she tried, but what could she do?'

Julia laughs. Pete is notoriously fond of his mum and of his cat. 'Hope you're not making her feel too bad. We should get together for dinner soon.'

'Soon? You? Superwoman makes time for her sweet old poofter mate. It'll be a headline.'

'We'll keep it quiet then.'

'Jules, why don't you come back to us? Our CEO only needs a small push. I don't mind being your underling. Mum will send in lunches.'

Julia looks down at some papers. 'It might be a good idea. Right now, I've got work to do here.'

Pete lifts an eyebrow. 'Are you trying to fob me off in the immediate, or forever?'

'I truly have to get on with this work.'

'Julia, you are stuck in this office like a – oh, I don't know. I'm worried you're losing your vibrancy. I mean, you look fab in the clothes and all, but you're my Docs-wearing Diana, goddess of the good hunt, the moon, out there shooting for the stars. You'd better be careful or you might end up like that husband of yours.'

'Soon to be ex-husband. Come on, he's done wonders for us over the years with his pro-bono work.'

'Yeah, yeah, and now he's a businessman, his generosity is financial. I know.' Pete leans closer, again giving off a hint of sweat. Honest sweat, outdoor doing-stuff sweat, Julia thinks. 'Thing is, you don't even know what his business is, do you now?'

'Pete, you're sailing near an iceberg.'

'Rubbish, Jules, absolute rubbish. We talk, we always have and we will again soon. It's time I took you on a field trip, see a bit of the old Oz this time. No wars or famines and a damn sight better than ruining your feet in those high heels you bureaucrats go for. Good prep for your job application too.'

'Attractive idea, I'll put it to Vanessa, she has the diary strings.' It occurs to her that Pete isn't just relaxed, he's pleased with himself. She makes an educated guess. 'You found yourself a new fella in the outback, didn't you?'

'Thought you'd never get there. In Darwin on the way in, there he was, and waiting for me on the way out. Luckily for me, he's coming down this way for a visit real soon, so I need you round to impress my new love. He's a French aid worker, here on an extended holiday and he'll love you. The French always go for the good looking types.'

'You are so politically incorrect.'

'Previously noted. Got to stop you nestling too far into this haven for depressives. Pettiness is an addictive drug around here. That's what I like about you, Jules, you try your damnedest but you've never really fitted the mould, any mould. You're too cool for conformity. Like me.' He grins.

It's tempting to throw something at him. But her computer is heavy, the papers would only flutter, and there's nothing else to hand. 'Pete, I really must do some work. Honest.'

'Sure thing. Promise me you'll think on your ol' Uncle Pete's advice and come back to us. We truly are gonna be looking for a new CEO real soon. Heard the word. For whatever reason you think is good enough, you're still thick with a husband you want to ditch, a department that values you only for the hours it can wring out of you, the boxes you can tick and the vacuous policies you can oversee – and doesn't even give you an office with a decent window. Not to mention you're embroiled with family who demand undying devotion. Too much being nice ain't good for you, it'll suck you dry.'

'Got it.' She hears the ping of another email. So many of the little cyberfuckers, as Pete calls them. 'Pete, we'll talk soon. Cross my heart.'

When he leaves, taking the scent of freedom and hard yakka with him, Julia starts on the emails. She is an organised woman, she tells herself, and this is her organising habit. It is hard to concentrate, but she manages the first cascade of emails, heads to the conference room for the meeting, chairs that, returns to emails and phone messages, responds to Vanessa as she flicks in and out, tries to ignore the list of reports, briefing papers and so on she needs to direct her staff to write. Lunchtime comes and goes; she finally gives in.

Tom Challinor will be easy enough to track down. The blind barrister. Everyone knows him, many fear him. When in court, he's quiet, a stealthy leopard who will, when perfectly situated, pounce and consume its prey. Or so it is said. He avoids the limelight, and photographs, which is eminently reasonable on his part. He was definitely not what – or who – she had imagined.

His mobile number is not publicly available. His chambers, though, are readily contactable. Julia chews the end of a pencil – another twentieth-century habit, she notes wryly to herself.

Should she, should she not? What is she doing? Why is she doing what she's doing, or not doing, or about to do?

It's complicated. *Shit!*

16

SONYA AND AVRIL STAND IN THE ORNATE PORCH ON THE WESTERN SIDE OF the street. The hour is early and if it weren't for the reproduction Victoria gas lamp they'd be entirely in the dark. Avril wraps her arms tightly around herself. 'It's fricking cold here. Maybe we should just go over the road. That building's got a ramp, it really could be the right one.'

'Many building have ramps.' Sonya is watching a middle-aged man rolling down the ramp. He pauses at the base, surveying the street. Even from a distance and in the low light, she can see his wheelchair is top quality. His overcoat too.

'Come on, Son, you got us here. It looks right to me.' Avril grabs her friend's hand, pulling her forward.

'Wait, Avril, see that man come out.' He turns right onto the footpath as she points him out to Avril.

'Rich looking bloke, hey,' Avril comments, uninterested.

The light above them flickers off. Sonya disentangles her hand, replaces it on Avril's arm, urging her back further into the darkness. 'I think I see that man before.'

'You reckon, then, that's really the main office? We found it! Cool.'

'Have you seen the man?'

A bus roars up to a stop. It sits, obscuring their view, doors cavernous, the rest of its blue body a block of brightness in the wintry street.

'Nah. Can't really see his face, but I don't reckon I have. Where'd you see him? You think it was here? We only met the boss and she's a woman remember, even if she sounded more like a guy. Maybe she's trans.'

When the bus sets off, the chair user is whistling away. He's really thin but he's pushing himself really fast, Avril notes, and it looks like he's enjoying scaring anyone silly enough to be in his way.

'In hotel. I see him in hotel.'

'A client?'

The shake of Sonya's head says "maybe" rather than "no". 'I see him sitting in foyer. He watch a lot.'

'You reckon he's security?' Avril pushes some of her curls away from her face, stares out. 'He doesn't look like security, hey. Did you see him anywhere else? Like in a room, or following us or anything?'

The man in the lift yesterday was big and broad and could've been security, Sonya thinks. This man is different. Sonya doesn't want to mention the man in the lift. Her body cringes as if expecting a blow when she thinks of him. 'No, only in foyer. Three hotels, or four.'

'I've got it. He's one of the organisers. He's hanging around on the job to see everything is going right. That's why he's here too. Besides, why's it matter so much, Sonnie?'

Sonya bites her bottom lip. Avril tilts her head and looks up at her friend. Seems to her it's good to have the bosses around. That way they can really keep them safe. She decides to change the subject. 'I just can't believe how smart you are. I hated them making us wear those blindfolds when we came in for the interview and sign up. No way I could've worked out where we were. And, wow, you got us back here again. How did you do it? Like you was always good with numbers and directions and stuff, but this was totally over the top, working this out.'

Sonya's smile is sharp-edged. 'I learn very young. Sometime we move in the night. You have to keep good track.' She pauses, more confident now. 'Sydney is easy city with lots of different sort of houses and hills and freeways and water. We come in all this way, we feel the big bridge, the Anzac bridge, we come to end of city. The sea smell in the air.'

'Wow. Really wow.'

'This is little street, short. Remember we work that out even in blindfold.'

'Yeah, right, well, you did. You're a genius, Son. And you must be spot on. 'Specially if that guy's one of the bosses. Cool. Now we know where to come if we need to talk to them.'

A heavily-coated office worker brushes past them, peering,

undeniable shock on her face. They both ignore her. What's the point? This kind of regard is a daily – no, round about an hourly – occurrence. Particularly for Avril, even more particularly when they are together. Then the woman smiles, almost grins. 'Apologies,' she says, 'shit of me to stare like that. Are you waiting for someone? I can let you into the building if you need to get in. It's freezing out here.'

'We are going to Botanical Gardens,' Sonya offers as Avril waves the young woman away with a hint of a conciliatory smile. She doesn't want to go too far, though, and anyway, isn't all that interested in the woman or her worries about politeness.

'Liar,' Avril whispers.

The worker opens the door with a swipe card, letting out a brief blast of warm air.

Sonya moves forward, out of the darkness, and peers out around the thick stone columns. The footpaths and car lanes are thickening with work traffic, but the man in the wheelchair is gone. 'I see that man several times. He is lurker – that's what my mother says,' she announces. 'Not in English,' she adds.

'What! How does your mum know about that guy?'

Sonya's giggle is genuine. 'She doesn't see him. Just she say that about men who wait around, don't do nothing, only look. Look funny and bad.'

'I get it – a dirty old man who could be up to something. But couldn't that guy be keeping an eye on us? Like, looking after our welfare. He's dressed smart, like one of the bosses, so he's probably protecting us.' Avril pauses, grins ruefully. 'Yeah, or maybe protecting his own interests. Anyhow, he hasn't hurt you or anything, has he? Sonnie, what's weirding you out?'

'Maybe you are right, maybe he's a good guy.' Then, turning directly to her friend, Sonya asks. 'What about you, Avril? Why you want to come here so much? Why you want to find where the boss is?'

Avril adjusts her shoulder bag. She fiddles with the bright badge that signifies it's a designer label. It's a fake, but she's practising for the time she can afford the real deal. 'Nothing in particular.'

'What is no particular?'

Avril doesn't respond immediately. She watches the wind whip litter along the street for a moment, wanting to be able to fill the silence but unsure herself why she is here, why she asked Sonya to see if she could find the old building they'd been brought to in the van. It wasn't like the escort agency lady who'd interviewed them was the sort of person you'd want to run to for help.

Besides, it isn't like she needs anyone to run to for help. Or is it? That cheap porno video has put the wind up her, as her own mother liked to say. She was always thinking people were having the wind put up them, her mum. Maybe this time she's right. Thing is, Avril really doesn't have a clue what that wind is carrying or saying or trying to scare her with. It's just strange and makes her feel like an earthquake is shaking her around. A little one, some small number on that scale they have, but one that goes on and on. So maybe she's here 'cause she's been checking rooms more carefully for cameras, been on the alert in the lobbies and the car parks, freaking about anyone near or behind her. Her own safety isn't her issue. It's her job. If the agency finds out there's recordings, there'll be trouble. Innocence won't save her; they'll say she must have agreed. As if.

The litter keeps up its little dance. Sonya keeps up staring at Avril with big questions in her beautiful eyes. The pain that's recently invaded Avril's guts intensifies; her job is the biggest and brightest key ever to escaping from poverty and from the grinding boredom her life had always seemed fated for. She refuses to have that job taken away by a total nut case voyeur. She thinks that she has talked Sonnie into this excursion on the hope that seeing where the really big bosses are, she can demand to talk to them if she has to, make them take action. That having their address is a back-up. Like, if she spills the beans first about the video, it might save her. Something like that.

'I dunno Sonnie,' she eventually says. 'I really don't. But come on, you promised we'd go shopping. And we haven't got too long, gotta get back to work. Come on, we can have a coffee on the way, we'll have a great time.'

She can see and feel and taste that Sonya doesn't believe her.

17

Ivan's excited about a lead. 'It's like string theory,' he says, 'things look different in different scales. An ordinary particle can turn out to be a string. And if you believe some of the theorists, there's a zillion parallel universes each ever so slightly different from the one we're conscious of sitting right up against us. Something like that. I'm going all quantum to find the portal.'

Tom figures Ivan's understanding of quantum theory is about as good as his own, if the truth be told. 'Meaning?'

'Disguise what's close to you, so you – or another person – can see but not recognise it. You – or they – can't decide if it's real or alive or dead until the box is opened and that is an event that does not occur. Schrödinger's cat. Although I could be mixing stuff up here.'

'I'm not sure I'm getting the new geek speak either. Are you suggesting there might be a coded website or social media site that is just a pixel away, but absolutely ungraspable? Except that you're hoping to get hold of it by the short and curlies?'

'You're onto it.'

The taxi driver mutters in Arabic. Tom takes it as swearing of the first order. The accompanying banging on the steering wheel and blasting of the horn are giveaways.

'Sounds good, keep at it, got to go,' he says, still not sure what Ivan will be keeping at. However, he'll trust Ivan's expertise. He has little of his own when it comes to the back alleys of cyberspace.

The corridor to his chambers smells of wet shoes, baking slowly in over-elevated air con. Janice buzzes with a call the minute he's in his office, hissing the name of the solicitor on the other end of the line. 'Tell her I'll ring back in five.' He is supposedly on a holiday week, after all.

Janice hurrumphs.

He calls Marcia. 'Jesus,' she says, 'where the fuck have you been?'

'I didn't get a message from you.'

'Got better things to do with my time. I'm on your missed call register. That should be enough!'

'I take it there's another doll?'

'There's a pile of shit in our letterbox. Complete with body parts.'

'Plastic parts?'

'Fortunately, yes. Tom, this is totally out of hand.'

'I won't argue with that. Marcia, I'm not sure I'm the best person – this has a very warped mind behind it.'

'And you think I should talk to a psychologist or a shrink. That drip Clif Johnson's offered his services–' She's about to say more when two or three heavy-footed someones come into her room: the police.

Marcia demands that he call her back as soon as she is free. He stops himself laughing aloud at the mild illogic. 'Text me when you're finished with them,' he says.

Tom calls Warren.

'I'll talk to Marcia,' Warren offers. 'Get the CCTV footage. They mighta missed something. Needs practice to really see what's going on.'

'Ask her if there's anywhere to attach an extra camera; a decent one. That's cheaper than funding you lot picking your teeth all night. It's safer, too.'

'You trying to put me out of a job?'

'I'm trying to save your marriage and pay my mortgage.'

'Reasonable.'

Call finished, nothing on his desk grabs Tom's attention. The law interests him, but the law does not equal justice. It's simply the most efficient way currently available, in a large, diverse society, to get something akin to an agreed-on process. The law is thoroughly utilitarian.

Janice interrupts his thoughts, putting through yet another call, with no introduction or opportunity to refuse. Pay-back.

'Tom, it's Julia.'

He decides jumping out of his skin is not useful.

'How are you?' he replies, feeling programmed for a stultifying politeness.

'Good, fine,' she answers, as mundanely polite as he. 'Tom, I know I've broken the rules, tracking you down–'

'You knew who I was all the time.' Tom stops. 'I am hard to disguise,' he concedes.

'A leopard pouncing is the description of your courtroom performance.'

'If only I were that stylish.'

'Ah, I was hoping we might meet up sooner than the allotted week. Oh, shit, hang on. I'll have to ring you back. Can you give me a mobile number? You have a dragon at your reception and I'm not keen on being burnt. I'll only be a couple of minutes.'

'Sure.' He's not sure at all, but he refuses yet another call Janice wants to put through. His popularity with her, never high, is dropping like a lost ring down a sinkhole.

'Sorry about that. Work,' Julia says when she calls back on the number he gave her. Her voice is wider, more generous now. 'I need to fess up. I'm Julia Prettie. I work for the Department of Social Services. Will that do for now?'

'We can google each other as soon as we get off this call.' He knows she does not work for the department so much as run it.

'I might not have the time, work's intense at the moment. Well, work is always intense. It'd be good to have a break. Tomorrow late afternoon is possible if I do a diary stretch. How about you?' He hears the clatter of a keyboard. 'Are you worth it?' she suddenly asks, the music returning to her voice.

'I am.'

'I suspect you are.' She pauses. 'That could be a problem.'

'Julia, is there anything I should know before we meet again?'

'We're not kids, there have to be complications. Absolutely unavoidable.'

He runs his free hand over his head, controls the pleasure in his voice and makes a couple of mundane remarks. All the time, he's thinking the heart can't really fly, it's simply a slimy internal organ that responds to a limited set of stimuli. Including fear. And lust.

'I'm not in court this week, and I'd really like to see you,' he finally admits.

He hears a phone in the background, the movement as she checks the caller ID. She ignores the call. Then she laughs; sudden, low and generous. 'Sorry to be so inarticulate. I think I'm having some sort of adolescent moment. Does tomorrow work for you?'

He could make a show of rustling pages, clicking keys, checking his diary. Rubbish, of course. He knows both that he has no free time and that there is nothing recorded he isn't prepared to change. Besides, she's far too astute for any pretence. 'Good. I'll see you at the café. It's their late closing day. And I understand the adolescent moment.'

'Yes, I think you do. It's all very strange.'

When they've said their polite goodbyes, Tom sits still, discombobulated. What brought that on, he wonders. He decides he's game for it, whatever it is.

In some cultures the voice is the essence of the soul, the perfect representation of the inner being. In many religions it is the only true means of communication with God. Voices raised in unison are power. Despite the hesitant words, Julia's voice lacks the wariness he often hears in new acquaintances who don't know how to interact with a blind man. As if the outer shell made all the difference. Perhaps it does. Even without seeing, he found her physical presence an unavoidable attraction. Or distraction. He certainly wants to know more – much more – of the shape and feel of her. It's one of the irritating aspects of being blind; there is no simple observation, no possible voyeurism, innocent or not. He can only know the shape of woman's lips, breasts, curve of the elbow, tautness or not of muscles, by touch. It's a wonder more blind men and women aren't wildly promiscuous.

Janice buzzes again; the previously rejected colleague is insistent. Tom puts the office phone on speaker and listens to the irritated solicitor doing pro bono work she considers below her level of expertise. He asks her to email him the papers, but before he can relax Janice buzzes again.

This time it is Caroline Zammit from Acqui, wanting to know if there are any developments in their investigation. Caroline's interest makes him wary. He must remember to ask Clare if she has uncovered any activities in Caroline's past or present that might signal his response is warranted.

Once he's finished with Caroline's mild inquisition – he gives away nothing – his thoughts return to Julia. Her voice is enticing, but much about her puzzles him.

He stands and opens the window: luckily his chambers are in an old building with actual windows. Outside, there is none of summer's humidity to trap the fumes in the air, which is crisp and refreshing on his face.

It strikes him Julia thinks that in some way he poses a danger to her. It's better than being treated as vulnerable; at the same time, it is odd. Perhaps he's projecting. She unsettles him, not entirely in a good way. He could ask around about her, but the escort agency and the threats to the refuge are more pressing concerns. Besides, taking a gamble could be fun.

18

Later that day, Tom's taxi drops him beside the El Alamein fountain in King's Cross. He stands, meaning to be noticeable. Up here, the city takes on the quality of a film set. Sound and movement everywhere, people calling, knocking into each other, others hiding in the shadows, waiting for the unnamed. Officially he doesn't know Warren meets Lexi here. However, he does know her windows overlook the fountain.

He moves, cane out, to a bench. People pass with the tapping of high heels, the slippery, slouch-gait of young men on the prowl, children giggling in pushchairs.

His seat reverberates as a heavy body lands beside him. 'Got a smoke, big fella?'

'Sorry, I don't smoke.'

The man smells – stale food, staler urine, recent drink, the usual. He leans closer and the scent becomes a stench. It is extraordinary, Tom thinks, the different values different humans place on each of the five senses. For Proust, with his madeleine cake, the sense of smell was a portal to a precious past; for this man it is presumably irrelevant.

'You looking for trouble, consolation, fun or what?

Tom considers. It's possible the fellow has borrowed his clothes, his slurred speech and his rank odour from a guidebook to good surveillance. Yet, if he is genuine and this is his patch, he might have useful gossip to exchange for the price of a good meal or a bottle of scotch. 'Do you know of anything out of the ordinary?' he replies.

'Nah, nothin' real special.' The man shuffles away along the bench. 'Wish I could help you out, mate.'

'You could help me for a few minutes, if you wouldn't mind,' Tom says, measuring the effect of his words by any change in physical alertness and, when it comes, tone of voice.

'Got nothin' better to do. Is there a few bucks in it?'

'Fifty. First, I want you to stay here, see if anyone shows any particular interest in me.'

'Fifty bucks?'

'Yes, if you do that for five minutes and then discreetly watch again as I walk in the direction of Darlo.'

'I'm your man. When we get going, you can pretend you're trying to shake me off from begging. I'll just bang inta ya now an' then like I'm really hasslin'. Anythin' else you need?'

'How good are you at clocking trouble before it happens?'

Tom hears the man rub his calloused fingers together, blow on them, rub again. Cold? The smell suggests a stockpile of clothing, but heaven knows what warmth there is in any of it. 'I used to be a cop,' the man says as if speaking to himself. 'I reckon I still got it in me.'

'I guess you meet a few of your old colleagues around here.'

'More of 'em dressed like me than like you, mate. Y'ready? Name's Ted.'

'Peter.'

'Don't bullshit me. You're Tom Challinor. S'not that long since I left the force.'

'Apologies.'

'Nah, normal.'

They stay on the bench. No action. They set off along the footpath, Ted attaching himself to Tom's cane as if trying to trip him up, while too pissed to have the co-ordination to manage it. Now and then Tom loses the intensity of his scent. He's doing the job properly, urinating against a bin, collapsing on the edge of the gutter, pulling himself up and bumbling after Tom as if he's suddenly rediscovered his prey. Tom is on high alert, reasoning that a man as well-trained as Ted could well have better reasons than the proffered fifty dollars to keep track of him.

When they near the intersection with Victoria Road, Tom stops suddenly, forcing Ted to collide with him. 'Okay, okay,' he says, feigning a tolerant anger at the alcoholic loser, 'I'll buy you a drink.'

They head for the bar nearby.

'There's trouble brewing.'

'Details?'

'One of the places we passed is a brothel, right? Well, more'n one is, but you know the one I mean. Upmarket, old school. There's a window in the front room all decked out in finery – red velvet style. Hipster's love it, reminds them of the Wild West or somewhere like that.' Ted guzzles his drink then pushes his glass noisily across the table, indicating his need for another. Tom signals. 'Well, in that room were a coupla characters who don't usually spend a lotta time together, if you get my drift. In fact it could be said they generally prefer shotguns at close range.'

'They were in discussion?'

'Deep confab and they're not hidin'. The curtains're open, they wanna be seen together.'

'A show of strength. Good. That's where I want to go.'

'No way.'

'Every way. First, though, is their window visible from the lane opposite it?'

Ted scratches for a moment, releasing more odour. Tom is surprised he's been allowed into the bar. 'Yeah, what's the interest?'

'Do you happen to know a shop down that lane? With unusual sex tools inside.'

'That pervert place?'

'That's one way of putting it. Would whoever is in the shop, or coming and going from it, be able to see the group in the window? Would they feel like they're being watched?'

Another scratch, a cough. 'Maybe.'

'And there's no indication of anyone interested in watching me? Except yourself, of course.'

'You bored the pants back on everyone within cooee.'

Tom nods. 'But the people in the window saw me?'

'Yeah. They took a good gander.'

'Good. Now, before we head there, tell me – did Lexi send you?'

'How'd you come up with that?'

'We all like to think we're famous but I've only been back in Sydney a few years. You wouldn't have known me when you were in the force.'

'Smart bastard. Lexi says to say hello. Saw you by the fountain. She passes a bit o'work my way, must've known why you were hanging around.'

'If I'm a smart bastard, she's a Mensa mind. Give her my love.' Tom lifts his glass. 'Now it's time I paid that visit.'

'Tom,' a throaty voice says as he walks in.

'Angela, good to see you.'

'You too. I don't believe you've visited me at work before. To what do we owe the honour?'

Tom smiles. He defended Angela's daughter Molly three years back. Molly's boyfriend accused her of fraud, producing all sorts of excellent documentation. Tom had had to involve Warren to uncover the counter evidence. It turned out the boyfriend in question, scion of a wealthy family, had gone haywire when he discovered what his girlfriend's mother did for a living. In his twisted logic, he was destroying Angela's evil influence on the world by framing her daughter for fraud he had committed. Luckily they found the holes in the elaborate scam.

'No, but I have the impression you might know why I am here,' says Tom.

'I admit to a good guess. In a minute, I'll introduce you to a few of my colleagues. Some you'll probably like more than others. On account of those others, we have to go through the formalities first.'

Tom is approached by a burly bloke who smells of hair oil and leather. Tom hands over his mobile, is frisked – as if a gun would be any use to him – and promises never to mention any person in the room by name or description.

'Apologies,' Angela says, leading him into the inner room. She does a brief introduction, a warning in her voice: she wants, and expects, those unwilling "others" to behave.

The sumptuous décor muffles the direction of sound. Tom has to listen intently. The sense of discomfort and annoyance around him is strong. The irritation is not directed at him, yet. Tom focuses his thoughts, knowing he must play the game their way. The men and women in this room are powerful and with that power comes ruthlessness.

'You want this escort agency stopped obviously, but may I ask why that's so important?' he asks politely.

Glasses clink and chairs creak. The three women and two men

around the table are presumably exchanging glances, assessing each other's silently expressed opinions of how much should be said and what information might work against them. Even with Angela behind him, he'll have to be very careful.

A cigarette is lit, a tut of disapproval comes from a corner.

'It's a matter of principle,' offers Pamela, sitting to Tom's right.

'We're losing custom, as you can imagine,' Angela admits.

'And,' Tom says slowly, 'previously you could charge a premium for supplying similar services, mostly with imitation disabilities?'

'Vijay speaking. Naturally, we recognise each person has their own predilections and it is our job to meet those needs. We use actors. We're not in the business of preying on the most vulnerable members of our society. I am a patron of the Paralympics. We have very good makeup artists and some excellent equipment. In fact, some of us have invested considerable capital.'

'I cannot speak for each business represented here, but I am not charging anything like as much as these newcomers,' Vijay continues. 'Recently our clients have been demanding properly deformed workers – for the original price, of course. Plenty are prepared to pay a premium, too. Authenticity is all the rage. Soon we'll have to show medical certificates, outlining the workers' most intimate problems. Passports and proof of age will be old hat.'

'There'll be a good market in proven virgins then,' a nasal voice adds.

'So, the advantage this agency has is its ability to recruit people with authentic disability, as you say,' says Tom.

'Correct.'

'And none of you have any idea of their sources?'

A pause. 'We admit, no.'

Pamela isn't going to let her righteous indignation slip, or admit she's been outsmarted by some new kids on the block. 'All those poor people who've been injured or born with half-arms – what was that drug? Thalidomide? How do we know they're being protected? We all have very good health practices. We've been thinking of introducing counselling for our staff.'

Tom politely ignores her. 'So, you each are, as any business person would be, troubled by a loss of revenue. Is there any other aspect of this agency that's concerning you?'

'As I said, principle.' Pamela again. 'We've been fighting for years to have sex work properly recognised. It's the oldest trade in the world but our girls and boys are kicked and spat on and have doors closed in their faces. And that's just what happens when they take their kids to school. There is far worse.'

If it all weren't so serious Tom would laugh at brothel owners as moral crusaders. 'Are they attracting some of your S & M customers too?' he asks.

A glitch in the soundscape and then Vijay says, 'If the truth be told, yes. Many.'

Apart from Vijay and Pamela, the others are quiet, probably keeping a studied eye on him. The centralised sex industry has been under threat for years now, with small, local businesses proliferating, able to provide services with much lower overheads. The larger operators have coped by being flexible, but this new service is expensive, specialised and available only to those in the know – making it a new, highly desirable fashion indulgence. Sado-masochism is a particularly lucrative market, too, so if their clients are suddenly being offered women and men whose very bodies apparently declare suffering, money will indeed be moving away from them.

As well as that, the people in this room enjoy the status of fashion icons, the most in demand. For decades – undoubtedly ever since white invasion – being the owner or the Madam of a first-class brothel has meant close contact with many wealthy, well-connected Sydney identities. You garner invitations to openings, rub shoulders with glittering stars of stage and screen, get privileged real estate deals and your own table in the most fashionable restaurants. You are also well-placed for a word in the ears of the law and policy makers. In the normal course of life, the individuals in this room vie with each other to top these invitation lists; making this recent problem the beginning of a turf war that could get very nasty.

'And some of the customers you are losing are perhaps wealthier than your average punter? Men and some women willing to pay a premium for secrecy – which this agency is already renowned for offering?'

'Ah, well, yes.'

'Perhaps you have a name or two of customers who may have changed his – or her – allegiance?'

Another glitch in the soundscape, a tiny but perceptible collective intake of breath. 'We will consider this. Once you have shared information with us.'

'How much do you *know* of the operations?' someone asks with constrained eagerness.

That they haven't yet got the gen on the agency's MO confirms how effective this new business is at keeping its skirts and shirt-tails away from the mire and mud of ordinary prostitution. It further confirms the set-up money hasn't come through regular channels, and that those behind the agency haven't risen through the ranks of the sex worker industry. Good-to-know information.

Vijay speaks up. 'One piece of your information for one piece of ours.'

'A fair exchange. Before we get down to it, I'd like to ask you about a series of threats recently received.' His description of the dolls is brief and to the point. 'Have any of your workers – those who imitate disability – had any similar experience?'

The shock in the room is mild but feels real enough. 'That is terribly tacky,' Pamela needlessly points out. All deny any knowledge, however. Vijay suggests surveillance and consulting the police. Tom merely nods. Then they set to business.

The trick is for each of them to reveal just enough of the right information to whet the appetite of the other party. They could be playing Texas hold 'em poker.

When Tom is politely ushered out with a promise for future cooperation that is extravagant and not to be trusted, he leaves behind enough reliable information about vans and hotels that the brothel owners are comfortable.

He carries with him a mental record of four names that could well prove useful. Each name is attached to a man who can ill afford the slightest besmirching of his pristine public image.

THURSDAY

19

Innocence must be protected. A woman rejecting he who loves her most is forsaking the protection she must have to survive. You ignore this truth at your peril. I was prepared to love you forever but you have sold yourself to the devil, you have thrown yourself upon others and let them succour you.

The letter continues in this vein, finishing with, *You are dirty, you are defiled. It is beyond even my power to forgive you.*

Tom is about to close the file when the electronic voice produces a set of violent expletives. The effect is alike a suddenly emboldened wild man strafing his target with an AK47. It is also inconsistent with the previous repressed and contained violence. Is the man losing control of his own plot?

This letter came speared through the detached breasts of another Barbie doll. No wonder Marcia is hysterical, in her forthright way. Everything about this letter is disturbing. As with the earlier letter, the indications are that the writer is educated and has a strong sense of both entitlement and betrayal. Psychopaths have that immeasurable, deeply rooted belief that what they want is right and proper and theirs for the taking. Devotees, like the general population, are rarely psychopaths, but "rarely" does not mean "never". Unfortunately, as the brothel owners are well aware, people with disability are also attractive to sadists, those who are excited by witnessing, as well as inflicting, pain and suffering.

Tom shifts on his chair, listens again to the first letter Marcia sent him, noting this second letter shifts from "we" to "I". The writer has become more frantic, and more personal in his attack. Together, the two letters suggest the writer ticks the sadism box. And the male dominance box. And a sadist, particularly one who thinks of himself as duped and betrayed, is a far greater threat than a devotee.

Warren's associate, Alan, failed to see the note delivered. The night was quiet, he'd reported, and he was probably right. The doll, its slashed breasts and violent note were in a padded bag in the letterbox. They could easily have been pushed in there after Alan had finished guard duty. An ordinary-looking passer-by, a kid paid to do the job, or a lad dressed as a delivery boy would raise little curiosity in daylight. Has the man behind the dolls realised there is increased surveillance? If so, how? Has he got a mole, an accomplice inside the refuge?

Tom forwards the electronic version of the letter to Warren. Marcia is showing the actual paper letter to the police. She has increased staffing and introduced monitoring of movement in the refuge. She is not happy but it has to be done. He runs his hand over his head, grimaces. He's got people to see, places to go.

Harry Montague is not a solicitor who passes briefs to Tom, but his secretary has no trouble recognising him. The secretary – Brian – fusses in an irritating manner, explaining that Harry wouldn't keep Tom waiting, only he is with an important client who's overstaying her welcome. Perhaps Mr Challinor would like to come back tomorrow. Tom can't decide whether Brian is worried about professional hierarchies or the fact that an infirm person is sitting in the waiting area.

One reason Harry doesn't pass Tom briefs is a simple one – Harry's area is company and corporation law, a field that bores Tom more than television with the sound turned down. The other reason – and this would apply no matter what – is that Harry distrusts him. Like many solicitors – and coppers, court reporters and criminals – Harry sees the law as an adversary that can, if tamed, make him a lot of money. The law as a means of guiding or reinforcing half-way decent social behaviour makes no sense to him at all. Harry provides services to those who might otherwise have difficulty finding a lawyer sympathetic to sailing very close to the legal wind. Which is why Tom is there.

When he is finally shown in, Harry is short on his handshake and quick to return to his seat. 'Like the new premises?' he asks, leaning back in his chair. He is a big man and the stress on the mechanism is audible. Tom presumes Harry has perfected a way of arranging himself so the panorama of the city remains on show. An office with a harbour view is *the* badge of success in Sydney.

'Very nice. It's an expensive part of town. You seem to forget I can't see the vista.'

Harry leans forward. 'Challinor, you can smell it. Or something. We all know that.'

Tom doesn't demur. 'What I want, Harry, is for you to help me find a name.'

Harry sips a coffee. He doesn't offer Tom one. 'A small enough request, but why would I do it?'

'Because I have a list of names myself. People associated with very special service. A unique escort agency. Your name, well—'

Tom waits. So far, no intel directly links him with the escort agency, but Harry's name came up in the search of businesses and companies, and in the exchange with Angela and friends the previous evening. Harry is not on the list of lost customers which the brothel owners provided, but he is associated with two of the four who are. Also, and interestingly, Clare turned up a photo of Caroline Zammit and Harry together. Caroline was glittering – heavily made up, in a very tight dress and immense jewellery. The two were cosying up at a charity function. Given the way the city works, and Harry's brilliance at polishing money that's laundered, these links are not surprising.

Indeed, Tom had briefly considered Harry as a possibility for the eager philanthropist Bec brought to his attention after the Acqui meeting. But Harry is really a very straight kind of gay bloke, careful with how he splashes around his money. Simple tastes, it's said, a wife who doesn't mind as long as he pays the extravagant mortgage and the school fees for her one child (previous marriage). Tom finds it sad that Harry feels he has to parade a specious normality, but right now he needs to exploit Harry's penchant for keeping up the appearance of conservative respectability.

Harry exhales. 'Haven't a clue what you're talking about.'

Without a word, Tom extracts a sheaf of papers from his leather satchel. 'I printed these off just an hour or so ago: a list of companies, all purchased or set up locally. Shall we say, very locally?'

The chair makes the smoothest of sounds as Harry eases forward. The papers are on the desk between them. If blackmail occurs to Harry, he is both wise and wily enough not to mention it. 'They're in bloody Braille, what's that supposed to mean to me?'

'Ah, wrong order. Apologies. Your printed pages are at the bottom of the stack.'

'All bullshit, Challinor. I'm as clean as a new washed window and you know it.'

'Harry, I'm not interested in you. I'm sure whatever you've done is legal, or near enough. You're too smart to do it differently. It's the movers and shakers I want to stop.'

'A bloody saint, are you?' Harry scoffs.

'Who knows, I might be that boring; it's not relevant.'

'If you're sure I haven't done anything – which of course I haven't – why are you coming to me?'

'Have a good look at the papers, Harry. I made a visit to some associates in the Cross late yesterday. We put our heads together. Further to that, I called in a favour from a friend who can trace ownerships better than you or I can. What you'll see on these pages are companies coming off shelves, new ventures being established, other fascinating coincidences of place and people not unknown to you. Makes good reading. You're probably too self-protective to go any further than aiding and abetting, but some of those companies and some of those names – well. And, if there were anything too close for comfort, you no doubt referred your clients to another legal mind. One without your, shall we say, ethical concerns.'

Harry takes the pages and noisily tears them into several pieces before placing them in the waste-paper bin. Or does he? He's quick and clever enough to have left the print ones behind for future reading. 'You're asking me if I know the solicitor? I don't.'

'Harry, you can find out.'

'Challinor, you're an arrogant bastard. You still haven't told me why the fuck I should do anything for you.'

'No particular reason, Harry, other than it's potentially dangerous not to. Never forget your reputation, Harry. It's important to you.'

Tom leaves, confident Harry will contact at least some of the people Tom'd like to have the winter wind whip into a mild fever of fear.

Frightened people make mistakes.

20

'YOU KNOW, WHEN I WAS KID YOU COULD BUY EVERYTHING, I MEAN *everything*, here. Humungous plasma TVs, laptops, clothes, shoes, drugs, booze. All sorts of good stuff fell off the backs of trucks, my dad said. These days it's all stupid dealers.' Avril waves at the hectares of open space with its scratchy grass, formal rows and irreverent clumps of trees, its unexpected hills and small, deep valleys, its sunlight sliced by the shade of the taller trees, the old buildings. In the distance, a group of school kids is walking slowly up a hill, on an excursion to Old Government House. 'My mum never let me come here.'

'Is that why you want to come here now?' asks Sonya.

'To piss my old lady off? Nah, too old for that sort of thing. To be honest, I've been thinking about what happened to Melanie.'

'Yes, me too. We will look.'

The long road through the immense park is largely empty. An occasional passing car, a small pack of cyclists, a few dog walkers. On the footpaths, elderly women chat about their grandkids and yummy mummies – one rearranging her stylish hijab while on the move – jog jauntily behind well-sprung baby carriages.

'Look at those show-offs,' Avril says, pointing at a slim blonde woman pushing a particularly large carriage.

Sonya sighs. 'I want to have a baby. When we finish.'

'That'll be great," Avril reassures her, knowing Sonya is scared she won't be able to have babies after this. She figures there's more worrying Sonnie today than babies, and it's not just Melanie. Has she been given a video too? Avril narrows her eyes, begins to ask, but Sonya is focusing on a middle-aged man coming toward them, arms pumping, legs jerking up and down, eyes flicking over them. The man slows. Avril eyeballs him, daring. He's old and ugly in her opinion but she's never seen him before, which is good news. In fact, she can see he is shocked by the two of them. He's one of those who thinks disabled people should be kept at home, out of the normal peoples' way. She pulls a face at him. If Sonya weren't with her, she'd put a finger up too. And a finger up to normal. Who ever wanted to be normal? Normal is totally boring.

'Look, Avril, here,' Sonya calls, pointing to the blue and white police tape, one end tied to a wooden fence, the other trailing off onto the dry grass. 'This is where Melanie was attacked.'

Avril checks the now retreating jogger, then slips through the fence and races toward the water on her very short legs.

Sonya follows. When they reach the grimy corner of the lake where the tape begins, she stops, assessing the place.

'Do you think Melanie was threatened? To keep her quiet, like, while the guy wheeled her?' Avril asks. 'Course, he could've drugged her. I mean, it doesn't make sense. Why would some businessman or whatever bring Melanie into the park in the middle of the day to dump her in the water? One of those nosey mums'd notice for sure.'

Sonya shakes her head. 'Nobody can see here. So many trees and it is very dark.' She pauses. 'But they do not kill ladies like that. In Iraq they kidnap people and they torture. They do it when night come. They do it a lot, like it was a game. Play over and over.' She bites her lip. 'Maybe they kidnap Melanie? Something go wrong.'

'You reckon they were going to go for a ransom? That's an idea.'

'No ransom. Avril – think who want to take Melanie away? Her family? Her father? He is feeling betrayed?'

'Melanie's like Anglo or whatever. Anglos don't believe in honour killing, do they? 'Sides, her dad's a butcher. He could kill her real easy if he wanted to. Doesn't need to throw her in the lake. And she *likes* her dad.'

'What about her customers? Was she afraid?'

'We're all fricking afraid, mate.' Weakness is not Avril's strong point; her expression dares Sonya to comment. 'Let's look for some clues. Maybe the police missed something. They're all thick-as, if you ask me.' Avril heads for a copse of tall fir trees. 'Might be stuff in here. We used to play in the cubby under these trees when I was a kid.'

'You say you never come here.'

'Wasn't supposed to, was I? Made it heaps more fun.'

Sonya moves a branch aside and follows Avril into the tree-cave. 'Avril, I go to see Melanie in the hospital,' she says, quietly, cautiously. 'She have visitors now.' Sonya explains the clever way Melanie introduced her to her parents as a friend from a support group for accident victims. Her parents left them alone. 'Avril, she tell me the man, he is not the man in the hotel. But she will not tell me the real man. She is very scared.'

'What do you mean? The guy confessed, right?'

'Yes, but I think the agency, they pay man to confess to police. Maybe he is illegal refugee and need money. They dress him up, make him look like wealthy man. In Iraq they do these things. Same thinking.'

Avril pushes the cherub curls back from her face. 'Nah, they'd notice if he had a foreign accent.'

'There are many British and Irish and American illegal people. Nobody think they are foreign.'

'Yeah, okay, could be. Who's the real kidnapper, then, hey?'

'Big question,' Sonya says slowly. 'You know man in wheelchair we see in city. Why is he in lots of hotels lots of times? What if he looking and waiting? For opportunity to steal?'

'Money? Jewellery?'

'Maybe people?'

'That's super-creepy. Kinda makes sense too, like with Melanie and what happened to her.' Avril pulls a few fronds from a low hanging branch. 'Thing is, it's no use to us. We don't know he's doing bad stuff for sure. And we haven't got his name or anything.'

'We see him come out building, we have address.'

'And the coppers'll go knocking on account of what a couple of disableds say, hey? Like I said, we haven't got any proof and he's maybe part of the organisation. He really could be looking after us.' Avril kicks into a pile of beer cans. 'Come on, let's go home, I'm sick of it all.' She puts a hand on Sonya's arm. 'Awright, we'll look out for that wheelchair guy. And we'll be real careful.' She kicks more cans. 'Sonnie, I don't want anything to happen to you. Not to me neither.'

'Melanie tell me another important thing.'

'Yeah?'

'Melanie tell me it was *your* time in that hotel. She and you swap shift time that day.'

'Fricking hell, I'd forgotten. Fricking shit! My 3 o'clock Friday.'

'Probably it is coincidence.'

Avril picks at the bark of the tree, swearing softly. Flicks the bark away. 'Yep, that's it. Coincidence. Like you said before, could be an honour thing. Some old boyfriend or something like that. They've been following her – did she say anything about being followed? And that hotel has crap security. Like, anyone can wander on in. That's what they did, hey? Followed Melanie in and waited. For her.'

Sonya looks at her friend. Her stomach feels empty, sore. She stares out through the branches of the tree-cave. The sun is high now and, without shadows, the landscape is flattened and ugly. The smell of stale urine is rising despite the insipid winter heat, blotting out the scent of fir. She remembers Stephen, the dress, the throne, his perverse speech and demands. She has not told Avril about Stephen.

Before that day she had not been ashamed. The use of her body had seemed a small exchange for funding a future in which she could study and travel and speak English out loud as beautifully, as poetically, as the words sounded in her imagination. Now, it is all different. Now there is Melanie and the man who has confessed to a crime he did not commit. There is the idiot girl who is already pregnant because she wants love and does not understand to take the little pills, there is the boy with his broken, misshaped legs who has been beaten and left alone in the gutter outside one of the hotels. And there is the shaking she perceives in Avril's voice despite her attempts to be brave and to laugh. Sonya reaches for her friend's hand, clasps it wordlessly. Long ago, she'd learned to smell danger, to know when it was close. Right now it isn't on top of them. It isn't far away either.

21

IAN LIKES HIS GROUP OF RETARDS. CAN'T SAY RETARDS PUBLICLY. THAT'S old psych nurse speak. Get him fired, even though "people with intellectual disability or cognitive impairment" takes a bloody hour to say. Yeah, he's pretty fond of the buggers, 'specially Ahmad and Graham, who totally enjoy a laugh. Sensitive too: they come up and hug him if he's in a bad mood. That behaviour is outside the department's rules too. No touching makes for some peculiar interactions. Touch is comforting. Nice.

Government departments are also real good at keeping their policies away from the people they affect, Ian thinks, filling in yet another form. They put them on web sites – but, gees, reality-check – how many clients of departments dealing with disabilities and social services could get anything from websites filled with big words and legalese? How many clients have the computers in the first place, seeing as how poverty and disability are such enthusiastic bedmates? As for the staff – half his team is barely literate. That includes Danny, whose complaint is driving him around the bend and down a ditch.

Ian scratches the back of his neck. He's planning on a chat with Jean's "person responsible", as they call the family member in department-speak, at her regular visit this evening. Tell her about the harassment charge Danny's pulled on Jean. Good idea to make a few notes first.

Suddenly the door slams open. Ian jumps, sees Jean, half-naked, looking like she's about to cry. For a moment he stares, surprised by the best pair of tits he's seen in years. Full, high, perfect.

'Go get some clothes on.'

Jean grabs at his desk, sending papers, folders and lever-arched files flying toward Ian in one direction, the floor in another. She's clearly very pissed off.

'Holy shit.' Ian stays sitting. He'll lose his job if he touches Jean, 'specially with her being half-naked. He can't stop her destroying the office. She grabs more papers, her breasts fortunately not colliding with the stapler or scissors. Ian gets that hardware in the drawer as fast as he can.

'I found these,' a male voice suddenly announces from the doorway.

One of the casuals comes into view. Ian can't remember his name, although he's pretty sure it starts with a J. Everyone starts with a J this week. The casual holds out a clutch of dolls and soft toys, completely ignoring Jean, who plonks herself on the floor and begins ripping paper in a satisfied fashion.

'I found these in Jean's room,' Justin/Jason/Joshua announces angrily. 'They're not age-appropriate. Jean is over thirty. The guidelines say we must select age-appropriate activities.'

What the fuck? thinks Ian. What the fucking fuck? Fortunately Jean isn't taking any more notice of the casual than he is of her. Bloody good, seeing they're her dolls he's holding. The fucking guidelines don't say that anyway. Not anymore.

'Personal choice, person-centred, that's what the guidelines say,' he throws back. Choice is the trump card.

Jean is obviously impressed with Ian's argument. She's off the floor and lunging for her dolls, scrabbling to get them out of what's-his-name's arms.

'She scratched me!' The dolls fall on the floor.

'What'd you expect? You're hanging on to her favourite things.'

'She shouldn't have them. She shouldn't attack me.'

Jean drops back to the floor, cradling a doll, beginning one of her long gabbles. She's happy.

Ian decides ignoring her is the way to go. 'Bring her some clothes,' he says, 'and go do the bathrooms. Her sister'll be here soon.'

'Will she take the dolls away?'

It's only as Justin/Josh/Jason leaves that Ian wonders why Jean only has a skirt on. He shrugs; she must've been getting ready for a bath. Funny time of day, though.

The reliance on casual staff is driving him crazy: can't get funding for permanent. Casuals cost more! Also, he doesn't have a bloody clue why Danny – who's well enough trained – couldn't do his job properly and has instead put in a complaint against Jean. For harassment. For pity's sake, the woman doesn't and never will know what the word means. She grabbed Danny's crotch, so what? Probably just a bloody accident. Besides, just 'cause she's retarded doesn't mean she wasn't looking for a roll in the hay. How else is she gonna ask? Ian's willing to bet a month's pay no one else'd propositioned Danny in years. Bloody disability service world: a Luna Park of moralists who think if you have intellectual disability you're a perpetual kid and never need a good bonk. And a sacred citadel for workers who want haloes and can't get them except by caring for someone who can't protest.

Jean wanders out of the room. Ian follows, checks there's staff around before going outside for a ciggie. He drags deeply, not bothering to think about giving up. A neighbour turns her car awkwardly into the driveway next door and grimaces at him through the tinted glass. The neighbours hate the staff nearly as much as they hate the residents. They all lower the tone of the area.

Ian resists the desire to give the woman the finger. Instead he decides on another ciggie. With the packet comes the card he was handed the day before at the local area meeting. A suggestion of work, big dollars possible. An attached note explains he must forget quite where he got the card. Which is easy enough, as he found it in his folder after the tea break and has no idea who put it there. Also says that the offer, and the number, will be deleted in three days. Figures it can't be too great an organisation if it has to delete or replace its phone number; still, more money is highly attractive. Might give 'em a ring. He wanders round the back – flat grass, drought-dry – lights another ciggie, gaining a bit of time to think about it.

'Ian,' one of the staff calls the second he's inside.

'Righto,' he replies, then remembers how his father had driven him nuts using that expression. Righto. Sicko.

'In Jean's room,' the disembodied voice directs.

The staff member sounds anxious, but things seem to be as usual. Graham's sprawled on the couch, his fly undone, watching 'Home and Away'. Ahmad's walking around slopping a cup of coffee over the tiled floor. Dave's singing away. Jean isn't in sight. He avoids Ahmad and the coffee, tells Graham to do up his fly, and goes down the passage to Jean's room.

Justin, or Jason, or whoever, is standing in the room, frightened. 'Where's Jean?' he demands.

'In the kitchen?'

'No.'

'Bathroom? In one of the boy's rooms? The laundry? Shit, you haven't lost her, have you?'

'We'd better look again.'

Ian pulls open the three possible doors and sends Justin-or-whoever to check behind the shower curtain. Jean hates showers, but you never know. Not there. She likes practical jokes – Ian checks cupboards that couldn't hold her size anyway, but you never know that either. Ahmad grunts and comes over to help, coffee cup still in hand, innards doing their final cascade. Ian calls to Sanjiv, who's just come on shift, to clean up the mess, otherwise someone'll slip and the bloody tiles are hard.

Jean isn't any-fucking-where.

The sense of desperation is sickening. Jean is in his care. He might not be the most dedicated of workers, but losing one of his residents is pretty end-of-the-world scary. For a few seconds, or it could be minutes, Ian sits on the couch, the TV still blaring, and thinks seriously about crying. Or chundering.

Sanjiv is more sensible. The streets here, he points out, are not very interesting and the houses are all very similar. Jean probably got out somehow and got lost. She has a history of absconding, they've documented that. This gives some comfort, 'cause round here she'd be noticed. He suggests a search outside.

Ian directs the other staff to go with Sanjiv. He bites his nails. He hasn't done that since he was a kid. He'll have to phone Jean's sister and declare the emergency. Scary. But then, Jean might reappear before the sister visits. She'll be here soon: she's more organised than a Google calendar. Gorgeous too, but that's none of his business. And there's the Danny complaint. Ian leans against the filing cabinet. They call this place a typical house. A bloody cardboard box, he calls it: brick veneer, low ceilings, cheap laminate in the kitchen, a second bathroom that is a cubbyhole off a pokey bedroom. Whenever anyone pisses, the whole household hears. He hates it. And he pities the staff out there knocking on the neighbours' doors. It'll be the biggest thing since the council changed bin night.

Half an hour later, Sanjiv and the casuals return. No sightings, no news. 'We have gone a long way. No person has seen her.'

Ian pushes frustrated air out of his mouth. It's shift change time; he'll keep on the A as well as the B shifts. It's like herding cats to get the searchers in – warring cats, once they're in, all of them with different opinions as to how or why or where Jean has gone. He calls them to order.

'We look after her really well.' Dee is clearly more determined than most. 'She doesn't always want to be with us. She hates staff being in her face.'

'Jean's a law unto herself,' he agrees. 'One of the things I like about her. You're right, Dee, but we're stuck with doing what we're told.' He holds up an official dot-pointed list of instructions. 'We're not supposed to let the clients out of sight. We've got to interrupt their down time, always give them something to do.' He stops. The banging in the background is rising to a dangerous crescendo. 'Will someone please see to Graham? I can't stand the noise.'

Sanjiv leaves the room.

'Why can't you do it yourself, Ian?' Rose asks.

There is no sensible answer so he ignores the question. Being house manager of a small group home is a petty power and he knows it. He walks over to the window. The back garden is still uninspiring. He considers the possibility of a weekend away. Camping. He hates camping, but can't afford anything else. His ex-wife insists the kids go to a Catholic school and his portion of the fees wipes out what he could save for a wicked weekend. It's lucky they're not going to one of those seriously posh schools, his wife says, ignoring the fact they could never have afforded a school like that even if they had stayed together. Maybe Dee needs someone to amuse her for a while; she's a woman who might think camping a romantic choice. He reckons she'd look good bending over the fire.

'Did anyone upset her?' Ian asks, turning back to reality.

'You mean other than Danny?' Dee says, curling her lip in a way Ian finds attractive.

'Where is Danny?' Rose asks.

'Stress leave,' Ian replies, caustic.

Rose's eyes glitter. 'We're not trained for this sort of thing.'

Ian looks around the circle of staff. A couple nod in agreement. Others are red-faced. Ian doesn't know what to say. Bugger training. The staff all think their way of doing things is normal and normal is right. Fucking normalisation isn't policy anymore but the idea has wormed its way into disability support like a computer virus. Who the fuck wants to be normal anyhow? Look at Justin with the dolls. Ian knows plenty of adult women who still love their dolls.

'What if she's been abducted?' Rose calls out.

Predictably, there's an explosion with everyone talking at once.

'That's it. Finish panicking. I'll ring the police, they can deal with the idea of a snatch and grab. It's their job and they might even be good at it.' At least that raises a mild snigger from his audience. 'You lot get back to the door-to-door. Sanjiv will delegate who goes where, he's marked off where he's been. I'll hold the fort here, sort out the paperwork too. Who's volunteering to help? How 'bout you Dee?'

'I, well, yeah, I could do that.'

Ian nods. She's picked up his vibe, he reckons.

22

'It's like the early scenes of Hitchcock's *The Birds*,' Tom says, aware the sun is slipping behind the bridge. 'When the birds are beginning to collect and form a mass. We understand their vengefulness because of the absence of ordinary sound. You're on tenterhooks, waiting for the first single flap, the prelude to horror.'

'Surely it's not that bad,' Julia replies.

'Probably not, I'm prone to exaggeration.' Tom laughs. 'Although when the court is gowning up and growling about the mooring fees for their yachts, current mortgage rates for their holiday homes or the filthy coffee that's supplied, I'm very glad the defendant doesn't have to see us all together.'

Julia remains silent.

'I'm sounding pompous, aren't I?'

'A little.' She laughs. 'More embarrassed – like me. Do you think it's because we're too old to flirt?'

Not at all, he thinks, but perhaps we keep coming up against the reality that we shouldn't. 'As we are flirting,' he says, ignoring his own cynicism, 'we should decide where to eat.'

He feels her pull her coat closer to her. Rejection? Pleasure? Both? Tom waits, having nothing to lose except an insipid dignity – much less consequential than desire.

'On one condition,' she says slowly. The staff begin to move tables, the metal legs scraping on the flagstone floor. They both wait for the distracting sound to subside. 'That we still don't tell each other facts. Living life by a check list – what part of the city you live in, who your parents were and who your family is connected to, whether there's a gym in your building and/or you have a portfolio of real estate – is dull in the extreme.'

'Opinions?'

'I'm sure you already know who I vote for, and what I think of the state of the environment.'

He smiles. The promise of continued mystery is enticing, including its potential for danger: he's always enjoyed being near the edge. Her insistence on privacy has to raise the question, though – why is she so secretive? Well, he'll play her game for the time being, all the better to find out what the game is and where it is headed. 'Excellent. Shall we go somewhere for a drink first? It's too early for a meal, but the waiter here will have us fined for loitering soon.'

'I feel a little over-dressed in my work clothes,' she says, standing up and moving closer to him so that the warmth of their bodies joins and provides a small protection against the encroaching cold.

'Umm,' he takes her cue, giving a good impression of looking her up and down. 'You look lovely, but I was thinking of a cheap little trattoria. Perhaps they'd be overawed.'

'I'll have you know that this suit comes from Florence. It's a town in Italy, you may have heard of it.'

'You could inform the waiter I suppose...'

'There's time, we could shop. I could buy something more casual.'

'Excellent idea. Now you mention it, I wouldn't want to go out dancing in this outfit either.'

'You have Y chromosomes and you're agreeing to shop? I was only joking. Partly – I really would like something more relaxed. I hardly ever wear suits like this one – it's natty, a little *Breakfast at Tiffany's*, except I'm far too tall for Audrey's elfish elegance, and the skirt's almost impossible to walk in. Movies do cheat. This morning I had one of those meetings where we all have to look professional.'

'I enjoy shopping. Seriously. We don't need to go anywhere extravagant.' Particularly if that means this evening goes on, with no interruptions of home and husbands, life outside this pleasing bubble. He wonders if and when she will contact her partner. And if not, why not? There must surely be one: she definitely doesn't have the aura of a woman who lives alone. Or of one who readily damns the feelings of others. Interesting. 'I'll have to make a few calls later,' he says, thinking this might provoke an admission.

Julia makes no response.

A cab ride later, the street vendors are unravelling cloth studded with cheap jewellery, boxes of imitation Rolex watches, incense, and T-shirts proclaiming the wearer had participated in various obscene moments on Bondi Beach, the Harbour Bridge, or Opera House. Bunches of British, German and Spanish-speaking tourists gather – laughing, describing holiday exploits, discussing where to drink, eat, sleep, taking little notice of the merchandise. Julia and Tom are in Bondi for the pragmatic reason that shops are always open and the unstated reason of likely anonymity: Bondi is overcrowded, a hectic part of the city neither of them visits regularly.

People push and shove and call. Julia describes what she sees, speaking as if discovering the joy of words. Tom smiles. It happens occasionally, that his companions find an unexpected pleasure in translating their perception of the world into speech. 'It's good here,' he comments. 'Often when I shop, people walk around me. It's out of some sort of consideration but it feels like I must have a contagious pox on my face.'

Julia responds after a few seconds, 'I presume it has occurred to you that being six-foot-five, dressed like a film director, and looking like you own the street has some impact too. Some people might be too awestruck to go too close.'

He grins. 'Touché.'

'And there's mystery, too. Tell me why you need to know a good PI?' she continues their conversation from the taxi.

He knows she isn't going to accept this is simply because a blind barrister needs a set of eyes. Still, he doesn't want to give too much away. 'Much of the advocacy I'm involved in needs behind-the-scenes investigation.'

'An unusual way of mainstreaming disability support, isn't it?'

'There's more than a few in the advocacy movement who'd agree with you. One hell of a lot of people are convinced that either church fundraisers, on the one side, or street marches, on the other, are the best way to support people with disability. And that anyone who has an impairment is by nature innocent, or especially wise – either way, certainly not in the least capable of, or interested in, having any dealings with the underworld.'

'As if neatly mown lawns are the only reality?'

'Experience speaking?'

Her arm tenses. Always a give-away.

'I'll tell you my experience with disability sometime. Right now, we're here to enjoy ourselves and we're allowed a few hours off saving the world. And here's a decent-ish clothing shop.'

They exit the shop half an hour later with Julia in comfortable black jeans, shirt and a gorgeous leather jacket, her work clothes in the parcels. The store manager was pleased to see them go. She'd been solicitous of Tom, panicking politely when he selected items for Julia to try on, offering him a seat – kept for American tourists, who're often over-sized and need to sit down, she had explained, digging herself deeper into unconscious prejudice.

He'd continued to assess the clothing on offer: feel being an essential ingredient in what you wear. Julia is beginning to think there's a lot more about him she'd like to assess by feel.

As they step back into the clutter of the tourist strip, she catches his hand. 'Where did you learn to shop? I mean, most men don't. Or maybe I'm just being hopelessly gender specific.'

'My mother taught me. And she would've agreed with your gender specificity. My father was wonderfully academic and domestically incompetent, while my brothers are both the sort American sit-coms are written about – you know, hilarious scenes of them over-cooking a frozen meat pie in a microwave: the pie explodes. My mother wasn't going to let all of us get away with it and, as I had to cling to her skirts more than most boys, I was the patsy.'

'And a very good thing, too.'

'My mother always did say it would make me attractive to women.'

'Absolutely right. Where is she now?'

'Julia, it's not a great story but I'll tell you in a minute. Right now, do you have a sense of being watched? Over and above the ordinary staring at the blind bloke and the great looking girl?'

'Being watched?'

'Perhaps followed.'

'I've been tempted to look over my shoulder a couple of times. I assumed it was just being out of my usual comfort zone. Should I look?'

Tom keeps walking. 'Might as well. Try the shop windows, it's clichéd but it works.'

'I can't see any signs of suspicious activity,' she reports.

'Good, although a professional doing surveillance will melt fast in this crowd. You're probably right; we're both just out of our usual frames of reference.'

'Why would someone be following us?'

'Good question. Do you have any ideas?'

'Not a clue.' Her frown is in the stiffness of her body against his, the sharp shift of her arm.

'Don't worry about it. I'm like most blind people – I can be over-sensitive to the idea that I'm being watched. I'd better tell you what happened to my mother,' he says and briefly describes the accident that killed her.

Julia accepts the distraction. 'You were there when she died?'

'I got home a few minutes after it happened. My cab pulled up and there was commotion everywhere. The accident was just outside our house. I'll let you imagine the rest. She was a wonderful woman.' He moves his hand to her shoulder; her hair falls upon it. 'We're getting a bit up close and personal, aren't we?' he asks.

'We're about to become more so. Here's an attractive menswear shop. I think a tight T-shirt over those pecs will be just the thing.'

'Excellent.'

She laughs. 'After that – food. I'm beginning to curdle with hunger.'

23

IAN PARKS THE VAN. BEFORE HE GOES HOME — WHICH HIS BOSS INSISTS HE must do — he'll have another go at contacting Jean's sister. She sent a text saying she can't make it and then closed her phone off, which is decidedly out of character. Officially, he's not suspended, but without doubt this is the first slice across the neck of his employment — trust all gone, Ian responsible for Jean's disappearance, et cetera. Jean's sister not turning up is making matters worse: it's like both sisters have dematerialised. The police aren't too concerned about Jean and not at all about the sister. Well, it is logical that Jean isn't far away.

Sanjiv has been waiting by the carport for Ian's return.

'I dropped Graham and Dave off,' Ian tells him. 'They're safely in the bowling club and Marty's keeping an eye on them. Ahmad's at his parents tonight.' He hands over the car keys. 'Pick-up's in two hours. And hey, Sanj, seeing as nobody's in for dinner, I reckon you might go out again and look for Jean. Take Jason or whoever with you.'

'It is not procedure to leave the house empty.'

'Bugger procedure, mate. Keep the house mobile with you. Police've got that number, and my personal one.'

Sanjiv is both relieved — wanting to find Jean — and concerned about the breach of procedure. Ian throws his stuff into his old duffle bag. The bag is an emblem of an earlier, freer life.

'I have tried to ring her sister again,' Sanjiv says. 'There is no response. Should we ring another member of the family?'

'There's only the sister, mate. Mother dead, father pissed off.'

'Her husband, Jean's brother-in-law?'

'Dunno, isn't there some story about him not having any involvement? He sure as eggs never comes near the place.'

Sanjiv swallows. 'It is possible that we do not have such information in the files. Families have many disputes with which we need not involve ourselves. Would it not be better to speak with Jean's brother-in-law, as a family member should be informed?'

Ian knows that Sanjiv is telling him he's looked and there's nothing written down. It could be a staff beat-up anyhow. Lots of those stories turn out to be bullshit and they are duty-bound to talk to a family member of some description. 'Yeah, right, don't you think the police will do it?'

'That would not look efficient on our part.'

'Yeah, you're right. I'll do it before I go.'

In the office, Ian pulls up the house contacts list yet again. 'He's not under P,' he mutters. 'Isn't his name a pissy double-barrelled one? Prettie-Jones?'

Sanjiv hands over a phone number with a smile. 'I think that Mr Jones is his proper name. It is possible he considers Prettie-Jones sounds more important.'

Not a bad bastard, Sanjiv. He and Ian respect each other. Ian might look like a drop-kick, but he is bloody well-organised and Sanjiv acknowledges it. Same goes the other way.

Less than a minute later, Ian gets off the phone. 'Not available. I've left a message. He'll ring back. Listen, Sanj, we'll find Jean before it matters. Okay?'

'Of course. Jean must be very sad, being lost.'

Ian raises an eyebrow, says nothing. He is outta there, and now. He'll be fired straight up if he hangs around.

He's being kind of compensated for the stress. He's picking Dee up outside the Pavilion at Bondi, then heading down to Coogee for a meal and music at the pub. He has the old Holden; they both live nearish. No need for the rest of the staff to see what is going on. Especially 'cause maybe nothing is going on.

It's hairy crossing town at this time of day. Ian has to get in on the arterial, join the distributor, lob off, and thread through Darlinghurst. Half of Darlo's streets are not much wider than the original dunny lanes and are chocka with cars and trucks and bikes.

Stuck in the traffic, Ian looks out at footpaths remarkably free of debris of the human variety, though saddled with an extravaganza of other crap. He's gonna be late. He drums his hands on the wheel and swears more than once.

Finally he squeezes out onto Oxford Street and lane-hops through Paddington, over the expressway, before sweeping down to the beach. He's proud of the Holden's performance, but Dee isn't outside the Pavilion. He cruises past a couple of times and is about to assume she's ditched him when a gleaming new Beamer pulls in front of him and, dangerously, stops. He slams on the brakes and the Holden, bless it, grinds to a halt. Ian hates to imagine the cost if he'd run into the back of the bastard. Then he's stuck, traffic everywhere. Ian peers out in the hope of spotting Dee.

He nearly spits chips. There at the pedestrian lights is Jean's currently uncontactable sister, Julia Prettie. She's standing with some outrageously good-looking bastard who is not her husband, but is very bloody close to her side. Ian can't believe his eyes as he watches Julia, the most dedicated, determined relative of a retard he's ever met, looking at the guy in a way that Ian can only describe as naked. It's one wild look. He wishes he'd inspired it in someone recently. At any time, come to think of it.

How come the guy isn't returning the look? He sure would if he had the chance, with her looking at him with such open lust.

Ian turns at a knock on the window. It's Dee. He signals to her to get in, leaning over when he realises he's forgotten to lift the lock and she's pulling at the door handle and it's going to fall off.

'Hi,' she says and he grunts in return. Not rudely, it's just that he's concentrating on the other couple. They've linked arms now and are moving off. Then he sees what it is about the bloke's failure to respond to that shining beam on his face. The bastard's blind.

The car in front finally moves, but for a second or two Ian doesn't put the Holden into gear. He's dumbstruck. He turns to Dee and is about to point, when suddenly he thinks he shouldn't. Dee and he are hardly an item yet and he doesn't know in which direction her loyalties might go. 'You're late,' he says.

'No, you are. I was here on time. I went and bought a drink and was going home. It's only by accident I saw you.'

Ian shoves the car into gear. He likes a woman who doesn't stick around for a bloke. Not one like him. Maybe this was gonna turn out all right after all.

'Didn't see anyone you know, did you?' he asks, flicking the indicator on.

'No, should I have?'

'Nup. Just making conversation. I reckon we're gonna have a good night.'

24

'BULL'S BALLS,' WARREN MUTTERS. IS CHALLINOR OUT CLIMBING KOSCIUSKO or what? Sort of thing he might do on a Thursday bloody evening, in the middle of winter. Warren presses into a doorway, sheltering from the wind. Lexi'd rung as he was parking in an innocuous spot near to the refuge. Gotta call her back.

'You talked to Tom yet?' she demands when he does. 'I gotta confirm with those young women real soon.'

Already had three goes. Not telling Lex that. Tom won't want to miss the next morning's meeting; it's a miracle Lex has arranged that event in such a short time. She isn't saying how she performed the magic, but unlikely she'll do it again. Decides to take a punt. 'Yeah, it'll be cool with the boss,' he says, thinking the guy he's masquerading as would be proud of this show of bravado.

'Okay, I've gotta get back to the contact now. He'll be set to go?'

Warren drags out a packet of cigarettes, fiddles with them to provide a further reason to shelter in the doorway, which is readily observable from the strip of pho eateries opposite.

'Lexi, trust me.'

'Wazza, I do. Same time, I don't want to lay anyone on the line for nothing. These girls must be freaked, or they wouldn't agree to talk. They'll be jumpy, scared.'

'You can't come along with them?'

'Gees Waz. They're meeting in Parramatta and from where I sit that might as well be the moon, 'cept the pollution's worse and the drugs are heavier.'

'He'll be there. Now, I'm working, gotta head, Lex.'

'Cool. See ya.'

Warren steps out of the doorway. The high wind hits like it's waving a cricket bat toward his face. Make that two bats. He needs to get a quick but thorough picture of this area around the refuge and then find a good pozzie for keeping an eye on the women.

He pulls up the hoodie. The hoodie's the sort worn by middle aged men who go to the gym and sit on benches staring at their mobiles, never to raise a sweat. A cool dude wouldn't be seen dead in it. He phones Marcia. Nothing doing inside the refuge. Kids squealing in the background. The homely sound soothes, even if it's the wrong time of night for youngsters to be up and about. Has a bit of a wander around, easy enough to do a pissed suburban dad look. Eventually, he fetches up outside a pub, pretending he's deciding whether he can have one last wee drink for the night.

He finally gets a result with Tom. 'Where the hell are you?' he demands.

'Out for dinner and dancing.'

'One minute you're as serious as a ship's ballast and the next you're a hot air balloon.'

'I take it you have some news I should've heard earlier.'

'Thing is, you gotta be in Parramatta on time,' Warren says, cursorily explaining the Lexi's arrangement.

'It's nearly midnight.'

'You could've answered your phone earlier.'

'I'll be there.'

'Clare's coming too. I could get through to her.' He hears the groan in Tom's voice but he's got no time for anyone's love life right now. Ends the call. Wanders past the refuge. Gloomy looking place. Continues his perambulatory "mildly drunk married man on the street not wanting to go home right yet" act. He drizzles into the neighbour's yard next to the refuge. No lights on, his movements not disturbing anyone (he's been practising for years, after all). He pretends to have a whizz against their garage wall. Gives him a good sight line. Decides he can afford to stay there awhile.

'Wazza, ring me,' a text from Lexi unexpectedly declares. Hell to pay if the meeting's cancelled. He picks himself up, makes his way back to the street. Interest in him appears to be zilch.

'I want you to listen to me, I want your full attention,' Lexi growls into his ear.

'Okay, listening.'

'What you have to do, Waz, is to be careful. Real careful. And tell that good-looking employer of yours the same. I just heard some stuff. Big money's involved. And big money that's not the same as your common or garden variety dirty money. It has a different set of connections.'

'Any idea who this big money comes from?'

Look, Waz, I don't know and I'm not going to try to find out. Carrie's telling me that we've got other work that's safer. I've got the girls sorted to talk, so that's enough for now, okay?'

Lexi's best friend, work- and flat-mate Carrie, is usually more gung-ho than Lexi: if she isn't willing to put a toe in the water there's some real serious talk on the street. 'What's giving Carrie a case of the old reverse-rickets?'

'Dunno. She's closer to some of the out-of-area workers than I am. You know, the girls who do the pricey escort work, more than one of them have the jitters.'

'Any full-on action? Likely to be anyone laid out on a shelf in the morgue?'

'I don't think it's that simple and it hasn't gone that far either, yet. An' I don't wanna be involved in making that happen any faster than it has to. From what I hear, the girls and boys are being treated all right at this stage, if you don't mind a bit of real kinky stuff. Maybe they don't need me too much. I'm going to back off.'

Warren is desperate to have a real whizz. Bad timing on his bladder's part. 'Turf war?' he asks, making his way toward a dark patch off to the side of the road. One of those pocket parks used by old ladies and alcos; sometimes one and the same.

'Nup. We're used to the turf wars. Something different about this operation.'

'Interesting.'

'Yeah, mate, fascinating. Look, I need some sleep. Got a meeting of the women's cooperative first thing in the morning.'

'Fair enough. You've done one fine job getting those girls to agree to chat. Couldn't ask for better than that.'

'Ta, Waz, invoice's in the post, as they useta say. I'll keep it in mind and let you know if anything turns up. I'd just prefer not to be too active on this one. Got Tina to consider after all.'

Warren looks around the yard for a convenient tree. Lexi really thinks something serious is brewing. He needs to get hold of Tom again, pronto.

He drops his phone into an accessible pocket, rather than its usual hiding place. Doesn't hear the man close behind him as the steam rises from his own piss.

25

'THE GULLS ARE SPYING ON US. I'M SURE THAT'S THE ONE THAT STOLE MY lunch,' Julia says as they dodge the late-night gaggles of young men and similarly raucous flocks of birds.

They step down toward the sand. It is foolhardy, but the wind has dropped and they are both warm from the hours of eating and talking and drinking. As yet there's been no discussion of how the evening will end.

'Are you going to tell me more about this investigation you're on?' Julia asks as they scuff their feet on the sand.

'It's truly too late to talk shop.'

She is quiet for a moment and he is reminded of the confusion he detected in her voice on the phone the previous day. 'Reasonable,' she agrees. 'Let's sit down – there's a set of stairs over there, they'll do.'

Nearby the waves suck and slap, a couple snort with desire, adolescents, out too late, squabble or laugh as they cavort on the sand. One twitching, stoned young man almost trips over them as he tries to find his way back to the Corso. Other consumers of softer drugs sprint and fall about on the sand, finding it all hilarious.

Tom's whole body registers the simple touch of Julia's shoulder as they sit, close. They've ranged across dozens of subjects over their hours together. He's found she has a good command of irony and rarely tiptoes around subjects many think of as out of bounds; at the same time, each of them is holding a lot back.

Julia describes dogs, their owners nowhere apparent, the bag lady settling to sleep in one of the small shelters behind them. 'You pick up at least half of what can be seen without the slightest need of me, don't you?' she asks, that wonderful smile in her voice.

'Maybe more sometimes, less other times. But it's good to know we're sharing a world. Mine could be very different from yours, otherwise.'

Grains of sand scatter as Julia kicks off her shoes. 'Do two people ever share a world?'

'That's a deep a question for this time of night. Particularly after that much wine.'

'True. The cocktails were good, too.'

He is about to ask what she wants to do now when he hears her take a breath. Both instinct and experience detect a confession of some sort is about to come. He waits.

'Tom, you've noticed I have experience in the "disability world". Apart from my job, I should tell you about my sister Jean.' Her voice curls, a wave hesitating before breaking. 'Jean is my younger sister. She has intellectual disability, tactile hypersensitivity, poor hearing, reasonable sight, a great sense of humour, and lovely hair and eyes.'

She stops.

'So that's why you were resistant to sharing your lunch table with a disabled person. You had to turn into an adult too early, behave like a carer, fill in all the gaps, make amends?' he asks, taking an educated stab at a psychological interpretation.

'It sounds so awful but yes, you're right.' The wave of her voice breaks now. 'I had to be there for her and to clean for her and to think for her and to amuse my father for her so that he wouldn't notice how much was wrong. You see, he'd get very angry and he'd take it out on her. I had to keep her out of the house and keep her quiet when all she wanted to do was bash things, or giggle or scream – Jean is not a person who responds in shades of grey.'

The arm and shoulder against him are tense. 'Go on,' he says quietly. 'Siblings usually get a really raw deal.'

'It's much tougher for you.'

'Rubbish, I've had – I have – a great life. There's many much worse off than I am, I can assure you. What was the hardest part of having to live with your sister?'

He could hear her scraping a layer of sand back and forward across the step. 'The hardest thing was trying not to love her,' she says eventually.

'The other kids called her retard or spazzie, idiot, half-wit, you know the sort of things kids say. I was a coward, I'd cringe in my room, making sure I only left home as the school bell rang so I didn't have to face them in the playground. I'd stick my fingers down my throat so I vomited, I'd do something at school that put me on detention – anything to get out of taking her to the park or the shops when the other kids were looking. I guess I should be ashamed, but that's just the way it was. In the end, though, I loved her so much. Her face would light up when she saw me. Still does. She listens to me; she became my confidante. She doesn't understand ninety percent of what I say, not literally, but that doesn't matter because her love is so complete.'

Julia stands up quickly. 'I need to walk.'

She strides away, the squeals of the sand confusing his sense of her direction. 'I can't reach you there,' he says, testing the void around him.

Minutes later, she returns, her voice sharp now, provoking distance. What the hell, she asks, what the hell was she doing there on Bondi beach with a stranger who'd picked her up in a cafe? Whom she'd picked up too, like they were teenagers in a bar. She hasn't spent so many hours in the company of any one person for God knows how long. She hates bleeding hearts and sob stories. There's nothing that can be done about Jean or their childhood or their dead mother and long ago disappeared father. Who cares and why the fuck should she cry?

'You did this,' she accuses. 'Just don't say you're sorry. I hate sorry. I hate it, *hate* it. Do you understand?'

'I'm not sorry. Not at all.'

Ten minutes later, they are sitting together, his arm around her in what he hopes is a comforting and non-demanding way. Her breathing is more regular. Tom scoops sand with his free hand. He holds the grains, enjoying their coolness, before releasing them slowly back to the ground. 'I've booked a room in a hotel,' he says quietly.

'You booked a room? If I may ask, why?'

'I take it you're not being disingenuous. You know why. You're asking why I haven't offered to take you to my home.'

'Is there someone waiting for you? Did I guess wrongly?'

'No one. My assumption is that you have a husband or partner waiting for you, though. I thought it might be easier to stay in a hotel room.'

'Then I will feel less like I am betraying him? If there is a him. Or her.' Julia's tone of voice gives nothing away.

'Yes, and so you might be able to say, more or less truthfully, where you slept the night. If that is what you decide to do.'

'Good thinking. Where are we going?'

Tom reaches down, finds her shoes. 'Do you need to let your husband know you're not coming home?'

'I don't have a husband anymore.'

'Is that a bad thing, the not-any-more? Hurtful?' He is pleased, but surprised to be so wrong. Perhaps it was her relationship with Jean that lent her the sense of being committed emotionally elsewhere.

She remains close to him, no agitation in her body. 'Not now.'

'What does your ex-husband do?'

'Why do you want know?'

'It's not entirely personal, while somewhat revealing. Like doing up the zip on a woman's dress.'

'That's quite an image. My ex-husband makes money. Share trading, that sort of thing.'

'Ah.'

'You don't approve?'

'It's not my business. Although it might explain why you're no longer married; you don't strike me as the financial market type.'

'He was different once,' she adds and falls silent.

'Pardon my cynicism, but weren't they all? Let's go now, there's not much of the night left and I have to leave earlyish in the morning.'

'Sad, but it's that kind of world. Let's find a cab.'

26

Julia's husband, Phillip, sits on the couch, phone in hand. 'Colin,' he says, 'do you remember the weekend we all went to Merimbula?'

Colin's sleep-soaked voice is slow. 'Who the hell is this?'

'It's Phillip, Phillip Prettie-Jones. My wife has disappeared off the face of the earth. That's why I'm ringing you at two am, so don't bother asking.'

'Julia doesn't disappear and what would it have to do with me anyway? She's probably gone to Canberra or somewhere for a meeting and stayed over. Most organised, dedicated woman in the known universe. It's too late for you to be her gatekeeper.'

'I am drunk now. I was not so when I made all the appropriate checks. We were supposed to be having dinner. She left a message. It was not truthful.'

'You're so frigging precise when you're drunk. Now, I'm tired and grumpy and my wife's snoring. Go to bed, Phillip.'

'And Jean's disappeared too.' But Colin has hung up.

Phillip regards the phone. Newest model, but a disconnected smart phone is still an empty shell. The voice has no substance, surely?

He continues to sit on the sofa, folding and unfolding the corner of the doona he's dragged in, paying no attention to the dust it might pick up from the unswept floor. Phillip hates dust, but not enough to have a cleaner. Cleaners are nosy, they are spies, ready to pounce on any piece of nylon clothing or cheap shampoo that might show he is no different from them.

Perhaps he should try Julia again. Or the police. Not that the police believed him either. 'How long did you say your wife's been missing?' the telephone voice had asked. No police stations to visit any more: it would've been good to bang on a door, have an interested face open it. Over the phone, they were free to snigger. When he told them about Jean being lost too they passed him on to someone who asked a few pissy questions about family feuds. He dreads having to ring them again in the morning. Of course, he could pull a few strings, speak to people with more power, but well, he doesn't want them to know. Especially not about Jean.

Phillip throws the doona back, collects his glass and makes for the kitchen. Might as well put the dishwasher on. Then he tries Julia again. No answer. He's damned if he's going to leave a message.

He doesn't have her contacts list, as he doesn't have her phone. What he does have, however, is her old book, her pre-smartphone book. She is loyal, Julia. Most of the entries are still real people in her life. He dials a number scribbled in the front of the book. Doesn't have any idea whose.

Another murky middle-of-the-night voice. 'Ian McIntosh speaking. Is there a problem?'

'Is my wife in bed with you?'

A pause. As if the guy is checking the woman beside him to make sure.

Phillip decides to be helpful. 'She's tall, dark-haired and good looking, mid-thirties.'

'Nah. Sorry.'

'That's fine. Tell me, did I have you worried for a minute?'

'Yep, but she's blonde, always has been as far as I know. I reckon Northern European.'

'Good arse?'

'Great.'

'That's excellent. Sorry to disturb you.'

A new glass is called for. He pads back to the dining room for a crystal one, eschewing the quaint blue-glass tumblers Julia bought for the kitchen from Mexico or somewhere else poverty stricken. They'd had enough poverty in their childhoods, both of them, surely. He smiles at the whisky. This is beginning to be more enjoyable.

Colin is in Julia's book under "D" for Derby. He's already tried the

Alcots, the Alaverezs, Barbara, Aaron Beatty, a number of Cs. "D" means there are many more names to come. Hundreds. His suspicion is that Colin and Julia had an affair. A brief one. He is a handsome bastard, old Colin, and witty, well paid and well connected. The three Ws. What more could she want? Not her husband, apparently.

He settles back on the couch, the phone book by his side. Who else might she have had sex with? Who else might she have confided in? Were they one and the same? Phillip is pondering this question when his phone rings.

'I have a message for you, Mr Jones. Listen carefully. The message is simple. Take better care of the company your wife keeps. She could cause you a great deal of inconvenience. It is advisable to act on this message immediately.'

With that, the voice – a monotonal male voice – stops dead. Phillip is again left with the empty phone in his hand. This time, though, it isn't the alcohol making his hand tremble.

FRIDAY

27

THE DOLL IS BEHEADED. THE BLOOD COAGULATED ON THE PLASTIC NECK smells real. One of the adults finds it; the children are all being kept away from the front porch. The staff member doesn't scream, but she does vomit her early morning cup of tea carefully to the side of the step on which the doll has landed. This morning there is no note.

It is just after sun-up and Marcia sends one of the staff out to find evidence of Warren. She is not impressed with his performance and she can't reach him on the phone to tell him so. 'Probably went home to his missus, forgot about us,' she says caustically when the staff member returns to report that no van matching the description can be seen, no extra person is walking the streets, only the usual dog walkers and the couple of homeless people who regularly doss at the back of a house a short way down the road. 'Least there are some decent people in the world,' Marcia says, knowing the residents in the house down the road offer the homeless use of their shower. The staff member merely raises an eyebrow and heads off for a cup of coffee. In her books there are plenty more decent people around than Marcia would ever allow.

'What are you doing after the interviews?' Julia asks, turning over in the large hotel bed.

Tom is coming out from the bathroom, his tall, strong body so very attractive to her. 'Long answer or short?'

'Real answer.'

'What I'll be doing depends on whether Warren's been able to uncover anything of interest. I've got hold of some names – through reliable sources. People who might be involved in the escort agency. A lot of money's going into it, and these are people with wheelbarrows of the stuff. Warren's doing the background work – financial dealings, connections between the persons behind the names, any previous interest in devotism – Ivan's also onto that. After the interviews I mentioned, I'll be stuck with paperwork and, if I'm lucky, a polite interview or two. So, a complete lack of excitement. And you?'

Julia stretches under the sheets. 'Work, work and more work.'

Tom reaches for the shirt they'd bought the night before. He smoothes the fabric and Julia recalls again the thrill of those hands on her body. He has such passion.

'I'm also trying to trace a lawyer. The operation is so well-crafted, so superbly convoluted, that I think it's the legal aspects – or person – who'll lead us to the key players.'

'Don't you trust your own profession?'

'Does anyone? It has to be a solicitor with good knowledge of the disability laws and agreements,' he says, doing up the shirt-buttons.

'A solicitor with knowledge of the disability laws and agreements?' Julia echoes.

'Yes. And yes, I was hoping you'd know someone. Do you?'

She pulls up the covers. 'Well, I come across a few solicitors through work, naturally enough. Specific possibilities, no, I don't think so.'

He waits for her to say more, but she remains silent. 'I'd appreciate it if you could think on it. Julia, I've really got to go. I suspect you, too, were expected somewhere some time ago.' He moves toward the bed again.

'I'll go in soon.' She wills him not to touch. He is so hard to resist.

'Hold on,' he says. 'I don't have your mobile number. You rang me on your work line.'

'I'll text you, then you'll have it.'

'You could do it now.'

'Soon. My phone's in my bag. I've got a few things to think about it.'

'All right,' he says mildly, then adds: 'Julia, I don't give in easily.'

She wonders if he is reading her thoughts.

28

THE WINTER MIST IS THICKENING AS IAN WAKES. HIS PHONE IS ON AND messages are absent. More evidence that his job is starving to death before his very eyes. Where is Jean? Curled up on a back verandah in the cold? That'd be a good option even if an unpleasant image. He texts Sanjiv. The theory that Jean has been abducted is gathering pace and credence, Sanjiv tells him. Ian decides he's going in, management or not. He wakes Dee. It's been a good night. He apologises for not having anything decent in the flat to eat, suggests he go to the 7-Eleven to buy a packet of frozen croissants.

'It's all good, I'll go home, get some clean clothes, come in to work. The extra hands'll be needed. No problem if you can't pay me for the extra shift,' Dee responds.

'Are you sure you don't want a lift to the station?' he asks, really meaning it. How could he not, with her standing on his doorstep, bag over her shoulder, pert bottom turned toward him in a way he finds particularly enticing?

'I like to walk,' she replies. 'Keeps me fit.'

He resists the desire to pinch her bum. She mightn't like the gesture. 'Guess I'll see you soon.'

'Guess so.'

And she is off without kissing him goodbye, which kind of excites him 'cause it shows she isn't going to fall swooning into his arms, which in turn shows style – as well as saving angst, at least in the short term.

He's heading toward the car when he stops suddenly, nearly colliding with an inattentive young Labrador. Didn't some bastard ring him in the middle of the night? It wasn't a dream, he's dead certain of that. He and Dee didn't even drink all that much.

A bloke who couldn't find his wife had rung him in the middle of the night.

Ian looks for a stick to throw for the over-sized mutt that's now yelping around, trying to make friends. He chucks a plastic bottle from the gutter instead. It doesn't travel well, too light, wobbles around in the air in a silly bloody way. The dog doesn't mind.

The bottle reminds Ian that he'd got up and had a glass of water after the guy rang him about the missing wife. The dark-haired woman. Good looking, he'd said.

Something odd's going down. Ian kicks away the bottle, now covered in saliva. The dog scurries off. Ungrateful bastard.

Then it hits him. He'd only met the bugger once, months back, but he'd lay his life the bloke with the poncy voice and the misplaced family member is Phillip Jones, Jean's brother-in-law. And the person he was looking for wasn't Jean but the very gorgeous Julia. The very same woman Ian saw lusting after a blind bloke down at the Pav.

In his car, Ian checks the incoming call register. He presses the number sitting there. 'Mr Prettie-Jones', he says formally, 'I believe you may have rung me during the night, looking for your wife.'

'Did you lie to me?' Phillip snaps.

'Nah, now listen, I've rung to see if I can help.'

He can hear Phillip's confusion and realises that it's a stupid way of introducing the issue. 'Sorry, look, it's Ian here. I manage Jean's group home. She hasn't been found.'

'Yes. I talked with someone called Sanjiv a short time ago. I apologise – did I wake you? I didn't recognise the number in the middle of the night. I was a little inebriated, and worried of course.'

'Not a problem.' He bites back the "mate". He does feel quite matey but Phillip PJ would have no idea why. 'Look, it's just that I – ah, it's a bit difficult – I think I saw your wife last night when I was picking up, ah, my girlfriend. The blonde,' he adds, placating.

'Of course, the blonde.' Phillip's voice is precise.

'She was good,' Ian offers.

'I'm pleased to hear. Now, how could you have seen Julia?'

'Is she back?'

'No. I have no idea where she is.'

'I saw her outside Bondi Pavilion. About six, maybe six-thirty.'

'Bondi? Why would she go there? Are you sure?'

Ian thinks this is worse than getting a tooth filled, which is worse than getting one pulled. Especially on the hip pocket. 'Yeah, it was her. She's unmistakable. She was with a bloke.'

'A bloke?'

'Sorry, wrong description. With a well-dressed man, very tall, blonde. Strange thing was, he was blind. Well maybe that's not strange, but you know what I mean.'

Phillip's intake of breath is like a westerly wind down the phone. 'Tell me more about this man.'

'He sure made an impression,' Ian admits. 'Handsome, kind of self-possessed, a coat which musta cost a mint.'

'And you are definite it was Julia with this man?'

The way he enunciates "this man" makes Ian think Phillip is more interested in the bloke than Julia. Still, who is he to say how a man who's misplaced a wife and a sister-in-law in one day should react?

'It was Julia all right.'

'Did you notice anything more I should know about?'

'Sorry, I was just waiting for my girlfriend, like I said.' What is he, some sort of frigging detective? 'That's all I know, Mr Jones. Good luck.'

Ian sits in the car when the call's finished. He wouldn't like to be Julia Prettie right now. Her much-loved sister missing, her husband not giving a fuck about that, but right up his own bum about Julia being with a blind bloke who looks like a movie star. Ian swears. Phillip's response makes the hair on the back of his neck stand up. He hadn't meant trouble.

Phillip too sits, stunned. The pieces are falling into place, like the settling of an avalanche. He catapults out of the chair, refusing the hangover's vicious attempt to hold him back. He can see, feel, hear, sense disasters – on every front. How did this come to pass? He grabs suitable shoes. He needs to walk, to think, to develop a strategy. There are choices to be made. He needs to decide how to save things. Who to save.

29

The taxi hurtles up the slipway to the Anzac Bridge. Tom sits with one arm on the vinyl-clad armrest. Julia is next to him and he is not entirely easy with her presence. He was leaving his chambers for the interviews with the escort agency workers when she'd rung, wanting to come with him. Why? Romance? Perhaps: but they are hardly teenagers out taking recreational drugs all night, sleepily and ostentatiously showing a presence, hand in hand, at lectures late the next day. Her stated reasons are the desire to understand the agency and to spend time with him; reasons that do not fit with her work position, her way of life (as he knows it), or her responsibilities. He is unsettled. It is a risk – he'll take it head-on, but it's a risk nonetheless.

Julia is silent as they swing across the arc of the bridge. He suspects she lives nearby. Balmain, the narrow, hilly streets of Rozelle and the wider, tree-lined ones of Annandale and Leichhardt are now the most expensive areas of the expensive Inner West. The mixture of Victorian grand homes and earlier workers' cottages is populated by a few remnant aging Italian women, the occasional dock worker who's been unemployed nearly as long as he's been alive, and, much more plentifully, by families with green to pink social justice views, and by academics, artists, writers and public servants, also with left-wing tendencies. Her arm beside his on the arm-rest is tense and Tom recalls her insistence on maintaining privacy and mystery. Why? Soon he will ask a few direct questions.

They crest the hill and join the Western Distributor. With further unease, he recalls last night's impression of being watched. Normally he'd ask the taxi driver to keep an eye out for a tail – it wouldn't be the first time he's been the subject of a counter-investigation. This driver is not friendly, nor does he want to alert Julia to his concerns. If nothing else, "welcome to my life, which is often under threat" is not a good pick-up line.

Julia shifts on the seat and Tom feels her gaze on him. The slight pull away from him, the straightness of her arm, suggests a certain critical regard.

'Who are these young women?' she asks.

'I've told you as much as I know.'

The tension in her arm increases. 'I don't want to make them feel bad about what they're doing. It's a job after all.'

'It is. And probably well paid at that.'

Julia ignores this agreement. She has evidently been worrying at the ethics of what she is about to take part in. 'I know I'm teaching you to suck eggs, but even the best advocates sometime lose sight of how tough life with disability is out in the 'burbs. So many people stuck on the receiving end of charity, at best. At worst – and it's often at the worst – among the most abused: physically, financially, socially, sexually – anywhere, everywhere, at any time.'

She taps her fingers on the arm rest. 'For heaven's sake, at Jean's place, freedom is totally dependent on which staff member is on. The manager is relaxed and treats the place more or less like a home. Other staff? I've seen an adult sent to their room because they only drank half their cup of coffee and left the dirty cup on the side of the sink. Such a petty erosion of dignity is coercive.'

Before he can say anything, Julia goes on. 'I know you're worried about safety and exploitation and all of those things we should worry about. But, really, we so often forget how easily a person with disability can also be denied any – and I mean *any* – form of sexual expression. Cerebral palsy doesn't change desire, any more than deafness does. Neither does cognitive impairment, although so many otherwise decent family members, supporters, whoever, pretend that it does. It's as if having disability must obliterate lust, ensures the person can only be a holy innocent. It's so demeaning.'

Her tone changes. 'You know, when Jean was an adolescent, she strained her beautiful eyes at every good-smelling man – I'm sure the smell was the thing – who walked past. At home she rubbed herself against her clothes, the bed, the furniture. My mother cried, my father – well, he was very annoyed, to put it mildly. If anyone took Jeannie up on her advances – and believe me, she continues to make them – he'd be accused of rape. Society insists Jeannie can't give "informed consent", and it's assumed she couldn't possibly *want* to. Jeannie chooses to eat, she chooses to play games, to like or dislike people – and she's very good at all those! Why can't she choose to have sex?'

Tom senses the strength of feeling in her body. This isn't the diatribe of the self-opinionated outsider. History, experience and years of consideration inform what she is saying. 'What about Touching Base?' he asks mildly. 'It's still going. An agency bringing sex workers and people with disability together is acknowledging active sexuality, isn't it?'

Her voice turns directly to him. 'From what I hear, it's a great service. If you're wealthy enough and in the know. Realistically it's only available to those who can make contact themselves or have sympathetic supporters. Most women with disability, especially those with cognitive impairment, are confined to the graveyard when it comes to sex. Besides, if a person with disability is hiring a sex worker, then someone's still being a prostitute. Which raises the question – why can't people with disability be sex workers themselves?'

The driver pulls up, too quickly, at traffic lights. They are jolted against their seat belts. Julia ignores the man's evident displeasure. 'We have the most peculiar morality – like it's all right to sell your hands to massage a back, feet, hands, even the whole body. Which is pretty intimate, when you think about it. It's all right to pay to stimulate the aural sense, the visual sense, the tactile, the olfactory sense. You can pay, or be paid, to stick just about anything in someone's mouth – except your prick or your cunt.'

The driver turns the radio up. Julia leans toward Tom. 'The driver doesn't approve, but I'm not going to apologise. Although I have been haranguing, haven't I?'

'Reasonably, very reasonably. By the way, do you ever resile from the positions you believe in?'

She laughs then, the arm against his finally relaxes. 'Only if I'm convinced by another argument, or find another way of looking at the problem,' she admits. '*Have* I said the wrong thing? From your point of view, am I being insensitive?'

'To be honest I was more interested in the passion in your voice. So it's me who is being insensitive. Sexist, reductionist, totally inappropriate, in fact.'

'Haven't we made a pact to be attracted to each other, making a bit of lust within the rules?'

Tom thinks of her skin – like satin – against his body, of the ease with which her voice has found its way deep into his consciousness, his desire.

The taxi wrenches to the left, throwing Tom against Julia, Julia heavily against the door. They take a moment to right themselves.

'I'll give him the benefit of the doubt and think he only saw the sign at the last moment,' Julia says, as they are emptied out on a private road with uneven curbing and a disconcerting absence of sound. The driver almost throws the receipt at them, and refuses the proffered tip.

Tom takes Julia's arm. 'There's a small matter I haven't mentioned. Clare, my ex-wife, will be here as well.'

'Has anyone ever wanted to kick you? Why didn't you tell me?'

'I could say your coming was last minute, you didn't ask, and you must admit we've been talking about other things.'

'I invited myself along. So, my problem. I'm not usually this stupid.'

'We can call another cab. I can meet you in Parramatta.'

'I'm a big girl now. Who does your ex-wife think I am, by the way? You've let her know?'

'My new girlfriend. I'm training you up to be a disability rights activist.'

'Tom!'

'What was I supposed to tell her? That we'd talked half the night and had fabulous sex the other half, so now we're checking each other out some more? Or give her your full name and job description so she's wary and potentially wanting to take up an argument with you. Seriously, I thought it best to say that I'm interested in you and that you had a family interest in the issue. That's true enough; I didn't go into any more details. Okay?'

'Shit.'

'Number 206. Did I say?'

'Arrogant. That the other description I've heard of you.'

Tom smiles. 'It's accurate.'

The foyer tiles are scratched. Dirt grates underfoot. An old signboard lists names and room numbers. The office of the small advocacy agency they're looking for is at the bottom of the list.

'Hi, Tom's told me about you,' they hear Clare say almost before they are in the door. She's speaking in a bright voice. Julia notes that Clare's lipstick has just been renewed.

'Clare, this is Julia—'

'The two young women are waiting,' Clare says. 'They're both scared we'll tell their parents. It's all so hopeless. They're in their twenties and should have some independence. Instead, because of their disability, they have to stay living at home. The economic and practical constraints are extreme.' She suddenly directs her gaze to Julia. 'I hear you have a family connection?'

'My sister,' Julia replies. 'You and Tom should go in. I'll be comfortable out here.'

It is her olive branch and Clare takes it. She almost smiles. She and Tom discuss a few points, then Clare says quietly, 'Times change. You and Tom go in. I've got another interview to do soon, a young man who's coming in about a different issue. You two will be fine.'

'Hang on, don't I get a say in this?' Tom asks.

'No.' Clare and Julia respond at the same time.

'Just what we need, female solidarity.'

'It is.' Julia is emphatic.

The cleft in Clare's shoulders relaxes. 'It's fine, Tom, you and Julia go in. Like I said, everything's ready. And,' she adds, 'life goes on.'

30

'WE'VE BEEN SET UP, IS MY ESTIMATION. FED JUST ENOUGH TRUTH, BUT NO detail to take us anywhere,' Tom says when the interview has finished. 'Or am I being paranoid again?'

'They certainly seemed to be doing a sales pitch for escorting as a profession, and the particular agency as employer of the year. Of course, they may have got cold feet and covered up their concerns. Maybe scared the agency would find out they'd talked to us,' Julia replies.

'Is that what you really think, or are you taking my role and playing devil's advocate?'

'Barristers aren't the only people who explore all sides of an argument, you should know. In fact, aren't barristers paid to be one-eyed in favour of their client?'

'Fair point. Let's talk over lunch. I for one didn't have breakfast.'

They are walking along the Parramatta River, once a sludge-thick, polluted stream running between concrete banks. Now it's a high fashion water-view address: the river's been dredged, storm-water rerouted, the river ferries slowed to avoid eroding the mangroves along the banks. Developers are bragging about European appliances in the kitchens of apartment blocks sprouting up along the river like fireworks on a Sydney New Year celebration. With its multicultural edge, Parramatta has long been a great place to eat, and a further plethora of cafes and restaurants has accompanied the area's growth.

'How about an older, family-run Italian? Just off the to-be-seen strip. Excess oil and garlic and entirely delectable,' Julia suggests. 'It's my go-to place when I have a work meeting I can insist happens over lunch. Or when I sneak away between meetings.'

'Perfect.'

'I don't want to over-interpret those young women,' Julia notes after they take a table. 'Still, neither of them truly seemed like the women they said they were. Their clothing was almost a parody of high-class sex worker dress. Reading facial expressions is actually incredibly unreliable – except in crime fiction or TV drama – but I would say they rarely looked uncomfortable or frightened. That doesn't mean the theory they were scared and covering it should be canned.'

'Interesting. I thought they had the wrong accents too – seamlessly middle class for women who claim to have been born, raised and residing in the tougher suburbs of the south-west. They both sounded much more like you and me. We hardly rate as the proletariat.'

'Step back a little there. I'm acquired middle class myself. More or less. I'll admit my mother came from very faded gentry. Making her family, such as they were, even more unhappy about her living with my father, who was a perennially underemployed, good-looking bastard – with an emphasis on the bastard. She was a good mother in many ways, although lacking in gumption. She hoped her family might come to her rescue and insisted I learn to "speak well" in case they did. It's been a useful attribute if for no other reason than it's much harder to classify me. I prefer not to be too easily pigeon-holed.'

'Indeed, you fooled me and I'm well-practised at listening. You should think about working undercover. Now, I heard an article on the ABC recently, arguing that sex was a substitute for eating, therefore eating is the ultimate pleasure. We could test the theory. Would you run through the menu with me?'

Once they order, their drinks arrive quickly. 'So, we're left with two theories. One, that the agency has been monitoring my and my associates' movements and sent along some employees who could paint a picture of an employment idyll. Two, that Tanya and Jasmine are who they say they are. At the last minute, they were found out and threatened.'

'One more hypothesis – they actually meant what they said: Jasmine and Tanya are workers, they love the agency. Against that, neither of them sat or moved in their chairs in the way most chair users I know do,' Julia notes. 'Static legs, sure, but their spine control was excellent. Jasmine, in particular, wriggled her toes as if she were cold.'

'Their arms?'

'Jasmine was thin, with little muscle development for a woman who uses a manual wheelchair. Tanya's arms were covered, even though her cleavage certainly wasn't. Both their legs – in very attractive silky tights with remarkably high heels on their feet – showed little or no signs of wasting.' A child bangs against Tom's chair, staring briefly before racing off to tell his mother he's seen a blind man. 'Do you get very tired of that?'

'Water off the proverbial duck by now. Basically you're saying they could be imposters. They could also be pretenders – people who want to have a disability, dress up and present themselves as having an impairment. The information to date suggests the agency is not employing pretenders. That could be wrong.'

Tom pauses as a waiter arrives with their meals – superb smells. 'I don't think we can fully resolve the issue right now. Better – safer – to accept the worst option as the default: the agency's got wind of our investigation. Worrying, of course. However, right now, the food smells excellent. Let's eat. After lunch, I'll try getting hold of Clare again. It's unfortunate that she was in that other interview when we left. She needs to be warned there could be a mole, and there could be danger. I also have to talk with a few other people.'

'Ditto. But food is the priority.'

The risotto is pleasing; rich, traditional, the texture perfect. While enjoying it, Tom again wonders how Julia is managing to take this amount of unplanned time away from her office. He thinks better of asking, judging too much enquiry could sour the moment, if not the future.

'I'll just go to the loo,' Julia says, putting her cutlery down with a mild clatter.

Tom nods. He finishes his food and pulls out his phone. Warren isn't answering. Neither is the refuge. Marcia's personal mobile goes straight to message. Julia is taking her time. He checks in at his chambers: Janice is her usual self, doing grumpiness with verve.

'Did you get hold of Clare? What about Warren?' Julia asks, setting her handbag down on the seat beside her.

'I left messages. Otherwise, no answer was the loud reply. Hopefully Warren will get back to me soon, I need the info on those names.'

'Do you still think the brains behind this has a history of disability connections, rather than someone with a background in sex work or escort agencies who saw a new opportunity?'

'Seems so.'

Two cars, sound blaring from front and rear bumper bar speakers, pulse up the street, the drivers looking for their lost egos. In the cafe, the volume of chatter adjusts to overcome the disturbance; a child cries as the bass beats against her fine eardrums.

'Why did you leave Clare?' Julia asks, after the car turns with a dramatic flourish into the busier main street.

She's jumpy, Tom notes, before answering what is a reasonable question in the circumstances. 'Clare's a fascinating, complicated, clever woman.' He hesitates. 'Perhaps it's as simple as we'd both got as much out of the relationship as there was to get.'

What he doesn't say is he feels that for Clare, he could have been black – which he knew he wasn't, he'd asked around – or someone of another marginal status currently on the progressive thought barometer. She was attracted to the exotic, to the cause. He doesn't say it because he could be wrong, and because he didn't think it was conscious or even necessarily a bad thing. Without such attractions, the world be even more rigidly pre-packaged and boxed, surely. 'She does have a tendency to be nice a lot of the time,' he does admit.

'Ah, that's why you enjoyed my rudeness.'

'One of the many reasons.' Seagulls, eager to find their way upriver, flap by. 'More spying seagulls and enough said. We'd better get on with finishing today's commitments so we can meet again for dinner. We can share a cab into the city.'

'One more night out of reality? Tempting. I have to think on it, life being what it is.'

'You have the length of the cab ride.'

'Who's being rude now? Besides, I rang in. I'm going to work out of the Parramatta office this afternoon.' She picks up her bag. 'But, yes, let's meet this evening.'

Tom wonders why she hadn't said earlier she was staying in Parramatta. 'How would you feel about coming to my place? I'm not a bad cook.'

Her breath catches. 'That might work,' she says quietly.

'So, say seven-thirty-ish?'

'I'll try to be on time. I have a hell of a lot of work to catch up on, you know.'

He stands up. 'I'm probably exaggerating about Clare. Maybe I'm lazy where she's dedicated; sometimes I just want to enjoy myself.'

31

ROBIN PARKS HIS CAR IN HIS UNDERGROUND SPACE, TAKES THE LIFT, SMILES at his assistant and, with apparent calm, makes his way into his sumptuous inner office. Under his layers of fine clothing, however, he is breathless and has a concerning numbness in fingers and toes. He takes his own pulse; elevated, slightly.

The surveillance firm he has engaged appears to be doing a decent job. Cyber-investigation is their main *modus operandi*. Unlike most current services, they also retain a group of highly trained real-life operatives who don't object to being out on the streets or scaling a wall or fence, and are willing to engage in real-world contact. Very useful. The firm has indicated obliquely that other services may be available, should extreme circumstances arise. At this stage, he has pretended not to fully comprehend.

He stands by the window, tapping his fingers on the deep wooden sill. Outside his solid walls, the city is still jangling with the wind. On the harbour, discombobulated ferries smack hard against grumbling piers, while on the streets below, hair is whipped into eyes, ties appear set on strangling their owners. If there were trees, they would be swaying wildly.

Robin continues to watch. How has the careful fabric he created come unstitched so suddenly and so quickly? Should he desert? He is, he realises, tapping out SOS in Morse on the windowsill. Stupid skills learned at school. Robin straightens, takes out one of his phones. He will speak with his "friend" in the police.

'I have tickets to the Grand Final, including entry to the after-party,' he offers.

'Not a bad score.'

'Do you want to take your young ones as well? I can probably swing it.'

'I'll get back to you. How's business?'

'Good, very good.' Robin never knows quite how much to offer, what words to use with his police contact. The criminal underworld really isn't his area of expertise and although naturally the police can't be called criminals, they certainly excel in the language and behaviour. While he himself fails to be fully gung-ho, no holds barred. He fails to be amorally ruthless.

Robin sighs internally. The imperative is to discover whether there is any truth in John's claim there is a kidnapper and potential killer on the loose. Secondly, he must stem the flow of information from the police to John and vice versa. John's secret sources make Robin some sort of uninformed flunkey. Undoubtedly, his police contact will not want to appear uninformed either, nor want to lose those extra payments that make his officer's life more viable.

'It appears one of my colleagues has been speaking to one of your colleagues. Perfectly legitimate and I wouldn't want to step on anyone's toes. I know your information is most reliable – you've been exceedingly helpful and I can't imagine any other officer is as knowledgeable. The difficulty is that, as you would know, if colleagues are not on the same page, well, the smooth running of an operation is challenging.'

His contact, whom he calls Frank, grunts. 'You're hoping I'm going to give over the name of the officer who's handing intel to your mate?'

Robin wants more than that, but it would be a start. 'Some silly gossip is being aired. Knowing who is muddying the waters would be extremely helpful. As you always are.'

A definite change in tone. 'Don't lay it on so thick, pal,' Frank says, his voice loud, rough, making Robin wonder whether there is another person in the room whom Frank wants to impress. 'If you're hoping I'm going to dig around, set cats among pigeons here there and everyfuckingwhere, all for the chance to watch some pansy AFL longlegs jump around after a ball that's the wrong fucking shape, you've got another fucking think coming. Or maybe it'll be your first think coming. Listen, Robin or whoever you fucking are, I've only got so much free time to be speaking to the public like you. I've been kind and generous. Like most real workers – not a breed you'd be greatly familiar with – I've only got so much fucking patience. So fuck off right now and get yourself another errand boy. I've had enough.'

Frank is gone before Robin can respond. He unfolds a handkerchief and wipes his forehead. It is only after he has taken industrial scissors to the sim card and sent the remains off via the sewerage system that he understands Frank might be the very person John is chumming up to. John might simply be paying better. Or calling in favours. Favours are the premium. Alternatively, Frank might know exactly who is feeding John his tidbits. If that person is high enough up, Frank'd be wiser to date the wife or daughter of a Mafia boss than interfere with that cosy arrangement.

How to deal with Melanie and the event in the park? Although at the time he assumed John had unintentionally let something slip, it could have been a ruse. He could have told Robin the man in custody was not the perpetrator to throw him off-balance. Behind the irritating façade, John is a genius and a performer, as brilliant marketers must be. He could have been getting back at Robin for refusing John the names of his devotee friends. How, then, to find out if there truly could be further attempts, attacks? Without Frank, whose information he'd been relying upon – perhaps rather stupidly.

Robin streaks his fingernails down the thick windowpanes. The high-pitched screech drowns out his internal scream. He hates foolishness, and yet here he is, playing the fool, bells on his toes, a pointy cap on his head, chortling, making rhymes, doing the bidding of men whose arrogance, whose infantile surety of their superiority, is unshakeable. He's letting himself be shoved around like a kid who's sold himself to the playground bully.

Suddenly he hates silver spoons and yacht clubs, he hates the bloody salt water, the stalking of wind, the winding of ropes, the commands of the petty captains; all of it, he hates it all.

Robin breathes in, breathes out. The problem of the sightless man with the best set of eyes in the business is troubling him too. It is a problem he must find an immediate strategy to combat.

He looks down at his fine hands, which show no sign of the work he does – dirty work some of it, it must be admitted. The surveillance team has assured him that tomorrow at the latest, he will have useful details of those threatening that work. So much to lose. Is he going to have to stoop to gutter level? Use the surveillance firm's other, special, services to get out of the mess? A sickening thought. But all types of men – and women, he mustn't forget that another significant problem is a woman – get twisted into shapes and actions they never imagined possible. Can he claim to be any different after all?

32

The cab driver's a taciturn man who prefers the heating turned up to scalding. Tom shifts uncomfortably in his seat as he answers Ivan's call.

'Success!' Ivan announces. 'Sorry, hold that, could have been an exaggeration. It's potential, real potential.'

'I'm listening.'

'I'm only in the front yard yet. Gates are locked but we'll storm them.' Ivan stops, reorganises his voice into mainstream professional. 'It's a website, disabilitymed.com.au. From the front it looks like a forum for medicos searching for information about amputees and other disabilities. A list of papers is available – I've checked; most are real and come from peer-reviewed journals. The others look similar but they exist in no database or library reference I can find. Those have way more photographs of stumps and discussions about the effect of amputation on the sexual interest and response of amputees. Devotism is also covered – as a medical condition.'

'Aren't there a plethora of these sites? From the voyeuristic to seriously pornographic, through real discussion to just plain chatter?'

'Absolutely. Put an extra website up and who'd think to question it – that's the clever bit. I doubled back, looked again at this one because of the attached Facebook page. The number of posts on that are off the scale, for a comments page on a specialist medical site. An over-the-top number of conferences and special guests too. So, maybe if we view it differently we might find it's not an ordinary particle. Could be a string.'

String theory again? Tom had hoped quantum physics had had its day, at least in this investigation. 'When you said you were only in the front yard…?'

'I need to get into the back end. Hack in, basically. I've got enough to tell you the participants on Facebook are very limited – aliases are being used, but overlaps in ISP addresses, that sort of simple give-away, show there's only a few real bods. Also leads me to tell you they're Sydney-based. Harder to get into the website, it's got better protection.'

'So, a secret society?'

'Seems so.'

'With nefarious intent?'

'Good word, nefarious. Your department, though.'

Tom loosens his collar, not wanting to draw the driver's attention by asking him to modify the car's heating. 'It being a world in which voyeurism is everywhere and flaunting a paraphilia could lend you a desirable air of mystery, or give you coveted victim-status, it certainly seems a good bet the ulterior motive for this site is not one I'd find pleasing. I'm going to send you a short list of names I garnered from acquaintances in the Cross. Presumably they will have fake Facebook profiles but, you never know, the names could be useful. Keep on with it.'

'Onward and upward. Who said that? Names might help with the code. I'll get back to you as soon as I've got more.'

Before Tom has time to ponder the implications of Ivan's find, Marcia's deep contralto is filling his ears.

'We're all scared shitless over here. The doll this morning was actually filled with shit and blood. Real human shit as far as we can tell. Don't know yet whether the blood is human. Smells like it, but who sniffs animal blood so often they can tell the difference?'

Tom wishes he didn't have to take this information on board. A symbol of defilement or simply a mess as disgusting and as harrowing as the sender could make it? It's very possible the perpetrator is a man with more than one fetish – co-morbidity of paraphilias is common and attractions to faeces and blood are surprisingly popular.

'A bit much,' Tom agrees. 'Warren observed nothing of the drop?'

An exasperated sigh. 'Warren pissed off. He hasn't been seen or heard of since midnight.'

'Marcia, hold on, that's not Warren. Have you looked for him, tried to text or call him?'

'He isn't responding.'

'Have you called the police? He doesn't desert.'

'I will go to the police. The residents have all voted for it. Except Marie, but we won't go there.'

'I meant have you called the police about Warren!'

'Why should I?'

'I will.' He'll ring Warren's wife, Karen, first. If no joy there, Lexi might know something, but he's never had her phone contact. Could he find Ted again, get a message to her? 'In the meantime, give me more detail. We really do have to thoroughly interview the residents and staff as soon as is feasible. No more prevaricating on that.'

Marcia's grating voice irritates as he listens to her adamant protestations about the innocence of all in the refuge.

'I can accept they're all totally uninvolved – actively. But you need to accept that someone must be linked to this vicious behaviour. This woman may have no conscious idea she is the target – although I think there'd have to be a lot of pigs flying past, making a lot of noise, for me to believe that. Even if that is the case, or if she is simply scared out of her wits, she will have some information in the back of her mind that will come to the fore with decent questioning. And I mean decent by all standards. I will get back to you with a time and some details for the interviews. No argument.'

'Jesus fucking Christ.'

'Talk to you later. No, wait. Do you have notes on who has represented the women? Legally. We could go back over some years.'

'What the fuck has that got to do with anything?'

'Get the notes out. Send them. We'll talk later.'

He hangs up thinking Marcia would be a pleasant person if only she could relax. It is very possible that applies to him too. Right now, though, Warren's out-of-character absence is an unnecessary and very worrying complexity.

33

THE YOUNG WOMAN AT THE CAR HIRE DESK ISN'T TO BE HURRIED. 'The weather's beautiful today,' she says. 'I'm so glad the wind's dropped.' She taps computer keys, carefully watching her own manicured and accessorised fingers. 'My nails are new. They're great, aren't they?' she offers. 'I'm going to my best friend's engagement party this weekend.'

'That'll be wonderful. I'd like a car as soon as possible. Preferably a dark colour.' Julia tries to keep the impatience out of her voice.

'We've been told to recommend white cars because the colour stands out so well and it's safer.' She returns to tapping, her brow wrinkled. Finding a car seems to be an intricate process.

'That's important. Still, I prefer dark.' Julia smiles in a manner she hopes appears confidential enough that Kylie – that being the name on her tag – will experience a moment of bonding. 'Nothing too noticeable.'

Kylie turns slowly on her stool and bends to open a cupboard. She selects two sets of keys, which she holds up to the light as if they might mystically convey to her what she should do. 'Red or blue?' she asks.

'Blue.'

'The red car's got nicer upholstery. It'd go well with your coat.'

'Blue.' Although by now a bright pink one with stars would do.

Languidly, Kylie hands over the keys, gives directions to the parking bay and retires to the chair-swirling she was amusing herself with when Julia walked in. Car hire at 3pm in Parramatta on a winter's afternoon is not a high-demand business.

The car, a mellow mid-blue which would – Kylie is correct – be hard to see on a highway, is in a designated hire car bay at the top of the six-storey car park. Julia reverses out, feeling oddly vulnerable as she exits. The wheels squeal on the sharp curves on the drive down. Images of dangerous chases in empty parking lots slip from the cultural psyche of crime and action films into her consciousness. About half-way down, a sleek, blue Mercedes convertible pulls out and hugs her tail.

Outside, the sun glares, its lack of heat disguised by the sealed windows and air conditioning. The freeway is alive with wayward mid-afternoon traffic. She is hemmed in by workers fleeing town on flex-time, mothers and the occasional father suburb-hopping to pick up children from school, and older women returning from bingo, never sure which lane they should be in. Julia puts her foot down. The engine is sluggish.

Images of Tom flash through her mind. As would be expected, she notes, trying to maintain a mature distance. Already it seems as ridiculous to imagine a world without him as to hang-glide over Antarctica. On the other hand, the situation is intensely, horribly complicated. She stares out at the gathering clouds, exhorts herself not to anticipate a searing pain she may – somehow – be able to avoid.

The slip road off the freeway is thick with cars. Julia checks for the blue convertible. It is there, dodging in and out. The road ahead is a long, narrow snake, slithering down and through a valley filled with discarded children's blocks – hundreds of duplicated project homes, block upon block, internally resplendent with faux marble kitchens, Italian-look tiled entry foyers, and all with very thin, very white walls. Each house has more garages than a mechanic could utilise in a year. This is McMansion land.

Julia drops into the suburb. The convertible is behind her now. It stays with her as she passes through one roundabout and then a second. 'Shit,' she mutters, angling her rearview mirror. Worth noting the number plate.

And then it is gone.

Julia commits the first three letters of the plate to memory. No time to get the digits that follow. She swings through another roundabout, and another. Hugging her now is a different, more dilapidated car. One that sprang from a side street. Or did it? It could have been behind the expensive Mercedes and taken over after that peeled off. Tag teaming isn't uncommon in surveillance – as her work-life has taught her. This car is definitely staying with her. She doesn't like it.

It's no use taking a quick left or right, the roads are a series of intersecting, interconnected branches. The suburb was literally designed to minimise places to hide, sold as a place where crime could not flourish. All surface, no soul.

She passes a school surrounded by barren playing fields. The car – an older Audi A5 – remains in her rear-view mirror. Either side of her are empty yards where there should be gardens. No mowers or hedge-trimmers, no gossiping neighbours, playing children, barking dogs, loitering teenagers. The supposedly crime-free suburb is a disaster. A few hundred metres further, she pulls into a small carpark, watches the Audi dribble past.

The shopping centre is largely closed doors, broken signs and cracked glass. Graffiti on every available surface. Thankfully, there's one convenience store with a sub-newsagency. She walks into the poorly stocked store, selects a chocolate bar and a bottle of water – hating the waste of plastic – smiles at the woman behind the checkout, who eyes her with boredom.

Back in the hire car, Julia sees her tail has stopped just beyond the car park. Clear intimidation. She's experienced similar heavy-handed tactics in countries where violence is everyday currency. Aid workers are favoured targets, good for ransom, exchange, media coverage. She is not going to give in. At least they're unlikely to kill her in this backwater Australian suburb. And it is an unimaginative way to tell her to keep off their patch. The question is exactly whose patch?

Julia stops at each house with a For Sale sign – of which there are many – aiming to bore the tail to sleep. Each time she stops, the car slopes past, stops, waits. She yawns in their direction.

Eventually the dull voice of the GPS tells her she is at her destination. The house is much the same as the others, the yard neater than some. A van sits solidly in the driveway, its wheelchair hoist evidently retro-fitted. The house and yard lack signage to indicate this is a group home for people with disability, although that is what her information says it is.

She steps out of the hire car, in full view of a dozen homes. The Audi is parked behind her. Swiftly, she swings 180 degrees and walks towards it. Two can play the intimidation game.

The burly blokes in the car shift in their seats. Julia ostentatiously lifts her mobile, pointing it directly at the car's plates. They hardly react. False plates? Paid heavies who are simply bored? She keeps walking. Slowly one of the men raises a hand. Her adrenalin levels jump. The window slides smoothly down and the hand slides smoothly out, two fingers thrust in the air. And that is all. A gesture and they are gone, the driver gunning the car along the desolate street.

Julia scans the windows around her. She could have been shot and left bleeding out in the street and got less response than a corpse in a war zone. Still, she makes a show of shaking her mobile, acting as if it isn't working, and she's desperate to make a call. Her performance finished, she rings the bell of the house with the van.

She'll ask to use their landline, if they have one, or to borrow a mobile. And have a glass of water, use the toilet, whatever. She needs to get into the house. She can act innocent. Workers in group homes expect dumb curiosity and dumb questions from the public. Once she's made that visit, she has to hurry. There's another pressing job to complete ASAP.

34

The van reeks. A policewoman is tapping on the window. Warren greets her with a smile. He's just woken up, feeling euphoric. The policewoman taps harder. Warren smiles some more although it's gradually dawning on him that this situation is seriously askew. Slowly he sits up, the smile fading. He decides opening the window is advisable. His keys, he needs his keys. They're in the ignition. Why is he in the van, in what appears to be the dying moments of a cold bright morning, his keys in the ignition, a stupid smile on his face? Has to figure this out. Turns the key, presses the window button.

'You can't sleep here, mate,' the policewoman says prosaically.

'Didn't mean to. Long drive. Pulled over to be safe. Musta fallen asleep for longer than I intended. Heading off now.'

The officer looks quizzical. Not the troublesome type, however. Probably already run a plate check and had a good gander through the windows anyhow. Run one of those drug and explosive detecting wands over the van too. 'All right. I'll give you a couple of minutes to collect your thoughts. Toilets're in the park over that way if you need them.'

Warren nods, gives her the thumbs up.

She stares at him for maybe ten seconds, turns on her heel, returns to the car parked behind the van. Should he have asked her how long he'd been there? Because that is a puzzle to him.

In the toilet block – smellier than the van but not the worst he's been in by any stretch – he inspects his face in the stainless steel strip that passes as a mirror. No marks, no bruises. Pats his hands over his body. Ditto. Odd that his head is not hurting. Rolls up his shirt sleeves. Yep, a needle prick. Left arm, good vein. How did it get there? Something to do with the refuge? He's not there now and not in the car park that is his last memory of the van's whereabouts. Someone drove him away? Makes no sense, same time as rings a bell, albeit a very soft and tuneless one. Better get home, recce his own mind.

Karen isn't hysterical. She's used to him. 'You didn't tell me you'd be home this late,' she says, around medium-suspicious.

He uncovers his arm. 'Been drugged.'

'Let's look in the light.' Karen's a nurse. Management now, but she retains plenty of the old skills. 'No bruising, no sign you resisted the jab. Very professional.'

'That worries me.'

'Me too.'

'And I'm not sick or hung over or anything. It's like I've had a very pleasant night with a few party drugs. Can't remember a single event, person, how I got the van parked where it was, whether I had a piss all night, ate anything.'

'Peculiar. It sounds like an anaesthetic, administered over time. Pretty unusual drug to have out in the community, I wonder where they got hold of it. Stick out your tongue, I'll look you over.' Karen's got a few bits and bobs with which to assess him. 'I can't say for sure there's no ill effects. And that's peculiar.'

'I gotta ring the boss.'

Karen runs her eyes up and down him. Warren is wise enough to keep calm and convincingly in control. 'I really have to go,' she finally says. 'There's tea in the pot. My money's on you being okay. However, you're not getting back into my bed unless you go to the doctors. Murray's a good bloke. Take a cab. Hang the expense. And I expect you home for dinner tonight.'

He assents, appreciating her unflappability. Has to talk to the Boss first o'course, find out if anything seriously bad occurred while he was blissfully asleep. Although he's already listened to the radio, scrolled through ABC News Just In, rung a couple of contacts, and heard zilch of anything too worrisome happening in Ashfield overnight.

Warren texts Tom, who rings back immediately, demanding to know where he's been. He feels a right twerp, explaining it all. Derelict in his duty, blah, blah. Hears about the new doll, that nobody was hurt or more than usually harassed, that he is at the top of the list of Marcia's most-hated. That is scary.

'You can't recall anyone approaching you? No homeless person accidentally clocking the van, asking you for a smoke?'

'Used that one too often, myself. Wouldn't wash.'

'How do you think they spotted you?'

Warren feels like a kangaroo, immobile in the headlights, about to die. What can he say? 'Dunno. Don't fucking know. Excusing my language.' He swallows. 'I remember pulling into the council carpark, heading on foot past the refuge, talking to Lex, you, needing a piss. Mind after that is blank. Whatever knocked me out was one cool drug. Some idea in the back of m'mind about the old couple next door to the refuge. Marcia put me on to them as a possible place to hang out. Yet, I dunno that I got there. Reckon I was grabbed on my way, with that intention sitting in my brain all lit up. Can't tell you more. Sorry Boss. Really fucking sorry.'

'Warren, my advice – put the guilt in the bin. If whoever drugged you knew where the van was, they'd have to have been following you in the first place. Long before you could have stuffed up with making yourself obvious.'

'Unless they got me to talk.'

Tom is still on his way into his chambers. He wishes taxi drivers could cope with the windows down – a cold wind in the face would be useful right now. 'Without doubt, that's possible, although I imagine you'd shut down the sections of your mind you wouldn't want an attacker to access. Who knew you were due at the refuge?'

'Marcia. Dunno who she told. You thinking one of the staff might be a tattler.'

'Honestly, I have no idea.'

'Are you tying the threats to the refuge in with the agency?'

'Indirectly at this stage.' Tom again runs his hand over his head. His much-needed haircut is as distant as Mars. 'The information channels might be linked without the perp being associated with both, or vice versa. We also need to consider who could be aware that you and I – and Clare and Ivan – are investigating this new start-up. Who's close enough to one of us to have the operational information on each of our whereabouts and activities? Information is circulating.'

Warren hesitates. What about your new squeeze? he wants to ask, having picked up the Boss was out gallivanting last night. The timing of her arrival in Tom's life could be happenstance or it might carry more import. Can't ask about her – yet.

Other options also occur. 'That police contact of Clare's? I mean, you ever heard of a totally squeaky clean policeman? They love protection rackets.'

'A reasonable thought. Warren, I've got two callers trying to get through. I need to see what's up. We'll keep alert on this. In the meantime, we'd be safer with two people at the refuge tonight. Are you able to organise that? The two does not include you. I am not having you out and about tonight.'

'Al's cool for tonight. By the way, he isn't behind any leaks. I haven't told him you're the one paying, or anything about the agency. Just said he should look out for a nutter delivering parcels. Told him the guy could be dangerous, no further detail. I'll give Matt a ring too; he's the guy for heavy security when it's needed. He costs enough to refurbish a Rolls Royce – that what you want to pay?'

'No choice. I'll leave you to get onto it.'

Warren frowns as he presses off. Feels like a complete f-wit. Least he escaped a lecture on his own safety; that would've been galling.

35

Tom sits with fingers pressed tightly together, a classic lawyer pose. In fact, a lawyer in danger of losing a big case for no other reason than a small, innocent piece of evidence; or perhaps a connection, tenuous or half-seen in the shadows, is eluding him. In short, something's yelling at him from the edge of his consciousness, but he can't make out the words. It's irritating, to say the least.

Nearby, an office phone rings, insistent but ignored. Good. Work hours are almost over and he wants an empty building, with no chance of a colleague, jolly with the idea of a weekend, popping their head around the door, asking if he wants to partake in evening drinks. Barristers can be a dull lot.

Of course, he reminds himself, he's hardly less dull – right now he's set on working out why a man who could think up the vile threat of the dolls would merely inject Warren with a substance that wears off, leaving a peaceful afterglow. Why the man would have such a substance in the first place. First he'll ring Julia and check how her timing is going.

Her mobile goes straight to voicemail. He tries the department's Parramatta office.

'Julia Prettie?' the woman on the other end is disgruntled. It's closing time after all. 'She is based in our head office. I can email a message through to her.'

'I must have misunderstood,' Tom offers, implying he is a colleague who knows Julia well. 'I was under the impression she would be in the Parramatta office this afternoon.'

'I'm sorry, we haven't seen her. Head office will have her whereabouts. I'll try them for you.'

Tom is subjected to thirty seconds of dreary music before his call is answered.

'I know it's late in the day but is Ms Prettie available?' he asks.

'I'm sorry, she's on personal leave. A message will reach her on Monday.'

'Is she unwell? I was to contact her this afternoon: it was prearranged.'

'Oh. Well. We did expect her in after lunch. We're all a little worried.' The polite woman breaks off. In the background, another voice, mild castigation. The woman returns to the phone, formal now. 'I do apologise, I wasn't in possession of all the information. Would you like me to take a message? Ms Prettie will be in on Monday.'

He tries to extract more detail but they don't know him and he can hardly tell them he wants to find Julia because he spent the previous night having excellent sex and conversation with her. 'Thanks, I'll try her mobile.'

A call from Marcia prevents any immediate action. 'I've got that information you wanted. I'm in town. Meet me in the bar downstairs from your chambers in ten.'

Her style has to be appreciated, Tom thinks, grateful for the distraction. He slips into his coat.

Outside, the wind is whipping round to the south again, bringing with it yet more moisture and increasing cold. Tom recalls a trip to the snowfields beyond Canberra with a couple of colleagues who're avid skiers. He'd tried snowboarding while there. He came away without broken bones or other disasters, but there were better ways to get a few thrills.

He enters the bar. He's a regular and the waiter offers him his preferred table away from the door. He wishes he'd brought some work to keep his mind occupied. Julia's absence is worrying him, which is absurd. She is a grown woman and a clever one. She isn't lost and there'll be a reasonable explanation for her prevarication and absence.

Suspicion that she is covering up something damaging, possibly dangerous, keeps trying to worm its way into his consciousness. He firmly shuts the window on that as Marcia arrives, raucous voice landing before her physical presence.

'We had a special delivery this afternoon. A courier arrived with a parcel addressed to us,' she says, fitting her wheelchair comfortably beside him. 'The package purported to be from a tourism firm. No idea why I opened it. Stupid, really. Inside was a small, old-fashioned kewpie doll. In a cage. The whole thing is vile, Tom.'

'I'm in town to meet some detective,' she continues. 'More big-wig than the local area police. Fingers crossed for some response. Not holding my breath – might die of fucking asphyxiation. Before the doll arrived, I did get Anna to go through the files for those solicitors you wanted to know about. She's a wonder, that Anna. We started with the paper files, not the electronic, so these legal reps are not necessarily current.' She hands him two brailled pages. 'Like you asked, Anna also did a quick scan for the medicos too. The detail mightn't be as good – your request was last minute and she's not your PA. What's this interest all about?'

'A hunch, as they say in the classics, on the basis that the disability field is fairly contained. The power brokers, the professionals, the movers and shakers, tend to be one and the same. Given its operational modes, a legal adviser must be involved in the agency. There's very few specialist lawyers in disability – and oddly enough, I know most of them. It occurred to me that if a mainstream legal adviser is putting their hand up in one place, they may be putting it up in the other. 'Specially if they're motivated by money.'

'The medicos?'

'More of a trawling every available creek. You'd think the agency would have some sort of in-house medical support. There could be a link.'

The waiter approaches and they order from the extensive whisky menu. Tom turns to the list of medical practitioners. It's extensive, evidently filled with many local doctors, scattered geographically. Clif Johnson's name comes up three times.

'Do any of the doctors do house calls?'

'These days!'

'Clif?'

'Now you mention it, yes, he's come by a few times. We have to let him in despite him stinking of some disgusting male deodorant. Why do men's toiletries have more perfume than women's? Can't prohibit doctors and lawyers. Safety, human rights, blah, blah.'

Tom mentally files this info, turns to the lawyers and their cases – the clients carefully de-identified. Anna has organised these and highlighted three names: Caroline Zammit, Harriet Shanahan and Phillip Jones.

Harriet Shanahan he dismisses immediately. She's been in Galway working and exploring her Irish roots for a good two years now.

Caroline Zammit? Jumping on stage again, but, like Clif Johnson's regular appearances, hers is predictable. What had Clare said? 'Caroline's name is met with either enthusiasm or distaste. Little in between. Neither camp is inclined to disclose details, other than she is strident, had an affair with a senior barrister's husband – purportedly waving said affair in said (male) barrister's husband's face – or she's a terrific supporter of charities. Few of which have anything to do with disability.' Similarly, Caroline's online presence had rung no alarm bells. But she's shown herself to be interested in the agency and their investigation. And she is seen at the same functions as Harry Montague. Tom makes a note to ask Warren to dig deeper on Caroline.

Phillip Jones? Long ago, he and Phillip had been at school together; had been friends. Tom conjures up Phillip's voice. He, the blind boy, and Phillip, the lad from the poorer suburbs, had the fellowship of outsiders. Perhaps more than that – they both enjoyed philosophy, debating, fierce argument. Such serious adolescents they'd been, no doubt thoroughly irritating. At the end of their final year, they fell out and then lost contact when Tom went to the University of Queensland, where the services were better suited to his blindness. Tom had only run into Phillip once since he'd come back to Sydney. It was a legal event but Phillip was, he'd said, easing his way out of the profession.

'Law is interesting enough and I'll keep up the good fight here and there, but you know as well as I that being bright is not enough to make real money in the law,' Phillip had said when Tom politely asked why. 'In this town you must also have deep connections. Being a scholarship boy at one of the better schools – well, everyone who matters knows your antecedents. They curl their lip at you, no matter whether they belong to the Labor or Liberal parties or wouldn't declare their political allegiance if their next fuck depended on it. When you go to the school you and I attended, there's no hope of reinventing yourself with a more illustrious past.'

'And making money is important to you?'

'Money has a certain glamour, don't you think? I'm going into share trading. The suits are better.' He'd laughed. 'Honestly, Challinor, I don't enjoy the stuffiness of law, the repetitive jokes, the same old clubs. A sort of boiled cabbage approach to life.'

In a strange way, Phillip has all the qualifications of a man who might go into a niche-market escort business. An intellectual brilliance, a precise knowledge of commercial law, a desire for wealth, a chip on his shoulder the size of a Tasmanian old growth forest. And his pro bono work had involved disability discrimination work – a significant fact. Phillip would love offering a contraband service to those who'd bullied him in the past.

The whisky – Tom has his usual – arrives and is pleasing. 'How far back do these paper files go?' he asks Marcia.

Marcia gives a half-laugh. 'Too fucking far, too fucking many of them. For various reasons, we only moved on to computer for filing about two years back. Naturally, we don't have enough computers. However, I anticipated you'd ask, so we managed to eyeball the most recent files. Lawyers aren't always involved or named of course. Current residents have only a couple of mentions – a fellow called Marcus Weatherby – why the hell they go to male lawyers I don't know – and a woman called Sofia Carlotta. No Jones or Shanahan.'

'Does Caroline Zammit reappear recently?'

'That woman is a like a broken record. Her advocacy is all about her, her, her. No, we didn't sight her on the electronic files.'

Tom folds the thick braille pages, inserts them into an inner pocket. 'OK, I'll get some background on Weatherby. Sofia Carlotta, I feel I can vouch for. She's fun.'

'Fun?'

'Has a sense of humour.'

'Some people do, I suppose,' Marcia agrees dryly.

Tom smiles. 'Good to air it occasionally. Thanks for doing this Marcia, it's appreciated and useful. I'll follow up. Another drink?'

'Wish I could. Arriving half-under won't help my profile with the cops. Before I go, what's the deal with Warren? I've talked to him. He's convinced me he didn't abandon us voluntarily. He's all right, do you think?'

'He's ashamed, even if needlessly. You know he never likes to let the side down. Tonight Al and Matt will keep an eye on your place. I only hope Warren's conscience doesn't lead him to try to help them out. Karen's very understanding but she'll scalp me if he puts himself in danger again so soon.'

'Deservedly,' Marcia says. 'I'm off. Anna or I will get to the other files tomorrow. We've got to stop this horror movie some way or other.'

36

Tom rings Harry Montague, completely uninterested in the fact it is after hours on Friday and Harry has a life to lead. 'You haven't got back to me, Harry.'

'Christ, Challinor, I'm on my way home. I've got family commitments, you know.'

'Good on you. How do you feel about Caroline Zammit?'

'Why would I bother feeling anything about Caroline?'

'You've been seen out with her. And she might step on your toes.' When she isn't being a disability advocate, Caroline and Harry work in similar areas of the law.

'I wear very good shoes,' Harry responds. 'Why the hell are you asking me about Caroline on a Friday evening?'

Tom pauses. He isn't dismissing Caroline. He just isn't convinced she's the main game right now. 'The name I wanted is Phillip Jones, isn't it?'

'What makes you think that?'

'The way you just swallowed.'

'Arsehole.'

'Always good to do business. Speak soon.'

'Not a hope in hell of that.'

Tom chews the confirmation, tasting the bitterness, before again picking up his phone.

'Serge,' Tom says.

'Hey, it's Friday, aren't you going out with the new girlfriend?'

'There's no new girlfriend.' He is emphatic.

'Rubbish, you were spotted by Sylvia. She's jealous.'

Tom marshals his reserves of friendliness. 'Sylvia would be jealous of someone getting an invite to a Tupperware party. Serge, I know mates talk – you told me so yourself – but not over the phone. Not now.'

'Then what, pray, is the reason for this call?'

'Have you tracked down any interesting development applications yet? I have new information – a Phillip Jones is involved.'

'Fair enough, I should've got round to ringing you, I didn't realise it was urgent.'

'It wasn't, until just now.'

'I turned some stuff up. It's in the study.' The sound of footsteps; children, television and Imogen in the background. A keyboard springs into rapid action. 'Isn't Phillip Jones a character you went to school with?'

'Yes.'

'Un-huh. Say no more. All right, I've got two possibilities that fit your criteria. Apartment and town house development knocked back. Went stale for a while, recently revised DA. No Phillip Jones involved, but there's a disability organisation and the application stresses the development allows a larger than required proportion of community housing for the disabled. Local resident objections kicked it out first time round. Had to go out of my area to get the low-down on the other one. It's larger. A release of land, through the State Government. The tender included all the infrastructure and the rights to build nearly a whole bloody suburb.' Serge gets louder as he reveals Phillip Jones is a director of one of the two consortiums now being considered. 'This is so easy,' Serge almost chortles.

Easy, Tom thought, is not the word. Could Phillip really be that involved? Phillip, who'd been brave – and funny – in the face of persistent bullying, and who'd been game to go with Tom to seedy nightclubs, insalubrious concerts and generally do as much as they could – at seventeen – to experience the world. And was Phillip only the beginning of the horrors? 'Are further names attached with Jones'?'

'The name of the group – "Choice for All, Disability Support Services" – with directors Oscar Meyer and Sam Hasham. I'll forward the details. Phillip Jones is noted, too. Also Phillip Prettie-Jones. Same guy?'

And there it is. The fist in his guts punches again, and very hard. He should have known. 'Any reference to another Prettie-Jones? Or just someone Prettie?'

'Nup. You sound shit, Tom, what's going on?'

'Is there any more information?'

A cluck of Serge's tongue. A very Russian sound, emitted only when Serge is thoroughly disgusted. 'That's it. I'll email the details I've got so far. I have a colleague who can help, come Monday.'

'Do I need to read plans?'

'Come on, Tom, we've been mates for years.'

'Press the button. And thanks, I didn't mean to doubt you.'

'No worries. I know something I said has made you fly off your brain with worry. I'll mull it over when the kids are in bed.' Serge pauses. 'I get the impression that woman of yours will come through, though. It's written in the stars.'

'Since when have you been clairvoyant?' Tom's tone is bitter.

'There are times something unscientific like that is useful. Also, probably more rewarding than my day job. The information should be there now.'

Carefully, Tom places his phone in his pocket, as if it were a grenade with a faulty pin. Phillip Prettie-Jones. Husband of Julia Prettie. The memory he'd been repressing batters its way to the top of his consciousness. After their brief, stilted catch-up Phillip had moved on to a small group nearby. The champagne was flowing and this was a group of older, powerful solicitors and businessmen. Phillip became quickly and obsequiously ingratiating. The words had stood out at the time and they reverberated more loudly now: 'Yes, my wife, Julia, yes, she is indeed now Deputy Director.' One of the men had muttered a response, which Phillip had quickly affirmed. 'Yes, very useful indeed.'

Julia was – or is – married to Phillip Jones. Phillip Jones is the brother-in-law of a woman with significant disability. He has a legally trained and well-informed mind. He is behind? instigator of? – the escort agency. The very big question, then, is why is Julia sleeping with Tom, the man trying to chase that agency down, to grind it, or at least its patrons, into the ground?

Tom clenches his fists. He must find out as much as he can about Phillip Jones – and his wife – before he speaks with Julia again.

37

THE ODOUR INSIDE THE VAN IS OF TOO MUCH PERFUME. THE GIRLS ARE asked not to use chemical sprays: scents spoil the semblance of uncorrupted innocence. But they are young women who have mostly grown up in families with little money. Perfume represents their increasing wealth and, for some, the adulthood they had not expected to have recognised. Few take any notice of the prohibition.

Daphne, whom many call the idiot-girl, is sitting next to Sonya. Daphne sprays herself liberally and collects perfume bottles too, secreting them in the capacious bag that is her familiar, a pet-like object that she strokes and chatters to, despite it being an ugly oblong thing with a rip in the external plastic. Today, while she and Sonya and Jim drive around in worried circles, Daphne clutches the bag extra close.

Sonya finds Daphne's presence vaguely comforting. She's a nice girl, who enjoys a laugh, although she is also too romantic, sure that every client is the man who is going to marry her. Often, she plans her wedding, all white and shining and decked with big bows and ribbons. Daphne is not aware she is pregnant. Avril overheard the doctor who performs their health checks whispering the news to the lady who organises the drivers. Sonya is worried about what will happen to Daphne.

Avril, too, hopes the perfect man is around the corner, disguised as a client. It is Avril they are looking for now. Avril who hasn't returned from her last client. Already they have driven to the hotel, where Jim surreptitiously checked the room she should have been in. They have toured all around the streets. On Sonya's insistence they have driven around the park two times. Soon Jim will have to call in an emergency absence, an action he does not wish to take.

They park again outside the Mall. Sonya and Daphne are both fidgety: Daphne is desperate to be taken shopping while Sonya is concerned her mother, or one of the ladies her mother has cups of coffee and cigarettes with, will be annoyed by the van blocking the space their husbands use to pick them up. The windows are tinted and it is late in the day, but they will see her in the van. They see everything, those women.

The western sun reflects in the mirror-glass sides of the buildings across the road. Avril does not appear. Jim turns on the engine and drives slowly toward the train station. Sonya swallows repeatedly as she peers out, scanning the streets with the precision she learned in the refugee camps, where fear and enemies needed regularly to be avoided. Her lips are covered in balm and then in lipstick and then in gloss but the soft skin around them feels like it has been stung by a thousand tiny bees.

Hundreds of people are bustling around the station. Old ladies and gents, twenty or thirty countries of origin. Boys slouching, to be seen and admired. Tired-looking girls with too much make-up pushing young children, plastic bags slung over the handles of the baby carriages. Some push cheerfully, as if they've had some sleep, others as if each turn of the wheel is running over their own bodies. Sonya feels better about her job when she sees those girls, more than one of them from her school.

'Avril,' Daphne suddenly declares. Sonya whips her head, following Daphne's finger. 'Gone,' Daphne says. 'Gone.'

'Where? Show me where,' Sonya demands. Daphne tries to comply, pointing and smiling.

Jim pulls hurriedly into the bus lane outside the station. 'Did y'really see Avril?' he demands.

Daphne hugs her bag tighter, tears springing.

'Ah bugger it. You're all right, Daph. Don't panic. Probably you saw her. I'll let the boss know, hey.'

Sonya is determinedly watching the crowds. The direction Daphne indicated is the exit, near the taxi rank. It is possible. But Jim refuses to let her out of the bus. All the drivers are called Jim even though they are all different. This Jim is nice but she is fully aware he means what he says.

'What?' Jim says into the phone. 'All right, all right, I don't like it. I want that registered, we just made a sighting, we should be chasing after her.' Then a few more mumbled words before they drive away, fast. Jim goes round the back of the station, past the taxi rank, instructs Sonya and Daphne to keep their eyes open, goes back and forth once more, giving them time to survey queues, people already in taxis, the streets leading away from the rank. No Avril. 'We gotta move now, girls. Searching's not our job. I got orders to take youse two straight to work. Then I gotta go get another girl to replace Avril.'

A few more turns and they're in the confusing one-way system and into a car park and Jim is getting out and coming to the side door.

'Avril say anything to you today? Anything different or important or whatever? Give you a hint? I won't tell the boss.'

'No. No, we check our jobs like usual.'

'After that? After you got to work? She didn't ring or nothing?'

'Of course not. We are busy.' Sonya's lips tighten. She doesn't like the etched, unhappy lines on Jim's forehead. His worry escalates hers. Which is already great. This is the same time, the same appointment when Melanie was attacked last week. Already Jim knows this. It is why he is willing to break the rules, look for her. He even got out at the lake in the park. It was empty, they saw nothing or no-one suspicious.

The lights in the car park suddenly spit on. Jim looks over his shoulder, before climbing into the van and pulling the door closed, shutting off the sickly fluorescent light. 'Sonya, stop looking so bloody scared and think about when you last saw her. Where was she?'

'Going to hotel. You know. Close, so she walk. I walk other way to see client too.'

'Was she same as usual? I mean, like you really didn't get the idea she was going to skip, anything like that?'

'Avril? No. She want work. Money.'

'Y'right there. Turns out, she didn't even get there. The client's rung the boss and complained and they're all shitting bricks. There's near enough two hours between when you saw her and now. Daph here's probably just being hopeful, spotting Avril in that crowd. Listen, love, I better get youse sorted. Don't worry, I'll keep scouting around for her. She's easy 'nough to spot.'

Sonya folds her arm over her breasts. Folded arms is the position her mother and her aunts adopt in times of trial, and she takes it too, regardless of the fact that one arm stops just past the shoulder. 'I do not go.'

'Y'sure do. Otherwise we're all fucked. Avril too. This operation is supposed to run smoother than milk out of a cow's udder. No funny business. And that includes never being late for a job.' In the half-light, his hand is a skeleton's as he reaches for the door handle. 'Look, love, you're a nice kid. I don't wanna see no harm come to you, or your friend Avril, even if she's a bit high and mighty for my liking. Best way's to get you where you're going and then get meself back out there quick smart. She'll be 'round some place, don't worry. Prob'bly went shopping.'

Sonya feels tears at the back of her eyes. This annoys her. Tears are pointless. Tears don't repair the rips and gouges in the flesh, nor the deeper, darker wounds of the heart. Tears don't bring the dead back to life. She crosses herself and prays and slowly follows Jim out of the van.

38

THE FREEWAY INTO THE CITY IS ALL BRIGHT LIGHTS AND DERANGED DRIVERS. The wind buffets cars, vans, trucks, making drivers furious, frightened and dangerous as they wrench wheels in an attempt to stay within their lanes. Wives, husbands, partners will tonight tell each other of near misses, of clever avoidance, of nightmares that nearly came true, while learner drivers may well decide enough is enough and join a public transport lobby. Sydney lacks a decent underground rail system.

Thankfully the Audi is long gone, as far as Julia can tell – the distraction would be an added danger. It is wisest not to connect Bluetooth in the hire car. She uses Siri, yelling at the phone to ring Pete. Then – cheap phone, cheap mic – she has to shout to be heard.

'Pete, it's Julia,' she says.

'What's this number? It's not yours.'

'Got a new phone early this morning. I'll explain later. Now, remember when we were in Jordan? That women's program and the money being stripped from it?'

'Jules, it's Friday night, darling. I do not like new phone numbers nor remembering work, especially scary-shit work like that. It's party time.'

'And time to meet your friends. Your new bloke isn't in town yet, is he? You've got time for your old friends?'

Pete's dramatic sigh fills the car. 'What does Jordan have to do with us on a Friday night in sweet, safe Sydney?'

'Secretive Sydney, the seamy, soupy, sick underbelly. Like Jordan, we have to expose the secrets.'

'Jules, I have not a passing iota of an idea what you are talking about.'

'Buying you a fabulous cocktail in return for certain services. Or at the very least advice on how to go about certain explorations. I'll explain all when I get there. We should meet in the CBD. No, let's make it near you. The Continental in Redfern. The bar at the back. Come incognito and with an extra hat. We need to go undercover for a short time. A very short time, honestly. Merely avoiding recognition on CCTV.'

'Darls, you are seriously going to owe me after this, whatever it is. If I agree. Even if I don't agree, you are so going to impress Jean-Paul he will be salivating to stay in Sydney.'

'Rather too big an ask.'

'Huh! Modesty is so mundane. Luckily I love the Continental, they do a charming new-fashioned Manhattan. When shall I see you there?'

'Thirty.'

'You're on.'

Involving Pete is not the best option – putting your friends in harm's way never is. It is simply the only option. And the need is immediate. Unfortunately, Tom won't be as easy as Pete to convince of the rightness of her actions. She hums an old song, from Sydney pub band, Mental as Anything: '*if you leave me, can I come too, we could always stay.*' Fat chance. Fat chance of any of this coming out as she wants it to. Her message to Tom must be short, circumspect, and give nothing away. Ten deep breaths, and she again activates Siri. The message is recorded but is not to be delivered immediately. She can't risk him trying to call her again. She's using this one phone; her personal and work mobiles are tucked away.

The hire car shudders, its tinny body unwilling to protect her from the raging weather. The radio depresses with the news of yet more loss of life in Palestine, a child this time, the victim of a stray bullet, neither side admitting responsibility. Nearing the end of the freeway, Julia summons Siri again, instructing the AI to open voice record. Her intention is to record the details gleaned so far. Sydney is not Jordan or Palestine, nor any of the other troubled places she and Pete worked in over the years; this is not a case of internecine conflict, potential tribal genocide or even the simple predictability of drug barons fighting, with murderous ease, over territory. On the other hand, the stakes are high and the drug baron analogy is not too far-fetched; she could be stopped. What she already knows will be useful to others.

It should not be lost with her.

39

The aftertaste of whisky is bitter as Tom closes off the call to Serge. Leaning forward, he quietly directs the driver. 'I've changed my mind. Take me to Mrs Macquarie's chair. Just five minutes and then we'll head on to Randwick. Thanks.'

The desert-driven westerlies are giving way to southerlies that are dumping giant scoops of snow-cold into the already brittle air. Last night he was on Bondi Beach with Julia, the ocean a pounding presence. Tonight the water would be cut flat by the knife of the wind. Not that he wants the sea. Oceans suggest eternity, it is true – anyone's eternity, everyone's eternity. Oceans are impersonal and right now he wants his very own boundless time. He doesn't want to share.

Julia is not coming to dinner. Julia is otherwise occupied and her text, albeit apologetic, is uninformative about what and why and who she is occupied with.

'Do you know the concept of denumerable and non-denumerable infinities?' she had asked him as they ate together only a few hours ago.

'Maths was never my strong point,' he'd replied. Serious as usual, he thought now.

'This isn't maths, not entirely. It's – I don't know. There is clever stuff about real numbers and fields and other stuff hard to get your head around. Basically the idea that appeals to me, or the simple way of putting it that appeals to ingénues like me, is that if you count to infinity, using whole numbers, even if you never reach the end of the counting, it's defined; constrained. Counting is seeing only the spots on a straight line. Counting ignores the infinity of possibilities between each number. And all the possibilities around the line of integers – the arcs and so on.'

That's what he thought he'd found. The infinity of possibilities between each number.

'Ever been in love?' he asks the driver.

'Why do you think I drive a cab, mate? Dozens of times, sometimes every second day. How 'bout you?'

Tom relaxes briefly into a grin. 'More than once, I guess.'

He can feel the driver looking at him in the rear-view mirror. 'You got a new girl? Y'know I reckon there's one love that's always gonna be better than the others. I had a girl once, and did I have the hots for her. We were both bonkers about bushwalking. You wouldn't think so to look at me, would you? Oh sorry, you can't see, can you? Anyway, I'm a fat bastard.'

'What happened?'

'It's a short story. We was both married, and she had a young kid. I had me third on the way.'

'How did it end?'

'You mean did the jealous husband come and drag me out by the balls? Nope, nothing so exciting, just had to end. We both cried a lot – I don't mind saying that out loud – and that was it. But I tell you, if ever I get the chance, I'll be right in there again.'

The car turns right, the *thwick-thwack* of the indicator the only sound.

'Do you know how her life is now?'

'Too right I do. I drive past her house every bloody day. Just checking she's okay. Now and then I put the garbage out when she's forgotten. Her old man's hopeless at that kinda thing.'

'Does she know?'

'I reckon she oughta feel it in her bones.'

Tom smiles. 'I'm sure she does.'

The driver offers to walk him to Mrs Macquarie's Chair. 'I just need a moment of thinking time. And I've been there before,' Tom demurs.

'Like love.'

'Like love.'

'I'll wait,' the driver says, 'I'm good at that.'

Tom walks, now and then kicking at the earth, which is crusty from too much wind. He must face facts.

Phillip Jones has certainly trumped him. Finally. Their friendship had fallen apart twenty years ago over love. Wendy, the head debater from their sister school, asked Tom out, in front of Phillip, who was a year older, potential dux of the school, champion debater, and had been voted the best-looking guy at the school formal, despite his lowly social origins. Wendy ignored Phillip as if it were he who was blind – and deaf, and irrelevant. Tom remembers the tension in the room, Wendy's disregard of it, his own refusal, the way she walked quietly, proudly, out, while Phillip stayed.

'Well done, old chap,' Phillip had said, in that imitation public school style he had adopted then, and still carried on with. 'She's only a piece of skirt, shouldn't come between friends.' Tom had known then that Phillip was desperate for the girl. And that they would never be friends again.

He stops. He's forgotten to keep to the path. What must be dealt with is the fact that Julia is married – used to be married? – to Phillip Jones. Either way, she was associated with Phillip when they met in the café, when they walked across the sand, when they were in bed together. And Phillip is very likely to be closely linked with the escort agency that he is investigating.

Did Phillip send his wife to distract Tom? Was it a long delayed and particularly vicious pay-back?

Tom shakes his head. Julia is not passive, not a woman to be sent as a vehicle of the revenge of another. He removes his dark glasses. No light today and the air around him is a ferocious creature furious to be diverted by his bulk. He resists its anger, remains braced against the whirling air, willing himself to think through every last detail of their interaction. The recording of her voice speeds through his mind.

No. He cannot, does not, will not, accept he's been duped. Something is wrong with his logic or his conclusions. It's an unusual admission, but it must be the case. He must be wrong.

Tom assesses the wind direction, turns south to where the car must be. It defies all his careful intellect, but he feels an almost tribal attachment to Julia Prettie, the woman he has known for less than a week. He feels, in every cell of his being, that in some archaic and ineffable way, she is "his woman", and he "her man". He also knows, despite his hopes, that this does not make her innocent.

40

JEAN HASN'T BEEN FOUND, HER SISTER, THE POWERFUL JULIA PRETTIE, IS still somewhere floating off in space and Ian is aware he's a total fucking fuckwit failure. Which is why he can't take his eyes off this business card, even though the strain of focusing is making his headache worse.

He'd rung the number thirty minutes and two cheap wines earlier. It was his last chance, just before close of business for the week. The number was about to die. He got a woman – Carmen, she called herself (as if) – promising him work – special well-paid work. That hooked him straight away. Then things started to go belly up.

Ian picks up the card again. He's already chucked it in the bin and taken it out several times. In a vague way, he figures it is evidence.

He reckons he's rung a call agency, or the agency for a call agency. What else could you think when the woman purred out her spiel in such a throaty bedroom voice? She wasn't offering phone sex; her idea was obviously for a very different participation than him buying a few minutes of her breathing heavily down the line. He's heard of a coupla suburban brothels with workers who specialise in blow jobs for blokes with disabilities, but Carmen was wanting it all the other way round. Hard to imagine Graham or Ahman giving a blow job. Then, maybe not entirely. Graham was pretty interested in sex and every indication was he preferred the lads.

Carmen didn't say it straight out. Clever questions, sweet talking, exploring his thoughts and opinions like she was conducting some sort of survey. In reality, she'd been offering him high paid work as a pimp. Jeezus. That was the wildest thing ever.

Ian figures he musta done something badly wrong in a past life or whatever to've landed himself in this pickle. The Jean business being the sourest pickle of all. He really liked Jean, liked her toughness, her self-reliance in the face of crap odds. Those crap odds included bloody few real-world skills. It was dangerous for her to be lost, more dangerous than it would be for most people. But the police've come and gone, management have screamed at him (again), Sanjiv is doing his usual dedicated job, to no effect.

Ian has a thought – maybe he can track down the blind bloke. Might help him find Julia and that'd at least be something.

Does all this mean the end of things with Dee? She's nice, plain damn nice, and Ian likes nice. Sure as hell, she'll be giving him the big A. Tears prick at the back of Ian's eyes. He's a pathetic no-hoper of a bastard.

He decides to forget it, all of it. The curiosity about the card, the worry about Jean Prettie, the attempts at contacting her sister, his maybe overblown concerns about what the husband might get up to. Dee. Yeah, he might as well forget about Dee.

Ian squeezes out the last of the wine from the cask. Cheap muck, like his life.

Just as he's falling asleep, he twigs to something. That deep-breathing woman, Carmen, was real interested in the fact that Jean'd gone missing. Yep, when he mentioned Jean's disappearance being the reason he was looking for work, her shutters went down fast.

Can he take another puzzle? Only a void where there should be a brain.

Should he pass her number on to the police? Gotta be something underhand going on. Could they have kidnapped Jean? Was that it? Yep, better hand the card over. Before it's too late or whatever.

It takes him so long to consider that one, he's snoring.

Carmen's Friday was not supposed be extending like this. In fact, her plan had been a drink with the CEO. A drink she very much hoped would turn into a date. Instead she's tied to the phones that ordinarily wouldn't be ringing this late on a Friday. Or, if they were ringing, they'd be looked after by several people, not her. But they were desperately short-staffed – two of the office staff having taken sickies today and two field workers having gone AWOL. One of the missing workers is a driver – a stupid, unreliable kid. She has no idea why they kept him on. But the other is Avril, one of the Parramatta girls. Avril is usually a super-enthusiastic worker. Carmen had to find a replacement for her. All extra work.

Plus, if this guy who's called in is right, there's now another girl, also with disability – Jean, or some name like that – who's done a runner. Not one of theirs but Carmen has to ask what is going on? First Melanie – also in Parramatta – gets herself kidnapped or whatever. Now Avril absconds, and this Jean, whoever she is, too. Carmen sighs. Decides it isn't her issue, other than keeping the agency running smoothly.

She checks over the contact numbers gathered today. The last one belongs to that warbling maniac called Ian who reported Jean's disappearance. She'll leave that off the data base. Roger Macintyre, who'd rung in earlier, gets to stay. In fact, they'd been putting out feelers to him for a while. Amputees are so popular. Chair users are second favourite, and Roger knows men with both amputations and mobility aids. So much harder to recruit male workers. She enters Roger's data, flagging him red, which means he'll get a quick follow up.

Another call comes in about the missing driver who also takes the workers in and out of hotels. He's needed. She does her best to placate the team leader – they have one in each area – and sits back for a deserved sip of her coffee. If she hadn't taken on a mortgage and a car loan when she got the job with *Helpmates* – like all her Christmasses had come at once – it wouldn't be so bad. Between calls, she logs into her bank balance. Hardly healthy enough to allow a holiday, let alone another period of unemployment as an over-qualified accountant whose burnt-off arm, and burn-deranged face scared off every employee who'd read her resume well enough to let her in the door.

'Yes,' she answers the next call. She's tired and can't remember the correct salutation for each number right now.

'You must help. Avril, she is lost and police they only laugh. Jim will not tell you. I must. It is late now and she is not home for her dinner. Her parents, they will kill her. She is always home at time they say.'

'Who are you?'

'I not say. But you must help. It is your job.'

Not mine, thinks Carmen. 'If you give me some details I'll pass the information on to the appropriate person. Now who are you, who are you talking about and why do you think our service should have any responsibility for finding this young woman?'

Carmen curses herself when she lets this last line out. As if it isn't screamingly obvious that this is another worker calling in, thinking their employer should be their saviour. Didn't they realise that they were independent contractors? Sure there were rules they had to abide by – rules to keep the organisation safe, the clients out of any chink of light, the money flowing in – but the rules didn't make them employees, for pity's sake.

'Is this the girl who failed to attend a 3pm appointment this afternoon in Parramatta? We know about that.'

'You do not *do* enough. Avril want to work. It is her most important thing.'

Carmen sighs. She's seen Avril's stats and thought the very same only minutes ago.

'We are contract workers. But you have insurance, workplace must have insurance. You must find her or it will cost you lot of money.'

Carmen smiles briefly, acknowledging this young woman's style and determination.

'Am I speaking with Sonya?' she asks, having brought up the Parramatta screen by now. Girls who spend a lot of time together are flagged yellow. Carmen's never known why, but it is useful now. The incoming call, on an agency-supplied mobile, gives Carmen a code name which she cross-checks. The screen only displays first names but the fact her manager allows her access speaks volumes, she thinks, about how he judges her competence. She's going up in the organisaton and it's a pity the CEO won't have the opportunity to appreciate more of her personality this evening.

'I am Sonya. You get from phone?'

'Yes. Now, listen Sonya, I hear you. I understand your concern. I shouldn't do this but if you give me the details I'll have management take note of this immediately. You are right, the organisation has a duty of care.'

'You contact police?'

'I will escalate your concerns to CEO level. I am sure a report from him would be taken far more seriously than one coming from me. Now, please don't worry.'

Carmen keeps up the soothing speech. She really hopes Sonya believes her. For Carmen this job is essential. She must impress the men in charge.

41

The air in the underground car park is thick with the haze of too many cars and too little ventilation. Warren smothers a yawn.

He's seen the doctor. Without fuss, Murray stared at Warren's pupils, stuck a sphygmomanometer – now there's a word big enough to ward off starvation – on his arm, and so on. Murray declared him well, advised him not to drive for twenty-four hours, promised to look for medications that might explain the effects Warren described.

Back at home, Warren'd phoned a few people, made friends with his wife by hanging out with the kids while he pondered the problems. Then Karen's best mate called on Skype from the US and they set in for a fine old chinwag. He seized the opportunity and set off back to the Western Suburbs – not too far from home. After too much drug-induced sleep and too much failure the night before, he needed action now.

He spotted the van pronto. He also noticed, pronto, that something was out of kilter. Flies buzzing, no carcass in sight. A driver who jumped in and out of the van, looking around, leaving the engine idling. A couple of big burly types on foot, asking questions, demanding answers. A lot of cursing. Warren adds up the likely risks and gains of a direct approach – pathetic act, lost cause, needing love, been using the service, saw the van, could he get a last minute. See how the driver responds. While he's considering, the driver takes a call, legs it – the burly blokes on his heels – outta the carpark. Conclusion: they've lost someone or something.

He's left alone. The van's empty except for one girl, talking to herself in a corner. She's clasping a bag half as big as herself, stroking it. Warren gently tries the door; locked. The young woman takes f-all notice.

Several cars enter, exhaust spit and noise. He hastily returns to his own car. Sighs. It's only the hotel staff arriving for a change of shift. When they're all sucked up the lift, he lets himself into an aging Commodore – no alarm, no gadgets. A temporary measure; the bloke who owns the sagging car should be proud it's being used in the cause of justice. Settles into the driver's seat and chews a toothpick – doing his immigrant-worker look. When some action is on the way, he'll be out of the car and hunting around in the boot, performing as an electrician or plumber called to an emergency. Better be soon, car stinks; owner's a smoker.

Another ten minutes and the van driver is back, the van still stationary. Warren rubs his stubble.

A shadow at the car window. Shit, he's miscalculated, the owner's back. The shadow – an oversized bloke, head cut off from view – knocks. Owner wouldn't knock, surely?

'Whaddya wan'?' Warren asks.

Shadow doesn't move. Voice is like a fat fist. 'Get the fuck out of that car.'

'I bloody werk here,' Warren mumbles, fake Wog accent. It's a good accent; it's his father's.

'An' I bloody shit in a gold toilet,' the shadow emits, slamming his voice into the flimsy car.

Warren clenches the gear stick. Has a bad feeling he knows this slab of beefcake. Hundred to one this is Big Ray, as he likes to be called. Last time Warren tangled with Ray was when the over-sized oaf was head minder of a powerful media and betting agency mogul. They'd almost been on talking terms then, until Warren'd got a job with the mogul's ex-wife. Professional competitiveness can turn truly nasty in such circumstances. If it's Ray – and the gritty westie accent in a baritone that belongs in the opera makes it likely – the question is, who's parked the bastard in Parra, under a few tonnes of the kind of bland concrete Ray usually avoids along with his working class roots?

'I bloody werk here,' Warren repeats, reasonably confident he can't be identified under the cap, wig and bomber jacket.

'Not anymore you fucking don't.'

The body moves. Warren swallows. The door behind him opens. Warren calculates the stupidity of turning to look. Very high on the get-your-head-bashed-in scale.

'Pop the boot,' the body says, presumably having inspected the rear seat for dead bodies.

Where's the bloody boot button? He fiddles quickly. The boot lifts.

Beef-cake bangs the side of the car – hard – as he gets himself around to take a look. 'Ten seconds, you got to get your puny arse outta here,' is his only comment.

'I gotta job. I gotta do it.' He doesn't want to leave. From what he's seen the chances are a worker's gone missing. Their behaviour shows this is unexpected and unexplained. He thinks of Melanie, found seconds before death.

The shadow across him deepens. Beefcake is back near the driver's window, leaning further forward, pushing his huge belly flat against the glass – six pack plus fat – completely blocking out the light behind him. The smell of him begins to seep into the car. Warren figures Ray or whoever wants to grab him, screw his neck, shove a fist into a choke-red face, but for some reason he can't. Simply been told not to? No initiative? Or maybe the problem is Ray shouldn't be showing his presence right now. Maybe made a mistake. Warren approves of that theory.

The opera-voice growls again, face still hidden. 'Like I said, fuck off. Your balls won't be no use fried then frozen.'

This is a bland threat and they both know it. The man has other things to do, other concerns on his small mind. The voice shoots a few more expletives and commands Warren to watch himself, or else. A giant foot kicks the door. Warren stays put as the big body does its best to saunter away. Hard when you've got legs like bollards.

Warren waits: something he's good at. Ray's out of sight, the other guys appear and disappear. Without warning, the agency driver's back and the van exits. He needs to follow.

When the coast appears as clear as a beach in the middle of the night (meaning there's people still cavorting on the edges), he climbs out of the poor bastard's car – more damaged than ever – and makes his way to his own SUV, which will now need a new coat of duco and different extras added. He tries to drive quietly: can't be sure no one is watching and while the beefcake might not fancy plugging real flesh and blood right now, anyone's likely to have a go at some tyres if they feel the urge.

No movement, no sound. Conclusion: he wasn't recognised personally. Same time as it's likely there'll be someone up his behind real soon.

The carpark empties out onto a small side street. The van is out of sight. Warren pulls up next to a clump of garbage bins. It's dark but he's not fooling himself he can't be seen. But he's betting on big Ray or the other heavies taking off after the van.

Sure enough, a big black SUV exits the car park a few seconds behind him. The driver cruises slowly past his stationary car. Warren stares ahead. The SUV pauses in front of him, its engine a heavy purr. Nice machine. Warren continues staring ahead. The driver and his mate watch Warren in the side mirrors. They all stay like this for about a minute, until another car comes down the ramp, finds the small street blocked and blasts the horn. The SUV glides off. Warren smirks as he starts to pull out behind it.

The smirk fades as the other car glides rapidly past. A sleek, low-slung and superb machine he's ninety nine percent sure is the one he spotted following the van earlier in the week. Does the fact of it matter? It could indicate the driver is simply part of the team. If so, why was he being so covert the other day? Warren scribbles down the section of the number plate he can read. The rest is obscured by mud. Deliberate obfuscation? He's about to follow when there's a tap on his window. Scares the hell out of him.

It's a girl. In fact, it's one of the girls he saw the other day. The same day as the car. Nice looking lass, about twenty years old, one arm only. Should he ignore her? Can he trust her? Chivalry kicks in – her distress is evident, and Warren lets the window down halfway.

She asks for help, straight up. 'My friend is gone. She is missing. I am scared.'

Warren decides to give trust a go. Leans over, opens the passenger door. 'Quick,' he says, 'while nobody's watching.'

As soon as she's in the car, he makes for the main road, explaining they need to get away somewhere they can't be spotted. She directs him on a back route that could easily be a trap. Now they are both afraid.

They twist and turn, her talking, his tension rising. She directs him into a pub carpark. 'Good place to choose on Friday night,' he says to the girl who has confirmed that her name is Sonya 'What's the full story, what the hell is going on?'

They sit in the car, the air con running. Sonya talks. The story is not a good one. The disappearance of her best friend, the sassy lass he saw her with, seems to be just the beginning of it. 'You must help,' Sonya repeats several times.

Warren gets the impression she thinks he is undercover police. He explains he is not officially a law enforcement officer. Sonya is not pleased. She reaches her right arm across to the passenger door. Her exit is swift and determined.

It is dark outside and the carpark is not a place for a young woman alone. Warren jumps out of the car, calling to Sonya as she walks away.

Neither of them hear or see the man approaching.

42

THE BONES IN HER HANDS HURT MOST. THIS IS SURPRISING, SEEING HOW much else is wrong.

Avril tries to think of something, anything other than where she is and what is happening with her tortured body. That mad book she read at school. The one in the English countryside, in the big old house, with the lunatic in the attic. What was the girl's name? The one who was like a mouse, never game to say what she wanted, but who got it in the end. Kind of. Jane. That was her name. Silly cow. Was that an early book about devotees, in a peculiar, never-admit-to-it kind of way? After all, Jane fell in love with a bloke old enough to be her father when he had a mad wife. In the end she married him, when he was blind and had lost an arm.

Avril finds it strangely comforting to think of a woman as a devotee. Jane mightn't have had much going for her, but at least she wasn't into being cruel.

Avril had not expected cruelty.

She thinks about Sonya for a moment, who'll be freaking out. Sonya's the best friend she could ever have. Sonya is confused by all the peculiar stuff the clients want. Avril remembers one guy rubbing himself against her feet, spurting his stuff between her toes. Her feet are seriously deformed. That's never worried her – discomfort aside – but he made them feel kind of perverted. Can you have perverted feet? Another guy'd tried to hold one of her orthopaedic boots up on his prick. Why? Others wanted to pretend she was a kid, or a trapeze artist from a circus. Guys who've never grown up, she figures.

Some, thank the Holy Mother or maybe Mary Magdalene, wanted straight sex. A few times, it was really good sex. Occasionally they treated her like a lady and did the things you see on the movies. One guy told her she had the best boobs he'd ever seen, and she thought maybe he was right. Her boobs are exactly like they're supposed to be, good slope, great up-lift, fantastic nipples. Big for her body, but then anything decent is. She enjoys the guys who lick her nipples. Hard. Not vicious, she doesn't like vicious.

Zac isn't cold and calculating. Zac's a puppy dog that's been whipped way too often. The kind of guy her mum calls a wimp. He's one of the guys who takes them up to the rooms, and sometimes drives the taxi. If she thought about him at all, she'd've figured him as kind of nice. She was on her way to see one of her regulars, an easy walk from the last appointment, when he'd pulled up and offered her a lift. That was cool seeing he was driving a gorgeous old Mercedes, straight out of a movie. And he had the dark glasses to match.

'A spin around the park, then I'll drop you at your appointment,' he'd drawled, with a fake American accent. Playing the part for all of ten seconds. Immediately they took off it was obvious, despite his cool-dude attitude, he was scared out of his brain. His foot kept going on and off the accelerator, making her sea-sick. He rabbited on about nothing. Then he stopped the car, and he had a knife which he waved about, totally freaking her out. He pretended it was a joke but he tied her hands up and blindfolded her. Even then it was obvious he was pretty lost, direction wise. She asked him why he didn't use his phone's GPS. He didn't answer and she realised he didn't want her hearing where she was being taken. From the little he said and by the long curvy roads she guessed they were on the north side. Sonnie had taught her to think about stuff like that. Means she knows she's out of her territory, and his. Scares her, that. Neither of them know the kind of people who live across the bridge: nice people, conservative people, Liberal, National Coalition voters, nice houses, big blocks. The kind of people who wouldn't want to know a woman like her. Would they rescue her out of a sense of duty? Fifty-fifty, she'd say. Jees, she's getting cynical.

He kept her in the kitchen for a couple of hours. All white and stainless steel like in the magazines. Eventually, he untied her, offered her tea and coffee and food. Zac watched her nibble like she was a goddess whose every move was a demonstration of perfection. It made her want to chunder. She couldn't leave the room, except to use the toilet off the kitchen. Funny place for a bog. The small room smelled of new paint.

Then came a phone call. Zac jumped out of his skin, as her mum would say. Jees, her mum must be in a panic. Her dad too, he's a real worry-wort. She's not feeling too good about it all herself, either. When Zac put the phone down, he was practically smirking. 'Got it right, this time,' he muttered – he liked muttering – while the smirk only got bigger.

'You getting paid for this?' she'd asked.

'A motza.'

Within seconds he was dragging her down a hallway into a room with a door so heavy he had to thrust her and his own weight against it so it'd open. While he was stringing her up on the weirdo bloody cross, he almost cried. Yep, a total wimp. He was terrified of his boss so he bound her real tight, arms and legs stretched like Jesus in the pictures, her fanny exposed and her bra still on. Disgusting.

That was hours ago. She's getting sicker. Zac's gone somewhere. She's tried screaming, she's tried twisting to loosen the bonds. Dumb really – wasting the strength she'll need for the fight, whatever form the fight takes.

Besides, things might change soon. A bit of time ago – can't say how long time is any more – Zac'd poked his head into the room (it'd taken him a lot of swearing to get the door open). 'Got orders to feed you,' he said. Then he pissed off.

Is it worth praying he'll come back? Sort of thing her oldies'd do. She could try it.

If he does feed her, there'll be hope. If he takes her down to do it – won't he have to? – there'll be more hope. She'll demand her handbag – she needs her insulin, doesn't he know, the dingbat? Without it she isn't going to survive.

What the fricking hell – and it is hell – is going on?

She can't stand it much longer. Already she's passing out, only the pain bringing her back to consciousness with a zap that runs through her body like electricity. By now she's worked out everything is prepared ahead, including the soundproofed room she's hanging in. Even the floor is padded, which means Zac or the man he talks to on the phone could creep up on her if she's out to it.

The whole place is set up like a siege is about to happen – thick window bars, inside shutters, and she's seen enough tinned and frozen food for one of those mad nuclear bunkers they used to build in the old days. And what about the cross she's hanging on? That must've taken some planning. Someone – not Zac – really wanted to do this shitty thing to her. When will the mystery man, appear? What will he do to her?

Avril screws up her face, concentrates, asks herself whether mystery man – that's far too romantic a way to describe a cruel fuckwit kidnapper – could be the same bloke who gave her the USB outside the shopping centre.

But then she reckons the USB bloke isn't the kidnap bloke. Pretty much for the same reasons she kicks Zac out of the frame: the shopping centre dick was desperate, all lovey-gooey even if a bit filthy with it. That was the deal with the USB. Porn, yeah, but fricking nothing to do with nailing her to a cross or shutting her up and making her vomit and piss with pain. Way she figures it, she's in a much worse place than the soft bed full of petals – and cunts – that dick wanted. Her head hangs again. She raises it again. Might be worth that prayer.

43

Tom paces, his long legs swallowing the space. His home feels oppressive, with its carefully placed furniture, shelves of zealously organised files, books, and CDs, their sound so much richer than the streaming services. Every pro, con, possibility, aspect is weighed and measured – all thought, no heart. Only calculated risks allowed. Is he exaggerating? Probably. He has to think, to pull the threads together. He also has to admit Julia's potential part in it.

On the way home, he'd been practical and contacted Marcia. The residents had to be interviewed. 'They'll see I'm blind, unless one of them is blind too and then you can explain. They can have as much confidentiality as they like, but we can't leave this hanging any longer. One of them will know something.'

Eventually Marcia agreed. First thing in the morning she'll organise Skype interviews with him and the women. A great way to spend his weekend.

He step-measures the room, the hall, all the available spaces. Is there a relationship between the agency, the young woman thrown into the lake and the appearance of the sadistically mutilated dolls with their brutal notes? Does that relationship include the arrival of Julia, the fact that he and Warren have been followed and that Warren was drugged with an unusual substance?

Tom rubs the back of his neck, dismisses the desire for a massage, continues to pace. His stomach suddenly reminds him of the food delivery that arrived earlier. Still on the kitchen bench. Luckily, he hadn't planned an elaborate meal. He should scoff something down. Although he'll probably stick to whisky.

His phone rings. He swears.

'Why are you and not *we* making this decision about who gets involved in this project? How do you know this woman is kosher?' Clare demands.

He wasn't going to tell her that new evidence suggested Julia is anything but tried and true. 'You're right, and I have no defence.'

'No defence? You mean you have sold yourself to the devil for no reason at all?'

She's cutting close to the bone. 'That's not precisely what I said.'

'I'm sick of your precision. You're leaving out half of what should be said. It's a very obfuscatory precision.'

A branch screeches against a window in a nearby room. 'We all act on impulse now and then,' he counters.

'You're not telling me anything new. And you're not telling me you're madly in love with that woman. Whom I quite liked, although that is entirely beside the point.'

'Clare, I–'

'Oh give over, Tom. You're the best barrister in town and maybe the best fuck too. But there are times you are a total shit. And this is one of them. You've potentially ruined one of the most important investigations we've taken on, and all because you've let your emotions run wild. And you won't even admit to it.' He hears her light a cigarette, which means she's angry. As far as he knows, she, like former President Bill Clinton, never actually inhales. 'I've got some information; do you want to hear it?'

Do you want a scorpion to sting? he thinks. 'Go ahead.'

'As you know, that so-attractive friend of yours has a sister who lives in a group home. But have you been told that sister is currently missing? Twenty-four hours ago she disappeared from the little brick box she's trapped in.'

'Shit.'

'Wait, there's more. The manager of the home reported her missing, naturally enough – although he appears to have taken a while and, my sources tell me, the police response has also been on the slow side. However, by this morning a missing person's report was also being circulated by the *husband* of the competent and very powerful older sister, who is deputy-director of the very department that effectively funds her sister's home, through grants to the charity that runs it. This gives us several pieces of information: first – at the very time you and Ms Julia were interviewing young women about the escort agency, her own sister had disappeared. Oddly enough, she wasn't taking the slightest interest in this, while bringing out the violins about family trauma. Two, said Julia's *husband* was worrying *a lot* about her whereabouts. Three–'

Tom puts the whisky glass down. Does Julia know her sister is missing? She seems so dedicated. 'Enough. I get your general point. Right now let's keep to facts. Do you know anything more about her sister's disappearance?'

'Only what I've told you.'

'Contacts for the group home?'

'Come on, Tom, it's none of our business. Too much intrusion.'

'All right. Agreed. Julia is married to a man called Phillip Jones, whom you would recall I was at school with. Correct?'

Clare deflates. 'You knew about Phillip?'

'Late this afternoon. I also became aware that Phillip has acted in some capacity for a number of women from the Women Wear Wheels refuge. I don't have actual evidence there's more to it than him being a decent and proper advocate.' He remembers Harry's swallow, his own surety of Phillip's involvement. Not thoughts to share with Clare right now. 'Do you have anything of interest on that score?'

'I can ask Kurt.'

'Is Kurt your source for all of this? Is he a direct source?'

'He's not involved in Missing Persons, you know that.'

'Is he directly involved with the investigation into the attempted abduction and murder in Parramatta Park?'

'No. What has Kurt's police role got to do with anything?'

'Aren't you curious about why and how Kurt has information that's normally kept inside the divisions working the cases? He could, of course, be motivated to provide intel to interest and please you for reasons that aren't entirely professional. But how is he getting it? We've never had such detail so immediately before.'

'Pot accusing the kettle? Given what you've just told me about your girlfriend's husband.'

'Agreed. Julia is suspect, her husband also. However, someone's been feeding intel on what we're doing to people close to the agency.

I've been followed. The purported working women with disabilities I interviewed today are highly unlikely to be genuine. The agency is defending itself against us. I admit the possibility that Julia could be warning them; one never knows until all the evidence is in. But if her own sister has disappeared? That doesn't fit. And that brings us back to the only other person who is in on what we are doing – your police contact. Are you sure Kurt is sound?'

'Not a good enough argument to skate over Julia.'

'Clare, I agree I was a shit and possibly a fool bringing Julia with me this morning. Call me out for it. We still need to be certain *everyone* we speak with is trustworthy. There could be more than one bad apple.'

'I know why you are in love with that woman. You can protect her. She's beautiful and tough and she wants to rest her head on your shoulder. That's it, isn't it?'

'You may be right. I'm not sure that's such a terrible thing. The world's a better place for care – when it's wanted, and given freely, without obligation.'

Clare sighs a smoky sigh. So, she does inhale. 'Tom, it's fine, although I'm not sure you're totally free of paternalism. It's hurtful, but I think I finally understand why things went wrong with us. No, don't say it wasn't all my fault. I know it wasn't. It's going to be fine, I'll come up swimming, I'm that kind of girl. And I wish you luck with Julia, I really do. You shone together.' Another cigarette lit. 'I'll take on board your concerns about Kurt. Meanwhile, shine or not, it's not clear we can trust your new – ah – girlfriend.'

That was some phone call. He eases open the doors to the pool area. The rain and cold swoop like birds of prey. Tom considers going back and throwing his body under a warm shower. Instead, he wills himself to wind back the pool cover and descend into the narrow strip of water.

He swims, up and down, up and down, counting his strokes, counting the laps, measuring the metres, telling himself not to react to Clare's words. In a few minutes he'll return to working out the problems. For now, it's body over mind.

44

ROBIN POURS A COGNAC FOR THE THIN, CONSERVATIVELY DRESSED MAN known as John. Cognac is rarely a drink of choice in this day and age. Fortunately, the bartender is more than happy to visit the cellar for an appropriately aged bottle – clearly disconcerted by having a man in a wheelchair in his bar and overzealous to please.

'Our discussion must shift focus tonight, I'm afraid,' Robin begins. 'One of our drivers has gone missing – possibly of his own accord. More importantly, like Melanie, another Parramatta-based girl has disappeared. There is no suggestion she is a girl to abscond willingly. It seems your prediction of further attacks has been realised. As you would imagine, this has the potential to bring us undone.'

'Undone? Ridiculous.' John waves his hand sharply, swatting away Robin's words. 'Despite what you say, the girl has very probably run off with one of our customers, reaping the rewards of private work. We've already had more than one such case, as you well know. I want useful action, the protection of our *clients*. Solved, sorted, sealed. Now.'

Robin feels bile rise in his throat. What is John thinking? Just months ago he had presented as a confident, expansive, eminently successful businessman. His reputation was of a marketer *par excellence*, a self-made man, highly regarded in commercial circles. Even then he had a tendency to grandiose gestures but when Robin joined forces with him, his eye and mind were sharp and focussed on their success. Why now does he fail to understand the attention these disappearances could generate, the danger they are in?

'We should not take the girl's disappearance lightly,' Robin warns.

John again waves dismissively. 'Robin… No. It's time to dispense with other names, don't you feel? *Phillip*. Phillip, if you must know, I have taken the matter of the disappearance in hand. I have people working on it.'

Robin/Phillip stares into his cognac. How did John already know about the missing staff? Who are these people working on the problem? Phillip taps the side of his glass. Could Carmen be working for John? She waited more than an hour before informing him of the girl's disappearance. The girl whom she identified as Avril, although, as he would expect, she did not have a last name. Still, has he given Carmen greater access to data than he should have? It is all like a horror movie. No, one of those apocalyptic ones, where a switch is flicked and the world comes to an end. With a messy aftermath. John as Dr Strangelove perhaps? For a moment, Robin/Phillip smiles to himself. John is not educated in classic movies. He's culturally gauche, at best.

John – who is, in truth, Rupert Barton – is still talking. 'Meanwhile, we are having this meeting to clear up further and immediately important issues.' He swirls the cognac in his glass. 'We understand you have information, in particular about the recent leaks, that may enhance our ability to prevent further erosion. Our impression is that you are aware of who might be revealing damaging detail. Importantly, we all now know to whom much of the information is going. Is this not correct?'

Phillip, too, swirls. Perhaps the beauty of the liquid is worth the taste, he thinks.

'Our primary concern is names, naturally,' continues Rupert. 'Mud sticks. Particularly, in this town, mud can strongly adhere. You and I are associated when we can't afford to be. You do understand my meaning, Phillip?'

Phillip curses himself for agreeing to deal with this man. First the law and then the stock market were keeping him in comfort, almost opulence. Political machinations long ago ceased to interest him. As for the underworld politics that more nearly ran the show, he'd always kept himself resolutely away from that. Gus, his first partner, had turned out to be an obsessive devotee and therefore a mistake, but one readily dealt with. He really slipped up when he met "John" and allowed himself to be duped by the man's huge success and the casual mention of connections that Phillip dreamed about.

He suddenly feels feeble as he reiterates: 'Don't worry, we have been extremely discreet.'

Rupert tips himself another cognac. For this meeting he has minders; two B-grade movie muscle men. They are at another table, distant enough to observe more than just Phillip and their boss; close enough to watch a hand signal.

Rupert's tone changes. 'I, and my other colleagues and associates, are all very much aware of your continued attempts to ensure discretion, Phillip, and we thank you for it. Up until recently, you have been most impressive.'

The self-importance, the hubris of the man, curdles like stale milk. 'Thank you,' he mutters, disingenuous.

'However, the world is an unreliable place,' Rupert continues. 'Just one name might be enough to open a floodgate. Or close one. It is always so hard to predict who might feel inclined to shift the attention from themselves.'

Correct, Phillip thinks, just one gesture, one ridiculous discourtesy can change everything. 'This is all very well. The fact is, there is no way of proving who is behind the service. The charities have been an excellent means of clearing card payments.'

'Ah, but Phillip, it takes only one person – one believable, potentially knowledgeable person – to tell those who might listen that a business is not as legitimate as it appears. And then where are we? One thing inevitably spills into another.'

The room is filling up with after-dinner drinkers, their voices a thick background hum. It is out in the open now, as much as it will be. "A believable, knowledgeable person" is clearly his wife, clearly Julia.

Phillip pulls gently at his collar, wishing he had changed into something less formal. He is tired of having to spend so much on his clothing. The money he makes doesn't increase exponentially with the price of his shirts. Julia doesn't notice. The women he takes out are primed to be impressed with him anyway.

"John" continues to speak in that effete voice of his. Phillip pretends to listen. He has a plan to buy the time he desperately needs. It is a risk, potentially worth it in the end.

The waiter comes to Phillip's subtle signal. 'You must have just a sip of Horace's signature cocktail,' Phillip politely tells the man across the table. 'It's superb.' He nods to the waiter, who moves quietly away. 'I must tell you, Rupert. I have asked my wife to provide a little support for our enterprise.' By now, he is well aware that Rupert has been having Julia followed. 'I cannot go into detail, as you would expect. I can assure you, though, despite any rumour you may hear to the contrary, that she is an actress of some skill. She has Challinor well under control.'

SATURDAY

45

AVRIL REMINDS HERSELF SHE IS STILL ALIVE. A DEFINITE TICK, THAT. THEN she cries a little. It's so early in the morning her body would be screaming for sleep even if she weren't being tortured. She's back on that fricking cross, being treated like she's in a war zone and the invaders are proving their power by defiling the women. They do that sort of thing. Sick, very sick. What's the point of keeping a brave face? She's had to do that all her bloody life and she's tired of it. She's seriously ill, so thirsty she could put the whole country into drought just by drinking. She's hungry too and the fact that she doesn't give a monkey's curse about her own piss running down her legs tells her that if she doesn't get her medication soon, she will really, truly die. She feels so shitty it's getting hard to decide whether or not that's the best option. A coma and then death.

Her head's drooping. She can't change that, she's tried. But she wants so bad to keep her eyes open, to keep watch on the entrance – and exit – to the room. Avril is decidedly not prepared to let the fuckers have any satisfaction. That means death isn't an option – that'd be letting them win.

Trouble is, there's no insulin left. Last night Zac let her have what was in her handbag but she wasn't planning on being away overnight, so that's long gone. On the bright side, Zac also let her sleep in the kitchen. Heated up some gluggy macaroni cheese for dinner – did he think she was a kid, or what? She ate it, to keep going. He gave her cups of tea, never looking properly at her.

Scared the smile off Zac's face when another man arrived and dragged him out of the kitchen. It was dark and the guy didn't come properly inside, so Avril didn't get a good look at him, but they stayed near the back door so it wasn't hard to hear how pissed he was at Zac. He ranted and raved and carried on. Zac yelled back in his cringey, scared-he-might-get-hit way. Both of them kept a lid on the volume, like they didn't want the neighbours to hear. Well, they wouldn't want them to, would they? Least it gave her comfort there must be people around. Up until then she hadn't been sure there were people close. All she'd seen outside were trees. Couldn't see anything at all from the cross room.

Zac and the other guy kept at it for about five minutes, then the new guy stormed off. When Zac came back in he looked like a ghost.

Then he tied her to the chair. 'I havta,' was pretty much all he said. He sat in another chair and when he stopped shaking he closed his eyes like he was on some really comfy mattress. Made her wonder briefly about his life, that he could settle down so quick after all the hullabaloo. Probably been homeless, used to fights and stuff. Being homeless was pretty common round where she lived. Kids kicked out by alkie or druggie parents, tough kids who wanted to put a finger up to the whole fricking world, but mostly kids and families who were just dirt poor. It's a sad fricking world.

For a bit she watched him sleep. Then her well-developed survival instinct kicked in. She wanted a life. Didn't take too much to realise a night's rest was the way to go. Strength and alertness were essentials. Who knows who would turn up; who could predict what fricking shit thing was to be done to her? Took a while but she'd managed to fall asleep herself.

Before sun-up, the texts started pinging. Zac jumped around the kitchen, all anxious to be compliant (she figured he was one of the kids with the crap parents, who scared him into submission). In the mild glow of dawn, she was allowed some cardboard-tasting cereal. Then he dragged her back into this dark room and up on the cross. He could do it because she was small and light but how dare he? Probably he didn't dare, he was just so frightened. Of who? The guy from last night? She'd asked him straight up. That was a mistake, it was like he thought the phone mic had magic qualities even though it was off. Maybe there was a spy camera?

Working out who Zac's being controlled by still seems like a good idea. But how? And is there one guy or two? Or more? She'd picked up that some other girl had gone missing. Some retarded girl, who could've been Daphne but what Zac said gave her the idea this girl wasn't a worker. She didn't think the man on the phone was the one who yelled at Zac last night. This guy used a lot of words. Some of them big – Zac was pretty confused some of the time. Could he be the well-dressed eye-patch bastard USB man after all? Telling Sonnie about him was a good idea missed. Stupid, she is, as thick as those two short planks her dad is always going on about. Safety first should have been her motto.

Her eyes are closed to avoid the reality of the fortress-like room, the peculiar paraphernalia that decorates it. A sadist is coming, she is sure. Here comes the candle to light you to bed, here comes the chopper to chop off your, your, your head. 'Cept this chopper will do it slowly and carefully and with his dick standing to full fricking attention.

Avril lets her head really droop now. Fuck-all point wasting precious energy lifting it. She'll wait and rest till they make a move, whoever they are. She isn't giving in, not her.

46

THE MORNING SKY IS OPAQUE, ANY POTENTIAL FOR PLEASURE WELL HIDDEN. Phillip feels terribly alone, and fearfully inadequate. The phone calls he's already taken have shocked him more than he thought possible. He drives past the building that houses the office that belongs more properly to "Robin", who is him, but not him. How does he explain his agreement to that? He isn't delusional, he isn't in need of straight-jacketing and medicating. Is it the warped inheritance of a sad childhood, leaving him with a desperate, insatiable need to be both extremely good – he donates to all sorts of causes – and terrifyingly bad at the same time? Is it simply his willingness to think laterally, to accept that people with disability could have employment in a lucrative industry?

Such excuses sound pathetic, even to his own ears. Too late, too fucking late for anything. Or almost. Perhaps a small amount of honour can be salvaged.

He is parking his car – away from the carpark and its cameras – when he thinks better of entering his building. He's proud of his transformation of his office area into a green floor; lights dim at night, a cleverly designed ventilation system has replaced the air con, made more effective by the insulating thickness of the building's ancient sandstone. The problem now is that the day is only just yawning awake. He would need lights on inside and Rupert's palatial penthouse is within easy viewing distance. The man sees everything and could take it into his head to visit.

Phillip shudders deep in his bones. Better to go home. Julia is not there. It is safe enough, he has records enough.

Their wonderful old house, also sandstone, also high-ceilinged, creaks and echoes. Salvage what you can, he tells himself. Find the names. He owes that to someone. Himself? Julia? Perhaps to Jean. Bloody Jean. If there'd never been Jean, their marriage might have been different. Children, for instance. He wanted them, while Julia maintained that childbearing and rearing were, for her, stained with pain. That family of hers, that violent father and inept mother – so many "accidents" and overtly intentional incidents of harm that Julia had been threatened with. It had taken her a long time to share all this but, when she had, he accepted, of course, her fear of family life.

First, the necessary calls. The missing agency worker has not been found. The searchers he employed are precise, in their bullying way. They are convinced she hasn't taken herself off. They've questioned everyone, looked everywhere, found an excuse to bale up her parents – hysterical – and not a whiff of her anyfuckingwhere.

She's a money-making machine. Her voluntarily absconding is a ridiculous proposition. Police are out of the question; instead they'll – he'll – have to put in more resources, fast. "Robin" tells the surveillance/search team that *Helpmates* approves the spending. He discusses tactics, provides as much information as he can off the top of his head, although unhappiness wraps his brain in a maggot-filled dressing.

Then Jean. He rings Ian.

'Listen, Mr Prettie-Jones, Jean's still missing and we still can't get hold of your wife. She's as AWOL as anyone can be. And I've figured out that whoever's filched Jean is working for some kind of perverse escort agency. I made a call–' Ian's voice is hard, direct.

Phillip listens to Ian's story of contact with Carmen, imitating shock while the ache in his head pounds through his body. He's shaking like a man at the epicentre of an earthquake. At the end of the story, he mildly asks why this is his problem.

'Because the stupid police won't believe me. I'm just some failed group home manager with a bad haircut. The police like family members and they are scared shitless of people with more power than them. You can convince them to start really looking. You can tell them about this escorting business.'

Ian's voice has a break in it that Phillip can only respect. Does Ian know any more about the escort agency, he asks? The response gives slight comfort. At the end of the call, Robin/Phillip – he is himself becoming confused – gives Ian his personal email to send any further thoughts or information to. He promises to present Ian's summation to the police without implicating Ian in illegal or unsavoury activities. He does not say when he will do this.

His underarms are distressingly plastered with sweat. He'd been planning to destroy any evidence in his office, but that can't be the current priority. Finding Jean and the lost girl – Averil, or Avril, some proletarian spelling like that – has to be the main game. If he can't do that, he will truly be eaten by the maggots he feels are moving into his body and brain. In fact he might welcome them.

Phillip opens his home computer. Another of his phones rings. It's only 7 am, Saturday, don't they know?

Christ, it's an epidemic. Another girl is missing. This one is called Sonya.

His gut is gripped like an unbendable cramp after a very long run. This girl is the best friend of the already missing girl. This suggests a conspiracy.

Putting aside the mental images of engulfing flames, Phillip makes his way methodically through the clever computer web he himself has spun. He's done an excellent job, which is a pain in the buttocks at this moment. Eventually he puts together a coded list of names. Men who've seen Avril, those who've seen Sonya, highlighted overlaps. Other girls in their group – they are all in groups, little mini-battalions, which helps with the organisation now. He ferrets out other consumers who might be relevant. The computer sorts them, ranking by date and visits. Challinor would do it like this too; Tom always had a head for organisation. Phillip wishes he could really hate the man.

His brain already feels the effect of those maggots, munching mightily from one ear to the other. He closes and opens his eyes, forcing his mind to deal with his own codes.

Once upon time he'd imagined infiltrating ASIO using the very same tricks they employed. A sad joke. Eventually, he emails a newly coded list to his very private email address. Only a few days ago, he'd been puffed up with the thought that, if worst ever came to worst, he alone would have the power to implicate, to point fingers. It'd consoled him that he, Phillip Jones, scholarship boy, son of a minor clerk and an overworked hairdresser, owned the knowledge that it wasn't long-legged, tight-breasted, high-class whores who satisfied the desires of the men who featured on the pages of the major magazines and newspapers.

With three women now missing – one of them his sister-in-law – and Melanie still in hospital, but paid off and quiet, everything could well blow apart before he could put such knowledge to use. And he isn't brazen enough to forgive himself for that.

Phillip reminds himself he must not give in. Later he will return to the city to remove any physical traces. At least he can wipe the office computers remotely. He taught himself how to do that when he started the agency. The laptop hidden in the office – not networked with the other computers – does not trouble him. The secret drawer is superbly made, undetectable, and everything on the small, sleek machine remains protected by code and passwords. As soon as the computers are cleared, he'll be out, doing what has to be done. Silently he blesses the control he has continued to exert on the reins of the data. Carmen must have colluded with Rupert Barton – presumably he's paid her handsomely enough – but even she has had no access to the last names or any other identifying data on either the clients or consumers. The details Phillip now holds give him the edge.

Phillip sighs. He assumes Challinor, or his hired help, will be looking for the lost girls, especially Jean. Getting to them first is his priority.

47

THE WIND HAS FINALLY DROPPED. TOM PUSHES HIMSELF TO COMPLETE A kilometre in the pool, despite the half bottle of single malt he'd drunk last night to the strains of Tom Waits, also on a bender of one sort or another. Clare hasn't got back to him. Warren either. Definitely not Julia.

Interviews with the refuge's residents are anything but an uplifting start to the day but he won't abandon duty, as much as he wishes to. First he rings Beth, a forensic psychologist he knows and respects.

'Hang on while I grab my coffee,' she says. 'So, run what you've got past me. I warn you anything I say can't be taken as expert advice. It'll be a first guess.'

'Fine by me. Explaining to you will help organise my thoughts at least.'

Several coffees later, Beth has painted a plausible picture of the man behind the dolls and their accompanying letters. He's likely to be coercive, possibly covertly sadistic, both behaviours becoming more intense over time. Rape may be part of his hateful repertoire, but he would pretend – especially to himself – that it was consensual love. He's unlikely to perpetrate attacks involving fists, or other close physical contact. This perpetrator (most likely) prefers psychological torture. If he doesn't actually touch, he can see himself as innocent, a man who would never harm a woman.

After promising to have dinner with Beth and her partner, Izzie – 'but I owe you,' he protests – Tom finally eats breakfast, mentally preparing his list of questions. Beth has agreed that Warren being drugged rather than beaten or strangled sits well with her quick profile – drugs are a way of silencing that allows the attacker to be distant. How did the attacker acquire the drugs? That question is one place to start. Tom has names of doctors – and lawyers – to put to the residents. Should he also include those names the brothel owners handed over?

The video set-up takes too long, he can't see it anyway, and the first two residents are recalcitrant. They both dislike being in the stuffy office on a Saturday morning. Tom sympathises. He keeps the questions short.

Four more interviews and still no indication of a partner – among three male and one female partners – who presents as a person obsessed with "the one", the "perfect woman". One man reportedly regularly ripped his partner's clothes, preventing her leaving the house, but none have behaviours that suggest the ingenuity to develop a novel strategy of intimidation such as the dolls. Nor do any appear to have the means – the money, the geographical proximity – to enact it over time. Importantly, all six women describe partners who were physically violent, usually without warning, usually in a ferocious but disordered way.

They are all similarly adamant their erstwhile partners have no knowledge of, or access to, specialist anaesthetic drugs of the kind used in the attack on Warren.

One woman has had some dealings with Caroline Zammit. Tom makes a note for Marcia. He doesn't have the last names of the women. The first names could also be aliases. And he has no background information – Marcia will need to ask the more personal questions.

By the end of the sixth interview, a sense of futility has invaded him. Images of the unmitigated viciousness which some humans, male humans in particular, see as reasonable, even righteous to use in their interaction with other humans, especially women, are sickening him. He insists on a break. He unsuccessfully texts, then calls Warren, worrying mildly about his silence. He ignores his desire to make contact with Julia.

At the end of the allotted fifteen minutes, Tom stretches to his full height, deep breathes, and returns to his desk.

The penultimate interviewee, Penny, makes him sit straighter. She is – he is told – speaking Auslan with Marcia as interpreter. Penny describes intense flashing lights that were shone repeatedly, late at night, into her windows. Her mail was stolen, faeces (human) were left in her gum boots. All this began after she told her partner to leave the house he still occupies. Yes, the house is in her name, she only hopes he doesn't burn it down.

'Your partner's occupation?' he asks.

'He's a horticulturalist. I thought he was so gentle. Well, wasn't I taken in…?'

'Does he have any friends with medical training?'

'He works all over the place, he's a consultant. We were going to make the world greener together,' she responds, her sadness reflected in Marcia's caustic vocal interpretation.

The classic story of a man working odd hours? Another family hidden away? Tom will need to speak with Penny again later.

The light tapping of a mobility cane and Penny is replaced by Jane, the final resident to interview. Jane is legally blind, pregnant and very alone. Yes, she admits, her partner engaged in practices easily described as sadistic. He regularly left sharp objects on chairs and large objects in doorways. He moved her clothing and shifted utensils – including knives – in the kitchen. All these manoeuvres confused and were potentially dangerous for Jane.

Jane is hesitant on the details of her partner's occupation. 'He's a computer person,' she says. 'I don't know much about his work, I don't like to push people around with too many questions.'

Tom ignores the gentle jibe and probes further, asking how long the relationship had lasted (over three years), what she knows about his previous relationships (an ex-wife, no children), does she interact with his family? (never, apart from his brother).

'We liked to spend most of our time alone. I mean alone together. His work hours are unpredictable and we didn't always get the chance.'

'Did your partner make you feel you were the woman of his dreams?' She hesitates, swallows. 'To begin with?' Tom adds.

'Oh yes, yes, he was so kind, so attentive, he did everything he could to make my life so wonderful.'

'That changed?'

'I suppose it was too much for him, taking care of a blind woman.'

Tom swore under his breath. 'Jane, no one deserves cruelty.'

'I guess not.'

'Definitely not.' He lets that rest in the air for a moment. 'Was there any incident that incited or signalled the change?'

'Um, well, he did accuse me of flirting with his brother.'

'When was that? Did he make that accusation more than once?'

'Oh yes, you could say he became obsessed with the idea I was flirting.'

'Always with his brother. No other men?'

'He thought his brother was in love with me too. He is a very kind man.'

'And when did the cruelty start in relation to your partner's concern about his brother?' He has no name for the partner or brother – a confidentiality that is irking him by now.

'I really think he just got tired of looking after me.'

'You had the strength to leave him. That's great. You told him you were leaving, you said?'

'Yes, I said I was going to my sister's for a few days.' Her voice catches, quietens. 'I was worried about the baby.'

'He knows you are pregnant?'

'I don't think that would make him happy.'

Jane will not be drawn further on this. Tom returns to the immediate concerns. 'Did you let him know you weren't coming back?'

'I sent him a text. Then I threw away the SIM card. I needed to keep the phone because it has my screen reader on it.'

A computer technician – if he is indeed one – and a phone; a dangerous coupling. Of course anyone who could use google and YouTube could work out how to put a tracing app on a phone, but a skilled technician could do it more easily and probably more effectively. 'You didn't tell him where you were going?'

'I was frightened.'

'Women Wear Wheels will keep you safe,' he says, 'but tell me, Jane, what does your partner's brother do for a job?'

'He's a psychologist, I think it is.'

'Psychologist or psychiatrist?'

'Is there a difference?'

'A psychiatrist is a medical doctor. A psychologist has different university training, although they can work in very similar areas.'

'What does it matter?'

'I think it could be useful to know.'

Her voice is fading, unwillingness filling the spaces between the words. 'I don't know for sure but I think he's the doctor one.'

Tom quietly winds up the interview and asks to speak with Marcia again.

'I'll shut this Skype thing off and ring you on a proper phone,' Marcia declares. 'Get anything?' she says as soon as he answers his mobile.

'Possibilities, good ones. Penny's partner fits the profile, Jane's even more so. Plus, Jane's partner has an interesting brother. I should note too that Jane's partner apparently works with computers and she kept the mobile she left with. It's as easy as pie for anyone with tech skills to track a phone. That could explain how Jane's partner, or any other possible perpetrator, got your address.'

'Good deduction. The goddess only knows why we haven't thought of that. Our bad. Guess we better get cracking and check everyone's mobiles, probably replace their SIMs.'

'That's worthwhile, although I don't personally know whether ditching the SIM will disable a tracking device.'

'Now we have to supply new phones?! Where do we get the money?'

'Cleaning off all the stored info, deleting all the apps, and doing a manual restore might work. Now we need to consider that Jane's partner's brother is possibly a psychiatrist. Most impassioned men, aiming to threaten, frighten and cause mayhem, don't walk around with a pocket full of quality anaesthetic drugs like those given to Warren. However, a doctor might have access.'

'Yep, I got you were thinking that. Are you putting the partner or the brother on top of the list of suspects?'

'Let's call it a family thing,' Tom responds. 'Marcia, you see a bit of Clif Johnson – do you know if he has a brother?'

'Clif and I are hardly mates and don't discuss his family. Have a vague memory he might have mentioned a brother in passing. You can get that sort of info anyway, can't you?'

'Jane's – or her partner's – last name isn't Johnson? And before you remind me, I agree women shouldn't have to give up their own names. The sad fact is some still do and some take the man's name in defacto relationships.'

'I only know their partner's family name if the guy is harassing them or violating our other residents' rights. Guess I can say Jane's not known as Johnson, there's plenty of names left. Your job to find out about Clif and his family.'

'I will. So long as you ask Penny and Jane for permission to hand over their names, and those of their partners ASAP. The names won't go outside this investigation. We need more evidence. Some further gentle probing with Jane and Penny might help: I'll leave that up to you. Please don't wait too long – they might both clam up. I gather you know they've both been victims of sadists. So, it's not breaking confidentiality to say Jane's partner probably likes to watch her being hurt. It appears he sets her up so that he literally doesn't get his hands dirty. That's consistent with the characteristics Beth identified – a man who keeps his distance to enable him to maintain his sense of innocence.'

'Sick.'

'People are.'

'I'm on it. And Tom, thanks. I mean it.'

Small wonders, Tom notes as he ends the call.

48

Not again! Unbelievable. Time to tear up his license. Once he's out of this unnerving position, where his guts're shoved into his back by the handbrake handle he's either been thrown or fallen across, he'll – what? Doesn't have the foggiest.

A few minutes later, Warren's able to gauge where he is – an empty car park at the back of a seedy pub. Lured here? By that young woman? He reviews the event. Remembers the desperation in her eyes. Reminds himself that reading faces, and eyes in particular, is usually complete rubbish. Except for fear and love; they usually show. Most likely due to the sweat, hormones, adrenalin that these big emotions pump around the body.

He stinks. The car stinks. He knows he got out of it last night, tried to run after Sonya. After that he mostly remembers pain. He must've been thrown back into the car where he's vomited at some time – when? Warren opens the door now, climbs out, looks around. Sonya's nowhere to be seen. He sniffs the air. No blood, or faeces. His own or that of others. Right now, though, he could be shot by a person or persons hidden behind the overflowing skips that sit, rusting, at the edge of the car park. But who's going to hang around on this foul day waiting to pop him when they could've sauntered up to his car and much more neatly and effectively done the deed? Likely nobody's within cooee. He's got to find the girl. Needs somewhere to wash. A bloody cold tap at least.

Warren staggers to a tap not far from the skips. And lo and behold, his first piece of luck all bloody week. His phone's been chucked into the skip. 'Cept the thrower missed and here it is, lying only partly smashed on the ground.

The message from Karen is not cheerful. She's furious. Not too bad that: anger is way better than panic. Boss sounds irritated. Ditto on better than panic. Al's not impressed either, nor the insurance agent he was due to get back to. His head hurts and his own febrile, vomit smell wants to make him puke again. Hasn't got the time.

'Boss, there's a girl gone missing, maybe two.' Says it to Tom straight up. Explains how Sonya fronted him, having seen him being hassled by Big Ray – he's sure the beefcake was Big Ray. The girl, mistaking him for undercover police, thought he might help her find her missing mate. The other girl – Avril by name – had disappeared into thin air. Completely out of character. Thought he'd given Ray or his mates the slip. Wrong. The colour of the bruise on his head is only matched by the intensity of the bruise on his throat. Whoever it was – might not have been Ray, it was so neat – was well-trained, seeing he isn't dead. Trouble is he lost Sonya. She was abducted.

'You think Ray kidnapped her? And attacked you?' Tom's voice is curt.

'What else would I think?'

'Whose muscle-man is Ray, who does he work for?'

'Michael Bennett.'

'Bennett? He's a clever, well connected man whose reputation is very important to him. I can't imagine him involved in anything as salacious or as risky as the escort agency.'

'Bennett's also a media mogul with a large interest in real estate. You've been reckoning real estate's in the mix. And like you've pointed out as well, this devotism thing, it can be anyone. Fetishes or paraphilias or whatever you wanna call them, they can be irresistible. So they tell me.'

'Point taken. I'll think on it.'

'Before you do, there's more. And it's real worrying. According to young Sonya, the guy the cops have banged up for Melanie is the wrong guy. Melanie told her.'

'Oh Christ! That's serious. Means this is the second and perhaps a truly hysterical attempt at abduction.'

'Any way we can look into it? Clare's mate, maybe.'

'If the police have a stooge we have to question who got him there. Was it the abductor – how? Was it the clever man behind the agency?'

Tom pauses, thinking of Phillip Jones. And his wife. 'Or are the police themselves covering for one of their own, or for a very powerful person they are entwined with or in fear of?'

'Get you don't trust Clare's contact then. Because various someones know too much about what we're up to?'

'Correct.'

'Point. What do you want me to do now?'

'Get home, get cleaned up and call me as soon as you can.'

'That it?'

Frustration makes Tom's voice hard enough to sharpen a knife on. 'What else, Warren, can you or I do right now? You've just told me there's a kidnapper on the loose. Potentially a killer. About whom we know nothing. But who, potentially, holds two women in captivity – and captivity's the best scenario. At least we know he bungled it last time and may make mistakes again. He's presumably more desperate. I will activate as many contacts and favours as I can, dig as much as I can. You get your head sorted and be back on deck as soon as you can. But we're not the cavalry. We don't even know who we're looking for or where in heaven or hell they might be. Sydney's a big city, with a lot of crevasses.'

Warren gets himself home. Finds Karen's taken the kids to soccer and he's been left a list of jobs that require his immediate attention. Wishes he'd stopped to buy flowers – always a good cliché when truly meant – but he stank too bad to go into a florist. He calls Karen.

'Waz, I can't deal. This is total rubbish. I have a life, you have a life, all good. *We* should also have a family life. And don't jabber at me about duty or conscience or any such nonsense. Tom Challinor didn't know where you were, you flew off on an impulse all of your own 'cause you can't help yourself. It's time you got over wanting to be a character from a crap crime novel.'

'It is. I know it is. But those girls are missing and at least one of them being sucked into a gaping hole in the known universe is my fault, Kez. I've gotta head over to Challinor's. I have to get on with this, find that girl. Kez, you know that.'

Several quiet expletives – she's at kids' soccer after all – and a massive sigh. Thing about Karen is she gets it. Gets him. And he gets her too. Or so he likes to think. 'You owe me big time, buster,' is all she says. God, he loves her.

The smell of vomit is hard to eradicate. Despite showers, clean clothes, time, he feels it on him like a lizard skin, inseparable, metallic to the touch. Apologises to Challinor when he opens the door. The Boss gives every appearance of a bear with a very sore head and is not interested in politenesses. 'Sort your conscience or your psyche out later, the facts and the detail are what is needed now,' he directs. 'I'll get you up to speed on the refuge soon. So, your experience–'

The leather chair is frightening comfortable. Warren worries he'll fall asleep. His head still hurts. 'In the past hour, I've done a bitta delving into Bennett. Turns out he's been quietly buying up hotels or shares in hotel chains recently. And I know you shouldn't stereotype but the guy's had three failed marriages and no kids. Minded one of his ex's kids – wasn't his – for a time; she was definitely not happy with him. Lexi's heard a whisper that he's a kinky sex guy. I'm liking Bennett as a backer for the escort business.'

'Michael Bennett has the money and the wherewithal, I suppose,' says Tom. 'The Facebook page – PubDisMed – Ivan has identified around ten participants. He's narrowing down who they might be. Bennett hasn't been one of the options.'

'Aren't there a pile of aliases?'

'Yes. But if Big Ray is the muscle and Bennett's in some way entrenched in the agency, and they both know you, why are you still alive? If I may ask without offence?'

'No offence.' Warren scratches his ear. 'Reckon mostly 'cause Big Ray really is muscle. Gets off on being seen as a gangster type, without the worst trimmings. He's a draughts piece on a chess board. My money's on him having orders not to draw attention.'

'Does that make it likely Sonya is still alive if Ray kidnapped her? Relatively unharmed?'

'As these things go, yep. One good reason she mighta been nabbed was in the hope she'd have leads to first girl's whereabouts. I reckon they were trying to *find* Avril. And those two girls are obviously as thick as one of them gangster mobs themselves. So yeah, you're maybe right, Sonya might still be alive.'

'Hold that thought.'

'Will do. Won't make it reality, though.'

49

To Julia's left is Centennial Park, its vast grounds a reminder that the past was not always brutal or self-centred. Early Sydneysiders had forethought, setting aside the hectares of open land for the education and pleasure of the growing population. This morning, families are picnicking, children are playing a variety of sports and games, while adults are running, jogging, cycling or taking more leisurely strolls along the treed paths, chatting with friends. The park is a scene of jollity, although, when she'd driven past it late last night, she'd been spooked by the acres of night-time emptiness, the tendrils of blackness reaching to the silver sky.

Julia drives on, doubling back, taking intentional wrong turns, mindful of the cars in her rear-view mirror. All appears ordinary, veering to celebratory as the sun suddenly slips from behind scudding clouds and announces its presence with a brilliant smile. She finally parks a few houses away from her destination and checks the laptop is still there. It's ridiculous to think it won't be, but it provides a real if fragile backing for her arguments. She takes it with her.

'You're late,' Tom says with dead-pan sarcasm when he opens the door.

The game is up. Or that part of it anyway. Yet all she wants to do is to throw herself into his arms. Lust, drama, fulfilment. Instead, she has to face a world sullied with her past. And her present.

Julia straightens her spine and speaks as evenly as she can. 'I have a good reason for not coming last night. Are you prepared for me to explain?'

'Of course. I'm trained to listen to multiple points of view.' Stiff, resentful.

'It's not "of course" – I was followed last night, though not this morning as far as I can tell.'

'Then we shouldn't be standing in the doorway.'

He has evidently found out about Phillip. She expected that, although she hasn't fully anticipated the depth of his animosity.

'I have Phillip's personal laptop. We need it.' She is sure he'll sense her tears.

He gestures her in.

'Your house is lovely, though not quite what I expected,' Julia says, making auto-pilot small talk. He hangs her coat – the leather one they'd bought together, such a strangely elastic stretch of time ago – on a stand in the wide hallway. Julia keeps hold of the shining silver laptop, which is as naked as she feels.

'Does it feel too suburban? I need the space.'

'The colours are good.' Why can't she stop the small talk?

'Compliments of an interior decorating service, in consultation with me. I bought this house after Clare and I split up.' He gestures her forward, his manner minimally less intense.

It will be all right, Julia assures herself. She will convince him. She hopes. How she hopes. She is surprised to see another man in the living room.

'Warren, Julia,' Tom introduces them. 'You'd better explain why you are here, Julia,' he continues abruptly, sitting on a chair at right angles to the larger sofa he indicates she should occupy.

She is annoyed now. How dare he take the moral high ground without solid evidence. 'I'm not guilty. I am not here to be charged or sentenced.'

No verbal response. Warren eyes her with deep distrust. Tom's silence, she knows, is designed to make a witness speak, rush out words that they might not have intended. If only she could get her confession over and done without the anger and blame hanging in the air like an invisible guillotine.

Tom breaks his silence. 'I apologise. I am angry. At a personal level. I am also concentrating on more pressing concerns than my own emotions. There are now at least two young women – escort agency workers – who appear to have been abducted. I understand you to have a connection to that very service.'

'Abducted? How do you know? Have you gone to the police?'

'We'll talk about that soon. Let's hear your story now.'

'Surely those women are more important?'

'Yes. Still, we need to hear your defence.'

Julia taps the laptop in anger – her defence indeed! – and also to draw Tom's attention to it. 'This is Phillip's laptop. Last night, a friend of mine and I broke into his office and stole it.'

Warren whistles: good start to a story in his opinion.

'It took me a while to think through how to gain entry to the building itself. Phillip has an electronic tag. I could hardly ask him for it, if for no other reason than I've been out of contact and he's probably furious. He could even be worried. Anyway, my friend Pete is a tech fiend who was willing to use his skills in a good cause. You don't have to know the details. I knew where Phillip would have his private files stored. He's always done it the same basic way, modified as technology has advanced.'

'How long have you known Phillip is involved in the agency?'

'Since we woke up yesterday morning is probably the closest answer. I mean, I wasn't sure then. Various things you said about the importance of a legal mind and the links with disability…it's hard to put my finger on why and when it all gelled. All those years in aid organisations, living in very troubled countries… Turmoil teaches you to listen, put snippets together – and eventually to trust your intuition, because there's f-all else you can rely on.'

'And the laptop – why have you got that?'

'Proof. More information. I did get some information yesterday. After you left the hotel I caught a cab home. I knew Phillip would be out of the house by then. He's a workaholic, and in more recent years, a very wealthy one. He's also excessively neat with a penchant for old-school paper copies of his projects. I rifled his filing cabinet.'

'It wasn't locked?' Warren broke in.

'Phillip is fond of numbers and codes. He's brilliant at maths. I think his secret dream is to be a code breaker in a real war. At home, he's only worried about burglars, and what self-respecting burglar cares about a shoddy old thing like a filing cabinet these days? He uses combination locks but they're only a few digits. I figured out his possible codes while I was in the taxi.'

Warren is incredulous. 'His office, then? You can't just hack into a CBD building with a radio transmitter from Amazon.'

'Pete did the magic on the entry. The building only has a few tenants and no great call for high security. We avoided the CCTV. I wore an outfit of Pete's, kind of Cary Grant, including a very comfortable hat.'

Warren nods in approval. 'A real cloak and dagger drama.'

'No daggers, although we did have to smile nicely and look convincing for a tall guy who was exiting the building.'

'Guy get a look at you? He'd remember you?' Warren asks.

'Probably not. We also had wigs and other bits of disguise.'

'The laptop is going to lead us to what exactly?' Tom repeats.

'A fair and proper question. Raiding the filing cabinet, I found plans and references to several residential developments – one of them very large, and a smaller scale one in a perimeter suburb. These fitted with your comments, Tom, about the escort agency and money laundering. So yesterday afternoon, after we'd met the bogus workers and had lunch, I hired a car and drove to the address of the smaller development. Four new houses were there, one set up as group home, run by a new charity on the block.'

'Called Choice for All?'

'How on earth did you find out?'

'I'm good at that sort of thing. Or my friends are.'

'Then you know that it is a legitimate organisation in which Phillip has been one of a small group involved.'

'Bull,' Warren comments.

Tom continues: 'We have an informant who suggests that refuges are being set up as a means of recruiting workers for the escort agency.'

'Yes, you told me. But thinking Phillip is doing that – that's going too far!' Julia is adamant. And annoyed. 'Phillip may be many things but he is not a predator. It's not impossible he's laundering money somehow through Choice for All, but he got involved in it – innocently – years back. The disability sector was part of both our lives because of my sister Jean. Phillip also did pro bono work around disability discrimination. And the home I visited is kosher. Afterwards, I ran a check on it – I have some influence through work as you would imagine.'

Warren begins to ask for the detail he has missed but Julia is not to be interrupted. 'While I was there, I spoke with the manager and one of the staff. As it turned out, the manager has responsibility for several homes and was doing an audit on this one. He wasn't forthcoming to begin with but, well, I pulled rank. The Choice for All homes are funded through the charity, the national scheme's accommodation provision and, at the staff level, partially by my department. I did some probing about the recruitment rumour and the manager reported they had, in fact, been approached by a purported philanthropist, who supposedly wanted to fund further group homes and a specific refuge – personally and on the quiet. The manager attends Choice for All board meetings and knows Phillip. This wasn't him. In fact, the man who contacted them – a Gus Perkins – wasn't anyone they'd met as associated with the organisation. Discussions have faded lately, Mr Perkins has gone silent, and they now smell a rat.'

'Interesting. We'll file that for further investigation. But you said earlier you were followed out there, so something is going on. Do you have any idea who by?'

'A couple of unpleasant bully types in a coupe.'

'Bloody hell. Was it blue, metallic? A Merc?'

'Mercedes? No, but a blue Merc did hug me for a time. I wasn't sure it was actually tailing me – it hovered, then hived off. The other car was way less salubrious and much more intimidating. It was an older Audi A5. Phillip has the most recent one.'

'How the hell did they get on to tracking you?' Warren asks.

Julia speaks before he can ask more. 'Hold on, I have the licence plate of the Audi. You can check that?' She pulls out a cheap smartphone, finds the pic easily – it's the only one on the phone – and hands it to Warren, who is evidently impressed. 'And the Merc had personalised plates. First three letters, BEN.'

'Ahhh,' Warren responds. 'What did I say, Boss?'

Tom nods. He's been half-listening, breathing deeply, enjoying the lightness of oxygen entering his lungs. He believes Julia's story, although he's not letting his guard down completely. Clever liars are often the most charming of people. The worst of it, right now, is that if she is truthful and has truly been spending her time chasing after the nefarious deeds of her husband, she doesn't know what else is going on.

'What do the letters signify?' Julia asks. 'Or who?'

'Warren,' Tom says, 'are you up for keeping on that lead?'

Warren assents and mutters he's received the pic of the Audi plate while Tom turns in Julia's direction and asks: 'Have you turned on your personal phone lately? I'm assuming the one you've been using isn't your usual mobile.'

'No, why?'

'We'll let the question of why you've needed multiple mobiles rest for now. Warren, would you mind leaving us alone for a few minutes? It'd be good if you could make some coffee. We can all do with one, I'm sure.'

Warren rises slowly, his movements stiff and grudging. 'You're happy to be alone with her?'

'Do you want to frisk me? Tom's far too big and frightening for me to attack without a very good weapon.'

'Nah, I'll trust the Boss' judgement. Mine's buggered right now.'

50

A DISTANT EMERGENCY SIREN SLASHES THE QUIET OF THE ROOM AS JULIA and Tom sit, unspeaking.

'I recommend you turn your personal mobile on.'

'You're hardly in charge of my personal life.'

'Turn it on, Julia.'

She decides her best option is to accede. The pings of too many messages are interrupted by the phone actually ringing now it has the chance.

'Ian,' Julia says crisply.

'Shit, you're there.'

'Yes.'

'Haven't you listened to your messages?'

'Ian, I'm sorry I didn't turn up on Thursday evening. I've been busy.'

'I'm not beating about the bush. Jean's in hospital in Nowra and it's a long story.'

Julia's heart somersaults. Jean, ill, seriously ill, while she's – firstly and most pleasurably – been having illicit sex and then racing round the countryside, playing amateur detective, trying to save her own skin. The promises she's made to protect her sister disregarded, even her phone turned off. 'Hospital?'

'She disappeared but, like, well, now she's found. Like I said, she's in Nowra, which is fair way away, but she's okay.'

Disappeared? Julia stands up, asking Ian to wait a moment, quickly taking the two steps to Tom as she puts the phone on speaker. 'I think we both need to hear this.'

'Are you certain Jean is all right?' she continues. 'That's the most important thing.'

'The police reckon she's literally pissing herself laughing. She'll keep the hozzie staff busy. The problem is the police say they're not letting anyone near her yet, not until they've interviewed her.'

'Interviewed Jean? Have you explained that won't work?'

'Tried to. Coppers're thicker than, ah, yeah, two short planks.' He almost says, they're thicker than Jean, but stops himself just in time.

'I'll sort that out later. Tell me about her disappearance.'

She feels the alertness in Tom's body. Ian blurts out as much as he is prepared to admit to, reiterating how often he's tried to get hold of Julia.

'Is there a connection with those other missing women?' Julia asks Tom when Ian finishes.

'Who are you talking to?' Ian asks, suspicious. He's in enough trouble already without some random seeing his failings dance on the line like they're pegged on a Hills hoist.

'A friend of mine is listening, for good reason. He's looking for two other young women who've disappeared, possibly abducted. Did the police mention anything to you?'

'Jean wasn't abducted, s'far as I know,' Ian offers, aware it's lame. 'She was in the house one minute and gone the next. You know how she likes to go walkabout. Especially to the park and the swings. It's suburbia on steroids, y'know, and Jean's not, like, the easiest person to convince to get into your car if she doesn't want to so I don't figure someone got her in unwilling. She never has any trouble being in touch with her own mind. And I can't say she'd be up to working out a time and place to rendezvous if she wanted to stage a runaway with someone. Like, she can't tell midday on a clock or anything.'

Julia turns to Tom, all animosity forgotten. 'It's true, Jean's always wandered. When we were kids it was one of my jobs to find her. She couldn't work out how big a thing she needed to hide behind, so she was very easy to spot. Sometimes she liked to do it ten or twenty times a day – or night. She wasn't against two or three a.m.'

'Listen, dunno if this's connected,' Ian interrupts. 'Had this strange conversation with a lady of sorts who was looking for people with disabilities to do some work. She didn't say precisely what.'

'Work was offered to you as well?' Tom asks. 'For an escort agency which employs people with disability. Was that the work? They wanted you to pimp?'

'That's the one, how the fuck – sorry – how'd you hear?' Ian asks.

'Can you give us the phone number you called?'

Ian does a quick calculation on the advantages and disadvantages of telling Julia and her mate that he's also told Julia's hubbie. Maybe not, he reckons. 'Can do. Only it's probably run out of time. It wasn't connected forever.'

Julia cut in. 'Does Phillip know Jean was missing?'

He takes a moment to respond. 'Yeah, um, well, we needed to get in touch with a family member and your mobile was outta action and you weren't home. That EA of yours is off the planet with worry, y'know. We tried real hard to find you.'

'Did Phillip help?'

'Can't say for sure. The management haven't been too happy with me, and I don't have tabs on everything that's gone on. Um, I talked to him only a couple of hours ago, though. I reckon he might know about that agency too. Just something he said.'

'There could be problem there,' says Tom. 'Julia, I've got a message here I need to deal with immediately. Happy to stay, though, if I can be of help.'

'All good.'

'I'll be down the hallway, door to your right.'

Julia swiftly decides not to wallow in guilt. Guilt made a minefield of her childhood and has kept her far too long in a marriage to Phillip. It is a rubbish motivation for decisions. She plies Ian for information, then rings the police.

It takes far too long to be put through. Eventually she explains to an officer with significantly impaired social skills that she is Jean's guardian and they can't interview Jean without her being present 'Where is she now? How is she?'

The family liaison officer takes over the call. Why always a woman? 'One of her carers is on their way.'

'From her home?'

'Yes, someone called Sanjiv. I understand you were uncontactable.'

Ah, more guilt, and not a very good or sympathetic family liaison officer. But she is confident in Sanjiv's competence. And Jean adores him. 'I understand she was found only an hour ago.' Julia bites back the "why did it take you so long". It might not be their fault, after all. 'Can you please describe my sister's condition? And tell me exactly where she is.'

The officer softens slightly. Probably judges it in her best interests not to antagonise the public. 'Really, she's fine. Happy. Chirpy, I'd say. She shows no physical or, um, mental ill-effects, but she's in the local hospital for observation. The carer will accompany her in the patient transport from Nowra to Prince of Wales in Sydney. She will be underway soon. Luckily, she was listed as a missing person.'

The guilt continues piling, despite the women's politeness and Julia's best efforts. She shifts on the sofa and has a sudden desire to sink into its promise of fabulous comfort. Sleeping on the fold-out in Pete's studio had little to recommend it, other than the memory of youth and the warmth of his cat curled against her. She murmurs her thanks to the officer.

'Do you want to go to Jean straight away? We can organise it,' Tom asks, returning to the room.

'I can't. I'd pass her on the highway going in the opposite direction. The good news is Jeannie loves hospitals and flirts with all the staff and the other patients. Whether it's due to all the soaps our mother watched or the endless reruns of *Home and Away* and *Neighbours* they indulge in the group home, she's a romance junkie. If it's a real ambulance with equipment and lights, she'll be in seventh heaven.'

'Sounds like a woman after my own heart. The romance bit.'

'Well, she would be after your heart, and fast. Jean's rather fond of blokes. After my mother died, she moved in with Phillip and me. She soon made it obvious she hated being in a family. A male visitor who appealed to her – well, she was ready to leave with him ASAP. We tried a couple of supported accommodation environments. The one she's in now works because it's all young men apart from her. They don't seem to mind that she loves to cuddle up to them – she's thoroughly committed to heterosexuality. Like most of us, she much prefers to hang out with mates, rather than a too-busy older sister.'

'No flies on her, then.'

'Nary a one. Now, what was it that you threw Warren out of the room to talk to me about?'

'That Jean was missing.'

'What the fuck?'

'Exactly. Clare heard through her police contact and decided it might worry me. I, too, tried to contact you.'

'Oh, shit. This is all getting so out of control.'

'So,' he asks slowly, deliberately ignoring all other complexities, 'to briefly backtrack – you've had no contact with your husband in the past forty-eight hours or thereabouts?'

'Apart from a text I sent on Thursday, absolutely not.' Julia stands, walks across the room. There is the sound of a plane flying overheard. She returns and pulls over an armchair. When she sits, their knees touch. 'I nearly didn't come. I needed more time.'

'In what way would time have made a difference?'

'To what I know about Phillip, mostly.' The small part of her body that is against his is cold. 'I wish I could pretend we're back in the dream-time of Thursday night. You're so powerful, you know. Being with you is so exciting. Not like a roller coaster or anything ephemeral like that. And not just the lovemaking. It's the talking. I love serious talking.' She pauses. 'This isn't what you want to hear, is it?'

'It's exactly what I want to hear. What I want, though, may not be the most relevant thing.' He straightens. 'I don't want to – but I will ask. You're not here because you're Phillip Jones' wife? Has Phillip sent you here?'

'I have absolutely no idea what you are talking about.'

'Don't you?'

'Tom, stop this. Admitting I know Phillip is part of this agency set-up does not give you licence to think he's sent me to you. That's completely crazy. And extraordinarily rude.'

Their knees are still touching. Another plane flies overheard. It could be thunder; a storm seems apposite.

'Given the timing and connections, you and I meeting seems a spectacular co-incidence, don't you agree?' Tom says quietly.

No hesitation. 'I'll grant that. Spectacular and co-incidence are exactly what I thought. When we met – in the cafe – I had no idea about Phillip. Passing references had been made to a new business. I had no detail, none at all.' She sits back in the chair, her hands sliding from his. 'Phillip and I haven't been sleeping together for months. We've stayed in the house because his mother is dying and he reasonably enough argued that moving out was too much. He would never let on publicly – he has a very strange relationship with his own history – but he is extremely fond of his mother. We agreed we'd sell only after she died.'

Julia pauses. Tom recognises the silence of emotion. 'I like Barb a lot, too. And I'm loyal, you know. In some warped way I felt I shouldn't desert Phillip in his hour of need. I suppose I was holding on to the image of the energetic, inspired young man I'd once lived with. When I met you, I gritted my teeth and told myself that, while you were too attractive for words, that accidental, totally accidental, meeting shouldn't matter, mustn't matter. It did matter. A lot. The disjointed pieces of information you let out about the agency eventually fell into place with pieces I'd gleaned. I couldn't pretend there was no connection between Phillip and the escort business. I felt sullied, tainted, I had to find out.'

'And all these phones you have? The number you texted to me from clearly wasn't either your personal or work mobile.'

'Yesterday morning I bought a cheap prepay. I couldn't risk turning my work and personal phones back on – the world, all my worlds, would have come clattering in, fast and furious. Suffocating. I needed a number to communicate with you, and to use while I was delving into what Phillip was up to.' Suddenly, she sits forward. 'Hold on, was I supposed to be seducing you to stop you investigating him? That's outrageous! What sort of woman–?'

Tom rises and walks to the windows, tracing a long finger down the cold glass. 'I had to ask. It's my role to suspect and explore every angle.' He turns in her direction. 'For God's sake, Julia, you're a highly intelligent, beautiful woman with an established life, friends, commitments. And even if it's not PC to say it, you've had your life circumscribed by the demands of dealing with disability. What exactly was I supposed to think was the reason you were prepared to run off with me?'

He strides back to where she is sitting. 'I can't see you. I can't watch the way your face responds when you think. I can give you all the bullshit in the world about judging your reactions and it's good enough bullshit, but in the end I am never, ever going to be sure that you're not hiding something from me.'

A catch of silence like a glitch in time.

'Tom, for heaven's sake, you're standing there, towering over me, using the facial expressions you tell me you've been trained to use. You think that I can perceive more of what you're thinking than you can intuit about me? Ridiculous. I've just laid it all on the line and you are so concerned with your own issues you're not listening. I'm falling in love with you. But I'm not giving in to this nonsense.'

Tom's smile is broad. 'And I thought I was the leopard waiting to pounce. Should I get down on my knees?'

'You're impossible.'

For the first time in hours, they both laugh.

'Time to get on with finding those young women,' Julia says soon after. 'Let's have a look at Phillip's computer.'

51

THE SCENE AT THE HOUSE IN ASHFIELD IS UGLY AND WARREN ISN'T BEING allowed to leave. He's thoroughly pissed off. Just when he was finally restoring his reputation.

He'd been standing in Tom's kitchen – bloody big room – staring at the coffee-making equipment. Bemused him, it did. Didn't even like coffee. For some reason that tweaked his memory of the night he was drugged. A smell? Had the bloke who jabbed him smelled of coffee? Could be. Suddenly, a movie started up in his head, a kind of time-lapse doco of the night before last. Thursday night. Bloody hell.

He'd rung Marcia, asked if the older couple next to the refuge lived alone. 'Anyone regularly visit?' he'd added when she confirmed they did.

'Their nephew's been around on and off. Mowing the lawn, fixing a few things. They're really nice people, you can't think they're involved.'

Marcia as trusting? That'd thrown him for a second or two.

'We got a couple of photos of him – the nephew. He wears a stupid baseball cap, but I showed the residents, asked if they recognised him,' she'd added.

'Smart. What about the blind woman the boss was telling me about?'

'Jane?' Marcia's voice sharpened. 'Come to think of it she might have been at a doctor's appointment that morning. We'd have described him to her if she'd been there and I don't remember doing that. Christ – what are you suggesting?'

Warren had closed his eyes. Centre stage in the movie recreation of that night was the thick shadow of a body. A strong body. 'Big guy?' he asked.

'Yeah, tall, very solid. Baggy clothes though.'

'Dressed like he doesn't want you to notice him maybe?'

He'd heard Marcia pull breath in, swear on the out-breath. That was enough. He'd grabbed his stuff, briefly interrupted the intimate pow-wow that was going on with Challinor and that woman, got himself over to the house next door to the refuge. And got himself into trouble.

Another policewoman, gun large and clunking on her small, competent frame, materialises with yet another demand for him to go over a few details. How many times can he say he'd found the body slumped against the backdoor frame. And, yes, he'd had the temerity to break a window to get in to undo the ropes on the elderly couple who lived there. Yes, before the cops got there. Apparently it wasn't procedure for a member of the public to smash glass. Would the cops have preferred the couple dead just so they could tick the box against item seven point two, or somebloodynumber in the procedures manual? Had he called the ambulance first, she asks? Absolutely, why wouldn't he?

The policewoman smiles sagely. 'Goodo,' she says, before looking over at her colleagues nearby, huddled together like they're doing rugby scrum practice. 'Forensics are suspicious types. Goes with the job, and their new boss, he's a tough nut. Between you and me, he thinks you were breaking into the house for personal gain. My job is to get your version down. Prelim notes.'

Warren relaxes a little and returns the smile. A nice kid. Or ace at playing good cop. He carefully repeats what Marcia has also bellowed several times over in her deep contralto voice. That there'd been an intruder at the refuge, the police knew about it, that Warren was investigating, that he just stumbled across the near-dead body, that it was all kosher. He doesn't repeat Marcia's expletives for the record.

The policewoman writes. 'We'll still have to take you back to the station, do it formally. The tea and biscuits aren't too bad these days, they'll help you get over the shock.' With that she goes on her merry way.

Warren tries Tom again. Reckons the arrival of Julia – a handsome piece of skirt, with a scarily sharp mind, he does not deny – means Challinor's going to get himself into trouble again. He needs Warren, needs his advice. Look at the gold he'd struck with Karen. Look at the

time it'd taken Tom to extricate himself from Clare. This new one –
whose style is all too perfect, breaking into buildings, getting car plates
and all – well, she could be a hell of a lot harder to part with.

Joy of joys, Challinor picks up. 'Nearly there,' he says crisply.

'They're not arresting me or anything that stupid, but I'll tell them
you're legal support. We can do American crime-com, the lawyer flying
in, all dressed and coifed for the job.' More importantly, he tells Tom, he
has some information he wants to discreetly hand over. Material proof
that the three-quarters dead guy is not only 99.9% likely the stalker, he
is also linked to the agency.

Cars, trucks, motor cycles, bicycles merge into a thick blur as Julia
drives swiftly across Anzac Parade, comes to a standstill as they hit
the narrower lanes of Cleveland Street. Late lunchers are everywhere,
parking badly, taking their time to clamber onto buses, strolling across
intersections as they head for a much needed poké bowl of brown rice
and avocado after their morning's lie in.

Succinctly, Tom fills Julia in on the details they have of presumed
abductions of Sonya and Avril. 'It doesn't really help that we're fairly
sure it must be the same person, or gang, who took Melanie from the
hotel in Parramatta and very nearly drowned her,' he finishes up.

'No, particularly as it hints at police involvement. Unwise to go to
them then.'

'Exactly.'

'Let's leave that for a moment. You still haven't told me why Warren
raced off to Ashfield,' Julia says.

'Remember the violently damaged dolls? Warren was ambushed
Thursday night when he was doing surveillance at the refuge – very
different method from when he was watching the agency, it's worth
noting. In my kitchen today, it came back to him he'd been outside
another kitchen just before that attack. To cut a long story short, he
realised the stalker was probably using the house next to the refuge as a
base. He hoped to spring him there.'

'But the man is dead? Nearly dead? Isn't that what I heard?'

'When Warren arrived, a man was slumped against the door frame.
No visible injuries other than a needle prick. The elderly couple who own
the house were gagged and tied up. All have been rushed to hospital.

From what Warren gleaned, there's every chance the man he found is the stalker. He'd probably put location and listening apps on his partner's phone. After I interviewed the women at this refuge this morning, it seems his estranged partner rang a friend to talk about the interview. So, perhaps because we were closing in on him, or for some other reason of his own, he decided to take some of his own medicine – literally.'

'This may sound hard-hearted, but isn't it a good thing we can rule this guy out? As a kidnapper for Avril and Sonya, that is.'

'Sounds sensible, although Warren's found evidence of a connection with the perp and the agency. He'll hand over whatever it is.' Tom considers. 'It remains within the bounds of possibility the man now in hospital kidnapped those women. Plenty of scenarios can be imagined, unfortunately. For instance, he could have them hidden somewhere. He could have been intending to go back to them but was attacked by a third person – making it more urgent we get on with finding them.'

Julia makes a sound of disgust. She crosses King Street and heads down Carillion Avenue, briefly wishing it were spring and the jacarandas were in their fabulous flower gowns. Light-hearted glamour would be such an improvement.

'Has something been put in the water? A drug that turns everyone into an obsessive compulsive?' she comments. 'Or is it group compliance, some strange psychology of persuasion; it's now okay to be a crazy devotee kidnapper, it's maybe even a fashion statement? You know, it reminds me of young men in Yemen – I was there in 2014, not long before the Houthi rebels took over most of Sanaa, the capital. Kids, thirteen, fourteen, younger, suddenly felt part of a process bigger and grander than their ordinary lives, which were mostly spent scratching for survival. They joined up, whether they were Houthi or not, whether they had any idea of what the fighting was about or not. Kids as suicide bombers, kids shouldering weapons twice their own size, kids with hormones and – maybe for the first time – with hope raging through their bodies. But the hope was a chimera, the camaraderie a kind of cultural madness. They caused mayhem, they hurt many, they died, all for an idea that spread with all the lasting substance and destructive power of a wildfire. This is different, smaller and more directed. But like the young men's avid take-up of war, it's unreasoned, without compassion, infectious and growing.'

'Devotism as rampant cultural meme, a wild expression of entitlement? Sadly, I think you're not far off the mark.'

'The world's always fucked, somewhere, someplace, even if where you are seems near enough to sorted, almost perfect. Depressing.' She stops, changes tone. 'Right now, I'm going to concentrate on getting us through this traffic and safely to Warren.'

52

'GEES, I'VE EXPLAINED TILL I'M BLUE.' WARREN IS GROWING SERIOUSLY impatient. Before she was taken off in the ambulance, Mrs Paladino, the lady from the house, explained to the cops that he really had rescued her and her husband. She'd called him her "hero". So, the coppers know why he entered the house. They're still not buying it. Or if they are, they're having a laugh among themselves, putting the wind up the PI. Finally, Challinor turns up.

Constable Theopoulos whistles. 'You didn't tell us yer lawyer was blind.'

'I can hear,' Tom says, calmly.

'Shit, oh sorry. Oh shit.'

Tom ignores the constable. They're outside the house, traffic streaming by on the busy arterial road. 'I need to talk with my client for a minute,' he says, adopting his most professional manner. Such a con in its own way. Useful though.

'He's not charged with anything.'

'I recognise that. You are still holding him and he is still my client.'

'What have you got for me?' Tom asks when Warren indicates there's no officer within hearing distance.

'There's two old people. Mrs Paladino is pretty together still. Her husband looks sick and was carted off quicker. Anyhow, as the lady tells it, the near-dead bloke turned up a few weeks back, story of a broken marriage. Said the wife was working in the refuge next door and he wanted to keep an eye on her and their kid, dangerous place and all that. He's a middle-aged bloke, quiet, didn't marry till late according to his story. And he offered to pay for use of a room – they're pensioners, so that was a winner – and do some shopping, fix some plumbing, that sort of carry-on. After a bit, the lady started to get suspicious. First they thought he was a bit of a weirdo – coming in and out at all hours. Then they heard about the threats going on at the refuge. Finally, a couple of days back, Mrs P got wind of the fact the bloke'd told Marcia he was her husband's nephew. Now she's freaked that her clamping down on him holing up in their back room some nights is what set him off this morning.'

'ID? Is he Jane's partner?'

'Hasn't been formally ID'ed yet, not as they'd tell me anyhow. Name he gave the old lady is Charles Stone.'

'Any proof of ID?'

'Not yet.'

'Let me when you know.'

'*If* I know.' Warren surveys the police movements. 'They're pulling the joint apart like druggies going through a chemist shop, this lot. Better hurry, though, some of them are looking bored. My mate hasn't come up with the owner of the Audi yet, but that blue Merc is ninety percent sure to be one of Bennett's fleet. There's an executive car pool for Bencam, Bennett's media company. All of them have BEN personalised plates. On top of that I talked to Al who talked to a nameless person who can indirectly inform us Big Ray is still on Bennett's payroll. As far as the word goes, Ray hasn't gone rogue, although the word is that he's matey with a mate of Bennett's. Doing a bit of work on the side. Doesn't mean it weren't Bennett who sent him to Parra last night. Does mean it could be a ring, like a paedophile ring, or maybe a new individual who's pulling strings. As well as that, before I came clean about not being a copper, Sonya described being taken to an apartment in Darling Harbour. The building had a wall garden that matches Bennett's city pad. Could be his mate lives in the same spot as him. Sonya thought the bloke she had an appointment with there might be Avril's kidnapper. Apparently he was off the planet weird, had made the apartment into some sort of creepy sideshow. One of Bennett's neighbours – and a fellow traveller? All very cosy.'

'Fits with Ivan's covert society communicating through the PubDisMed Facebook page.'

Warren coughs. 'Bastard – one of the officers is sliming their way over here. We'll be broken up any minute. Boss, I'm gonna pass you cards. Our bloke here was familiar with the agency. Remember the cards I saw handed over at the shop in the Cross? Found a neat little package of them under the lid in the loo.'

'You were looking for drugs?'

'Anything of interest.'

'What's on the cards?'

'Instructions, contact numbers, and a coupla handwritten additions which could be useful. And you need to have a gander at the pics Marcia took of the stranger she saw mowing the yard. She's been busy giving the police heaps and only just sent them through.'

Warren hesitates. Now he's had more time to worry at it, he's thinking, given her connections elsewhere, Julia's style is impressive but her truthfulness could be another thing. On the other hand, he feels her attraction to Tom is real, and he's got a nose for these things. Plus, the Boss is a stubborn bastard. If he believes in her, Warren has bugger-all choice but to keep quiet. At least until the time is right. 'I see your lady friend is with you. Heard her say she's got some history with decoding. You happy for her to look at them all?' he asks, putting his doubts to the side.

'Absolutely,' Tom agrees.

Warren keeps the scepticism out of his voice. 'Goodo, and I got the address of Bennett's building, save you finding it.'

'Thanks. I'll have to leave you here. Shouldn't be for too long, I had a chat with a friendlier and more sensible member of the force on my way over. Hopefully that is her ringing them now.'

'Good one, Boss, see you soon.'

53

THE DAY IS GLOOMING OVER WITH CLOUD. JULIA OPENS THE CAR DOOR, drawing in polluted air, trying to make sense of where she is. She's seen so much of Sydney in the past forty-eight hours that places are folding over and falling into each other. Intellectually, she knows she's near the Ashfield shopping strip that has persisted as a busy community meeting point, despite gentrification and commercial imperatives.

But Tom Challinor is standing fifty metres away, she's holding a stolen laptop, police are everywhere, and they are desperately hoping to find two young women everyone else reportedly refuses to believe are abducted. She feels a long way from reality.

Julia moves into the rear of the car and opens the laptop on the bench seat. Phillip is such a private person. Stealing his laptop – and using the password he confided to her and to her only, in case "anything happened to him" – is a terrible betrayal. He deserves it, of course, but she can't hate him. He's too sad. Now she has to think *like* Phillip, follow his organisational strategies.

The most recent email was sent very early this morning. It has an attachment. Details of horse racing and boat racing. Phillip crews on racing yachts and aims to be captain, but he eschews horse races, except for those annual events that might get him on the social pages. Is she being too cynical? She scans the list, noting signs of a weak code. Can she break it?

Tom's footsteps approach. She calls him softly. 'We better go,' he says, his cane clicking against the car.

'Give me ten seconds, I think I'm getting somewhere with this email attachment. It was sent by a guy called Robin Nguyen. Know anyone by that name?'

'Nguyen's like Smith, very common. Robin's presumably Anglicised.'

'Smith – or Jones?'

'Interesting thought.'

She taps the keyboard, scowls. 'I need coffee to think. There's a Lebanese cakeshop-cum-café in the main street that serves coffee with cardamom. Let's go there.'

The café stirs slightly when they walk in, quickly returns to its business of servicing elderly men staying away from their wives and young people craving sweet food after an indulgent night. They sit in a rear corner, half-hidden behind a fake palm in a large pot. The woman taking their order gives the impression she's used to people who want privacy.

'Are there any developments with your sister? Are you sure you don't want to go to her?' Tom asks while they wait for coffee.

'I can't, she hasn't left Nowra despite police assurances she was on her way. Ian's keeping me up to speed. Besides, while everyone around will be confused, Jean is probably having a great time. She loves a good change in routine and she's tough. All that nonsense about people with disability being vulnerable does not apply to Jean. Or perhaps it doesn't apply to anyone – the idea's a product of seeing the world through an able-bodied lens: you think anyone "different" must be weak and suffering. Anyway, I love Jeannie to death do us part – truly – but we can best contribute to the world right now by finding Avril and Sonya. If those are their real names.' Julia places the computer on the table. 'I need to scribble. I don't have a mind like a steel trap or an AI.'

'And I do?'

'You give that impression.'

Their coffee arrives, strong, spiced, syrupy with sugar: they'll be wired.

'Before you get into the code, could you take a look at these cards?' Tom asks. 'Warren found a small pile of them stashed in the older couple's house.'

'Hang on,' Julia grasps his arm. 'I'm sure now: ninety-nine to one, Phillip's sent himself a list that matches workers with their regular customers. Possibly with meeting places – hotels – too. I'm not certain if that's the other piece of information yet. Tom, I'm willing to bet Phillip's looking for those missing women as well. From the little I can see, he's assuming – or suspects – that a customer is in on the abductions. And he's scared: I can't make out too much – it's all numbers, in the language of betting odds and form guides – but the horses have ordinary names. One is "Last Chance".'

'Scared for them or himself?'

Julia pauses, breathes out. It is painful to see her husband involved in all this. 'Both, I imagine. Though this suggests the agency isn't behind the disappearances.'

'The difficulty is that, if the agency is cracking, and Phillip has let go of the rudder, things could get more dangerous for Avril and Sonya.' Tom spreads his hands on the table, clearly weighing information up. Is he telling her everything, or is he still suspicious, she wonders? He continues, voice unreadable. 'I've garnered a few names of reputedly well-heeled and enthusiastic devotee types who were previously regular customers of particular brothels, or workers.'

'Excellent. This code is made for Phillip by Phillip. He was in a hurry, he'll have written his own memory into the code, his personal twists. More inputs will certainly help.'

Julia breaks up the names, orders the letters, the frequency, the combinations. Like Phillip she might have joined ASIO if she hadn't found national intelligence, and the ideologically driven ways it assumed the country and its citizens should behave, so narrow-minded, so often corrupt. She smiles with grim appreciation – the document's hasty creation is really showing.

'Getting there. Wish I could do it faster,' she says aloud. 'Anything could be happening with those young women.'

'Let's see if there's a further lead in the cards Warren gave me.' He pulls out his phone, puts in his ear buds to listen to his email reader. 'Oh, and here's the pics Marcia took of the possible suspect.'

'Oh, yes, I should have looked at them earlier. Cards first?'

The cards are thick, gilt-edged appointment cards, purportedly for an up-market hair salon. The blanks left for date and time are filled in by an accomplished hand, expertly wielding a fountain pen, making each card a small work of art. On each there is also a handwritten name, presumably of a hotel (coded). Julia flips through them. 'It's unlikely this code will match with the betting odds. Today's list is for Phillip personally. Hold on, here's one with a phone number, alongside the written-in word "driver".'

'We know taxis – not Ubers – are used to pick up the clients. Perhaps a regular driver? I'll ring the number.'

Julia scans the room again. Several tables have emptied and refilled since they arrived. A group of older, black-clad women, obviously long-term friends, and a larger table with two hefty middle-aged, gold-braceletted men remain in place. The women ignore them; the men show some narrow-eyed interest. 'Give me two more minutes before you call, a pattern's emerging.'

Within seconds, she grabs his hand. 'Yes! I used the letters in "driver", too. They really helped.' She sighs. 'Oh, god, I'm exhausted. But I can see some last names I take to be customers and Phillip's definitely scooped up the appointment history of a few workers – either working backwards from customers he has suspicions of, or clustered around Sonya and Avril – who spells her name without the "e" by the way. So far, I can see one customer who overlaps with your list from the brothels. A start, I suppose.' Julia sighs, rubs her eyes, continues. 'Let's discuss it more in the privacy of the car. Oh, first I'd better check those photos.'

Tom hands over his phone.

Julia enlarges, zooms in. 'Umm, we've got a big bloke – almost as tall as you, with shorter legs, thicker shoulders. He's wearing camouflage trousers. They look real but could be from an army disposal store – if those still exist. If you were sighted and knew him well, you'd possibly recognise him. But to pick him out from a line-up if you'd only seen him once? Nup. Is there anything I should pursue here?'

'Marcia is giving the pics to the police. Tragic as it is, the half-dead purveyor of terror at the refuge is not our primary issue right now. Of course, as I said, he could have kidnapped Avril and Sonya and then been attacked himself by another party. We can't even begin to find that out now.'

'And our priority is the women. I've been thinking about it – why? Why have they been abducted? The obvious police response will be because they are prostitutes and some men hate prostitutes. It's possible someone wants to display what happens to the despoilers of innocence

– although they should be attacking our patriarchal, hierarchical society in the first place, and the agency in the second. Not the women. But Phillip's data shows these two have been exceptionally popular in terms of bookings – so what if the kidnapper simply wants to keep them all to himself?'

'Or themselves? Devotees tend to have disability "types". Warren has seen both Avril and Sonya – and they are very different. Two kidnappers is my bet. Working in tandem, presumably. Possibly having met and communicated through the website Ivan unearthed.'

Julia closes the laptop. 'If they've been kidnapped to be kept, there needs to be somewhere set up to keep them. Sydney's a big place, spread out. It's overwhelming.'

'Let's start with ringing that driver we've got a number for.'

'All right, in the car. We're being overlooked and overheard here. It's probably all in innocence, but I don't feel absolutely at ease.'

54

AVRIL CAN'T LIFT HER EYELIDS. SHE CAN HEAR THOUGH, AND WHAT SHE hears is Zac freaking out. He's talking to Robin over the phone. Robin is the boss. Zac's sounding like a kid who's wet his pants in front of the school bully.

She tries to move her right arm. It's limp, like the muscles are all being eaten up now she's running out of insulin. The doctor explained it – she has to have insulin stuck into her cause her body doesn't make it. And she needs it to do something or other that allows the sugar to go into her cells to give her energy. Some diabetics have some insulin of their own. She's off the charts low, like she is for any body thing they can come up with a measurement for. Lucky her mind's good on the charts.

This being stuck on this cross really is too much, too. One of those straws her mother goes on about. The cross is weird, it's not made to kill her like Jesus or anything. At least she doesn't think so. It's got little platforms for her feet and her elbows which means she can rest and move a tiny bit. She really would already be dead if it wasn't for them. Although she hates to admit, she'd probably already be dead if it wasn't for that dick, Zac. The footrests are way below her legs, and the elbow ones in a stupid spot. He got some cushions and stuff so she could use them all right. Still her arms feel like they are filled with poison, the pain is so intense. And her left one won't co-operate with her will any more than her right one. It's getting too fricking awful.

What is the point of moving anyhow?

Is the guy who came up with this some kind of religious nut-case? Like her parents who believe in this weird thing called generational sin.

Somehow that makes her being way too short and having all sorts of medical problems a punishment for some stupid ancestor's sin. How do they figure that? 'Sides you can't put a sinner on the cross to die for the sins of others, can you? You put an innocent like Jesus Christ on the cross. The son of fricking God whose mother didn't even have sex to get him. The original IVF baby, Jesus. Her mum reckons Jesus never had sex either. 'Some people should never have "relations",' her mother says. 'It is not their destiny and we should not go against God's will.' Right! Can you believe it?

Although, come to think of it, a really perverted guy might want to string her up – or get that stupid Zac to the do the dirty work of stringing her up – because he thinks she is actually divinely innocent. That's what they'd kept on about at the Catholic school she and Sonnie went to. Handicapped – that was the word they used – handicapped kids could die before they were baptised and they'd still go to heaven. Handicapped kids were God's innocents!

A squeal from Zac brings her head half up. He's carrying on that he's on another job, he can't leave, no matter what, he totally promised he'd stay. Totally promised! Weasel! Speaking of religion, he probably made promises in Sunday School too – or in the mosque. She thought he was Muslim but who knew, or cared? Wherever it was, she'd bet on him having promised to be good. A promise already crushed under a mighty big truck, that one.

Zac whines on; he won't tell Robin where he is either. That makes her twitch in fright. Someone has to know where she is. Sonnie would rescue her if she knew where she was. She's almost surprised that Sonnie hasn't found her. She is so smart. All those years in refugee camps over in places Avril's hardly heard of. When she didn't go to school, or not properly, and then she came here and had to speak English even though she'd never learned it. They were in year 8 then, when they met. It was kinda love at first site. Friendship love. Which she suspected might be somehow deeper and longer lasting than most other types. That reminds her that her parents will be freaking out about her not coming home. Sonnie will be freaking too. Will she have gone to the police? Her mum and dad'll probably go to the pastor to have a good long yarn about how to redeem her soul first. Sonnie, she whispers, come on, you can do it, you can do it. Where is she?

She has another go at lifting a piece of her body. Any piece. Every muscle refuses. In fact she can't even feel her legs. Avril tries to look down, make sure they are still there. Impossible. Everything is impossible. And it's all giving her the shits.

55

Tom hangs up from his call. He and Julia are sitting in the car, a light drizzle puddling the road and amplifying the sound of the relentless traffic.

'Zac is indeed a driver,' Tom reports, 'and he's confirmed – unwittingly – that currently he's working for our one overlapping customer of both mainstream brothels and the agency – a Stephen Charters. Sonya, the woman Warren met, mentioned a client who called himself Stephen. A common enough name so could be simple coincidence. Or not. Our problem right now is that Zac became hysterical before I got an address.'

Julia's hands shake as she pushes the keys into the ignition. 'When you were pretending to be Robin, you sounded exactly like Phillip. I understand why Zac was prepared to answer your questions; he really thought you were his boss. How did you do that?'

'Acute attention to sound. I've always been able to mimic voices.'

'How can you know what Phillip's voice sounds like? Do you know him through work?'

Tom reaches for her arm, noting its stiffness. He should have told her. 'Phillip and I were best friends, of a sort, at school,' he confesses. The muscles in her upper arm flex. 'I've only spoken to him once in nearly twenty years, but I remember his voice.'

'Why didn't you tell me?'

'I suppose there hasn't been time. We've both been not wanting to talk about Phillip.'

'Tom, I don't think you ever "suppose" anything. There is some reason, which makes sense to you.'

'Perhaps, although I'm not really that deep, you know. I was shocked, too, to find out Phillip is involved in this. We spent a lot of time together as adolescents, enjoyable time, we bonded as outsiders. Perhaps I have some guilt about running off with my erstwhile best friend's wife. That's not relevant now. Avril and Sonya are more important.'

'We're going to do one hell of a lot of talking. Soon.'

She isn't going to make life easy for him, Tom thinks. Good: it is the challenge of her that he most enjoys. 'Agreed,' he responds, noting that the barriers he'd set up against her are falling much faster than the Berlin Wall. 'In the immediate, with luck, a good friend of mine can track an address for Charters, who remains our best chance.'

'As you suggested – what if there are two of them? What about Bennett? Although his name isn't among those Phillip has coded. Then, you'd expect someone as powerful as Bennett would cover his tracks better than most.'

'I can't square it with the Michael Bennett I've had dealings with over the years.'

'Come on, Tom, you're a defence barrister. You know that the nicest men can turn out to be criminals of the first order. Bennett's smart – I've met him too – and could be the instigator. His help would do the nasty bits.'

'I'm not discounting it. Merely surprised.' An incoming call, the digital voice announcing Marcia. Tom answers.

'Caroline Zammit? She's Jane's lawyer?' he questions, in response to Marcia's opening remarks.

Marcia's deep voice growls loudly enough for Julia to hear. 'No, Caroline is the lawyer Jane's partner wanted to have as their "family" lawyer. So they could make wills, among other – unspecified to Jane – things. The boyfriend probably wanted Caroline on board so she could save him from violence orders. For starters.'

'I won't argue with you. Right now, though, we have to weigh up whether Caroline's important to consider. Is the injured man definitely Jane's partner?'

'The Mastermind question – felt like a fricking game show where you make the contestants seem like fools, the way the police were carrying on – having to ask a blind woman about identifying the bloke. They'd be applying for trauma counselling – the coppers, that is – except Jane had some photos of her partner and herself together. Jane says he liked to take them with her phone so she could show her friends. But then he stopped her going out with her friends, most of whom are vision impaired anyway. Anyhow, he's the collapsed bloke.'

'Does Jane have a theory of what happened?'

There's a grimace in Marcia's voice. 'Ah, you know. Jane probably figured her bloke was the one dropping the dolls a while back. Couldn't admit it to herself. Right now, she's panicking that she's hurt him so badly he's overdosed or whatever – anyway, tried to top himself. She's full of guilt.'

Overhearing, Julia sighs. The story is too familiar.

'Marcia, you do an amazing job,' Tom says. 'All the best with Jane. In the meantime, do we have a name?'

'Adam Johnson.'

'Johnson! Hold on, didn't Jane say her partner had a brother who was a psychologist or a psychiatrist?'

'The unholy mother! I'd forgotten that in all the mania. You're thinking Clif Johnson is the brother? Clif as a devotee? That'd be a turnaround for the books. Can't stand him anyway, now I'm being honest.' Marcia sounds almost pleased.

Tom runs his hand over his bristling hair. Definitely wants the luxury of that haircut. Julia is silent beside him, her body attention-tense. Outside the cocoon of their stationary car, the sounds of irritated Saturday drivers spike and retreat and jump out like a kid trying to scare a scarier kid. Clif Johnson? A devotee? Or a man honestly in love with Jane, his brother's partner? That brother, Adam, sadistic, secretive, possessive? Is Adam why Clif put forward his explanation of devotism – being the outcome of a misguided, over-emphasised caring response to trauma? It had struck Tom at the time as an explanation concocted to fit with current beliefs of causation, one designed to excuse rather than understand. Could it also have been a protective explanation?

Has Clif recently decided to stop protecting and apologising for his brother? Did Clif discover what Adam was doing with the dolls and finally snap? Did he truss up the old couple, so he could inject his brother in peace? Or did they come to Adam's rescue and he wanted to prevent them calling for help? Is that why Adam Johnson is now in the Intensive Care Unit at RPA? Where is Clif now?

'Didn't you say your tech guy – Ivan, isn't it – was worming in behind a medical website that seems to be a front for devotism?' Julia asks when he finishes the call with Marcia. 'I could hear all that conversation, by the way. Is it possible, probable, the doctor you're referring to is in the ring of secret devotees?'

'Making it possible Clif's prominent in the abductions as well as the attack on his brother?' Tom considers. 'It's certainly possible. From what Ivan's already uncovered I'm fairly certain Stephen Charters is one of the group, but although Clif is a doctor, we have no evidence of him participating.' Tom runs his hand over his head again. 'Christ, I'm tired. You must be too. Angels can have evil undersides – isn't that the story of the devil, a fallen angel? But Clif? I can believe he'd go out on a limb to protect Jane but I'm having real trouble squaring him with kidnapping and attempted murder. He's too passive, too bumbling.'

'I guess the police will be onto looking for Clif, too. So let's start with Charters.'

Emily, the nice young officer, drives Warren into the station. 'The air con here is crap,' she informs him. 'I don't know who stinks worse, the staff or the crims. Either way, or altogether, their stink gets recycled and up our noses all day. Hold your nose and I'll let you keep your phone to amuse yourself with.'

Warren grins. Emily's also true to her word with the tea and biscuits. He figures she couldn't really confiscate his phone, seeing he's not arrested or anything, but she's a nice kid. He bends his head over the most recent text.

'Need more detail on Caroline Zammit, Dr Clifton (Clif) Johnson, and Stephen Charters asap. Are you out? OK?'

The enquiry about his well-being is obviously an afterthought. Warren spends a split second feeling pissed off. Hardly worth it. Those girls are still out there somewhere, there's a hell of a lot going on and if Tom wants to know more about these characters, it must be important.

He's about to text back, reporting his continued detention (it does feel like school) when another text interrupts. It's a busy place, the unseen world of communications.

'Audi business registered. Company name PSI, Sydney – Private Surveillance and Investigation.'

Warren looks up. It's a pity the sky through the smeared station window is turning so grey, he's feeling like Emily, cheerful, ready to get on with the next problem. Does a quick internet search. Sends a text to Tom.

Tom turns in Julia's direction. 'The second car tailing you isn't overtly linked with the first – entirely different companies.'

'That's popularity I can do without. I can't see we should concern ourselves with that right now.'

'Warren's looking into whether there is a hidden link between them. And he'll get on to Ivan who might be able to find more through the back doors. It's worth pursuing.'

A few minutes later, the air con on, Julia again tapping impatiently at the laptop, Tom rings Serge. Who, having demanded an explanation at the first opportunity, quickly finds three rates notices with addresses for Stephen Charters. One in the same building as Michael Bennett's Sydney penthouse.

'Shit! Unbelievable. No – believable. Fuck!'

'I haven't heard you swear. Much.' Julia takes a deep breath. 'But, let's think, would he keep Avril and Sonya captive in a residential apartment building?' Julia asks, her fingers hard on her forehead, trying to massage her mind. 'It's impractical to carry a bound or sedated body up in a lift for starters. Bennett – if you're thinking of him as co-conspirator – is a very organised bloke. He wouldn't go for that.'

'I do find your logic attractive. Charters has another apartment. It appears to be a studio in Glebe. You'd imagine access issues there too. He also has a property on the north side. In a quiet suburb, certain to have a driveway, garage, a garden big enough for privacy. When I was talking to that driver, Zac, I could hear wind in the background. Meaning trees, large ones. I didn't hear traffic or airplanes.'

'Good. Going back to our earlier theory – if he's kidnapping women to keep for his own pleasure, he'd want a large, quiet place to take them to. Hold on, while I google map the house and surrounds.'

Thirty seconds later, Julia is convinced. 'From what I can see here, it's perfect for a secret hide-away. Let's go.' Action is pleasing and, she has learned in war zones, often safer than sitting still.

'I'll speak with Warren on the way. See how soon he can get there.'

They strike out across the city again, the traffic snarling and nipping like a poorly trained dog. 'We're missing something, probably many things,' Tom says as they cross the Gladesville Bridge, its huge single span structure a sensation in itself. 'What I can't get is it's all falling apart so quickly and in so many directions.'

'In my experience, it's often the way. Structures erode little by little and then the final fall is sudden and dramatic. In the meantime, there's a car clinging to us and I'm trying to decide whether to worry about it or not.'

'I'm getting bored with cops and robbers.'

'Me too. Although I'm guessing it's everyday unmarked traffic police, from the look of the aerials and the dashcam. We will frustratingly proceed at an appropriate pace.'

The car peels off as they take a left turn. Julia watches for its reappearance, which would be noticeable on this wide suburban street. 'We're hypersensitive. It's gone,' she announces.

56

PHILLIP SHOULDN'T HAVE COME ALONE. HE CURSES HIMSELF FOR A FOOL. On the other hand, short of ringing the police – who would only snort through their hairy noses and further ruin his already completely ruined life – who could help? A short time ago, "John" would've lent him a heavy or six. Now it is more likely those very employees are out scouring the streets for him. And/or working on their plan to land him in the gutter.

He creeps forward. From the outside, the house appears an ordinary, expansive, expensive North Shore residence. Up this close, the story is more complicated. Faint outlines of bars can be spied behind heavy curtains, impenetrable double locks decorate windows and doors. Must be the right house.

Phillip takes the side path. The otherwise irritating light rain is reducing the likelihood of any neighbours being outside, watching. The rear of the house has an addition, its construction surprisingly ramshackle. The addition's iron roof, though, is more accessible than the higher, solid tile roof of the main body of the house. Perhaps his days of rock climbing will come in useful.

He runs his hands along the back walls, looking for holds, a safe enough way up the sheer sides. A ladder could be a simpler solution. He edges back toward the garage.

Phillip feels like crowing. The ladder is in deplorable condition, but he only needs to use it once. The tools he'd – with forethought he feels momentarily proud of – brought with him are the perfect complement, and much better looked after. Increasingly, he senses these abductions are like fireworks let off too early. Or too late. At the wrong time, whichever way. The fault of employing poorly-prepared help, he'd wager, if he were the betting type. Which on occasion he is.

Once on the roof, it doesn't take long to lever a sheet of roofing loose. He silently thanks the Australian architects who reintroduced corrugated iron as the residential roofing material of choice, as well as the builders who'd done such a shoddy job of this extension. With luck, the small window on the external wall denotes a toilet. If that is correct and he can get ceiling access he should be able to drop himself down onto the seat. Phillip is beginning to enjoy himself.

Soon, dirtier than he has been in a decade or more, he is listening intently through the partly open hole that once housed an extraction fan in the ceiling. He hears a suburban kitchen – the hum of a refrigerator and the soft tick of an analogue clock. Remembering film scenes, he drops a discarded nail onto the toilet floor. It resounds. Nobody investigates. Phillip quickly levers away more plasterboard, lowers his feet onto the toilet seat. He nearly slips. He bites the gasp back, his heart thumping with an unpleasant rhythm.

The complete absence of human sound is almost nauseating. He has to keep going. Skin prickling, sweat building, he edges through the kitchen and enters a dark hallway. He's just gaining confidence when an eruption of voices shocks like a spotlight, sending him through a door, any door, off the main corridor. Just in time. The room smells empty. Outside it is mayhem, Bedlam. In the dim light he spies opulent furnishings and heavy drapes that will provide some shelter. Now his panic is settling, the sounds are sorting themselves out.

One voice rises over the other. Whose? Phillip's data has led him to this house, registered to Stephen Charters, the man he'd met as a war hero of sorts, peacekeeper anyway. Is it Charters who is bellowing so menacingly? Is his chest barrel-shaped enough to make that sound? Charters is thin, tight, a body shape not usually associated with resonance. Still, without being able to see the yelling man, Phillip has no hope of properly identifying him.

'You got the wrong fucking woman,' the man repeats and repeats. Then suddenly the voice drops, seemingly half-strangled (by emotion?) and the words become indecipherable through the thick door.

The panic of moments earlier returns, flooding Phillip with

adrenaline. Has the speaker detected his presence? Is that why he's quieter? He could be coming for him. Phillip instinctively holds his breath. His heart thrums in his ears, making it hard to hear what is going on in the corridor.

Then relief, the second man is pleading now, although the words are incoherent. Is he also choking? Seconds later, thuds assault Phillip's ears: the sounds, he assumes, of hard fists hitting unwilling flesh. A heavier thud, followed by a scraping on the floor. Phillip again holds his breath.

The dragging stops and the kitchen door closes.

When the silence has continued for several minutes, Phillip sits down on one of the plush velvet chairs – tasteless, ugly – with his head in his hands. Terrible events have been occurring. Terrible things could happen to him. Tears bite his eyes. He berates himself in the effort to summon courage. Under his breath, he repeats a few Latin conjugations. He used the trick at school before he sat exams – the grammar stimulates a section of the mind far from the brain's centres for fear. It also reminds him that he is organised, he can do this.

Is there one women or two in the house? Charters was in Iraq, so it isn't unreasonable that he might feel a warped connection with Sonya whom he had recently booked for a long appointment. If that is the case, why is Avril also missing? Was she the wrong woman Charters was shouting about (he has to presume it was Charters he heard attacking the other man, doesn't he)? Is she silenced? Is she – dead?

Phillip shudders, then turns to marshalling his courage. *Amo, amas, amant, amamus, amatis* … the Latin for love. Stupid irony. With great effort he moves stealthily out into that corridor. Sounds can be heard when he is outside the thick door. Muffled, piercing at the same time.

An unspecified horror is underway in the kitchen. Which is his escape route. Is it burning flesh he can smell? He refuses to retch.

In the other direction, the corridor leads to a larger, grander hallway with several rooms off it. It is easy to identify the one the girl or girls might be in. The door looks like it is taken from an armoured tank. Unbelievably, it is open.

What Phillip sees inside that room does make him physically sick. He lets the vomit fall, bothering only to suppress the noise. When he can bear to look again he sees it is the dwarf girl, Avril, strung up on a cross. She looks dead. Phillip wipes the vomit from his mouth. He is about to close the door behind him when he realises it could have an automatic lock.

Instead, he walks over to Avril, pulling the insulin from his pocket. This at least he can do. The health files he insisted the agency keeps show the dwarf girl has insulin-dependent diabetes. He tries to ignore the way she is drooping and silent, moves up close like a good doctor might. His mother is diabetic, crumbling away and dying of it. He knows what to do.

It takes him a few moments – peculiar, elastic time – to work up to touching her. She is warm and her foot recoils just enough to convince him his effort is worthwhile. He could not, will not, have her death on his head. Phillip raises the insulin pen, Avril moans.

And then the bullet hits.

57

THE FRONT OF THE HOUSE IS SCREENED BY THICK GOLDEN PINES, PLANTED years before native gardens became fashionable. A driveway to the right leads to a garage. At the beginning of the drive, a letterbox announces number 5. Behind the trees lies a panther-like darkness. The quiet in the street is palpable.

'We could just bowl up, pretend to be Jehovah's witnesses,' Julia says. Then gasps. 'Shit. That's Phillip's car.'

'Is he in it?'

Elm St is actually a cul-de-sac of eight or nine homes. Julia scans the surrounds as she turns, stops behind Phillip's Audi, and flicks on her headlights. There is little point in pussy-footing around. 'The car's empty. What if he's actually–?'

'In on the abduction? I have considered the possibility.'

Julia bites her lip. 'No, he wants to be a hero. Pluck the women from of the abyss he's thrown them into. But then I could be wrong – who knows anyone really, deeply, especially when they're pushed into a corner? Most dictators are magnetically attractive. Until they are not.'

A car cruises slowly by, pulling to a halt fifty metres further along the road. A man stays in the driver's seat. Julia watches. 'They drive smart cars around here,' she comments. 'This one's positively Ian Fleming, or James Bond. Low on the ground, paint like shining velvet. Seriously sleek. I'm going to take a pic. We can't move until the driver does – seems he's checking his phone.'

Tom hears the soft *thluck* of the camera phone. Julia continues. 'While we're waiting, let's establish an open phone connection to use while I'm scouting around. Don't worry, aid work is great prep for this – in what are politely called "trouble spots" you hardly sit around on your backside doling out rice with a smile. It's more like espionage than we'd ever publicise.'

Julia hands the prepaid phone to Tom. 'The driver's getting out. Taking his time. Where is he going? All okay – he's making for the house two doors down from our target. I'm ready.'

'All good. Except that I'm coming with you. To the house at least. Obviously I know a blind guy is not generally considered an asset in the spy game. However, a nice middle class lady calmly walking down the street and onto the property while guiding a poor blind bloke will keep the neighbours interested enough, but not wanting to enquire. Your description suggests that if we approach from the north, we're likely to do this without anyone inside the house spotting us. The blind side of the house, as it were.'

'Ah-huh. You've put forward one advantage to this outrageous plan. What else?'

'Two people are always more threatening than one. I'm large, people get frightened because, no matter what, they don't have a clue what to do with me. Besides, I'm happy to wait somewhere within easy range of the house. And you.'

'And I suppose you are trained in martial arts. Close personal conflict might go your way.'

Tom decides not to reveal that his training is for strength and breathing, for immediate – and not prolonged – self-defence. His attack skills are limited. Confidence is important now, though. Hers and his. 'Naturally,' he says firmly.

'Arrogant, as aforenoted. Also smart. I like it. Shall we go?'

The smell of burnt flesh hits Julia with the violence of a car crash. She's smelled it too many times before. It is the stink of war, simultaneously acrid and sweet. It's collateral damage. It is hand-held mortars producing civilian casualties; it is children caught in the spreading fire of homemade bombs; it is cooking and heating accidents that occur daily in refugee camps. And once in the square of a large town in a war-torn region where self-immolation had seemed to a man devoid of all hope a reasonable response, it was the smell of a death she witnessed too closely.

Julia wills herself to breathe lightly and firmly. She presses against the outer wall near the small window at the rear. Faint moans. Crying. One voice. Above her, the roof-tin flaps and crashes in a small gust. Has someone broken in before her?

'Tom,' she says quietly into the phone mic, 'something awful's happened. I'll try all the entry points but I may need to go in through the roof. You'll have to be lookout.'

'I smell it too. If necessary, there's the police. I can alert the neighbours. Noise works.'

The moans are a desperate whimper as Julia rounds the corner of the extension. The back door is half-open. Small mercies. She pushes it just wide enough to listen, then slips inside. Slumped on a chair is a young man, bound with a light chain. The burning smell rises from wounds on his arms. His face is swollen, unrecognisable probably even to his mother. Julia stumbles as she takes the scene in, attracting what is left of his attention. He moans again. That is all he has the energy for.

'Oh shit,' she says quietly. 'I'm calling an ambulance,' she says firmly, standing close now to the twisted body. She doesn't touch. If she moves him, or he jolts himself, the chain that's around his neck is evidently designed to tighten. The perpetrator of this abomination was expert. 'The ambulance won't take long. It might feel like forever but it will be quick, really quick,' she says softly.

Julia assesses the young man as best she can. He is struggling, his breathing laboured. There's nothing minor first aid will help with. The chain is wrapped through the chair rails, crossed over and – she bends down – locked under the seat. Apart from the futility, any attempt to loosen it will increase the pressure and therefore his chances of dying sooner rather than later.

'Who is in the house?' she asks, as his left eye flickers, almost opens.
'Shot.'

Confusing: no blood is detectable among the mass of the blackened, blistering wounds, the intense discoloration of the face. Who has been shot? Is there another horror around the corner?

'Shot?'

The face contorts. 'There,' is what Julia thinks he says. 'Please,' he adds.

'I'm going to look,' she tells the mess that is the young man. Julia selects a strong kitchen knife and explains to Tom how to enter the kitchen from where he is. He has already rung emergency services. He will keep the boy calm.

58

THE SIRENS BOUNCE INSIDE PHILLIP'S HEAD, ADDING TO THE CRY HE IS suppressing. He has a vague idea Julia is near him and that she's somehow arranged the sirens. Or is it Tom Challinor's doing? He's in the house too, Phillip is not sure where. Can't believe any of it. It is the truth, though, a tiny piece of ordinary truth.

'The ambulance is nearly here, Phillip. So, as much information as you can. Now. Fuck your pain.'

'Reasonable,' he agrees. 'I am trying to think. Honestly.'

'Start with telling us where Avril is.'

'She was here. She was taken. I am not entirely sure she is dead. I got the insulin pen in, she may recover consciousness. The man carried her out. I have not the foggiest notion where he has taken her.'

'The man is Stephen Charters?' Julia asks.

'Ah, that's the thing. It isn't Charters. I expected it to be him too. But when I saw him – no, the man who shot me and took the young woman away was not Charters.' Phillip shifts his gaze to the impossibility of a giant Easter cross in a suburban living room. Tightens his nostrils against the smell of urine and faeces that mix with the metallic scent of his own blood.

'All your data? The house in his name?'

'My data? How do you have my data?'

'I stole your laptop.'

'You used very personal information that only you had access to. Such betrayal!' Phillip inhales and exhales as he would climbing a very high peak in low oxygen. The smell shatters his rhythm. He unexpectedly half-smiles. 'I suppose you can be excused. How on earth did you get into the building? And break the coded data? Of course, it was a last-minute exercise. Ingenious of you. You must tell me the story.'

'Another time. What about Sonya?'

'The other missing girl? To be frank, I have no idea. No sign of her here.' His breathing is more ragged now.

'Up to us then,' Julia says, business-like. 'Let's get back to the man who shot you. It's urgent we locate him. Who is he?'

'I honestly can't tell you. Classic, never seen him before in my life. Try the data, he must be associated with Charters, you'd think. Jules, I'm too tired to move. If I could I would plead my best intentions. Too late to forgive, et cetera, I do understand, but at least I could state my case.'

'Save it, Phillip. I need a key to really mine the data.'

'Understand, but it's a very limited set – I am assuming you have access to the full emailed list? You have; all good, too late for it to be bad. We have respected individual privacy and sold discretion, obviously. Cash transactions preferred. We have an outlet – one of Challinor's minions tracked that down I gather – in the Cross. To date it has worked very well–' He stops, gently wipes his hand over the blood collecting on his shirt, skimming it like taking cream from milk. Holds the hand with its gelatinous red film up to his face, grimaces. 'All very unpleasant, this.'

'Phillip, you're not dying. In fact, you're rabbiting on.'

'I do that when I am hurt. You know that.'

Julia ignores his further attempt at the personal. 'The code. I have some details. How do I get the rest?'

Phillip closes his eyes. When he opens them there are tears. 'Our student game.'

'Ah. Scrabble. Letter values?'

'Yes. Plus two letter words with squares. Jules, there's not enough information in the list. I don't know what else to give you.'

Tom enters the room. 'Charters' friends? Associates? There's a ring, like a paedophile ring. Is Charters friends with Michael Bennett?'

'Tom. Tom, I had forgotten you. All right, back to the task at hand. Michael Bennett? I don't think so. Charters parades as some kind of military hero. Dubiously, in my estimation. Why Bennett? Because

Charters lives in the same building? That's hardly evidence. Bennett has nothing to do with all this.'

'Bennett's security was seen in Parramatta, hovering around your van. Best guess remains it was they who abducted the other young woman, Sonya.'

'Puzzling. I repeat; we have nothing to do with Bennett. At least, as far as I am aware.'

'Can you describe the man who shot you?'

'Big, broad, middle-aged, hefty. Charters is all tightness and precision. This man wore military camouflage, too. I noted very little else. He was trying to kill me, after all.'

'Voice, accent?'

'The voice as the essence of the soul, Tom? Your thing, I recall. Possibly you're right. Not much to go on, just a lot of yelling and a few sentences. Educated, not old school, I'd say. Has he killed Charters as well? That possibility occurs to me.'

'What did he say?'

'He was furious and not entirely coherent. Told me he thought *Helpmates* – that's the name of the business – was worse than a Thai paedophile ring. Ridiculous – as there he was, taking advantage of it!' Phillip peers at the blood on his hands. Sighs. 'He muttered a lot to himself. I half-heard it while he was disentangling that girl from her obscene hanging position. That absurd cross – how could anyone do such a thing? He was saying she might die if he didn't do something. I noted he seemed to think he *could* do something. All very chivalrous and possibly just another element of his madness. The problem being she was probably already dead.'

'Could he be a doctor?' Tom asks. 'We've come across a website–'

The sirens are closer. Phillip's attention is fading. 'I have no idea,' he mutters. 'I hate websites. I don't have anything to do with them.'

'What about partners in your enterprise, Phillip? Who is Gus Perkins?'

'Perkins! How–? You've done well in your delving. He's gone, out of the country. Recruiting in our group homes! I couldn't have that. I replaced him with a wealthier partner.' Slowly, Phillip's good arm rises to his face, pawing at the sweat running over his lips. 'I am not going to die,' he announces. 'I will need to depart. A long way away.'

'Phillip, I really don't know how it came to this. But the best you can do now is give us any names that might be helpful. Your partner?'

'Did you love me once?' Phillips asks.

'You know that. I loved you very much.'

A long sigh. 'Rupert Barton. He helps finance and sees himself as King Pin. Several of our customers are his friends and associates, I believe. He never uses the service.'

'Barton? The alternative medicine tycoon? The charity king. Left field, that. Or right, I should say. He has open allegiance to the right of the Liberal party.' Tom shakes his head. 'How much do you trust him?'

'Personally, not one iota. If you're intimating he is behind the disappearances, I suspect he is much too self-protective. These days he's in a wheelchair, too. Plenty of money to order others to do his handiwork, of course.' He contemplates mentioning the recent change in Barton's behaviour. He's too tired to bother. And why should he?

'Does Barton happen to be friendly with our Police Commissioner?'

'I think not the commissioner. Barton sails with the Minister on occasion. I do hear the Minister has some patsies high enough up in the force to protect his own interests and those of his pals. I can't see any of them stooping to common crime, though. They're all so expert at the uncommon variety, why would they bother?'

'The man held for the incident in Parramatta Park was a stooge, was he not?'

'Yes, Tom, he was. However, not mine and I am unsure of the current relevance.' Phillip lifts his uninjured arm in a gesture of dismissal. 'The ambulance is nearly here. You two, I do not want to be your salvation. Those girls are a different story – to help find them, I am willing to pretend you have not been here. The police will be too distracted by what is here. I do not find myself able to walk to the kitchen. Tell me how that boy is. I will communicate with the paramedics.'

Julia regards her husband. A sad thing, wasted, diminished, hurt. 'Phillip, I really don't know how it came to this. But thank you at least for that.'

Phillips sighs. 'Go. No blessing.' And then he's had enough of these do-gooders. And enough of himself. 'Fuck you, fuck you, fuck you, fuck the pair of you. Fuck off out of my fucked, fucked life. Just fucking fuck off and find those girls.'

59

The drop in temperature indicates it is quickly getting dark. Tom pulls his coat closer around him. They climb into the rental car.

'Let's wait for the ambulance to turn up,' Julia says. 'Just to be sure.'

'Agreed.'

The pungent scent of burning eucalyptus unexpectedly invades the car. 'Someone's started a fire. I'm at least partially pleased that poor kid is no longer conscious. The smell of more burning would be agony.'

Two ambulances finally swagger into the street, their bright lights lending the quiet backwater a carnivalesque air. The first driver locates the house, the paramedics jump out, one half-stumbles over a tree root. Another calls out, reminding his colleague to go to the back of the house. They stride down the driveway, big bags in hand. Julia lets a long breath out. 'Thank someone who is not God, they're on their way in now. We can leave.'

The sound of the hire car engine is already familiar. 'We'll drive a couple of streets, find a place to unobtrusively park. We have more names, an idea of the key to the code.' Julia pauses, changes tone. 'Has Warren got back to you?'

'He will. He's reliable. But Julia, how reliable is Phillip? Could he have planted confounding information in that data, for example? I'm not saying he predicted you getting hold of his laptop and the email. More that he might have played around so that the police would not get to the centre. That might prevent us from identifying the real culprit.'

Julia slows for a particularly nasty speed hump. This is a wealthy area that likes its traffic to be calm and quiet. 'I don't think so,' she says slowly. 'He wanted to find Avril and Sonya, be their knight in shining armour. He couldn't afford to confuse himself.'

She pulls up under the deep shade of two overgrown Moreton Bay figs. Tom speaks with Warren. Julia checks the surrounds. No interest being shown in them.

'The plot thickens,' Tom says. 'Stephen Charters is Michael Bennett's half-brother.'

'Well, we knew there was a group. Blood beats water if you want loyalty.' Julia drums her fingers on the steering wheel. 'I need a photo of Charters. Military hero, Phillip said. The internet may supply us with a press photo, something ceremonial.' She pulls out her phone, googles his name. And there it is. There he is. The man she watched walk into a house two doors down from number 5, where they'd found Phillip.

'We're going back to Elm St. This time to number 9.' Julia hurtles into a U-turn.

Minutes later Julia walks with seeming purpose – but with extreme caution – along the driveway of the house two doors down from where the paramedics, police and, by now, neighbours are busily collected. Tom remains at the driveway entrance, out of public view, phone in hand. The house, smaller than its near neighbour, appears unoccupied. Julia reports a dismantled "For Sale" sign half obliterated by a transverse "Sold' sticker propped against the rear wall, suggesting this is likely the case.

If only they had known an hour – was it really only an hour? – ago that the man who drove into the cul-de-sac behind them and walked so confidently into this very tree-shaded yard was Stephen Charters.

Whether Charters is still inside remains a mystery. His car has gone but he may well have moved it out of sight. From his public war record it's evident he's practised at clandestine operations. He can keep out of sight, and out of harm's way. While at the same time being ready – and very much able – to attack his enemy.

A sudden beam of light catches her. Julia moves swiftly into a shadowed area. Her eyes scan. The sharp light slices through the trees. She waits. No flicker or shake. The source is hidden but she assumes it's a motion-sensitive outdoor light, over a door or patio obscured by foliage. Julia ducks below a darkened window.

Julia enters the rear garden. Lurking in the oncoming dark are piles of old furniture, garden implements, broken suitcases, the detritus of lives. The sale was probably a deceased estate. This gives her some hope. If neither the inheritors of the estate or the agents for the sale took the trouble to clear the garden, they may not have bothered either with fully securing the house.

The house is sixty, seventy years old. Its sash windows have no sign of window locks. Julia carefully tries the kitchen windows, those of the small eating area, the laundry. None give. Above her is a dormer, cut into the roof. It's difficult to see clearly in the dimming light but it appears partly broken. Like Phillip, she has rock climbing skills. She can scale the uneven wall, can lever herself over the gutter, get a grip on the tile roof, drag herself up and through the broken dormer window.

She does it. Her triumph is mild.

Inside, several candles are lit. A halo of light around a figure – anyone could be in the darkness beyond that?

She drops in as gently as she can.

No sound.

She waits.

The young woman is curled up under a brilliant-white doona. Only one arm, a sliver of the side of a face and mass of long dark hair are visible. There is no movement, either from her or from the reaches of darkness around.

Julia swallows, remembering horror. A child standing so near, waiting patiently for food rations. Her face, head, arms, chest shattered suddenly by shrapnel that should better have ricocheted toward Julia. The bloodied body carried carefully home. Keening women, furiously smoking men. Why does that scene, when the unfathomable entrenched hatred of one "tribe" against another became reality to her, come to mind now? The sense that humans are all too ready to perpetuate, and enjoy, the pain of others?

Then – fuck whoever is watching – she kneels beside the woman, slowly lifting the extended arm. It is warm. There is a pulse; there is hope.

'She's here and alive,' she whispers into her phone. 'Probably drugged.'

The girl stirs, her eyes opening wide, abandoned to fear. Julia reaches for her. She bites.

'I'm not here to hurt you.' Julia holds her wounded hand – nothing in the scheme of things – behind her: the blood might frighten. The girl's eyes close again. Julia gently shakes her. 'I need you to wake, Sonya – you are Sonya? – we must get away now. I am here with a friend to help. Your kidnapper might come back.' Julia watches Sonya's eyelids raise and lower, raise and lower, her mouth in a small, unwilling grimace. 'Are you able to move?'

Another set of sirens splinters the suburban air. Sonya sits up, turns, measures Julia with narrowed eyes. Deciding, she pushes herself to a stand, the muscles of her single arm strong, her legs visibly wobbling, her face set. Fortunately she is clothed and young enough that any traces of trauma are invisible. Sonya will not attract the neighbours' attention as they leave.

'We must find Avril,' she announces, as if she's merely been waiting for Julia and Tom to provide the opportunity to enact this very purpose.

'I think we should get you to a hospital.'

'No way. I am finding Avril.'

Julia grins, forgetting for a moment that the killer could be somewhere in the house they now have to leave, that beyond the house lie incalculable dangers. Particularly for Sonya. Forgetting also that it is likely Avril is already dead. 'I'm Julia. Let's go meet Tom and then we'll be on our way to find Avril. When we are sure we can get out of here alive and well. Is there anyone in this house?'

'Stephen?' Sonya shrugs. 'He is gone.'

'Where?'

Another shrug. Is this a good enough response? What does Sonya really know?

Julia grabs a couple of the water bottles stacked on a shelf beside the bed. She checks the seals. They're intact. 'Drink this, Sonya, it'll help. Then we'll check the house and simply walk out, heads high. Tom will meet us at the end of the drive. My car is parked just into the next street because the police are here – two houses down. I'll explain that when we're safe. We'll pretend to be a family, being nosey about the old house we're in now – so we'll leave via the back as if we've only been in the garden.'

Julia is already confident Sonya will understand and follow the directions. Their passage through the house, though, could be dangerous.

Charters may have feigned his departure, he may have helpers stationed downstairs. Julia draws in oxygen, takes Sonya's hand. They grip. Time to go, there are few other choices: they must leave.

60

THE POLICE CAR SLEWS AROUND THE CORNER, OVERCORRECTING AND shaving close to them. Julia waits, imitating a model citizen. The driver rights their car, takes the final few metres to Elm street. Julia starts the hire car: 'How many police do they need for heaven's sake? Didn't we just walk past two cars already? Anyway, where to now?' she says.

'Back around the block. We've got to talk.'

'No, we must go to Avril now!' Sonya insists.

Julia pulls onto the road. Tom explains the situation quietly to Sonya. The last thing they need is her resisting. 'Sonya, it's possible you have information that will help us pinpoint where Avril is. We can't rescue her without this.'

They return to the quiet position deep under the giant fig trees. Speaking quickly, Sonya recalls all she can of the past twenty-four hours. The man she knows only as Stephen is indeed the man who abducted her. Yes, he is the same one who frightened her so badly in the apartment in Darling Harbour. He wasn't intending to kill her, she's certain. He wanted to keep her for himself alone, secreted away forever. He wanted her because he thought she was Muslim, because she was part of the war.

'He has illness,' Sonya says. 'Illness is bad excuse, not good. Many people in war, they do not hurt other people after.'

'Was he holding Avril as well?'

'I do not see her.'

'Did you hear her, think she might be close by?'

'Last night, after Stephen get me, there was problem. I am – woozy, is that word? Stephen leave me in car and go into house. I think house where police go now. Where you say Avril is then. He come out very angry.'

'Of course. That's Charter's house – number 5, where Avril was. Charters had set it up for you, not Avril. At least that makes sense now. I don't know how the mix-up happened, or who is responsible. But Avril was taken to number 5, and Charters had to take you elsewhere. He'd have known number 9 was vacant.' Tom hasn't told Sonya the details of the cross. Too much information for now.

'So, there was no one else in number 9, where Charters took you?' Julia wants to keep to the salient points for now. The whys and wherefores will matter later.

No, I think he break in. The house, it is cold and very quiet. It smell of old people. I only see Stephen and the doctor.'

Tom's voice takes on a sharper edge. 'The doctor. Can you describe him Sonya? Did you hear his name?'

'I think I see him in lift at Stephen's building. He wear army trousers. Stephen call him "Doctor". He give me injection. I sleep a lot and do not remember everything.'

'We have the man from number 5, I think, the man who attacked Phillip,' Julia says to Tom. 'He seems to have a good supply of anaesthetics.'

'Indeed. Sonya, I am going to say some names. Stop me if one of them sounds right for the doctor who drugged you.'

Beginning with Anderson, followed by Walenski, Tom runs through a series of names that come to mind, carefully giving each the same emphasis. Julia controls a "gottya" moment when Sonya stops him at "Doctor Johnson."

'Yes, Johnson is name I hear Stephen say,' she says.

'Can you think of any more detail of what he looks like – from the lift perhaps?' Tom asks.

'I try.' Sonya taps fingers against the car seat, clearly trying to conjure the memory. Her description is reasonably generic: middle aged, tall, heavy-set, but all elements match Phillip's description of Avril's abductor and with what Tom knows of the physical presence of Clif Johnson, mild-mannered psychiatrist.

'So, the dolls, the abductions, above all the perpetrators, are all related.

I think we have our destination,' Tom says, keeping the excitement from his voice.

'The surgery of Dr Johnson, perhaps?'

'Avril needs treatment, it's not his home and, if I remember rightly, he works with at least one GP. There'll be medical supplies a psychiatrist wouldn't ordinarily have.'

'Warren?' Julia questions.

'Good idea. If you find Johnson's practice address, I'll get Warren to meet us there. They must have let him go by now.' Tom calls Warren's number. 'Clif Johnson's had years working with people with disability. How many has he abused?' he asks as he waits for Warren to pick up.

Julia googles Dr Clif Johnson, dictates the address of his surgery into her phone app. Checks the time estimate. 'Twenty-seven minutes, going over Ryde Bridge,' she says.

'Why so long?' Sonya asks, annoyed. 'The stupid traffic,' she answers her own question. She's recovering now she is hydrated and they are on the way to find her friend. 'Mr Stephen is very confuse, muddle. Like he keeps change his mind. Did he meet doctor at his work?' she adds a minute or two later.

'Professionally, you mean? Stephen Charters saw Johnson as a psychiatrist? That's excellent logic, Sonya.' Julia responds.

Tom finishes his call. 'Warren's finally free and on his way.' He pushes back in his seat. His long legs are cramped in the hire car. 'I wouldn't have put Johnson down as willing or able to handle a gun.'

'Perhaps he isn't, until cornered,' replies Julia.

'I can go with that. Why army fatigues? Why a sudden descent into extreme behaviour? What made him flip?'

'Are you sure we shouldn't bring the police in? The man is dangerous.'

Very dangerous, Tom privately agrees. Especially now when his — their? — careful schemes have gone awry. Thus, any predictability is lost. He might want to treat and save Avril medically but if the police scream in and he's about to be captured, he's unlikely to honour his Hippocratic oath. Wiping out a witness who knew too much would be, to most active criminals, common sense. That is, if she is still alive. This is not the time for cavalry.

'The problems are time and a mole in the police,' he says mildly and, he hopes, convincingly. 'We know that Barton — one of the main men behind the agency, Sonya – we know he is connected with the Police Minister. On a lighter note, Warren just informed me Barton is rumoured to have had an affair with the deputy police commissioner.'

Good heavens, Tanya Yenick? Isn't she gay?'

'Bi, apparently. Warren's sources are impeccable.'

'How times change. What else did Warren say?'

'That there was at least one unnecessary detective in and out of the interviews with him. A man who is most likely Clare's police contact, Kurt. Warren is going to warn her.'

They reach the Ryde Bridge. Julia continues to dodge and weave through the mess of early evening congestion, Sonya making sounds of approval each time they overtake. 'Not far now. We'd better discuss tactics.'

'To save Avril?' Sonya asks.

'Yes. We will find her.'

'Dead or alive. That is what they say in the movies.'

'Only about the bad guys. Avril's a good guy.'

'Yes, Avril has Australian guts.'

61

THE VENETIAN BLINDS ARE SHUTTERED, STREAKS OF LOW LIGHT BETWEEN the cracks. A car is in the driveway, parked askew, rear door flung open.

'They must have got here forty minutes ahead of us. That skew-whiff car and open door suggest they're still inside, possibly not sure what to do next,' Julia says.

'That is good. Good that he have no plan.'

'Probably,' Julia is ambivalent. She quickly describes the residence turned medical centre, the dour streetscape, the small warehouses among dilapidated homes. 'Odd place to have consulting rooms. I suppose the closeness to Concord Hospital explains it. It feels desolate though.'

'Advantage or disadvantage? For us.'

'Hard to say. Avoiding interfering neighbours is probably a benefit. In suburbia, most people would come out to defend their local doctor.'

'Our aim is singular,' Tom summarises. 'We're getting Avril out, safely. Capturing Johnson, or Charters, if he is here too, is not the priority.'

In the rear-view mirror, Sonya is grim-mouthed, the shade of herself at 80 across her face. 'That is good too. We keep alive.'

Warren's shadowy figure emerges from behind a nearby building. He slides into the car. 'What's the plan, Boss?' Then he grins at Sonya. 'Sorry I couldn't save you last night, but I'm a goodie, honest.'

Sonya smiles back. 'Is ok.'

'Are you armed?'

'Yeah, and legally at that.'

'Makes all the difference.'

'If I have to use it, it does.'

'Point. Have you had a chance to inspect the rear of the surgery?'

'Yeah, usual residential entrance and exits. Like going to visit your grannie. High fences too. Reckon he hasn't a hope of escaping that way.'

'Rest of the street?'

'Yep.'

'Excellent. Both Julia and Sonya have far more experience than either you or I in battle zones, including hostage situations. We're taking their lead. They need to know what you've seen.'

Warren wants to ask – can we trust this woman? Completely? But she's already asking questions, outlining the plan. And she probably prefers to save young women from dying, no matter what other allegiances she might have. 'As you know, our theory is he's come to the surgery to save Avril – a mercy dash that clearly wasn't on the original agenda. He's worried and won't have had time to consider or deal with contingencies.'

'What's his next move? He's got a gun, hasn't he?'

'He has. So, our plan is straightforward.'

Five minutes later, they are each in their respective positions.

Julia approaches the surgery door. She studies the nameplates, posing as desperate for a phone number. In fact, there are two Johnsons, a psychiatrist and a GP. No time to worry about that. She knocks loudly. No response. She calls out. Repeats her performance, making as much noise as possible.

Finally, the door is wrenched open. He's tall, wild-eyed, his stubble greying, sharp. 'What the hell do you want?'

'Doctor! I need a doctor.'

'Hospital's that way.' His body blocks the doorway, he gestures behind him.

'My son – that house, over there, we've just moved in, you have to come.'

'Lady, take him to the hospital. I'm no use to you.'

'I don't drive, I can't move him, I'm so scared he'll die. The ambulance hasn't come. Please, you must help.'

He remains rooted to the spot, confused now. Does he remember his oath, his early ideals of saving people? Children especially. 'Bandages,' she says, making to push past him, trying to enter. He blocks her, grabbing her arm roughly and, leaving the doorway unguarded, walks her off the verandah, down the path and away from the surgery. Julia smiles inwardly while continuing to outwardly wheedle and cry and threaten to scream. Insistently, she pulls at his arm, pointing to her purported house, keeping his attention forward and as far from the surgery as possible.

Warren, with a swift leap, is into the building. There is not much time.

In the darkened car, parked under one of the few spreading trees in the street, Sonya gasps for air. Holds it in. Her remaining hand clenches, her brain prompts her absent hand to mimic what it could once do. Both hands squeeze out the blood that gives fear its life. Sonya unclenches her remaining and imagined hands, letting small streams of fear fall, and reaches for the car door. She wants to slam open the door, push all obstacles aside, pull Avril free of this evil. She must wait. She is in charge of the signal. Her word has been given; she must be very alert.

She sits high in the car seat, watching. Julia's borrowed scarf shelters her hair and drapes over the severed arm. Obliquely she notes the fabric of the scarf is soft, warm, comforting. Her heart stutters as she watches Julia pleading, arguing, haggling with the large man. The darkness is encroaching, details are becoming hard to glean. They have set up for two options, each with its own possibilities and consequences. Each with its risks and dangers.

The phone in her hand is active. Now Tom is in place, her job is to speak into it at the exact moment. Not before. Sonya's remaining hand clenches, harder this time. In this moment she admits to herself that her friend may well be dead.

Tom settles in a position that is not at all comfortable. They parked diagonally across from the surgery, outside one of the few houses in the street. Warren's reconnoitre had suggested the house could be unoccupied and was surrounded by warehouses. As far as Tom can tell, no one saw him slip out of the car and walk, carefully directed by Sonya over the phone, into the yard and fold himself down near the gate and behind the fence. His is the only muscle available, and muscle they will need.

He crouches in readiness as Julia's voice comes closer, her volume increasing. The tension in his body intensifies. Can he do this? Tom swears to himself. Has he given Julia an exaggerated sense of his prowess? Has he fallen into the chest-puffing that men do when they are "courting"? He'd laugh at himself if it weren't so potentially serious a mistake.

'You're letting him die,' he hears Julia declare. 'You are a doctor and you are letting him die.'

Tom feels mild but troubled satisfaction. Julia is bringing Johnson nearer, appealing to his inner sense of self, his good self. The problem is the man may have long lost touch with that ethical self.

The sound of a blow. A furious whack of hand against flesh. Johnson must have slapped Julia on the face. No! Fuck. Fuck, fuck, fuck. Tom catapults into hating his blindness, its terrible, inescapable physical constraints. All he wants is to spring to her aid. His whole body reverberates with horror and need.

'How dare you!' Julia is outraged.

A second of silence. Has Johnson shocked himself in hitting her? The sense of ineptness increases for Tom – Johnson is losing control and there's nothing he can do to intervene.

A second, less, later, there's movement, a scrape of shoes against bitumen. They are closer now, moving faster. Julia is managing fine without him. He just needs to be ready to play his specific part. He deep breathes, telling himself firmly he can do this, he can.

Julia is near enough he can hear her breathing now. She's bringing Johnson with her. Option 1 is underway.

62

THE PHONE IS SLIPPERY IN HER HAND. SWEAT, SO MUCH OF IT, DESPITE THE insistent cold. Sonya lifts the phone. Her timing must be perfect. Julia is half-running, no longer talking, Johnson is following. No way he is a lamb but Sonya hopes he is going to slaughter.

Her eyes bore through the glass. If Sonya's image were captured at this moment, she could be a lost child, a deserted wife, a suicide bomber. She reminds herself she is doing a good thing. She thinks that the line between good and bad is as tiny as an ant crawling over a grain of sand. Or it is as wide a river, a sea, an ocean, a galaxy. The man is being drawn closer and closer to the house. Julia is nearly at the gate. There are no lights in the stranger's house towards which they are heading. That is good. Also, there is no movement in the street. Another good.

Warren is still inside the surgery, forty metres or more away and that is more worrying. Why isn't he carrying Avril out, racing to the car, ordering an ambulance? It is as if they are in a movie projected at the wrong speed. It is slowed down, its soundtrack distorted, its narrative lost. Sonya's heart heaves.

The squeal of metal; Julia is opening the ageing gate of the designated house – no lights yet. Julia calls, 'Help!'

Sonya speaks 'go' into the phone that has Tom at the other end.

Julia grabs at Johnson. Tom erupts from behind the fence, behind Johnson. Julia bars Johnson's forward path. He's trapped between them. It's all happening so quickly. Sonya's heart pounds. Tom swiftly throws the force of his body at the confused doctor. The large man is knocked to the ground. Tom follows. Sonya hears the crunch of bone on concrete.

So perfect. So far. Except if, even if, Tom is hurt.

Johnson is howling, a scream almost primal. Sonya scans the street. If a person comes out, she will jump in their path, explain. Apart from the scream, all is quiet. Tom rights himself, holding all the time onto Johnson, finding and pulling one of his arms behind his back. Johnson's other arm is still free and he is trying to grab, to hit, to escape in any way he can. Sonya watches Julia stamp on the free arm, hold it in place, the effort needed to keep the enraged man down evident even from this distance. Johnson screams again; pain and rage mingled.

Sonya presses 000.

'Which service do you want?'

'Police, ambulance, both.'

'Can you please locate yourself…?'

She responds efficiently, running through the script they briefly practised, finally grinning when he says: 'Putting you through.'

Sonya explains the urgency as best she can. She watches Julia and Tom work together to secure Doctor Johnson's arms with the cables Warren had in his toolkit. Strong cables, made for holding heavy furniture. Then, with some difficulty, they bind his kicking feet. The ambulance and police are coming, but where is Avril? And Warren?

63

Warren walks toward Tom and Julia, a photograph in his hand. 'Take a gander.' He hands the photo to Julia. 'Found it hanging in Clif's room.'

'There's two of them.' She turns to Tom. 'Identical twins. Clifton and Adam, it says on the back. Dr and Dr Johnson I presume.'

The Dr Johnson they have tied and are holding lets out a deep grumble. Fear? Pain? Anger? Hard to say. 'You're Adam,' Tom addresses him firmly. 'Clif is in intensive care.'

'What's it to you?'

Seconds later, the combined silence of Julia, Tom and Warren opens a floodgate. Anger and hatred spew as Johnson scatterguns violent expletives into their ears and minds. Warren figures adrenalin or drugs or both are helping him stay puffed up, a huge, hefty balloon of self-belief.

'Jane is very distressed by your stalking,' Tom says.

The mildness of the response evidently takes Johnson unawares. 'For God's sake, those dolls were little more than a joke. A bit of voodoo. If she'd bothered to get to know me properly Jane'd've got it that I'd always liked that kind of stuff. I tried it out when I was a kid – scared this dumb chick who wanted to beat me at maths with Barbie dolls I nicked from a kid across the road. I speared them with nappy pins from our stupid little sister who was born with massive congenital abnormalities. She was near enough dead then. Revolting she was.'

Is this Clif's childhood trauma explanation, a dying sister? Hardly sufficient causation for Adam's violence. Particularly if he'd found his disabled sister loathsome rather than sad. 'Did Clif follow your lead?'

'He's way too fucking pathetic. He's the good boy.'

'He used *Helpmates*?'

'You're fucking kidding me? Clif? He's a moralistic old biddy. Got himself all worked up when *Helpmates* made me get the shits with Jane. For God's sake any normal red-blooded man'd get irritated with her pathos. Clif calls me an amaurophiliac, says I'm fixated with blindness. I proved him wrong with the women I hired. Plenty of diversity there. He hated that.'

Warren sighs, looks over his shoulder. An ambulance is swinging into the street, followed by another. About bloody time. He half-listens to Johnson who's impossible, even for Tom, to keep on any track other than his own. Which seems to constantly reorientate itself to his hatred of his brother. He's complaining now that Clif couldn't see he had masses of empathy, couldn't see he thrived on looking after the weak. He'd joined the forces, gone to war-torn regions, treated children, children! with bodies half blown apart. That was empathy wasn't it? Clif was pathetic, Adam claimed, bleating about loving his, Adam's, partner Jane, really loving her for herself. Men profess love, Adam claimed, only when they want something, or are afraid of their own lust. Clif might have got to the level of medical specialist and him only a lowly military general practitioner, but the army would have done Clif a deal of good, knocked some discipline into him. And so on. Evidently the man had got lost in some time-warp, some fight to the death between two small beings in a womb. A fight he thought he should have survived while the other one died.

'Why did you tell Jane you were a computer technician?' Julia asks, breaking into the diatribe.

Johnson snorts. 'Wouldn't you? You women always want our money. The less she thought I had the better. I could pretend I got erratic work, sometimes in the regions. That gave me good reason to sleep elsewhere some nights.'

'Why didn't Clif unmask you?'

'To Jane? Mate, we're identical twins. We don't do that sort of thing. Honour among thieves.'

'Leave you to it,' Warren says, snorting in disgust as he walks back toward the car and approaching ambulances.

Tom continues with the questioning, keeping his sense of horror internal. 'Expert or not, we gather you knew enough to install a surveillance app on Jane's phone, locate the refuge and terrorise twenty or more women and children'

'I was disgusted with Jane's behaviour. I had every right to let her know,' is Johnson's only comment.

'And you set up the disabilitymed.com.au website?'

'What's wrong with that? The disabled can have their own medical speciality, and interest, can't they?'

'Indeed, but not if it's used to exploit individuals or groups. As a cover for devotee pornography, for example.'

'Huh!' is Johnson's only response.

'And you lured your twin brother to Ashfield and tried to kill him. So that he would conveniently be blamed for the fearful campaign you'd waged? What happened to that honour among thieves?'

'Anything that happened to Clif is on him. He's a complete fucking idiot.'

'You injected him – with what?' Tom persists.

Julia is recording this. She told Adam, as she should, and it seems he remembers. 'Clif deserves anything he got,' is all he says, carefully not admitting anything.

'Avril? Why kidnap her? And Melanie? And why vent your anger so excessively on that boy, Zac?' Julia demands.

'Stupid man. He brought the wrong girl the first time, some rubbish about them swapping times. The one in the wheelchair, he brought her into the park, straight up to me….'

'She'd seen too much?'

Adam looks away. They now have him propped up against the brick fence. For his safety, to avoid accusations of assault and to better observe his responses. Seconds later he lets out an arrogant snort. 'And it wasn't as if I wanted her. Or the other one, that dwarf girl. I'm not interested in dwarfs. Despite recoiling from her very existence, I brought her here, didn't I? I saved her.'

'Whoa,' Julia says. 'You instigated the kidnap of a young woman, two women – what? On behalf of someone else? What were you planning on getting out of that?'

Johnson's head snaps up, he regroups: 'Clif calls me a psychopath!' he declares, deftly deflecting the questions. 'He bought the medical practice in this dire place so he could keep me under his wing. Waste of fucking time. Arsehole idiot.'

Thirty metres away, the ambulance pulls up, paramedics bound out. Circus performers might envy their exit style, Warren thinks as he opens the car to the two young women. Avril's face remains pale and sweaty but her breathing is regular.

'Avril, drink again,' Sonya is saying, as she lifts her friend's head to one of the bottles of water Warren had left with her.

As Warren bends toward them, Avril's eyes open, begin to focus. 'Where. The hell. Are we. Sonnie?'

Warren grins.

'The ambulance is come. We are safe,' Sonya replies.

'You need any help?' Warren asks. By now he recognises Sonnie's not likely to need him to help her explain, but he wants to make sure they're sent off properly. And he wants to know exactly where they're being taken. The coppers'll consider them all witnesses, if not protagonists, and could try to keep them all separate. Thinking of which, where are the cops? Talk about a wet week of Sundays.

64

'FRICKING HOSPITALS, THEY SMELL DISGUSTING. I SPENT HALF MY LIFE IN them when I was a kid,' Avril says.

Sonnie, on the bed next to her in a small, tucked away Emergency room, nods, even though finally getting hospital treatment when her family made it to Australia was a blessing for her. 'Avril, we have problem, big problem,' she whispers. 'We must talk now, quick, before they take us to separate places.'

'The fun never stops round here! Don't worry, it'll be ages. We haven't even seen a nurse in yonks and that pissy guard has gone for a cuppa too. Least they believed us about the kidnap, hey? Anyhow, spill the beans, as my dad says. Oh, shit, what's gonna happen when our oldies find out?'

'The shit will hit fan,' Sonnie says, suddenly smiling.

'Good one, Son. Hope that takes as long as sorting out our health.' She pulls the cotton blanket up over her chest. That freako doctor who'd dragged her off the cross had helped her, but she feels pretty rubbish. 'So, what's this gigantic problem, hey?'

Sonya's eyes swivel around the small area. Her ears attend to sounds nearby, and further afield. Trolleys are being wheeled, people are moaning, questions are being asked. Is any of it threatening? She breathes in and out as quietly as she can, and decides no, they are relatively safe. Here. And for the moment.

'The man, the man we see in the city. I remember now, all drugs have gone. He was with Mr Stephen.'

'What'd you mean? That well-dressed guy? The one in a wheelchair?

He couldn't've got up loads of stairs, could he? Weren't you kept upstairs in that derelict house?'

'He walk up stairs.'

'Come on, Sonnie, he's like, mobility impaired.'

Sonya shakes her head emphatically. 'He walk. He pretend he need chair.'

'WTF! Whoa, that's totally creepy.'

'Yes.' Her left arm tries to cradle her face. But the arm is not there. When she is upset or annoyed – and she's both now – the perception of her loss is erased from both her body and mind. 'I wish I have telled Miss Julia. Or Mr Tom. But I only remember Stephen and the doctor before.'

'Don't worry, Son. We'll work it out.'

Sonya is sceptical. Stephen kidnapped her and he is hiding somewhere. The police will take many hours to begin searching for him; he could come to find her here in the hospital. This would be ordinary behaviour, she thinks – she and her family have been the hunted before. At the same time, she recognises Stephen didn't want to hurt her. He was horrible and terrorising and what he did makes the pain in her heart escape like broken glass to cut her sanity. But the well-dressed man was more evil. He took Stephen into a dark corner and made him afraid. That man is the one with power.

'Let's start with what he said to that Stephen creep.'

The memory is blurred at the edges. Sonya squeezes her eyes, hoping for clarity. 'He tell Stephen it is too late, the doctor man made mistake. Stephen, he try to change his mind, I think.'

'I get it. Kinda anyhow. Like, remember you said Melanie'd swapped shifts with me and maybe I was the one the kidnapper was really after that first time?'

'Yes, I remember.'

'So, it was the same shift and hotel and stuff yesterday as last Friday. Zac probably took Melanie to the park last Friday and that doctor guy came to pick her up and pushed her under water 'cause she wasn't me, hey? They got me a week later, 'cause that's when Zac was on shift. Maybe that well-dressed bloke was pissed having to wait a week.' Avril breaks off, shivering. Before Sonya can ask her what is wrong, Avril calls softly to her. 'I saw him too.'

'Avril! In the other house?'

'No. Outside Parramatta Mall. He's the guy with the eye-patch, you remember? He's the one pretended to fall over and I had to go and look after him 'cause those Muslim ladies wouldn't touch him. Couldn't touch him, I guess. Really likes pretending, that a-hole.'

'So he is big boss. True. And he is man with bad ideas, bad wants. I get it now. He organise them to kidnap us.' Sonya stops, holds up her one hand to tell Avril to wait. 'No, I think Stephen, he want to keep me. The man who kidnap you – he have his strings pulled. The pretender man is string puller. He–'

A nurse sticks her head in between the curtains that surround their cubicle, silencing Sonya. 'Be back in a minute, gotta check that drip of yours,' the nurse says, airily waving at Avril.

'It's working awright,' Avril calls to her retreating back. She's not totally convinced it is. She's not getting better real fast, but they don't need the nurse to return in a hurry.

Avril turns to Sonya, wishing their beds were closer. Sonnie's not real sick but the drugs they stuffed into her are making her body slow and weak. And what Sonnie is saying means they both need to be super strong right now. 'And, nobody knows about this guy. He's, what you call it, clandestine, real clandestine. He could turn up here and pretend to be one of our dads or our granddads or whatever and who'd stop him?'

'We need phone.'

'Those kidnapping bastards got away with all our stuff. I'd like to sue them. We're not gonna get new phones in here.'

'I have number for Mr Warren,' Sonya offers.

'Cool bananas. That's a start.' Avril purses her lips, bites down on her lower one, thinking. 'Hey, do you reckon we should tell that young cop? He's meant to be protecting us. We could give him pointers to what the boss guy looks like.' Her face brightens further. 'Anyhow they'll have to interview us properly real soon. There'll be heaps of police here, hey.' Her confidence is returning, Avril grins. 'Yeah, Sonnie, we'll be good.'

Sonya's long lashes come down over her eyes, secreting her emotions. She does her best to smile. What she hasn't said is that she has seen the face of the Boss-pretender. Seen it clearly. One of the candles that surrounded her had flickered high, he was illuminated. Their eyes had met and held for several seconds before he withdrew into the shadows.

In the cloak of darkness, his anger had been sharp: 'Give her another dose, quickly. The agreement was the girls would have no memory of any of us. If you break that agreement, you will lose her. Do you understand?'

Stephen had whimpered but the doctor-man had assured the man she could not possibly remember anything. Lying in the hospital bed, Sonya is sure the Boss-pretender will not risk her identifying him. Throughout her childhood, still now all across the world, women and men 'disappeared' to prevent them identifying those who abused them, or who abused their loved ones, or just other people in the street or neighbourhood.

None of this does Sonya now say to Avril. Avril has nearly died – all the nurses have agreed on this – she has had enough alarm for one day.

65

Caroline Zammitt opens the door. 'Tom, come in, we were hoping you'd turn up.'

Warren goes to step forward, to put his weary body between Tom and this sharp-faced woman in a wheelchair. Both the body driving it and the chair look designed for speed and agility. An attack is not out of contention.

'Caroline, a surprise.' Tom blocks Warren's move, speaks in his usual give-nothing-away urbane manner. 'I'd like you to meet Julia Prettie and Warren Hume. May we come in? Is Michael here?'

'Of course, follow me.' Over her shoulder she merely nods to Tom's companions.

Julia takes Tom's arm and they stride forward. Warren follows, eyes protectively swivelling, although the foyer is wide enough they could all walk abreast. The two immense Aboriginal art works are well known. Sell them and they could all just about retire on the proceeds. 'Pity the artists don't get a decent share of the market value,' Warren mutters under his breath, just before he clocks Big Ray, all bulk and silence, inside the immense living room. Which has a view to die for. And that is often what happens when you enter the lions' den – you die.

Michael Bennett is pouring himself a whisky. Tom hears his hand tremor in the sibilant ringing of crystal against crystal. Bennett is nervous – or angry.

'Michael, it's been a while,' Julia says, walking with Tom directly up to Bennett.

'My goodness, Julia Prettie. Well, this is an unexpected pleasure.'

'I wouldn't quite say pleasure,' she counters.

More subtle clinking of crystal. 'Perhaps not. Difficult times, difficult times indeed.'

'Didn't know you two were so well acquainted,' Warren puts in, having decided to ignore Big Ray. Ditto that Caroline woman who could be an S & M madam the way she's dressed.

Bennett disregards Warren's comment. 'Whisky,' he offers.

'Thanks. More importantly, we must get down to business.'

'Correct, Challinor, correct. Caroline here is representing me, or more precisely my brother. I presume it is he you are interested in. As am I.' Bennett gestures them to opulent lounges while he pours the drinks. Outside myriad city lights dance in the wind-pummelled air.

Warren sits on the edge of a chair. Has that Julia woman led them into a trap? She's pally with Bennett and it was her convinced Tom to come here, tackle Bennett, track down Charters, the minute they were out of the police station. The coppers'd kept them for hours. Despite plenty of evidence of the need to make a citizen's arrest of Adam Johnson. Grilled each of them in separate rooms, threatened them with charges of assault, withholding liberty, you name it, leaving them in the rank rooms alone to twiddle thumbs, coming back with photos of Johnson with cable-tied hands, that sort of thing. How could he or Tom know what truths Julia'd told or kept hidden?

Warren watches Bennett hand out drinks. Julia sips. His inclination is that she's on the level. But his inclination is the same as everyone's – sometimes swayed, induced or manipulated. Or just plain wrong. And that feels real relevant now they're behaving like bloody after-dinner guests in the home of the potential instigator of the abductions. Soon as they were out of the cop-shop she declared she'd "been thinking". Whoopee, Warren'd thought. Thing was she was right; the second car out the hotel carpark last night – about when Sonya jumped into his own car – well, it was the one Charters drove to Elm St. Julia'd taken a pic. Basic theory that got them into this room was that Charters waited till Ray and his mates left, having either clocked Sonya hiding or just struck it real lucky and seen her jump at Warren. His covert tactics training kicked in. He followed, bided his time till Sonya and Warren were out of the car and vulnerable, attacked from behind. It was dark by then and the place was hardly buzzing. Chucked Warren back into his own car, made off with Sonnie. While risky, it was clever and did not involve Ray. Julia'd argued Bennett had no way been in that picture, but he knew something. That something might just be knowing where Charters was. So here they were.

'Where the hell is your brother?' Warren demands, really getting down to business.

Bennett turns to Warren, dark crevices under his eyes. 'Ray is not guarding you or me. Behind him is a door, behind the door a hallway, at the end of the hallway, a room. Stephen is in that room. He will hand himself over to the police. Caroline is taking good care of all that. The condition is that – for his sake, and for mine too – that the architect of these abductions must first be identified and captured.'

'We are not suggesting physical capture,' Caroline addends. 'The instigator – who is not Stephen – must be placed in a position from which he cannot deny or escape responsibility. Stephen, you see, is suffering from post-traumatic stress disorder. This man, whose name he does not know, has been manipulating him.'

'A defence that is likely to fly. Particularly with Michael's money to power it.' Tom rises to stand. 'However, it is not in our remit or interest to help you make it. We're here because two young women – and possibly more – remain in danger, even if the police won't admit it. You're correct, the "architect" must be found. For their sakes, not yours or your brother's. We'll leave and get on with that now.'

Warren stands too. Julia, though, looks over the rim of her elegant whisky glass at Bennett. Who gives every appearance of a man at the end of his tether. 'Michael,' she prompts.

'Yes, thank you. Tom, please sit. We truly are on the same page, all wanting to find the source of this evil. The source other than your husband, Julia,' Bennett adds pointedly. 'I am offering you resources, Challinor. I am offering my own personal help. My motivation is to look after my brother. Our father was a violent, chauvinistic man. He sent Stephen into the defence force to make him "man up." I suspect Stephen is gay and has been shamed by our family into suppressing this even from himself. Lately his behaviour has become more erratic, more – how should I say? – hysterical, is probably a good word. He does not speak about it, but an event while he was on mission – something terrible happened.'

Caroline holds up a restraining hand. Bennett nods. 'Recently I found

Stephen had made modifications to his apartment. These worried me. He'd confessed his obsession with the escort agency some weeks ago. I brought Caroline in to help us learn more about its machinations, while Ray here has been monitoring Stephen's activities as best he can. Unfortunately, Stephen's reason is faltering badly. He is wily enough, practised enough to keeping dodging Ray and – he did what he did. He admits to kidnapping one girl. Whom he hoped, in his way, to make happy. He can tell you more.'

'Why then have you had us tailed? We're not the agency,' Tom asks, remaining standing. All this fits perfectly. As always the question then is, is it too perfect?

Bennett sniggers mildly. 'There's a positive battalion keeping an eye on you all. We've had intelligence, rather than being among that crowd. We suspect the unnamed "architect" has spent a small fortune on tailing you.'

'All right, likely,' Tom agrees. 'The "architect" has a police contact too. That no doubt helped him locate us.'

'Of course, why not? I should mention that Stephen's been purloining cars from the Bencam fleet and tracked Julia for a time, too. He's not aware enough of his actions to bother with an untraceable car.'

Warren, still standing, crosses his arms, plants his legs apart. 'You got anything useful for us then?'

'Fair question, Warren. I think it's best we hear from Stephen. He has solid information even though he's unable himself to properly process it. We'll go to his room – he's been mildly sedated and is most comfortable in the more contained space.' Bennett runs his eyes over each of them. 'Perhaps your combined bulk might be over-powering.'

'It's all or none. However, we won't crowd him. One of us inside, the others immediately outside the door.'

'We can manage that. Challinor, you and I alone inside, sorry Caroline. Stephen can become somewhat distressed in your presence.'

As they walk down the long corridor, Julia wonders if "distressed" is a euphemism for violent.

66

THE WAXING MOON IS VISIBLE THROUGH THE WINDOWS OF THE MAGNIFICENT bedroom Charters occupies. Even from the distance of the doorway, it signifies the promise of a quieter life. Julia gazes at it, briefly allowing herself to feel sadness that Tom will never see the moon, the sunset, the extravagance of colour in the paintings on the walls. He'd shrug this off, assure her of the excellence of his life, she already knows that. A reasonable argument, but....

Julia closes her own eyes for ten seconds, then turns to Warren. Who – to her surprise – gives her a thumbs up. Perhaps he's beginning to trust her.

'Stephen, Tom is here to help. He also needs your assistance. Those young women remain in danger.'

The greyhound of a man – strong, thin body, thin moustache, Nefertiti eyes – unwinds the tangled covers, pulls to a sit. 'At your service.' His graciousness is exaggerated.

Tom smiles. He will not interrogate Charters. Probing questions, especially repeated ones, try to inveigle information, work in court. They're counterproductive for a person in fragile emotional health. 'I'd appreciate it if you could tell me your story, Stephen. Your recent story, concerning Sonya and Avril. They're both in hospital now. We wish, with your help, to save them further trauma.'

Stephen reaches for the glass of water on the bedside table. He nods. Involuntarily, Julia wonders? Or true acquiescence?

Very slowly, Stephen speaks. He asks after Sonya, he regrets he was forced to keep her in that small, mice-riddled house. It was all Johnson's fault. Or the Tall Man's. The Tall Man is nasty and evil and could be the Devil.

Stephen's pace quickens. He jumps from one topic, one explanation, one point to another. But there is an underlying coherence, a solid narrative being told.

They learn that the cross was Stephen's idea. He loves symbolism and felt Sonya would look beautiful on it. So beautiful. It was designed to support her with leg rests and one arm specially made for her stump. She wouldn't have been hurt (Stephen could never hurt a woman, it was why he suffered so on deployment). He would have put her on the cross and shown that, like the Jewish Christ, a Muslim woman could save the world.

The words keep tumbling. Julia admires Tom's ability to let them fall out as Stephen chooses.

The Tall Man ordered Johnson about. It made Stephen angry. But Johnson tricked him, Stephen. All the time, over and over. Adam gave him nice drugs, and Adam's brother – did they know he had a nice brother? – the brother was kind, he didn't make Stephen do nasty things. The Tall Man, he was a gigantic sack of nasty things. He looked nice but he wasn't. The Tall Man made promises.

When Stephen has repeated these points several times Tom begins quietly to direct the unfolding story. 'The Tall Man wanted Avril?'

'Of course,' Stephen affirms clearly.

'But he didn't want to get his hands dirty, so he employed Adam Johnson,' suggests Tom.

'I would like to shoot him. I have never shot anybody. They threatened to court martial me when I threw my gun away.'

'Adam Johnson was on deployment with you?'

'He looked after me.'

'You were upset when Johnson placed Avril on the cross. For the Tall Man.'

Stephen's eyes snap up. They gleam. 'It was that boy, that silly, pretty boy, Zac. The Tall Man wanted to take the dwarf girl away, to the country or the mountains. He gave Adam some keys and then he took them away after that other girl was stuck in the lake. He told Adam to forget it, forget getting hold of the dwarf, but Adam didn't. Adam made Zac help him again. We were friends, he had keys for my house so he took her there. Zac put the dwarf on *my* cross. I think he was in love with her and Adam agreed to it because he was angry.'

'Did Adam hurt Zac because of the cross?'

Charters raises both his hands to his head, grasping himself, pushing himself. 'I hate disloyalty, hate it, hate it, hate it. Michael taught me that as a boy. Being friends is better than being enemies.'

'What did the Tall Man promise Adam?'

Dropping his hands, Stephen shifts his gaze to Tom, looking directly at him for the first time. 'Vengeance,' he says. 'He said he would destroy that place, that – what is it? – that refuge? The Tall Man has the power to make their money go away – zap, just like that. He promised he'd throw all the women out on the street. I do not like the Tall Man, he has no chivalry.'

Julia suppresses expletives. Tom speaks calmly. 'He was lying. The Tall Man did nothing. He betrayed Adam. Because Adam and Zac made the mistake with Melanie, the young woman in Parramatta Park. Am I on the right track?'

'The Tall Man was never, ever, ever going to do anything, do you hear, anything? Something is going wrong with his business and he wants more money. That's all he's interested in. Money.'

'I believe you,' Tom says quietly. 'Now we need to work out who the Tall Man is. It's very important, Stephen. Especially for Sonya and her friend, Avril.'

67

Twenty minutes later, they reassemble in the living room. Caroline is irritated, having been left there alone so long.

'You knew!' Bennett growls at her as soon as he walks in.

'What did I know?'

Warren is stunned by Caroline's disingenuity.

'It's Rupert Barton, isn't? Behind all this. Stephen is not carrying any cans for that charlatan.'

'Michael, please. Stephen's not making sense most of the time. Yes, I thought Barton may have been involved in the agency. That's all. Kidnapping – good grief, that's completely not Barton's style. He's a seducer with a history of predatory behaviour with young women. Very dull, ordinarily beautiful women. It's possible that dwarf girl got under his skin – some idea of the exotic, one presumes – nevertheless, I can't imagine him abducting her. Besides, he's in a wheelchair now. Very adept with it for a novice user, but take it from me, kidnapping even a midget when you're in a chair isn't going to happen.'

'You're fired!'

Caroline lifts her chin, eyes glittering. 'No longer retained would be a better term. Honestly, Michael, you need me–'

'Apologies for the interruption, but right now your business relationship is irrelevant. We have to fully pool our intel. As you know, Michael, Caroline has a sharp mind. We must use her information and opinion.'

'Coffee?' This and a sceptical glare are Bennett's only responses.

'Good call,' Warren responds to the coffee, liking Ray being sent off to make it. He'll drink the putrid stuff just for the pleasure of being served by him.

'Let's summarise,' Tom begins. 'Stephen's convinced us his intention was to look after Sonya. That he was essentially subjecting her to torture escapes his reasoning. He's convinced us the abduction of Avril had nothing to do with him. However, he's seen and heard a lot. Phillip Jones confirmed Barton's involvement in the agency, Barton fits with Sonia's observations, the data Julia had accessed on Jones' computer, and the matches made just now by Ivan on the basis of more names, connections and so on. We are all in agreement Barton is the "architect" of the kidnappings. Motive unclear and method very messy. The impression is that he's recently become disorganised and is behaving out of character. Reasons unknown, although probably to do with money.'

'Stephen let out more than he intended,' Julia continues the tale. 'Including that Barton appeared in Elm Street last night, furious. He turned up unexpectedly at number 9, the deceased estate Stephen broke into when he found Johnson had taken over his house. Barton was walking, I should add, and scared the life out of Stephen. Barton threatened who knows what – Stephen avoided the detail, violence obviously disturbs him.'

'Our father beat him badly,' Bennett puts in.
'Sad.' Although Julia's voice is dead-pan her response suggests experience, Tom notes.

'Barton was walking?'
'Seems so, Caroline. He's probably a Pretender.'
Caroline bristles. 'Christ! Now that really annoys me.'

'Agreed. Setting that aside for now, in the current context it's important to note that the first – failed – kidnapping last week in Parramatta was set up by Barton, enacted by Adam Johnson, who very foolishly drew in the driver-cum-delivery-boy, Zac. Barton was furious when they tried again this week. For unknown reasons, this was too late as far as he was concerned. We'd already heard, and Stephen's confirmed, there's a fall-guy in police custody for that kidnapping. Totally unclear whether Barton sorted this, or the police did it themselves.'

'It's like a microcosm of how communities can behave in civil war,' Julia says.

'Meaning we can't go to the police? If they're part of the set-up.' Caroline asks.

Tom drops his chin on one large hand, classic thinker pose. 'I don't think so. Warren? Julia?'

'Apart from potential police involvement or pay-offs, what have you, that Barton's off the planet, I reckon. I'm worried about those girls in the hospital. Bugger the police.'

'I agree.' Julia looks down at her phone. 'I've got the PubDisMed Facebook page here. There's a recent post from "Sean". It purports to be about an event tomorrow night – cancelled because the main speakers have not arrived in time. "Sean" is, according to Ivan, most likely Barton or a trusted person who works for him. This "event" had been due to run last weekend. Obviously that's when Avril was to be abducted and transported to a secret location out of the city.' She hands the phone to Warren to read. 'So, to tonight. Barton is presumably aware – via his police contact – that Adam Johnson is in custody and that Stephen isn't. Stephen has agreed to do a post. His code name is Charles Stone – a name Adam Johnson "borrowed" as an alias. Stephen as "Charles" will post that he is able to collect the aforementioned "speakers" immediately. This should attract Barton's attention. He won't want Stephen getting away with Sonya. Or Avril.'

'Smart, very smart,' says Bennett, as Ray distributes the coffee and Warren smirks.

'You see,' Julia turns to Caroline, 'Stephen is certain Sonya saw the "Tall Man" last night. Saw him clearly enough to identify him. Stephen has some paranoia but I believe him when he claims the "Tall Man" will – and I quote – "need to rub her out". Luring Barton to Sonya and Avril will not be difficult.'

'Playing with fire, but necessary,' Tom comments. 'We must act now and not give Barton time to organise. In fact, his recent MO suggests he won't use employees. He's been relying on men, Johnson in particular, over whom he has some manipulative power – knowledge of their devotism and their own crimes for starters.'

'And whom he doesn't have to pay. The rumours are ricocheting everywhere recently. The scandal about his herbal formulas is just the beginning. Rupert Barton's big on pride though – he won't be seen dead in a petrol-powered car even on a mission like this. His Tesla is adapted.

That's what he'll drive. It's late but I may be able to put in some calls. I know people who know Rupert,' Caroline offers.

'Harry,' Tom says. Caroline does not deny it.

'I'll get my surveillance people onto it immediately.' Michael pulls out his phone.

'All excellent moves. However, time is getting away. We must run this ourselves. Michael, we need your help.' Tom straightens, energy returned.

68

THE SOUNDSCAPE IS CROWDED WITH THE PEEPS AND BEEPS OF MONITORS, moans, a cacophony of snores, the squeal of shoes on vinyl, trolleys on vinyl, the hushed conversations and the strident demands of doctors and, less often, patients. The hospital is over-full, short-staffed and Avril and Sonya are still waiting for beds on a ward.

Sonya finds the sounds of a crowded hospital comforting. She and Avril are still together, their guard has been replaced by another guard although he, like the first, wanders off. She suspects both men feel flirting with the nurses is one of their duties. Better they stay close to Avril and her. Avril is sleeping, but Sonya is on high alert. The man will come to silence her. Or will send someone to do that dirty work for him. She has seen him, so what else can he do?

The night settles in. Sounds lessen, movement slows. Neither of their families has visited yet. The policeman told them their parents were informed they are both safe but in the hospital. Why have they not come? Don't they care about their daughters? Perhaps that would be a relief. Sonya is fearful of her father's reaction. Will he try to kill her for her work? Her mother would surely not allow such a thing, she has become stronger in this country which acknowledges she has some rights of her own. His anger, though, will be immense. And his shame, their shame, the whole family's shame. They will be tainted with her sinful behaviour.

Sonya tries to settle against the pillows in a way that does not impede her watching. Rest is important, staying awake more so.

Sometime later – how long? – a smell, acrid and ugly, wakes her. The smell should not be present. It is the sweat of the man bending over her. When their eyes meet, his hand swiftly drops over her mouth. Hard and tight. Worse, a knife is pushing into her left side, where the arm is missing and cannot protect the rest of her.

It is only a dream, it is a horror movie in your mind, she tells herself. It is not.

What happened to their police guard?

Her mouth is dry with the shock that is all the greater because the imagined has actually come true.

Sonya fights her exhaustion, sets her eyes to search. The night-light illuminates only the centre of the room. She can just make out another man, tall and thin, leaning over Avril's bed, his fingers reaching for the cannulas in her arm. The man sees Sonya move, holds fingers against his mouth. His message is obvious – if Sonya resists, Avril will be damaged, perhaps die.

Why is the man hurting Avril? It is her, Sonya, he needs to silence. This is wrong. But of course it right too. Right for him to know she will protect her friend before herself. To save Avril, she will accept her own kidnap. Again.

Time is suspended. Such weakness, such stupidity that she has slept. Avril is much sicker than she is. Her job was to be at the ready. In her mind, Sonya curses.

Then, nearby, an emergency bell shatters the thick glassy silence in the room. The men react. Sonya understands they are not practised at this sort of behaviour. That is good. The hand over her mouth loosens, the knife withdraws. Her breath expels in a squeal, her lungs too empty for a scream. Before she can pull more breath in, cloth is being thrust into her mouth. If only Avril would wake.

And then Sonya feels the object in her hand. Such joy. It is small and can be concealed. Even in sleep she has held it close. It is power, she has power.

Strong arms gather her up. She mimics compliance. One moment, she has one moment. It must be used to full effect. She allows her arm to flop. The man carrying her takes no notice. Her hand squeezes the item, activates it. Her heart jumps with pleasure. And then, the tall man leaves Avril, opens the door and Sonya is rushed out of the room.

69

WARREN ENTERS AT THE SUB-BASEMENT. LUCKY HE KNOWS PEOPLE WHO know people who know places. The service lift stinks more like the dead than the living. He avoids close contact with the walls, who knows what's stuck to them. His overalls and bag proclaim him an emergency service electrician. Between them Bennett, Tom and Julia have hatched a bloody good plan. Never would've come up with it himself. If for no other reason than it takes connections, money and power he doesn't even want to have. Way too many ethical compromises required. Albeit useful now.

At the first floor, he exits the lift, moves to a window and peers out at the carpark. Cars are quietly collecting, several blocking the exit of the currently empty target vehicle. A grin spreads across Warren's face. Stephen and Ivan did the thing with Facebook. "Sean" reacted quickly to the alert. Bennett was true to his word. Did a ring around or whatever and got a truckload of journos pissing themselves to be first to get the scoop of the day. 'Cept in the middle of the night, and at this very hospital. Gave them co-ordinates for the carpark, described what they should look out for. What a send-off Barton and his mate are going to get. Hopefully.

What's more, Caroline got Harry Montague to finally cough up and has the rego plates for Barton's car, while that Julia, well, she did a pretty cool job of pretending to be Sonya's Mum, Iraqi accent and all. First Julia got the gen on where Sonya was located. Her friend was with her, the nurse had also added, comfortingly. Unvisitable for the time being, a message would be passed on. Oh, and yes, in the circumstances, she'd give Sonya the phone as soon as her uncle dropped it off. Family contact was so important for recovery. Half an hour later Warren delivered the phone and a wireless emergency pager. The staff were too busy to question the detail and decent enough to deliver. Pretty soon after that Sonya rang, confirming receipt. Next thing they knew, via Facebook, they were on.

He watches, ears attuned. It's in these minutes the risk is reaching a crescendo, as he'd've said in his journo days. Some crescendo – he just feels a bit sick and a lot exhausted. Barton arrived fifteen minutes ago. He'd walked in – that was interesting – accompanied by a bloke way bulkier than himself. Beanie pulled down low. They obviously had intel and took a narrow set of back stairs, but too eager to notice they were being filmed. At least until they were fully inside the building. Sonya, plucky kid, got the buzzer out when she was lifted. That was six minutes ago. Time is moving on. He has to go inform and protect Avril but he's getting worried. Surely they should have reached an exit by now. And every exit should have a camera pointed at it. Should have. But it's possible – and looking sickeningly more likely – there's a way out of the hospital they don't know about.

Tom's also alerted the local police of a bogus incident in the car park but there're no sirens yet. Could be a good thing. But where the bloody hell are the bastards? Warren takes a deep breath and heads through the backdoors of Emergency, past the various cupboards and stacks of medical paraphernalia, to the cubicles.

'You okay Avril? You got the message?' he asks, hoping his appearance doesn't make her scream.

Her voice is small but steady. He already likes this girl, both girls. Can't keep them down. Now she's checking his credentials: 'You rescued me from that doctor dude, hey? You're helping Sonnie get rescued?'

'Yep. And I reckon that's happening as we speak. I'm here as your muscle. Just in case, you know.'

'Jees, can I get outta here and see Sonnie rescued? They've taken me off the drip – look.'

'That might be going a bit far.' Warren looks around, listens. 'Fuck it, mate, why not? I'm carrying you, though. And we're watching from up here.'

Warren almost feels like crossing himself as they head back to the windows. 'Cept he was never a Catholic, any sort of believer and he's holding a small but fully grown woman in his arms. He hopes hard that what she sees is success.

The commotion in the car park is big. Phone cameras are flashing, curious onlookers are leaning against the barrier of cars that blocks the exit for the parking area. Closer in, women and men with large on-the-shoulder cameras and microphones on sticks are milling around the men, who have catapulted out of a small side door and are momentarily trapped in the glare and their own complete confusion.

'Is Sonnie–? Jees, she's alive isn't she?' Avril wriggles in his arms and tries to point through the glass.

Barton's mate in the beanie is still holding Sonya, Barton is seemingly helpless. Warren's fairly convinced neither of them'll have weapons. Sure doesn't look like they've had practice in rapid assassination. Saying so would be little comfort. 'Look, there's a nurse rushing out now. Three of them in fact.'

The three nurses command, yell, push, shove their way through the phalanx of Bennett's best and worst and most available journalists. They reach Sonya and her captors. The men appear glued to the spot. And then, at the last moment, Sonya is half dropped, half deposited on the ground and the men turn, making a run for it back into the hospital. If it weren't so serious it would truly be funny. The sirens are closing in, and a pile more cameras are in place inside (and out). Influence – in this case, Bennett's – gets you everywhere.

Avril's eyes are straining to see her friend, who's almost hidden now by the nursing staff. The nurses are yelling at everyone to keep back, for heaven's sake, but being stolidly ignored. Warren, on the other hand, has his ears straining for the chase, and what is surely the inevitable capture of Barton and co – those two being real amateurs.

The nurses finally succeed in pushing the crowd back, getting Sonya some air.

'Look, look, she's waving. Go Sonnie! Woo hoo.' Avril reaches out and bangs the window.

Warren staggers. 'Hey mate, I might drop you too. Come on, we're getting you back into that bed before we get booked for breaking some public health order or other. Sonya's good, you'll see her soon enough.'

Avril grins up at Warren. He grins back, bloody tired but feeling pretty good.

SUNDAY

70

FOR TWENTY SECONDS AFTER HE WAKES, TOM FEELS BLISSFUL. JULIA IS curled around him, they are naked, the sun is warming the room, the wind is only an occasional rustle in the trees outside.

Reality hits like the worst of all hangovers. What a night.

Julia turns in her sleep. Tom resettles her on his arm, careful of the bruised, swollen side of her face – the injury Johnson gave her. She feels so good there. Fortunately, he'd restrained himself last night – the desire to punish Adam Johnson had been strong and right now he would be in a cell if he'd acted on the impulse. Instead, he can imagine a holiday, he and Julia together. Three weeks in the Bahamas, she'd said: 'I dream of lying on a lilo on crystal water.' Perhaps he could arrange that.

Julia slowly unfurls. 'My head hurts, it's too early. How long have you been lying there, thinking too hard?'

'Only a few minutes. Do you drink tea or coffee first thing in the morning? As soon as we can, we'll get going. No cocktails by the pool for us for a while, I suspect.'

'Tea, with a coffee chaser. Can't we stay in bed? No, I know. It's the morning after and it's all serious. Starting with top of my agenda, Jean!'

He runs his hand over her hair, draws her to him. 'No-one has rung yet.'

'Soon, I suppose.' She curls closer to him. 'I hope Ian doesn't lose his job over this. Jean's a Houdini. She took herself off, out of her own desires. Ian lacks polish but he's well organised and fond of the residents in a very real, human-to-human way.'

'Can you intervene?'

'Obviously, it'd be unethical if I acted as anything other than a family member. Well – perhaps, in the circumstances I can exert a little pressure. I owe him, and the staff. That Sanjiv is fabulous.'

'I owe a few beers too. Warren, of course. My friend Serge. You'll have to meet him and Imogen soon; they're fun. And there's Ivan, whom I must call later today. Might have to keep him working on the cyber side of the organisation. The police are going to be all starry eyed with catching the big crims, meaning they'll forget the agency.'

Julia reaches a hand up, strokes lightly across Tom's morning bristles. 'We'll have to deal with it. Later.'

'You're right again. Enough of the work talk. What about us?'

'Us?'

'Us. There is an "us" – agreed?'

Her sudden smile warms the air, he can feel it. 'I couldn't agree more,' she says.

'Good. Although I have to say I've never had a relationship start in quite such a complicated a fashion. Intensely pleasurable in its own way, but complicated.'

'How many relationships have you had?'

'Feel those notches on the bed head.' He holds her now in an easy fashion, as if they've been doing it for years.

'Trite. But not half as many as on mine,' she replies.

'You win. For the time being. I'll make tea. And then check the emails and make coffee. There's still a lot to clear up.'

Ninety minutes later, Julia and Tom make their way down the first of the day's hospital corridors. Jean is here. Later they'll traipse across the city to Westmead.

Outside Jean's door, Julia stops. 'Tom, you'll meet Jean, but I want to tell you a family secret first.' She rests her head against his chest. She loves the feeling he gives her of being protected. It is terribly old-fashioned, and perfect.

'You see, my father couldn't make sense of Jean's disability, couldn't understand why she couldn't speak, why she wouldn't – as he saw it – try. She was messy, food everywhere, threw drinks over the carpet, all the usual stuff. His anger built and he beat her. He left after a particularly bad beating, and he left her with a lot more damage than she started with. He also beat my mother – but not me, never me. I was his golden girl, is how he used to put it. So now you understand my tendency to guilt. There's a very good basis.'

'Julia, you were a child. A child isn't responsible for the behaviour of the adult. He was your father, he's meant to look after you, to love you. Beating your family was no way of loving them or you. Although, I'm quite sure you did save Jean, time and time again.' He pauses. 'Jules, we've got a lifetime to talk about this – let's see how Jean is now.'

A lifetime? She smiles. It's a very attractive idea. During which she'll have to find opportunities for Jean to have more adventures. Seems she thoroughly enjoyed this recent one.

CCTV footage at Jean's local station showed her jumping onto a train, by herself. She'd waltzed past the card reader, looking as pleased as the proverbial cat with the cream. At Central Station she was stopped by heavy gates that wouldn't open without an Opal card. Jean came up with a simple solution: she turned around and boarded the departing train on the platform next to the one she'd arrived on.

She alighted at the end of the line in Nowra, at Bomaderry Station. The largely automated station was only staffed occasionally. Jean found her way into the nearest "house" – the old Station Master's office. How she got inside in the first place and then into the back room to raid the vending machine stores was not recorded by cameras, although the station master was reportedly red-faced about his security skills.

Julia smiles at the thought of Jean, giggling among the chocolate wrappers, crisp packets and slopped drink cans. Jean as Princess of Mess of Great Magnitude. Having fun all of her own doing.

'I'll go in for a moment alone, 'Julia says, touching Tom's arm before pushing open the door.

And there is Jean, sitting up in the bed, hair neatly plaited, trying her best to destroy the cotton blanket that should have been covering her. The intent expression on her face turns to a wide grin when she sees Julia.

'Dew-a,' Jean calls, holding her arms wide.

71

IT'S ALL OVER THE NEWS, SOCIAL MEDIA, WHAT HAVE YOU, LIKE FAKE TAN ON a model. Facebook and Twitter spew moral outrage, shock at the debased misuse/abuse of vulnerable people, that sort of thing. As if those working as escorts had no capacity to make their own choices.

Bleary-eyed, Warren grazes through it all. Names haven't hit the shit fan yet, but the "allegeds" are everybloodywhere. A doctor, a man who served his country as a medico, is alleged to have kidnapped a "wheelchair bound" (the term they use) young woman last week and then alleged to have abducted another disabled – and therefore so-called vulnerable – woman a couple of days ago, and alleged to have attacked a young man... the list is long. And that same man's alleged to have developed an unprofessional relationship with a patient, a peacekeeping hero who, damaged by his experiences, is still missing. Fears for his safety, etc. They'll hopefully hear soon enough that Charters has handed himself in. Or his brother Michael's dragged him in.

No mention of the refuge and the shenanigans there. Good thing too: if any other ex-partners get a whiff of the address of the place protecting "their women" problems could multiply. Sad they've ignored the drugging of Clif – who remains in a coma. Seems he's a half-decent bloke after all.

Ditto complete silence on Rupert Barton and his henchman – Mario someone – being in custody. Too much power? Warren can only hope it comes out in court that Barton's behaviour isn't related to sexual preference or paraphilia. The man's a manipulative, power-hungry, money-grabbing predator bastard. Who shoulda stuck to getting help from professional crooks; they do a good job 'cause their mortgage depends on it. Look how he stuffed around with Johnson and Charters. They thought they were equals in a ring of like-minded warriors. Only to be double-crossed and discarded by a bloke who goes for dress-ups. It'd all make Warren smile if it hadn't hurt so many people, so badly. Including that naïve kid, Zac. Who may or may not pull through. Another poor kid getting a rum deal.

Warren scrolls. On one lot of footage, he spots himself, Challinor and that Julia woman, all looking like death warmed up, as you'd expect after the twenty-four hours they'd had. Tom'll be shitty being on the news, but he'll shrug it off, get on with the next job. Man is attracted to trouble, addicted to it. And now there's this new woman. Truth be told, she's a good 'un, even if, in Warren's opinion, she's trouble incarnate – albeit amazingly good at helping other people out of it. He has to agree – not that anyone has asked him – this makes her just right for the boss.

Warren closes his computer, goes into the living room where Karen's busy booking the pedicure he's promised her – while half-watching ABC TV's *Insiders*. Loves politics, does Karen.

'All right if I go off to the hospital for a bit?' he says. 'I'll pick the kids up from the party on the way back.' He feels good that he'll be able to keep that promise.

'Sure. Don't forget you're cooking tonight. No take-away, that's cheating.'

Warren stoops and kisses his seated wife. Loves her to death.

Westmead Hospital is the journos' place to be seen this Sunday morning. Warren steps over a sound boom and around a knot of his old colleagues trying to poach each other's titbits, one bloke interviewing a nurse who's seen f-all, from what she's saying. Good looking lass, Warren notes, she'll make the cut for prime time, and social media.

It isn't hard to find the girls' private room, although it takes medium-density ingenuity to get in. Supposed to be a relative, or the law. Forethought is one of his trademarks; he's wearing his janitor's uniform. He uses the service lift again, with its smell of blood and formalin.

He nods at the young constable sitting near the nurses' station. Asks what's up. The kid merely shrugs, looking more bored than a soccer player at a rugby match. Warren fiddles with the tool bag he's carrying, slips into the room. Sure enough Tom is there, with Juli-bloody-a.

Avril's sitting up in bed like a princess, talking about selling her story, getting enough out of it to buy an apartment. Only be a small one, she reckons. Has to start somewhere now the job has folded. '*Sixty Minutes* and Amazon Prime – can you believe it – are offering,' she says proudly.

'Sonnie'll be back soon,' Avril tells Warren when he looks enquiringly at the nearby empty bed. 'And, hey, thanks, you were totally cool yesterday. Did I tell you that doctor was just about to pack me into the car like a sausage in an esky when you turned up? He was gonna take me somewhere on the other side of the planet, like Dubbo, I'm sure he said Dubbo.'

Warren grins, appreciating her turn of phrase, if not her command of geography. They chat for a bit, going over the excitement of last night.

Avril turns her attention to Julia. 'I can't work all this stuff out. I thought you and Tom was married or together like, but they told me the first guy who also saved my life, back in that totally disgusting house, was your husband. How many husbands have you got?'

'None really, but I'm pretty attached to Tom. The man who saved you – well, he and I separated some time ago.'

'Thought so.' Avril nods with satisfaction. 'Is he going to be okay?'

'Hopefully. He's done some awful things, but he doesn't seem to be bad through and through. You know he was one of the people who set up *Helpmates*?'

'You think that was a bad thing? It sure got me out of house and on my way in the world.'

'Perhaps not entirely a bad thing, then. And, oddly enough, it seems that Phillip was donating a fair amount of his profit to real charities. Naturally, he paid himself a generous wage, but he also tried to protect the staff. He couldn't predict what would happen – not entirely.'

'No way. That Johnson is totally twisted. The other guy, too, the one that abducted Sonnie. And the top dog f-wit from last night. The lot of them want everything their way, all the time, no matter who gets hurt – so long as it's not them. An' they hype each other up like crazy.'

'Yeah, Ivan has a word for them – he likes words, Ivan. *Folie à trois*. Reckons that Facebook page made them all feel special and exotic and above the crowd. When you think you're better than everyone else, well, that's a recipe for real perverted ideas. Barton, Charters, Johnson, they all started with their own nuttiness, and then added their mates' loony ideas. Barton probably only got onto Facebook to see if he could flush out blokes he could bleed some money or favours out of, but by the end of it they were infecting each other and none of them was real rational. The whole thing got its own momentum.'

Julia begins to say it was the agency that truly opened up the opportunity for the obsessions – and abductions. But the website and Facebook page were not part of the agency. And Warren and Ivan are probably right about the contagion of the delusion – after all, all three of the main actors in the drama were already at messy points in their lives and not responding well to challenges. Meeting fellow "travellers" online would have justified and escalated their sense of the world being against them. And supported their self-righteousness about their own needs. Julia concludes she'd be best not moralising about the escort business.

'You sure pick smart blokes,' Avril says. 'Maybe you can give me some tips.'

As Julia begins to laughingly respond, Sonya walks in. 'Hello,' she says politely.

Avril's all concern. 'What happened, Sonnie? Are they real freaked?'

Sonya nods. 'I tell them it is my life. They not like that.' She lifts her head defiantly. 'They forget it is big and different world today.'

'Go you.' Avril turns to their guests. 'Sonnie's been dealing with her mum and dad, which is, like, massive. Mine have gone home to collect their tears in the bathtub, but they'll get over it in the end. We sort of love each other. Sonnie's mum just, like, adores her too.'

Sonya sits on the edge of her bed. 'My father, he is very upset. Being kidnap was bad. But scare my father and that is good. The worry make him not so angry now.' She smiles and then frowns. 'Mr Stephen, he want strange things. He dress me as a queen, he want me to be like Jesus. It is very creepy. But I think he is confuse, he have no plan at all. Mr Barton – did he have plan? What he want to do with Avril?'

They all hesitate. Tom finally speaks. 'We don't have the full details. The story seems to be that, at the start, Rupert Barton was simply investing in the agency – it was a great money-maker and he's always loved being the first to discover a new and exotic trend. Within weeks of joining up with *Helpmates*, though, it became apparent to him his other larger and better-known businesses were in serious trouble. Federal and state corruption and financial agencies, as well as health regulators, were all ready to start talking publicly about huge problems with the vitamin supplements his fortune was built on. In short, his world was about to crash, and crash hard. Barton couldn't deal. He thrives on being in control, being on top of the pile. He seems to have thought of blackmail fairly quickly, but Phillip Jones had brilliant data protection, preventing Barton getting hold of suitable names and details. Barton tried sweet talking and bribing *Helpmates'* operations manager, Carmen. When she couldn't supply those desirable names, he came up with a peculiar scheme. One that took advantage of Adam Johnson's obsession with the refuge as a place of evil. And further fragmented Stephen Charters' already broken understanding of the world.'

'He was gonna blackmail loads of people through me, that's it, isn't it? Like he wanted me 'cause I've had heaps more clients than anyone else. So he thought I've got the dirt on loads of rich guys. Which is kinda true. That's why he wanted to kidnap me, hey. And he gave me this USB and it's got the guys faces fuzzed out. Me and Sonnie always did reckon some of the rooms had spy-holes or secret cameras or whatever. That Barton coulda set the cameras up for his blackmail plot, hey. Sonnie saw him hanging around in the hotels plenty of times. Reckon he'll have the original videos – showing the faces and all that, won't he?'

'He was lure you with USB?' Sonnie asks.

'Sorry, Sonnie, I shoulda told you all the details. I'm pretty sure all the girls in the video aren't me – it's edited together or whatever – but he was pretending it was just me so he could say he loved me and wanted to meet up with me outta work time so we could be together for ever. Bull, hey. Probably would've put a bag over my head or something.'

'I should have telled you about Stephen, too.'

'Yeah, all good, and we'll both know next time. Anyhow, he's a real creep, that Barton. Why would you pretend to need a wheelchair? Or that eye-patch he was wearing. Normal people can be such weirdos.'

'I think you've just had the last and most appropriate word,' Julia says to Avril as there's a knock at the half-open door. A woman steps in, holding two fabulous bunches of Australian natives, another following with a hamper over-flowing with carefully chosen treats.

'Well said, indeed. Although we hope to hear more words and stories later,' Tom says. 'In the meantime, we hope the non-hospital food is enjoyable.'

'Shit, you think of *more* than everything!'

A nurse also bustles in, wordless, pushing her way through, picking up the observation charts.

'I think you two are going to be checked over. We'll drop in again later. Is there anything we can do in the meantime?'

Sonya is shocked: 'No more! You have saved our lives!'

Avril is more pragmatic. 'Yeah, go see Sonnie's parents. They're gonna hang around in the visitors' room all day. You stick up for her. Cops won't do it, somebody has to. Cause Sonnie's a hero.' She holds out her hand to her friend. 'You reckon that'll help?'

Sonya laughs. Avril has a solution for every trouble. This time, perhaps her idea will help a little. Only a little. Her parents will be impressed with Tom and Julia, who are so clever and stylish. And they must like Warren. In fact, her dad will be a bit awed by all of them. It will not hurt him to see his daughter as an adult with people outside the family who care about her. 'That is good,' she agrees. The she looks seriously around the room. 'I am sorry about the big dangers. I am glad you are all alive and kicking.'

'Hey, Son, listen to you, you're so Aussie!'

72

Journalists are still hovering outside: Sydney hates to give up on a good story, especially one with an edge of the perverse. Avril will definitely be able to sell hers, if she chooses to. Sonya too, they do a brilliant double act. Tom and Julia keep their heads down, wave away the microphones. With an eager journalism school graduate nipping at their heels, they reach the hire car that, under the smell of other people's lives, carries a hint of their own recent past. Julia pats the door as she gets in; it feels like a friend.

'The most extraordinary few days. Can't believe how tired I am.' Tom stretches himself as far back as he can go in the too-small seat. 'Of course, when we get home, we'll have to discuss the next job.'

'You're joking!'

'That escort business was like a university college in orientation week – with the right antecedents, the right money, the special wink and nudge, you can indulge in the rituals, bastardising, abuses, humiliations of your choice. We can, and must, expose more of the men who got off on all that power.'

Julia sends the driver's window down a little, to wake herself up and to enjoy the half-forgotten freshness. 'You're avoiding the mundane. Money laundering, for example. We'll need to look into the misuse of government grants and tax breaks.'

'And the links between its rich and powerful consumers and the law makers and enforcers they socialise with,' Tom adds.

'Vital to the survival of a decent world. We've also got lives to lead, remember. Don't you have to earn the money to fund all this investigation?'

'Do you really want to introduce the mundane? When there's such a good mystery waiting to be solved? And when I now have – hope to have – such an excellent partner in crime investigation.'

Julia spies the corners of his mouth turning up. It's crazy, it won't be easy, but with two of them – three, including Warren – they'll do it. But not today. Today, enjoyment is her priority. Eventually. Her voice drops into serious. 'What if a share of ill-gotten proceeds has come my way? Inadvertently. I was married to one of the bosses you know.'

'Julia, I like the emphatic sound of that "was". Okay, you're right, let's take the day off and have fun.'

'Tom Challinor, I'm planning on more than a day of fun in my life. More than a day in the next week, in fact. We've got that frock and suit to buy, remember. The museum stairs to storm.'

'The grand entrance to make.'

'But first, let's go back to bed.'

His smile is wide and welcoming and isn't at all strained. 'Agreed.'

ACKNOWLEDGEMENTS

Dangerous Devotions was originally presented as part of an M.A in Writing (by thesis) at the University of Technology, Sydney (UTS) in 2005. I would like to acknowledge the support of UTS and in particular of my supervisor, now Professor, Catherine Cole. Cathy was rigorous in her reading and enthusiastic in her belief the book should go to publication. It's taken a while, but we finally got there.

To my early and later readers – Heather Jones, Kim McClymont, Carole Hampshire and Drs Peggy Mares and Ray Tindale – very grateful thanks. Each and every one of you was generous with your time and incredibly helpful with your comments. Similarly, Sarah Mares has been an irreplaceable support through my many writing projects.

This book stars a cast of people who live with disability – as well as a few people who lack an identifiable impairment. I was born into two families – my mother's and my father's - each with an unusually high representation of people who live with many skills, interests likes/dislikes and a diversity of impairments. I have spent my work life with people with disability, as a speech language clinician, coffee-companion, fellow-parent, psychologist, advocate. Without the intimacies of family relationships and my wonderful and occasionally challenging 'clients' and their supporters this book would not have been possible. Thank you all for your trust.

My partner Andrew is and always has been a remarkable support and I cannot thank him enough. I also heartily thank my three children, Josephine, Nicholas and Toby who, throughout their childhoods, put up with me retreating to my study to write several novels (yet to be published, but there's still time), and several degrees. As children and adolescents they helped stuff the envelopes when I was editor of IDA (Intellectual Disability, Australasia) and they made welcome the many and diverse people (with disability) and their 'caregivers' who came to my home-office at the back of our house. This home-office was also the kids' computer and TV room, and they cheerfully gave it up and now and then made gentle friendships with those in the waiting area (aka our living room).

Finally thanks for Clan Destine Press and my editor Narrelle Harris for taking this book off the shelf and sending it out into the world. Great mid-wives.

ABOUT THE AUTHOR

A D Penhall is a psychologist who's been a vegetarian cook (when not a vegetarian), a cleaner, a speech pathologist, the editor of a disability-professional magazine, an eco-tourism provider (and cleaner, again), an activist, a volunteer, a university worker, a disability advocate. She is now and always will be a mother and grandmother. And always a writer. A.k.a. Ann Penhallurick, she is author of a number of prize winning and/or published short stories, various reviews, articles and degrees, including an M.A. in Creative Writing and a PhD in Social Inquiry. She lives happily in the Blue Mountains. Dangerous Devotions is her debut novel.

www.ingramcontent.com/pod-product-compliance
Lightning Source LLC
Chambersburg PA
CBHW022350020726
47500CB00002B/202